Hello! Welcome, adventurers!

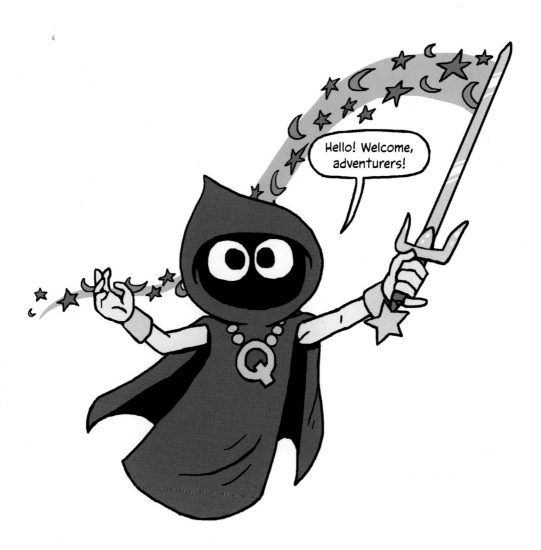

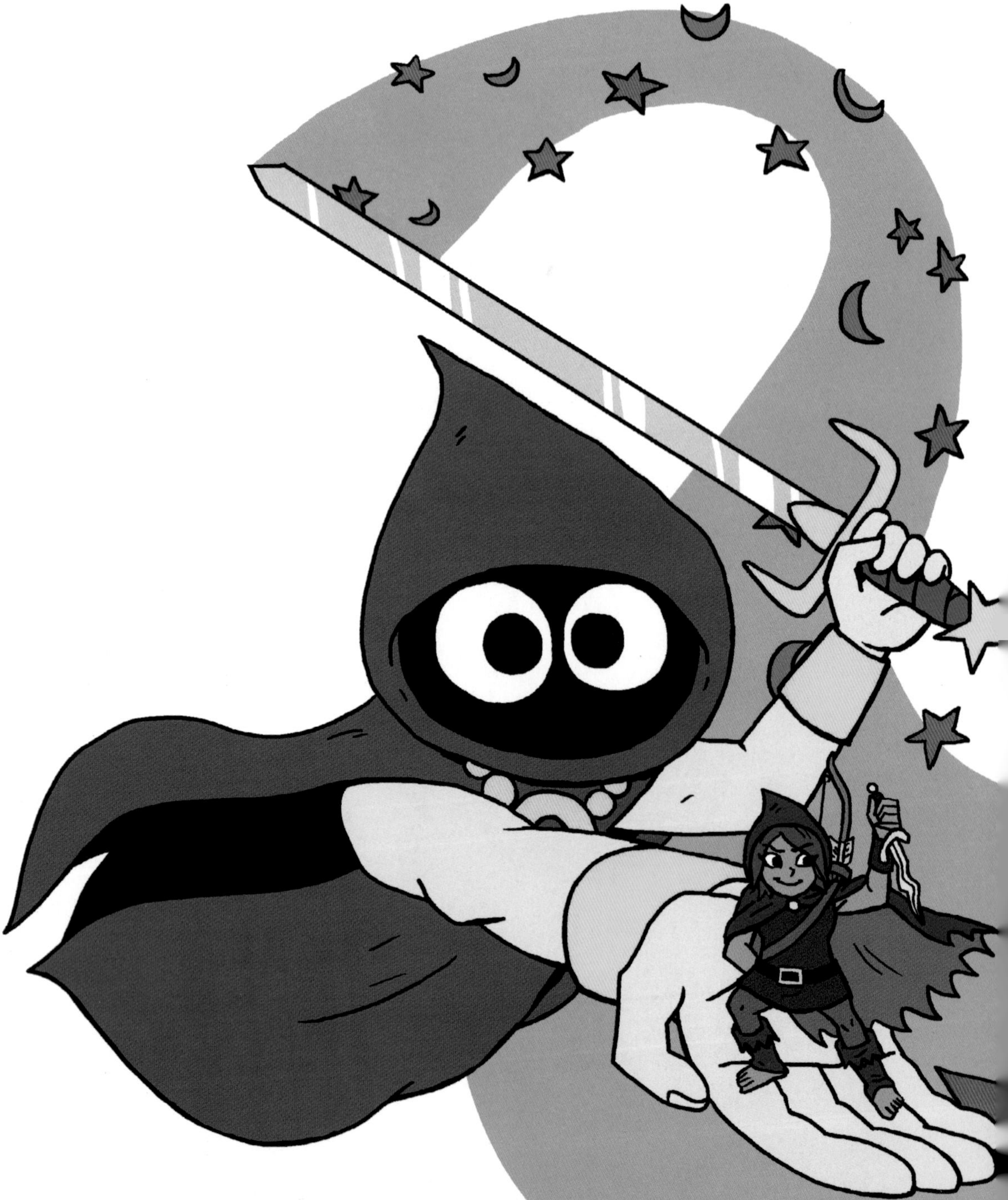

BRIAN McLACHLAN

COMPLETE THE QUEST

THE POISONOUS LIBRARY

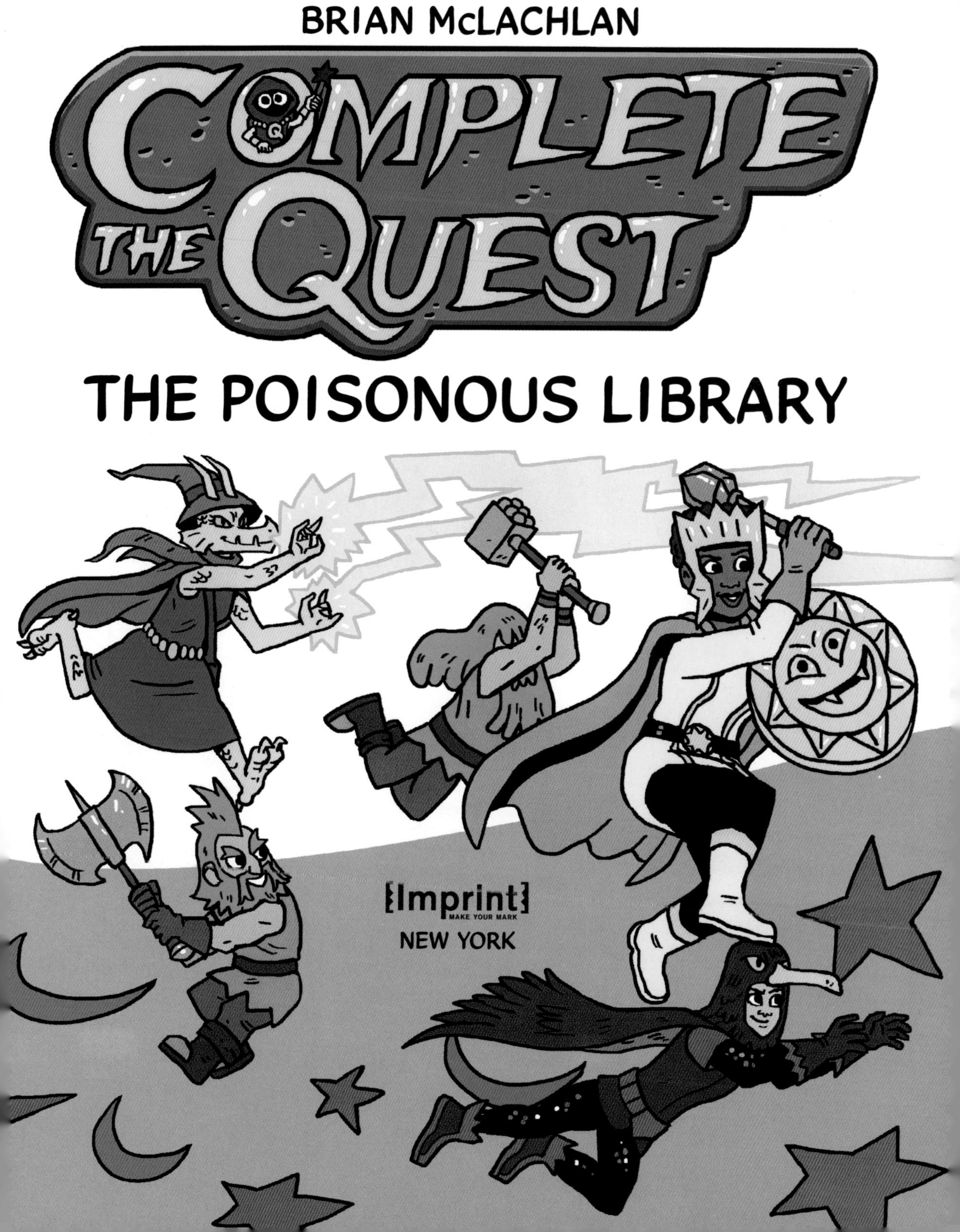

Imprint
MAKE YOUR MARK
NEW YORK

PICK THREE HEROES
TO GO ON YOUR ADVENTURE

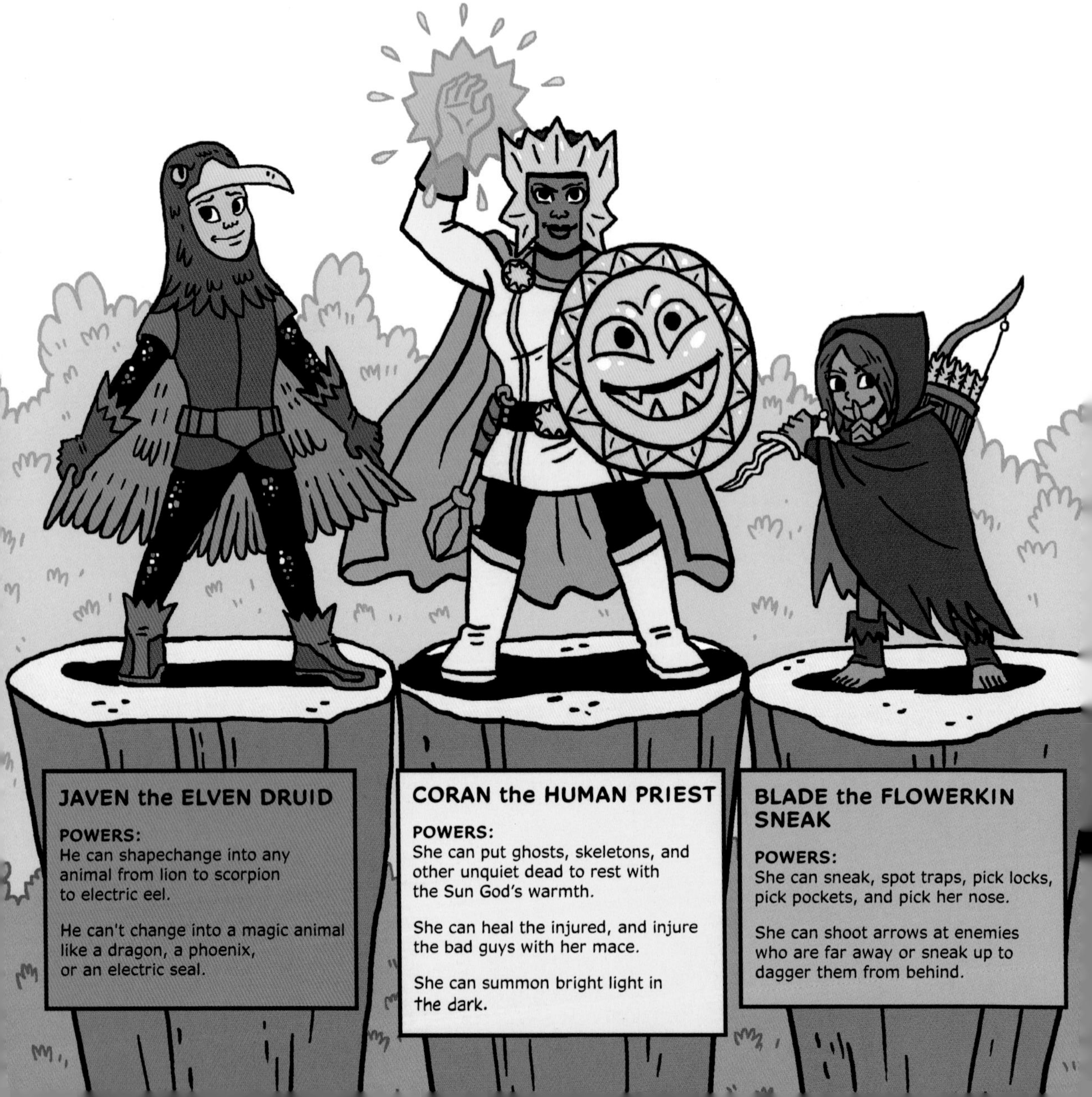

JAVEN the ELVEN DRUID

POWERS:
He can shapechange into any animal from lion to scorpion to electric eel.

He can't change into a magic animal like a dragon, a phoenix, or an electric seal.

CORAN the HUMAN PRIEST

POWERS:
She can put ghosts, skeletons, and other unquiet dead to rest with the Sun God's warmth.

She can heal the injured, and injure the bad guys with her mace.

She can summon bright light in the dark.

BLADE the FLOWERKIN SNEAK

POWERS:
She can sneak, spot traps, pick locks, pick pockets, and pick her nose.

She can shoot arrows at enemies who are far away or sneak up to dagger them from behind.

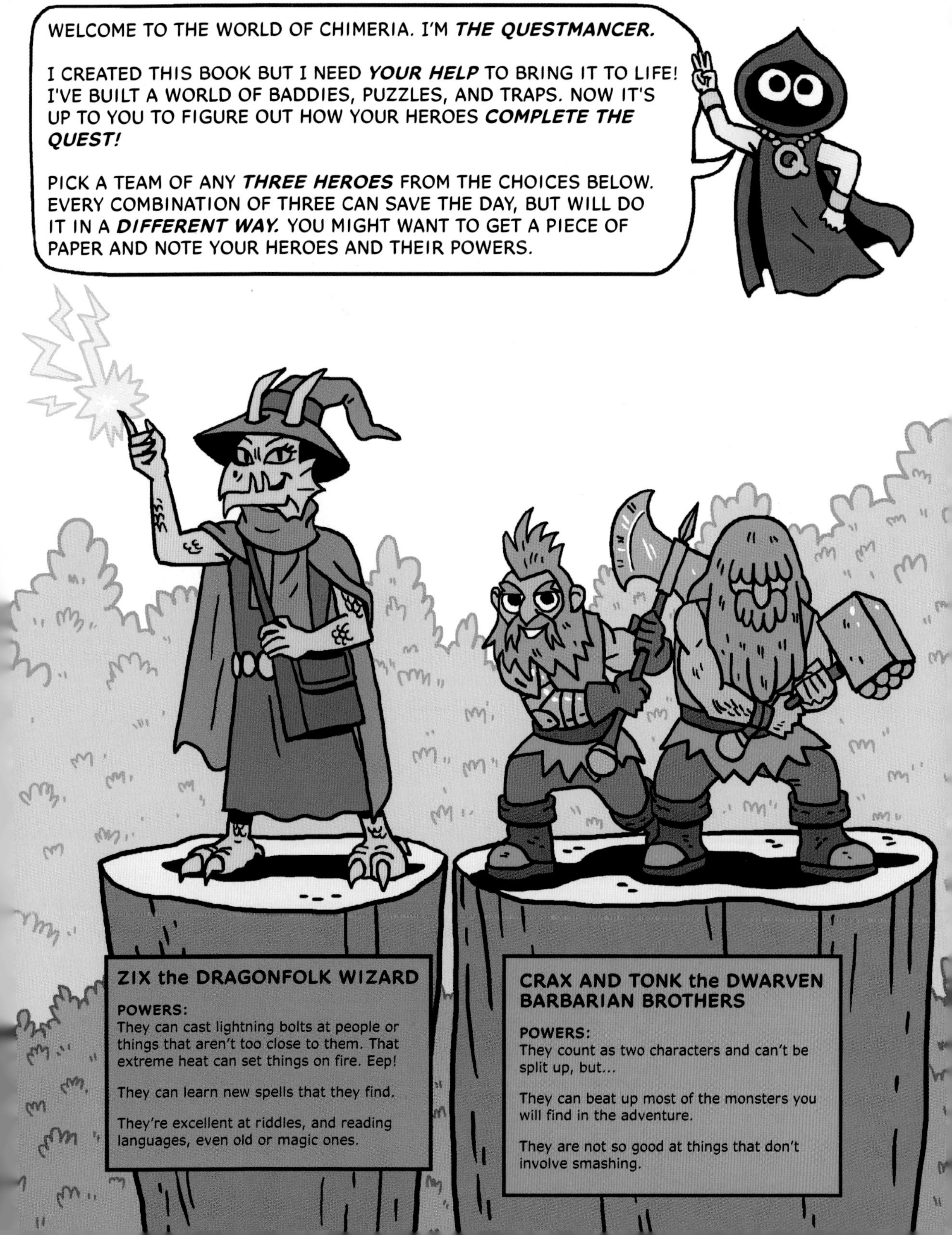
WELCOME TO THE WORLD OF CHIMERIA. I'M ***THE QUESTMANCER.***

I CREATED THIS BOOK BUT I NEED ***YOUR HELP*** TO BRING IT TO LIFE! I'VE BUILT A WORLD OF BADDIES, PUZZLES, AND TRAPS. NOW IT'S UP TO YOU TO FIGURE OUT HOW YOUR HEROES ***COMPLETE THE QUEST!***

PICK A TEAM OF ANY ***THREE HEROES*** FROM THE CHOICES BELOW. EVERY COMBINATION OF THREE CAN SAVE THE DAY, BUT WILL DO IT IN A ***DIFFERENT WAY.*** YOU MIGHT WANT TO GET A PIECE OF PAPER AND NOTE YOUR HEROES AND THEIR POWERS.

ZIX the DRAGONFOLK WIZARD

POWERS:
They can cast lightning bolts at people or things that aren't too close to them. That extreme heat can set things on fire. Eep!

They can learn new spells that they find.

They're excellent at riddles, and reading languages, even old or magic ones.

CRAX AND TONK the DWARVEN BARBARIAN BROTHERS

POWERS:
They count as two characters and can't be split up, but...

They can beat up most of the monsters you will find in the adventure.

They are not so good at things that don't involve smashing.

How to Play This Book

GREAT! NOW THAT YOU'VE PICKED YOUR HEROES, IT'S TIME TO SEND THEM ON A QUEST TEST RUN. BESIDE ME IS WHAT I CALL A **MAP.** MOVE YOUR HEROES FROM **"START HERE!"** TO THE PATH BEHIND THE **GUARD TOWER**, USING THEIR POWERS FROM THE LAST PAGES.

IN THE BOXES, I'VE PUT SUGGESTIONS FOR HOW HEROES MIGHT COMPLETE THE QUEST, BUT YOU GET THE FINAL SAY. FEEL FREE TO LOOK AROUND, BACKTRACK, AND REWRITE YOUR OWN VERSION OF THE STORY.

TO GIVE YOU SOME IDEAS, ***THIS* MAP** HAS COLORED PATHS SHOWING HOW THE QUESTERS BELOW HAVE FOUND DIFFERENT WAYS ACROSS THE MAP.

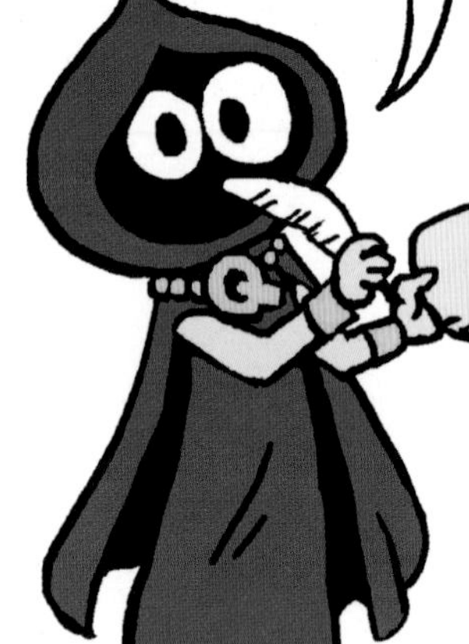

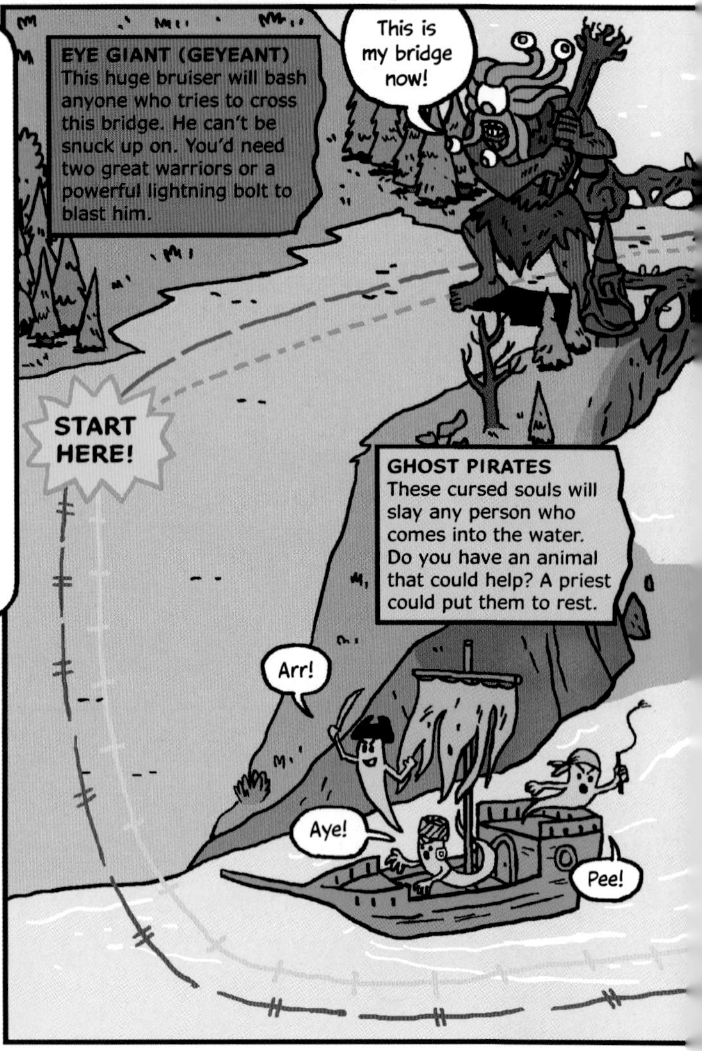
EYE GIANT (GEYEANT)
This huge bruiser will bash anyone who tries to cross this bridge. He can't be snuck up on. You'd need two great warriors or a powerful lightning bolt to blast him.
This is my bridge now!
START HERE!
GHOST PIRATES
These cursed souls will slay any person who comes into the water. Do you have an animal that could help? A priest could put them to rest.
Arr!
Aye!
Pee!

Questers

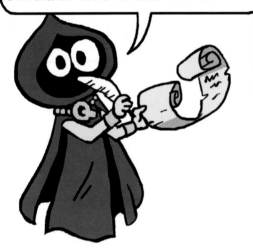

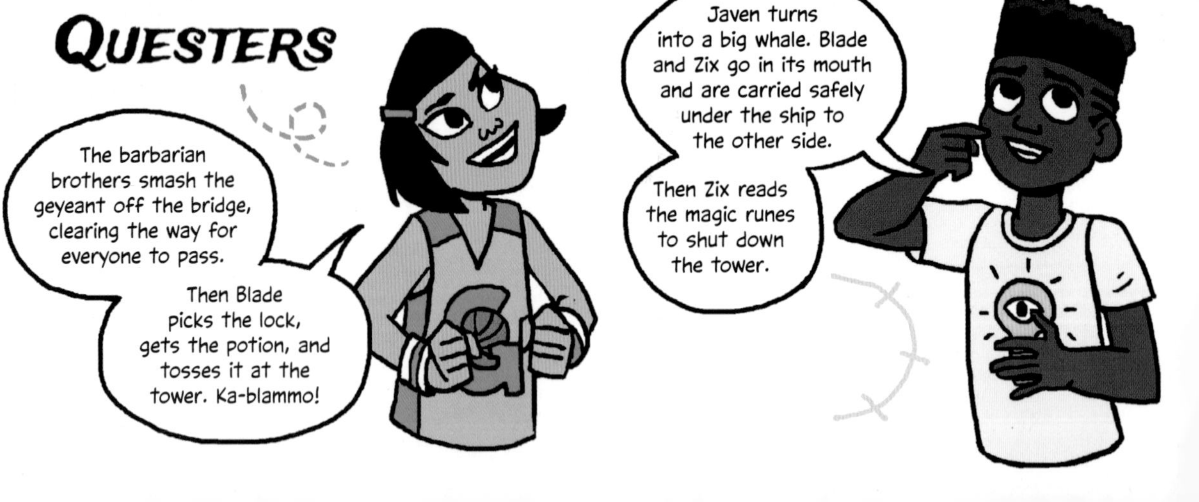
The barbarian brothers smash the geyeant off the bridge, clearing the way for everyone to pass.
Then Blade picks the lock, gets the potion, and tosses it at the tower. Ka-blammo!
Javen turns into a big whale. Blade and Zix go in its mouth and are carried safely under the ship to the other side.
Then Zix reads the magic runes to shut down the tower.

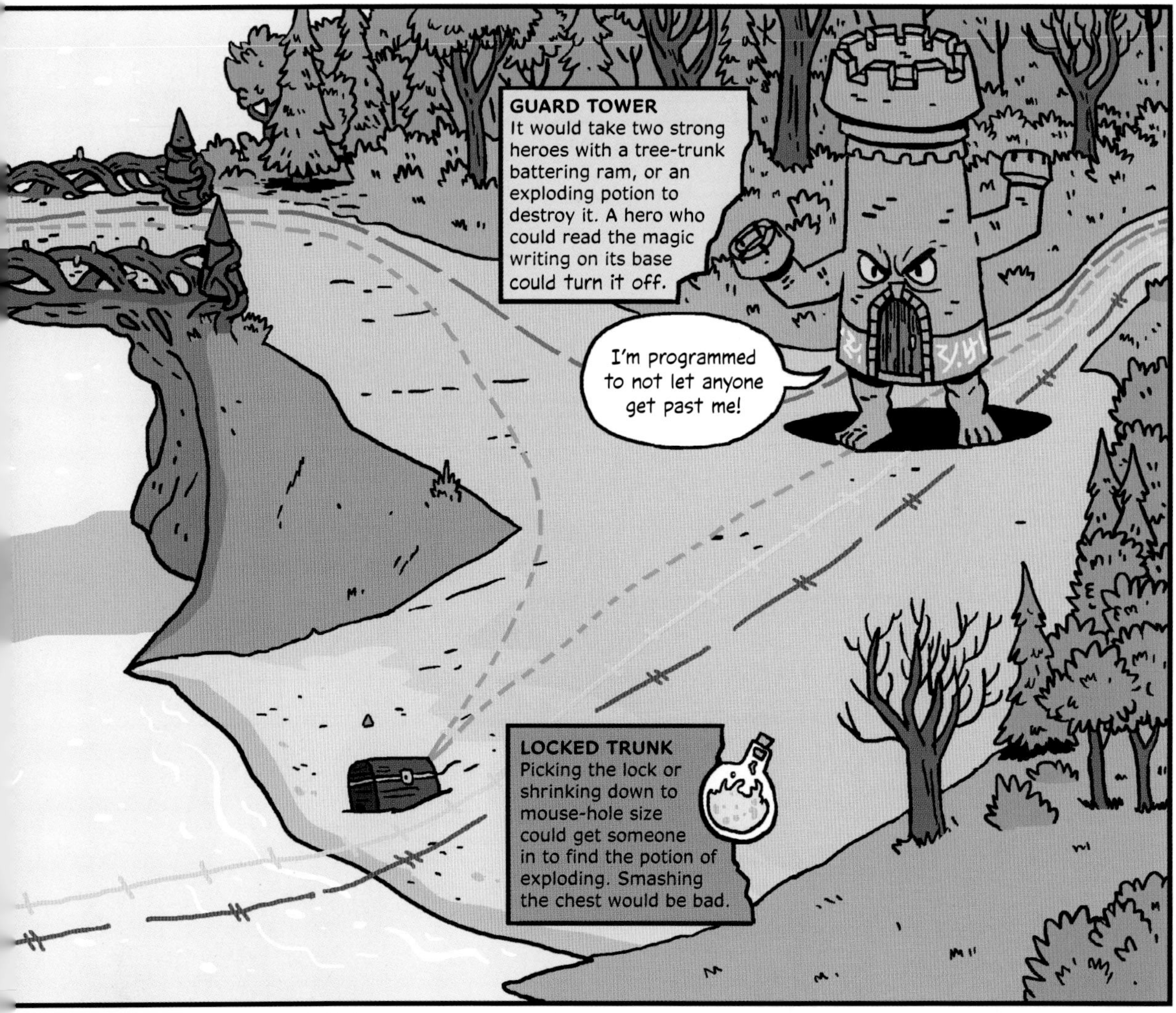
GUARD TOWER
It would take two strong heroes with a tree-trunk battering ram, or an exploding potion to destroy it. A hero who could read the magic writing on its base could turn it off.
I'm programmed to not let anyone get past me!
LOCKED TRUNK
Picking the lock or shrinking down to mouse-hole size could get someone in to find the potion of exploding. Smashing the chest would be bad.
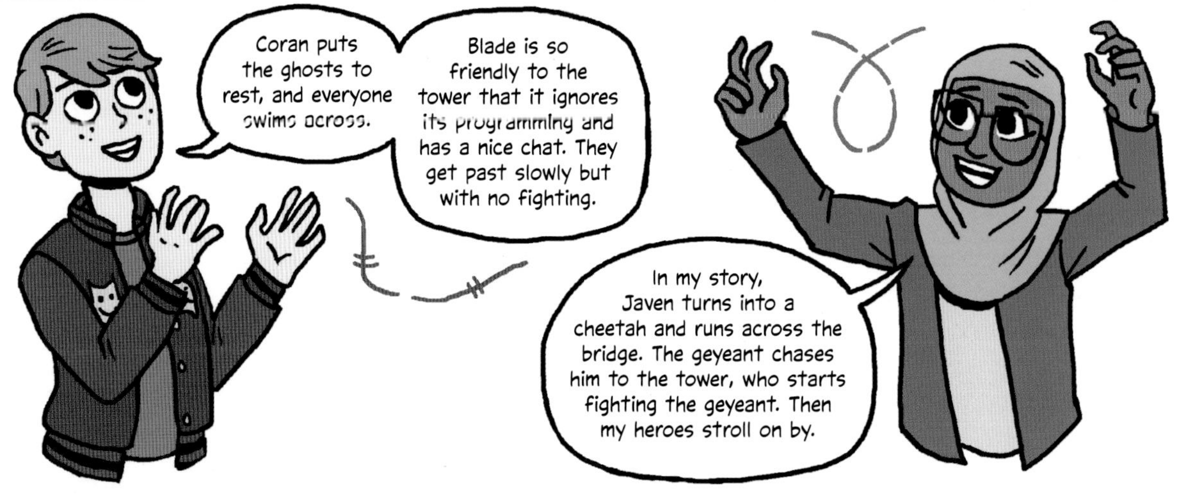
Coran puts the ghosts to rest, and everyone swims across.
Blade is so friendly to the tower that it ignores its programming and has a nice chat. They get past slowly but with no fighting.
In my story, Javen turns into a cheetah and runs across the bridge. The geyeant chases him to the tower, who starts fighting the geyeant. Then my heroes stroll on by.

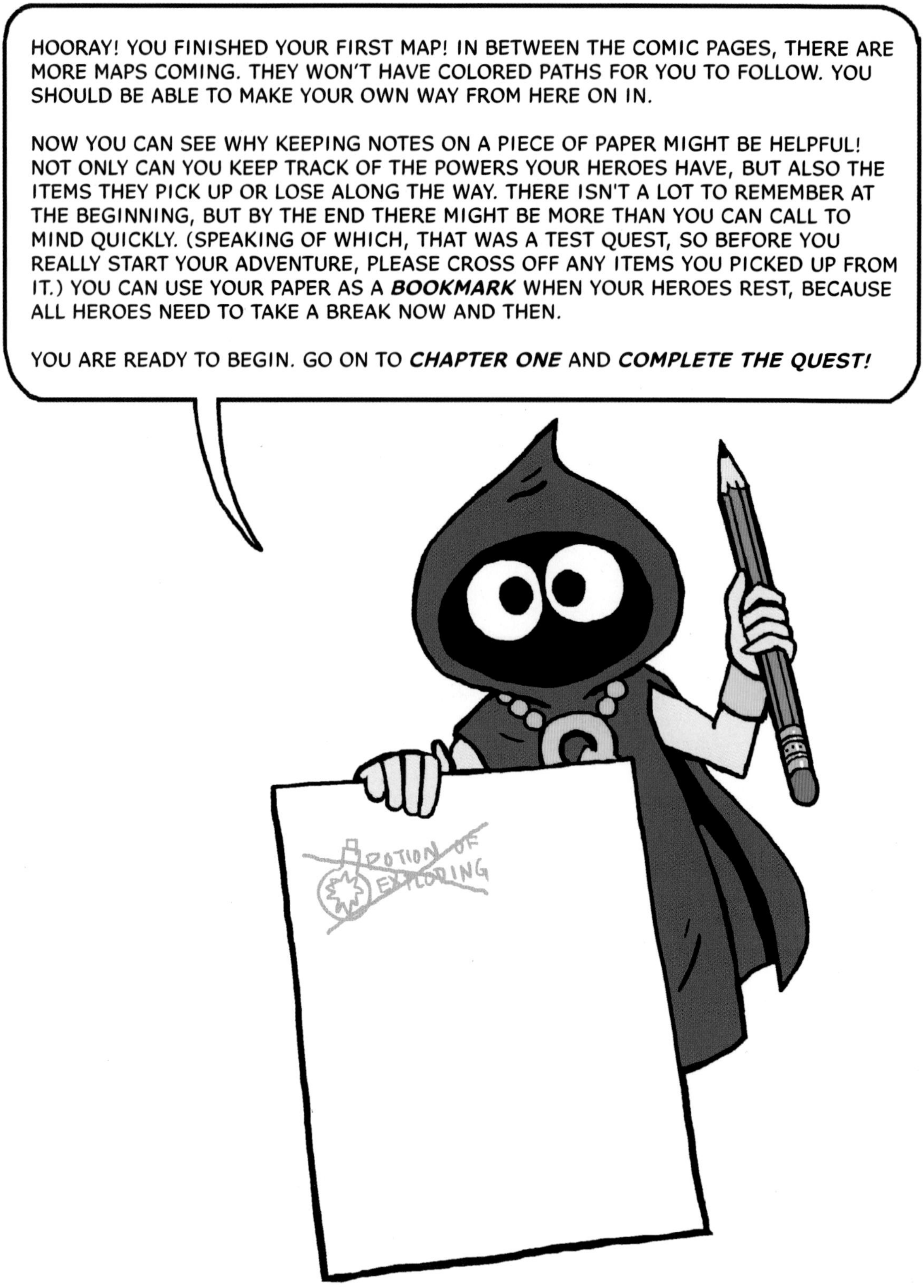
HOORAY! YOU FINISHED YOUR FIRST MAP! IN BETWEEN THE COMIC PAGES, THERE ARE MORE MAPS COMING. THEY WON'T HAVE COLORED PATHS FOR YOU TO FOLLOW. YOU SHOULD BE ABLE TO MAKE YOUR OWN WAY FROM HERE ON IN.
NOW YOU CAN SEE WHY KEEPING NOTES ON A PIECE OF PAPER MIGHT BE HELPFUL! NOT ONLY CAN YOU KEEP TRACK OF THE POWERS YOUR HEROES HAVE, BUT ALSO THE ITEMS THEY PICK UP OR LOSE ALONG THE WAY. THERE ISN'T A LOT TO REMEMBER AT THE BEGINNING, BUT BY THE END THERE MIGHT BE MORE THAN YOU CAN CALL TO MIND QUICKLY. (SPEAKING OF WHICH, THAT WAS A TEST QUEST, SO BEFORE YOU REALLY START YOUR ADVENTURE, PLEASE CROSS OFF ANY ITEMS YOU PICKED UP FROM IT.) YOU CAN USE YOUR PAPER AS A ***BOOKMARK*** WHEN YOUR HEROES REST, BECAUSE ALL HEROES NEED TO TAKE A BREAK NOW AND THEN.
YOU ARE READY TO BEGIN. GO ON TO ***CHAPTER ONE*** AND ***COMPLETE THE QUEST!***
POTION OF EXPLORING

CHAPTER ONE

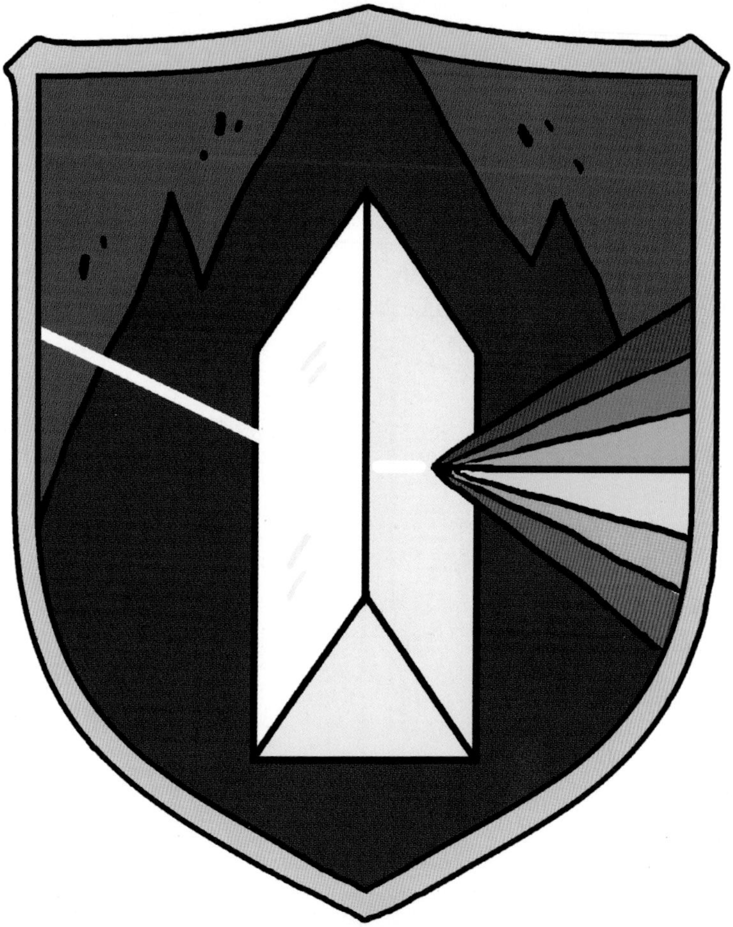

DEEP TROUBLE

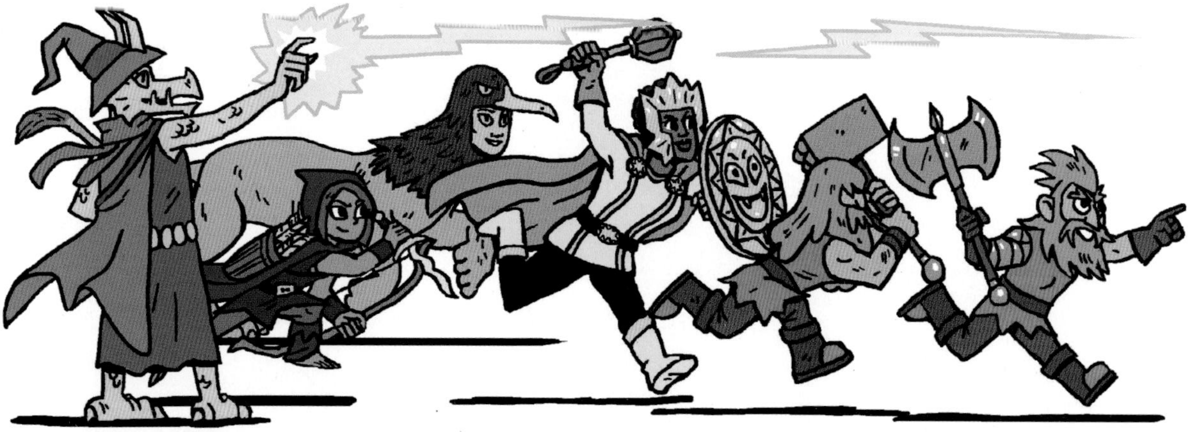

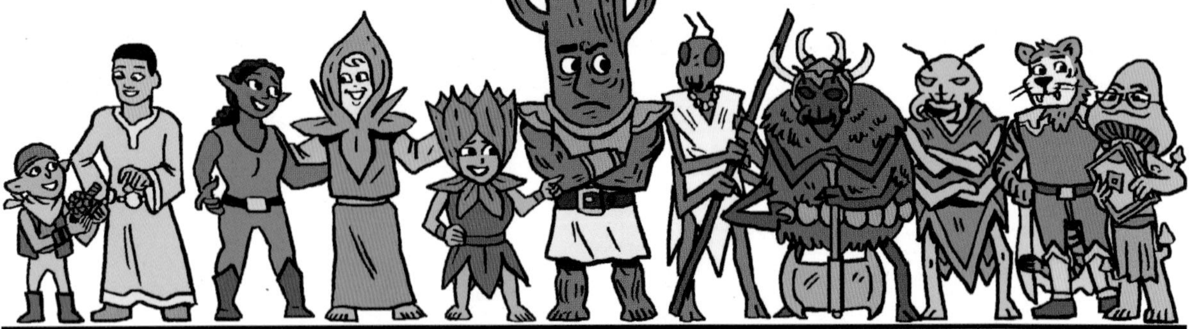

WELCOME TO ***CHIMERIA,*** A WORLD SHARED BY HUMAN-LIKE ***KITH,*** PLANT-LIKE ***FLORIN,*** BUG-LIKE ***SECTONS,*** AND OTHER STRANGER CREATURES. HUMAN ***QUEEN EVERGREEN*** DOES HER BEST TO MAKE SURE THEY ALL GET ALONG IN HER QUEENDOM AND BEYOND. SHE IS FAMOUS FOR COMING UP WITH SMART SOLUTIONS TO TOUGH PROBLEMS. HER BEST FRIEND AND WISE ADVISER, ***MARISHA,*** HELPS RUN THINGS AND TRAIN ***PRINCESS VIOLET*** TO BECOME LIKE HER MOM.

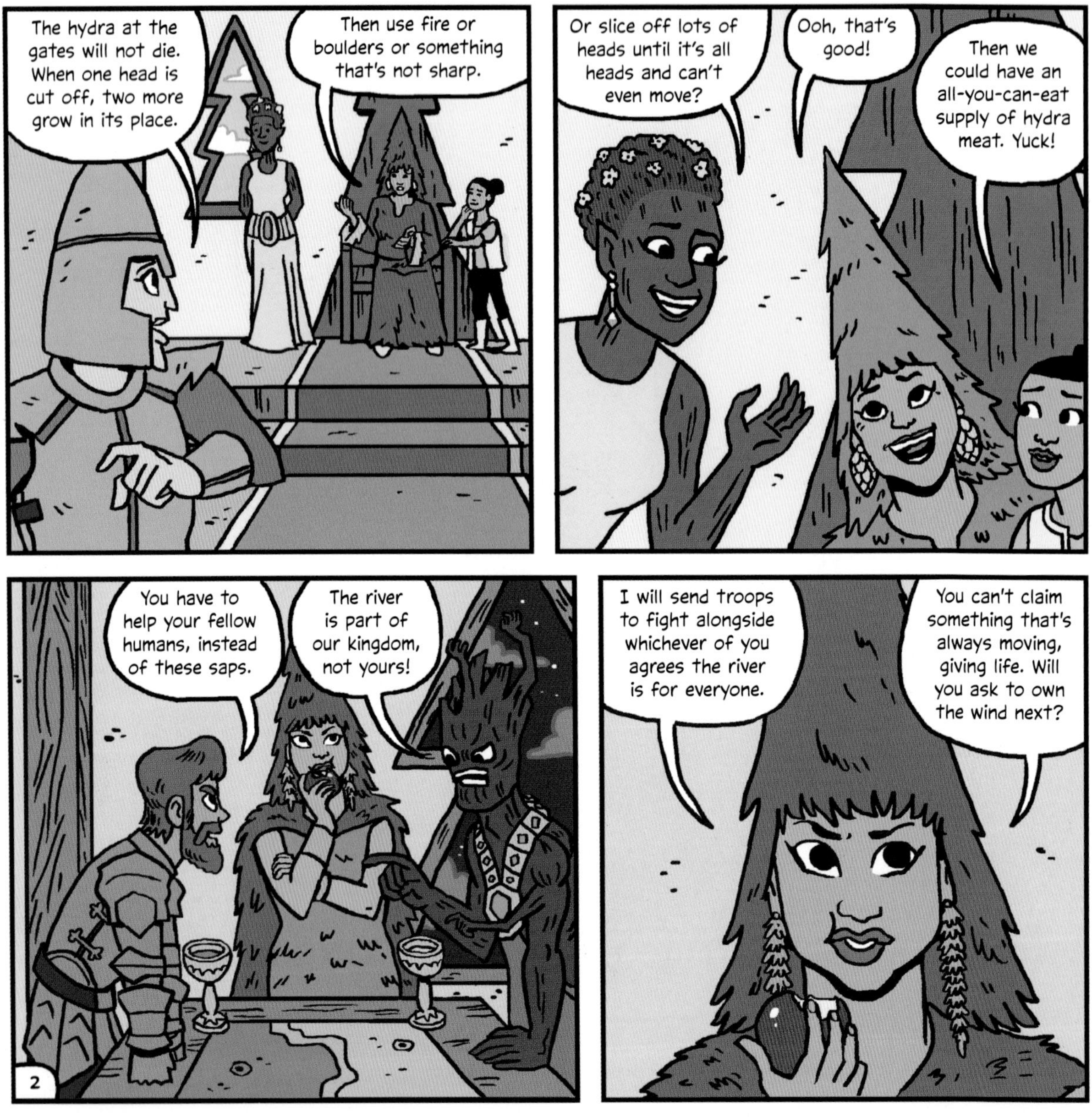
The hydra at the gates will not die. When one head is cut off, two more grow in its place.
Then use fire or boulders or something that's not sharp.
Or slice off lots of heads until it's all heads and can't even move?
Ooh, that's good!
Then we could have an all-you-can-eat supply of hydra meat. Yuck!
You have to help your fellow humans, instead of these saps.
The river is part of our kingdom, not yours!
I will send troops to fight alongside whichever of you agrees the river is for everyone.
You can't claim something that's always moving, giving life. Will you ask to own the wind next?

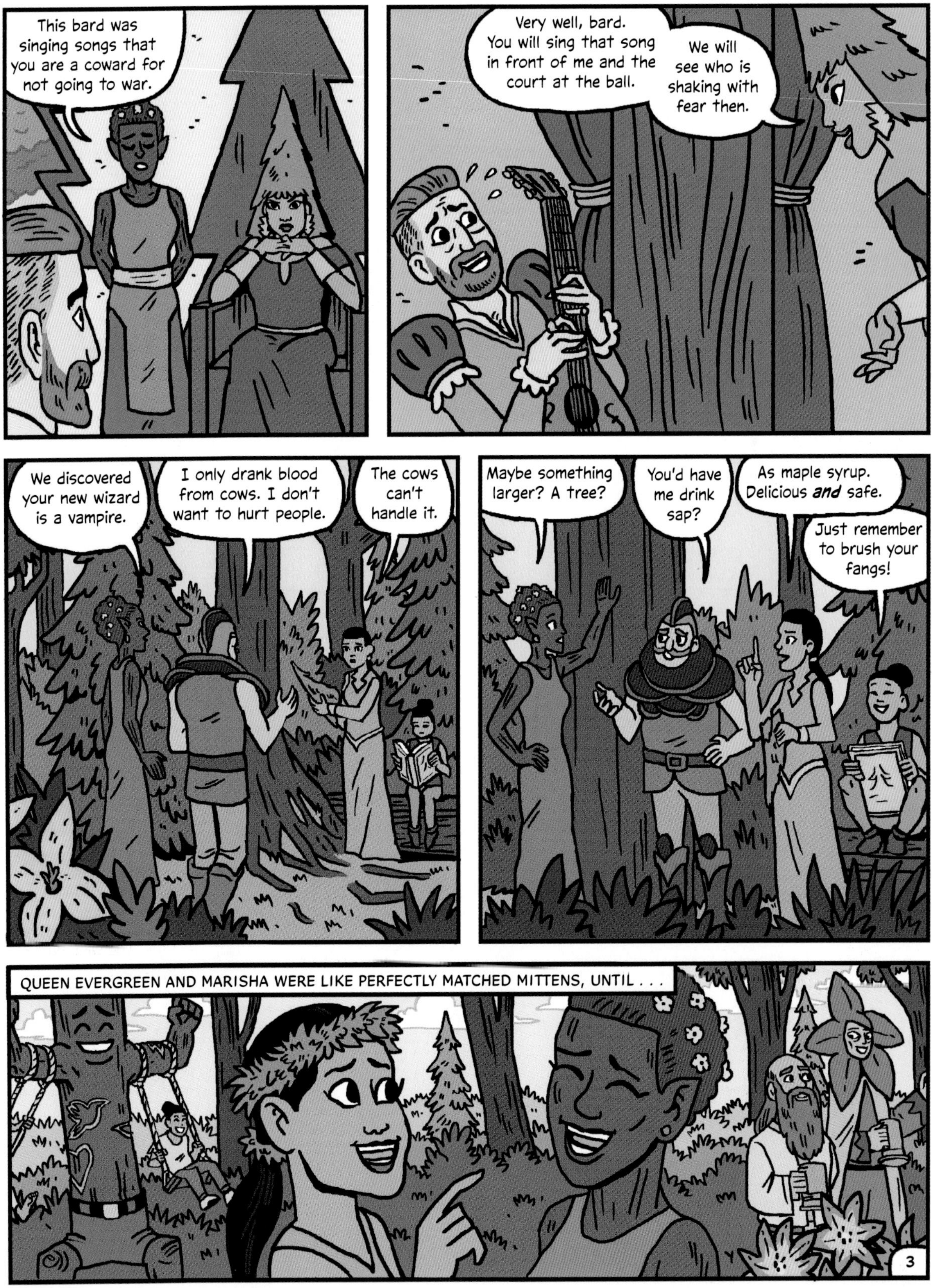
This bard was singing songs that you are a coward for not going to war.
Very well, bard. You will sing that song in front of me and the court at the ball.
We will see who is shaking with fear then.
We discovered your new wizard is a vampire.
I only drank blood from cows. I don't want to hurt people.
The cows can't handle it.
Maybe something larger? A tree?
You'd have me drink sap?
As maple syrup. Delicious *and* safe.
Just remember to brush your fangs!
QUEEN EVERGREEN AND MARISHA WERE LIKE PERFECTLY MATCHED MITTENS, UNTIL . . .

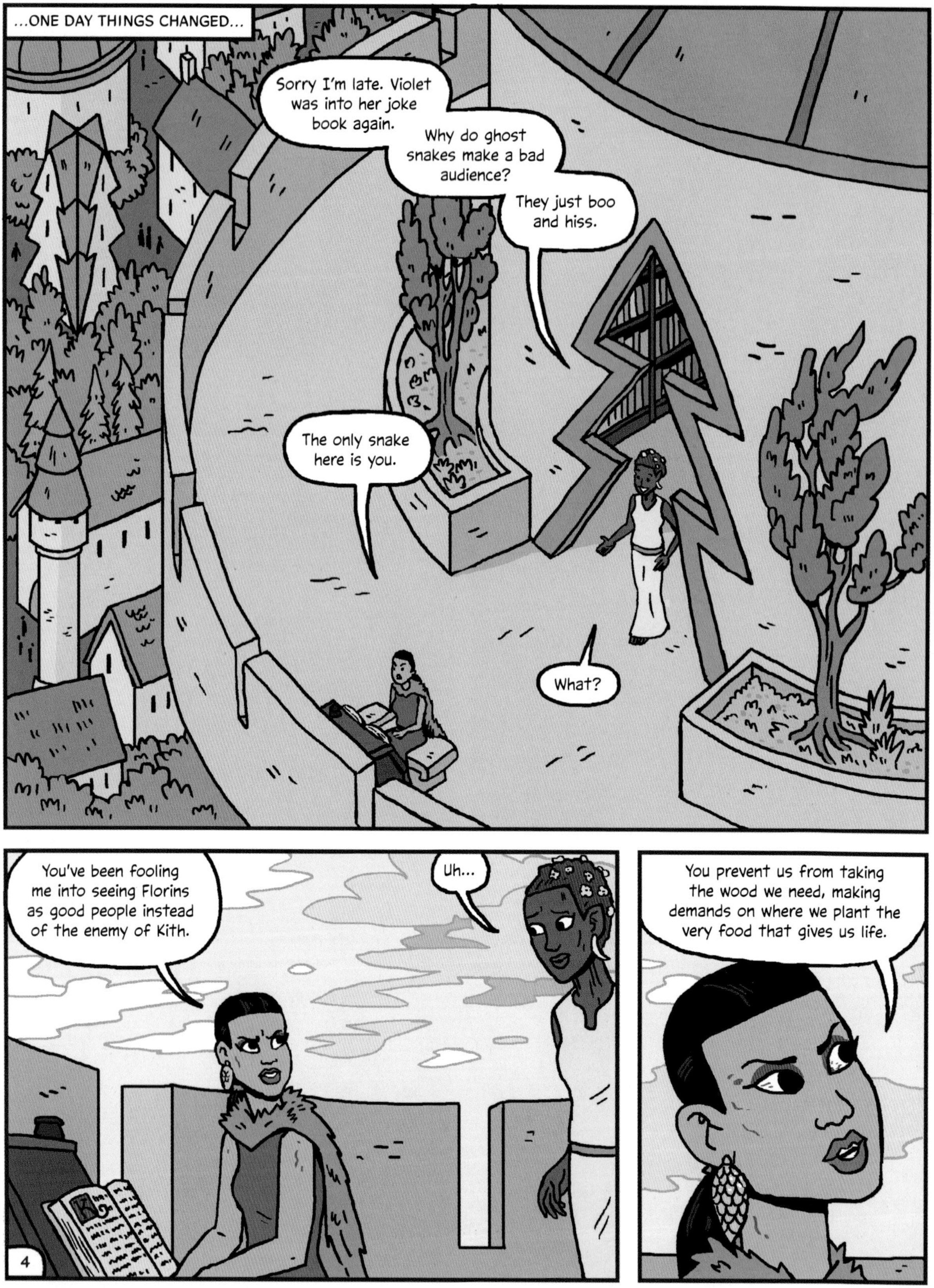
...ONE DAY THINGS CHANGED...
Sorry I'm late. Violet was into her joke book again.
Why do ghost snakes make a bad audience?
They just boo and hiss.
The only snake here is you.
What?
You've been fooling me into seeing Florins as good people instead of the enemy of Kith.
Uh...
You prevent us from taking the wood we need, making demands on where we plant the very food that gives us life.

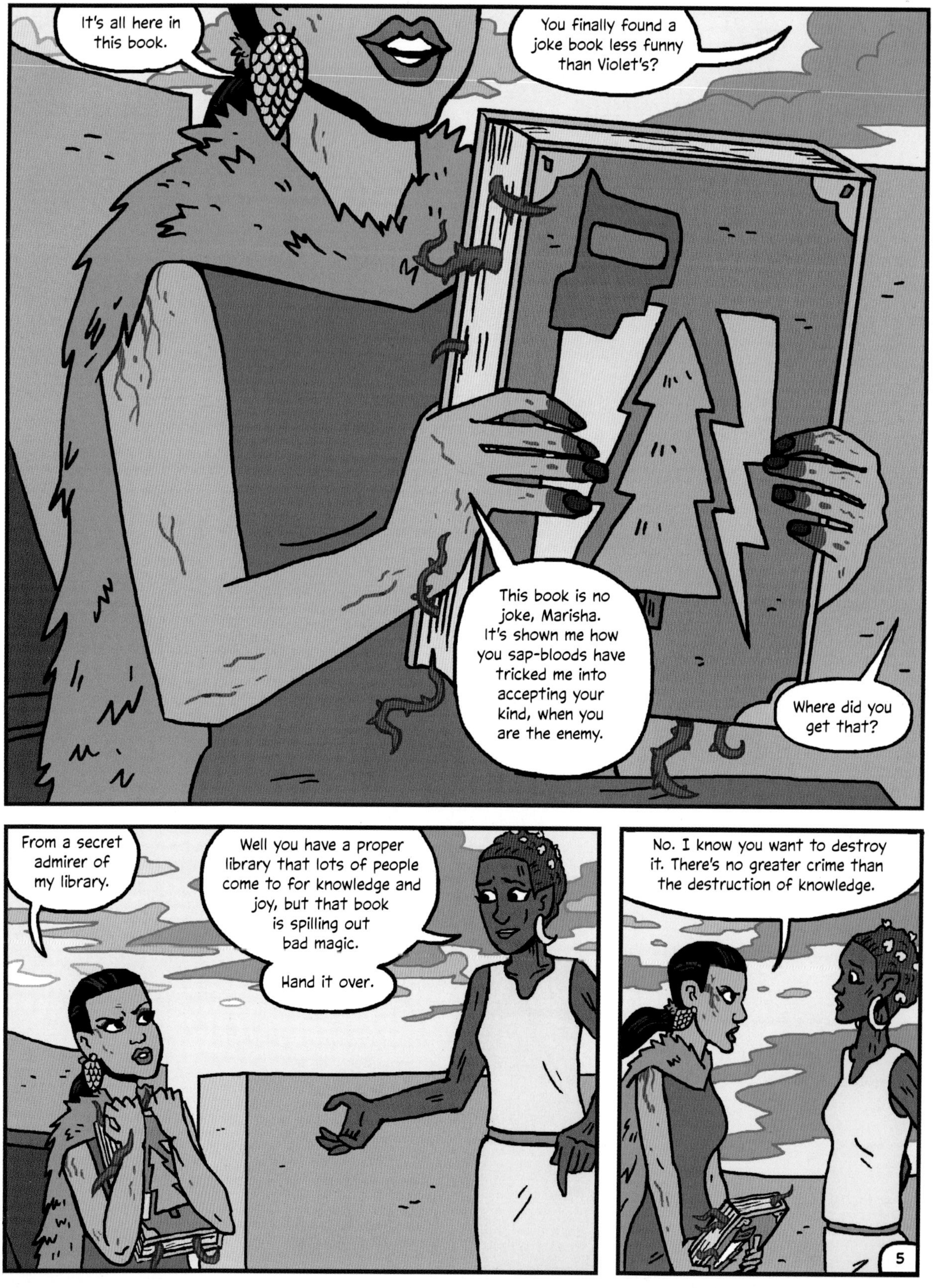
It's all here in this book.
You finally found a joke book less funny than Violet's?
This book is no joke, Marisha. It's shown me how you sap-bloods have tricked me into accepting your kind, when you are the enemy.
Where did you get that?
From a secret admirer of my library.
Well you have a proper library that lots of people come to for knowledge and joy, but that book is spilling out bad magic.
Hand it over.
No. I know you want to destroy it. There's no greater crime than the destruction of knowledge.

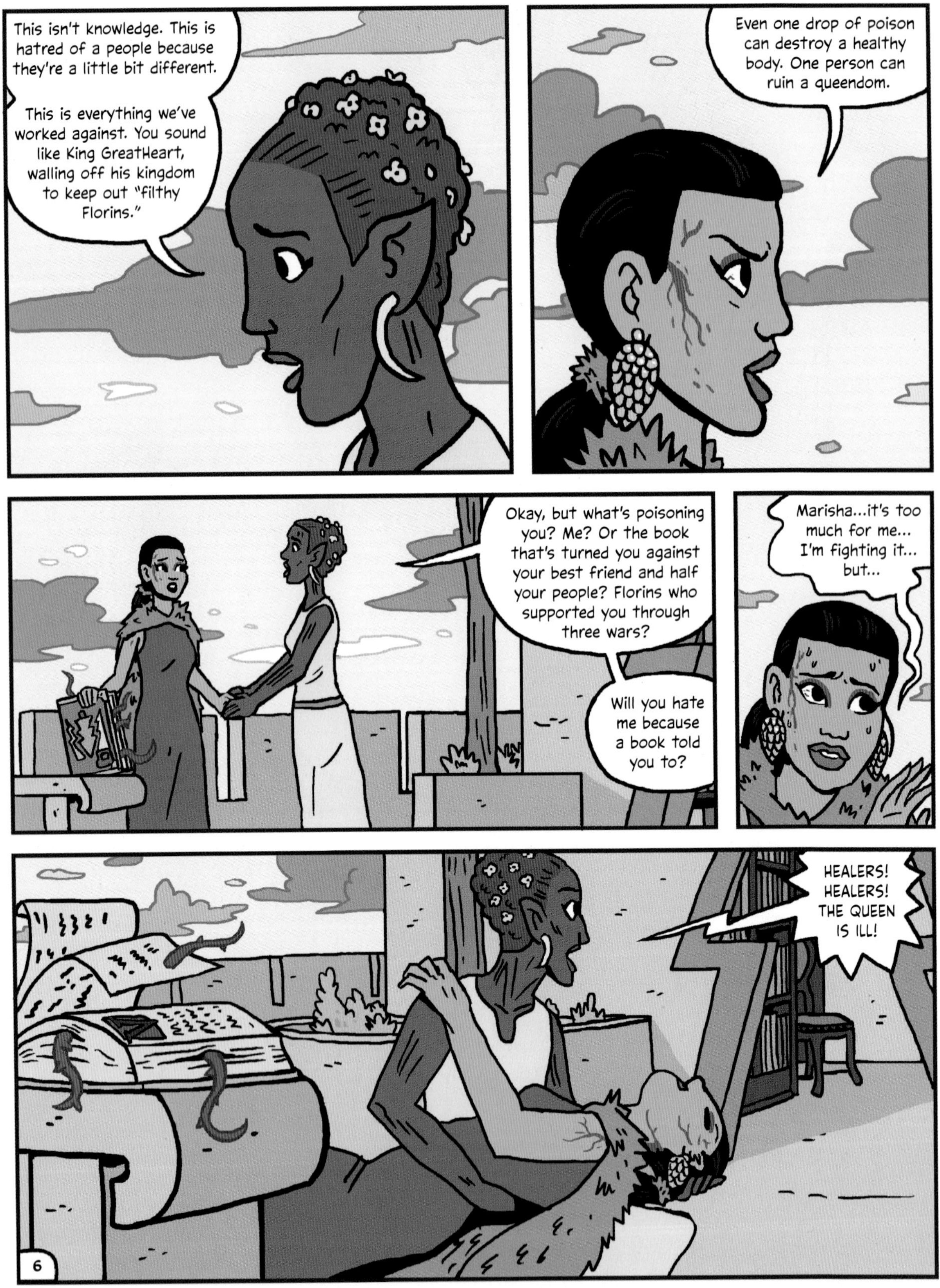
This isn't knowledge. This is hatred of a people because they're a little bit different.
This is everything we've worked against. You sound like King GreatHeart, walling off his kingdom to keep out "filthy Florins."
Even one drop of poison can destroy a healthy body. One person can ruin a queendom.
Okay, but what's poisoning you? Me? Or the book that's turned you against your best friend and half your people? Florins who supported you through three wars?
Will you hate me because a book told you to?
Marisha...it's too much for me... I'm fighting it... but...
HEALERS! HEALERS! THE QUEEN IS ILL!

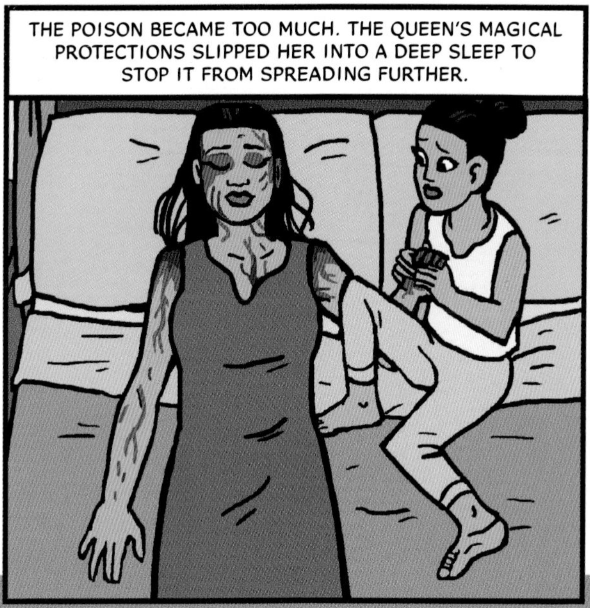
THE POISON BECAME TOO MUCH. THE QUEEN'S MAGICAL PROTECTIONS SLIPPED HER INTO A DEEP SLEEP TO STOP IT FROM SPREADING FURTHER.

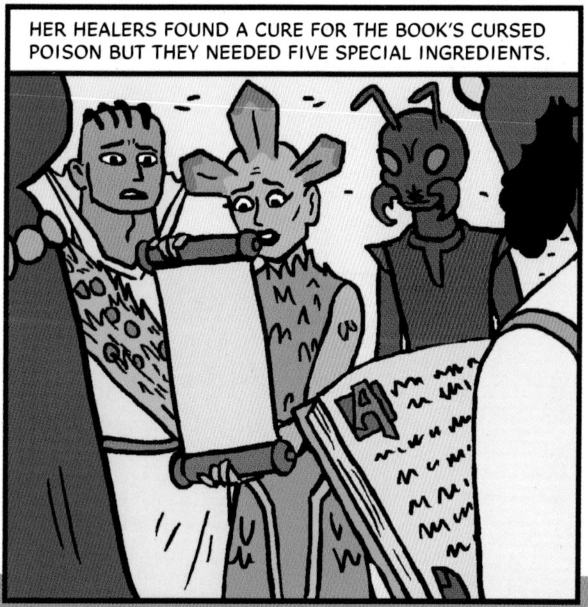
HER HEALERS FOUND A CURE FOR THE BOOK'S CURSED POISON BUT THEY NEEDED FIVE SPECIAL INGREDIENTS.

A STAR DIAMOND, MINED NEAR THE UNDERGROUND KINGDOM OF DEEPPRISM.

A BLANK LOTUS, FROM THE CRYPT OF THE WITCHQUEEN ICENAIL IN THE WHITEWIND DESERT.

A GHOST CLOUD, KEPT AS PETS BY SKY GIANTS. SOME CAN BE FOUND ABOVE THE HIGHTOOTH MOUNTAINS.

A DRAGON LIME, WHICH GROW WILD IN THE REDTHORN JUNGLE.

AND A ***SKRIM,*** THE BOTTOM-FEEDING WATER CRITTER FOUND IN SALTWATER SHIPWRECKS.

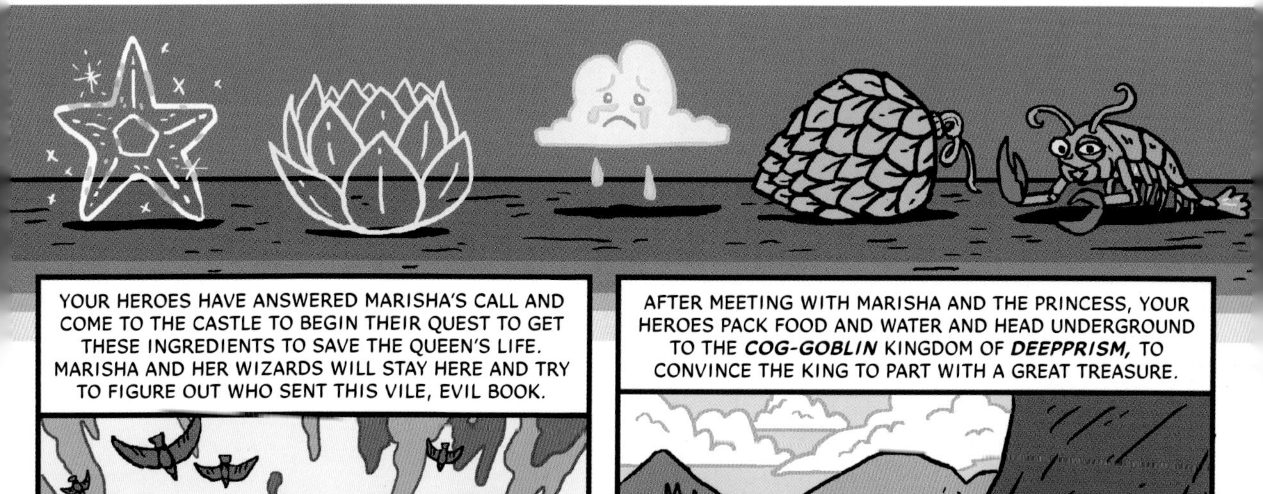

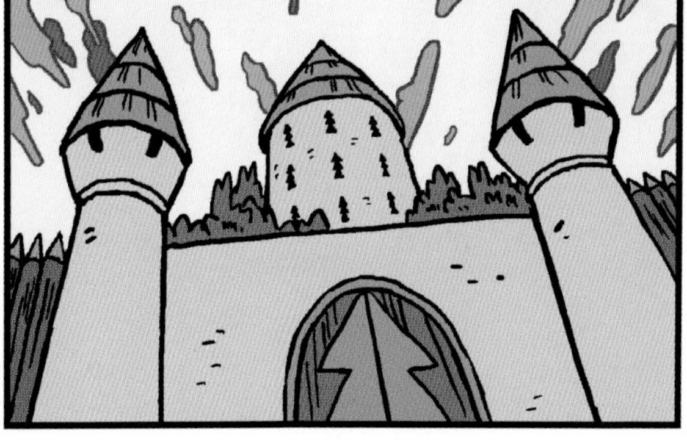
YOUR HEROES HAVE ANSWERED MARISHA'S CALL AND COME TO THE CASTLE TO BEGIN THEIR QUEST TO GET THESE INGREDIENTS TO SAVE THE QUEEN'S LIFE. MARISHA AND HER WIZARDS WILL STAY HERE AND TRY TO FIGURE OUT WHO SENT THIS VILE, EVIL BOOK.

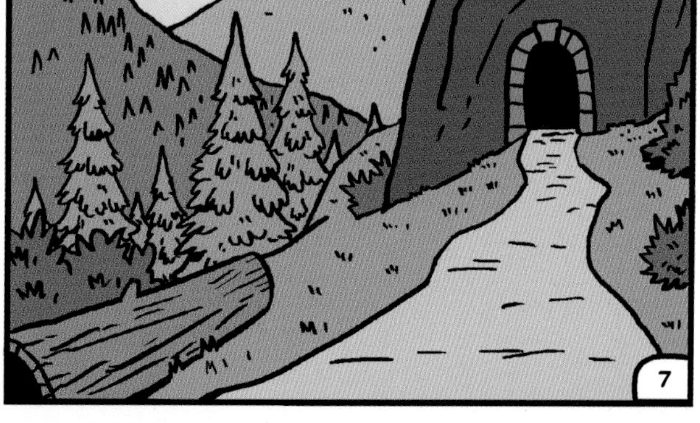
AFTER MEETING WITH MARISHA AND THE PRINCESS, YOUR HEROES PACK FOOD AND WATER AND HEAD UNDERGROUND TO THE ***COG-GOBLIN*** KINGDOM OF ***DEEPPRISM,*** TO CONVINCE THE KING TO PART WITH A GREAT TREASURE.

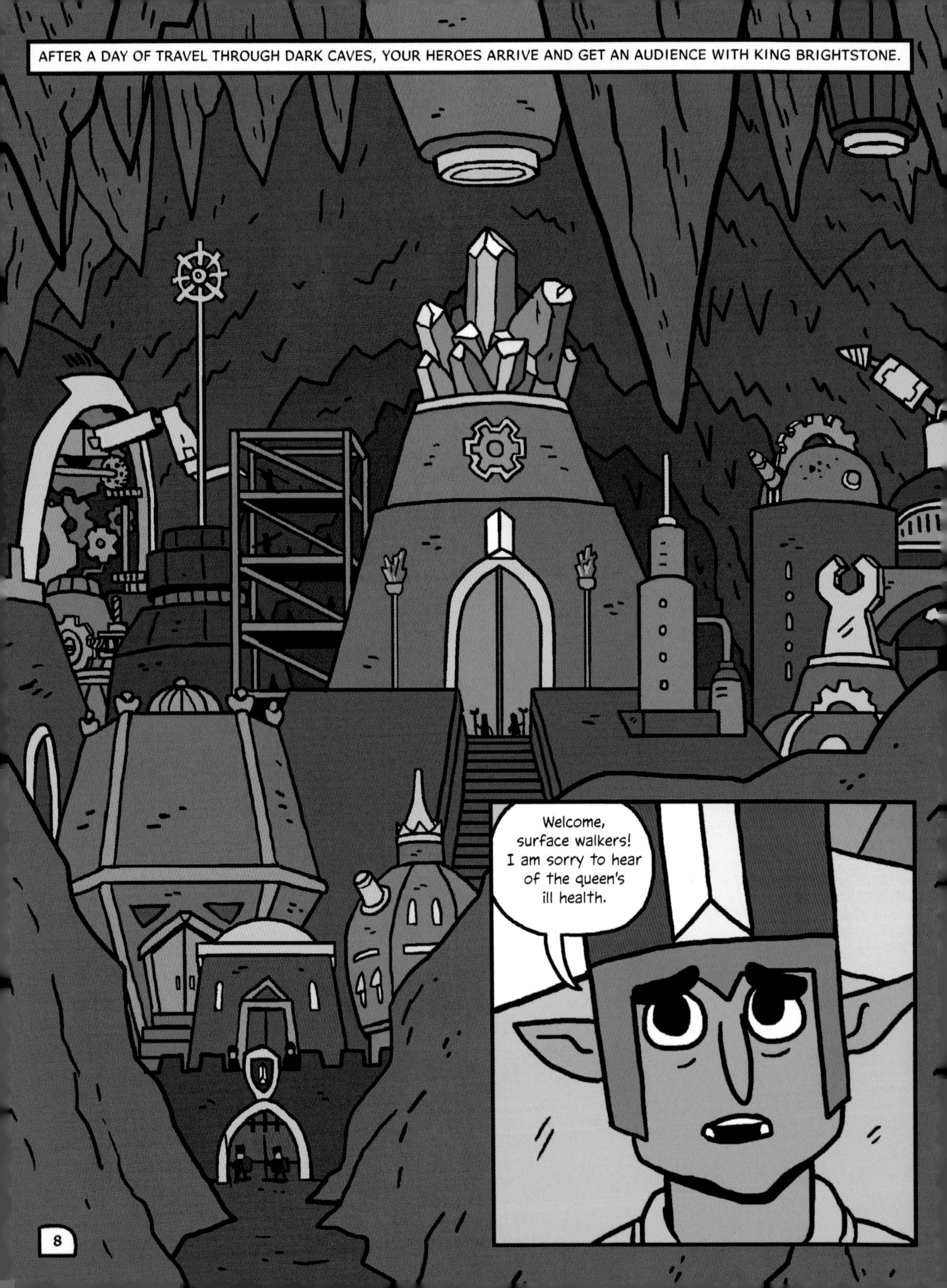
AFTER A DAY OF TRAVEL THROUGH DARK CAVES, YOUR HEROES ARRIVE AND GET AN AUDIENCE WITH KING BRIGHTSTONE.
Welcome, surface walkers! I am sorry to hear of the queen's ill health.

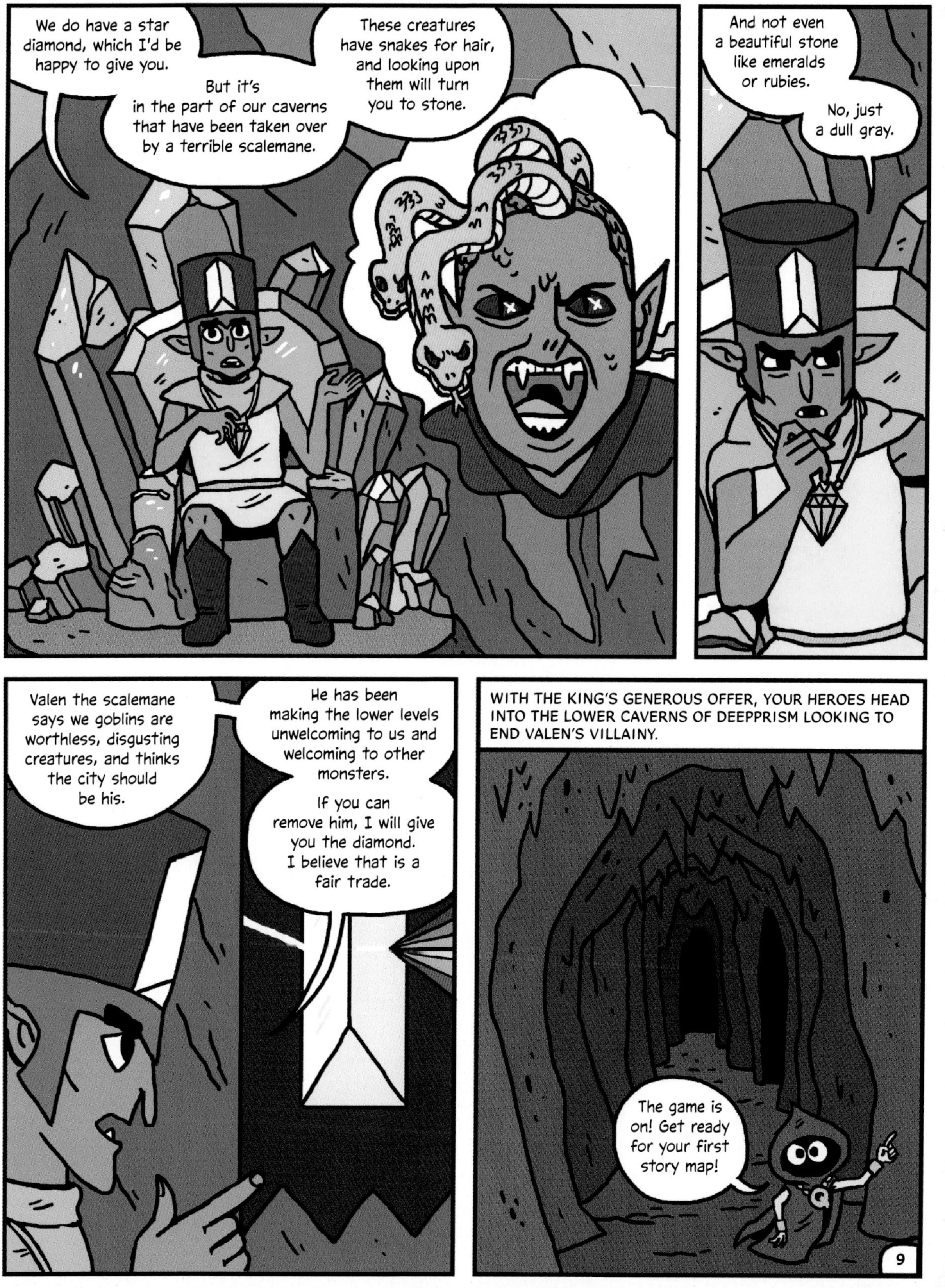
We do have a star diamond, which I'd be happy to give you.
But it's in the part of our caverns that have been taken over by a terrible scalemane.
These creatures have snakes for hair, and looking upon them will turn you to stone.
And not even a beautiful stone like emeralds or rubies.
No, just a dull gray.
Valen the scalemane says we goblins are worthless, disgusting creatures, and thinks the city should be his.
He has been making the lower levels unwelcoming to us and welcoming to other monsters.
If you can remove him, I will give you the diamond. I believe that is a fair trade.
WITH THE KING'S GENEROUS OFFER, YOUR HEROES HEAD INTO THE LOWER CAVERNS OF DEEPPRISM LOOKING TO END VALEN'S VILLAINY.
The game is on! Get ready for your first story map!

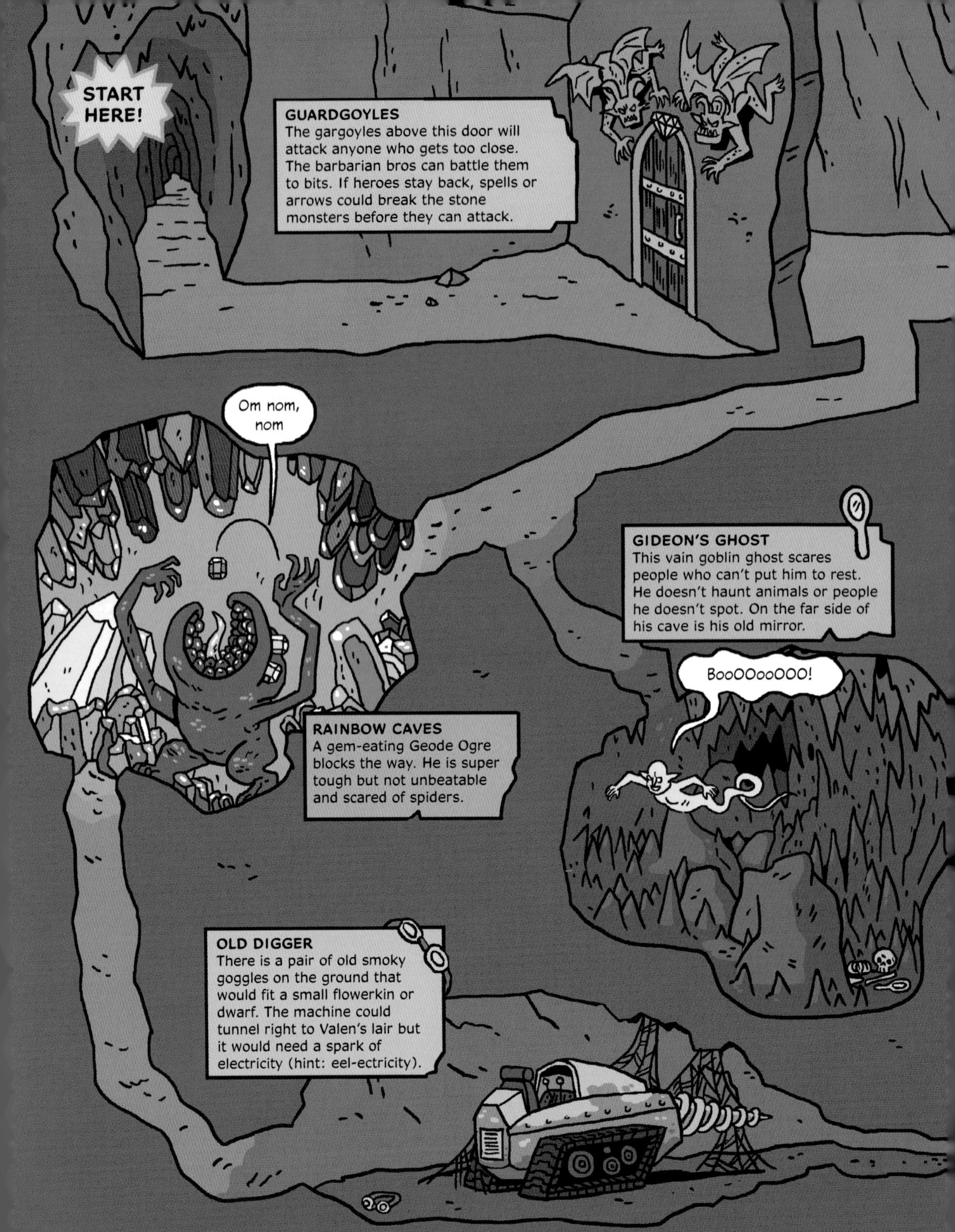
START HERE!
GUARDGOYLES
The gargoyles above this door will attack anyone who gets too close. The barbarian bros can battle them to bits. If heroes stay back, spells or arrows could break the stone monsters before they can attack.
Om nom, nom
RAINBOW CAVES
A gem-eating Geode Ogre blocks the way. He is super tough but not unbeatable and scared of spiders.
GIDEON'S GHOST
This vain goblin ghost scares people who can't put him to rest. He doesn't haunt animals or people he doesn't spot. On the far side of his cave is his old mirror.
BooOOooOOO!
OLD DIGGER
There is a pair of old smoky goggles on the ground that would fit a small flowerkin or dwarf. The machine could tunnel right to Valen's lair but it would need a spark of electricity (hint: eel-ectricity).

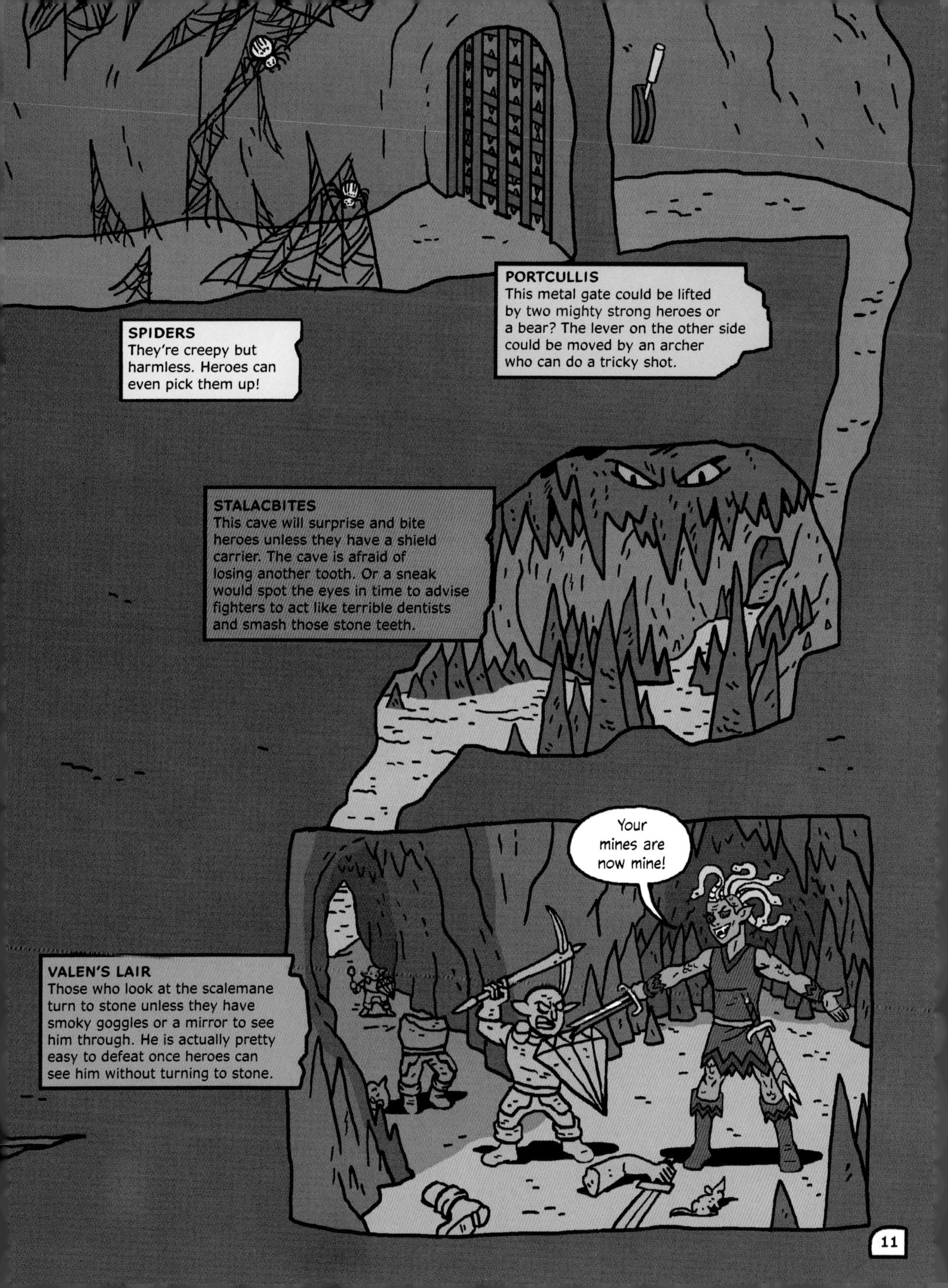
PORTCULLIS
This metal gate could be lifted by two mighty strong heroes or a bear? The lever on the other side could be moved by an archer who can do a tricky shot.
SPIDERS
They're creepy but harmless. Heroes can even pick them up!
STALACBITES
This cave will surprise and bite heroes unless they have a shield carrier. The cave is afraid of losing another tooth. Or a sneak would spot the eyes in time to advise fighters to act like terrible dentists and smash those stone teeth.
Your mines are now mine!
VALEN'S LAIR
Those who look at the scalemane turn to stone unless they have smoky goggles or a mirror to see him through. He is actually pretty easy to defeat once heroes can see him without turning to stone.

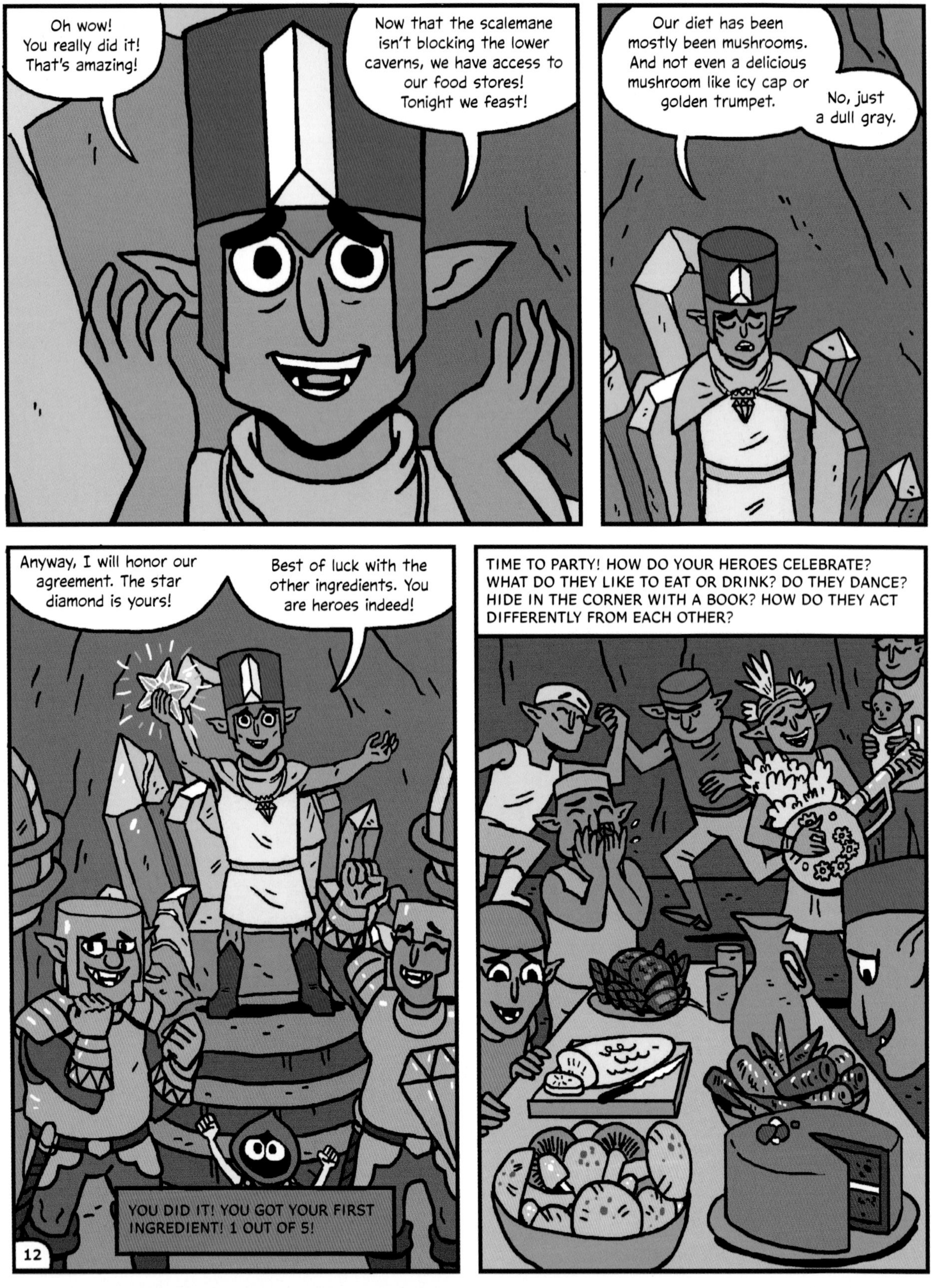
Oh wow! You really did it! That's amazing!
Now that the scalemane isn't blocking the lower caverns, we have access to our food stores! Tonight we feast!
Our diet has been mostly been mushrooms. And not even a delicious mushroom like icy cap or golden trumpet.
No, just a dull gray.
Anyway, I will honor our agreement. The star diamond is yours!
Best of luck with the other ingredients. You are heroes indeed!
YOU DID IT! YOU GOT YOUR FIRST INGREDIENT! 1 OUT OF 5!
TIME TO PARTY! HOW DO YOUR HEROES CELEBRATE? WHAT DO THEY LIKE TO EAT OR DRINK? DO THEY DANCE? HIDE IN THE CORNER WITH A BOOK? HOW DO THEY ACT DIFFERENTLY FROM EACH OTHER?

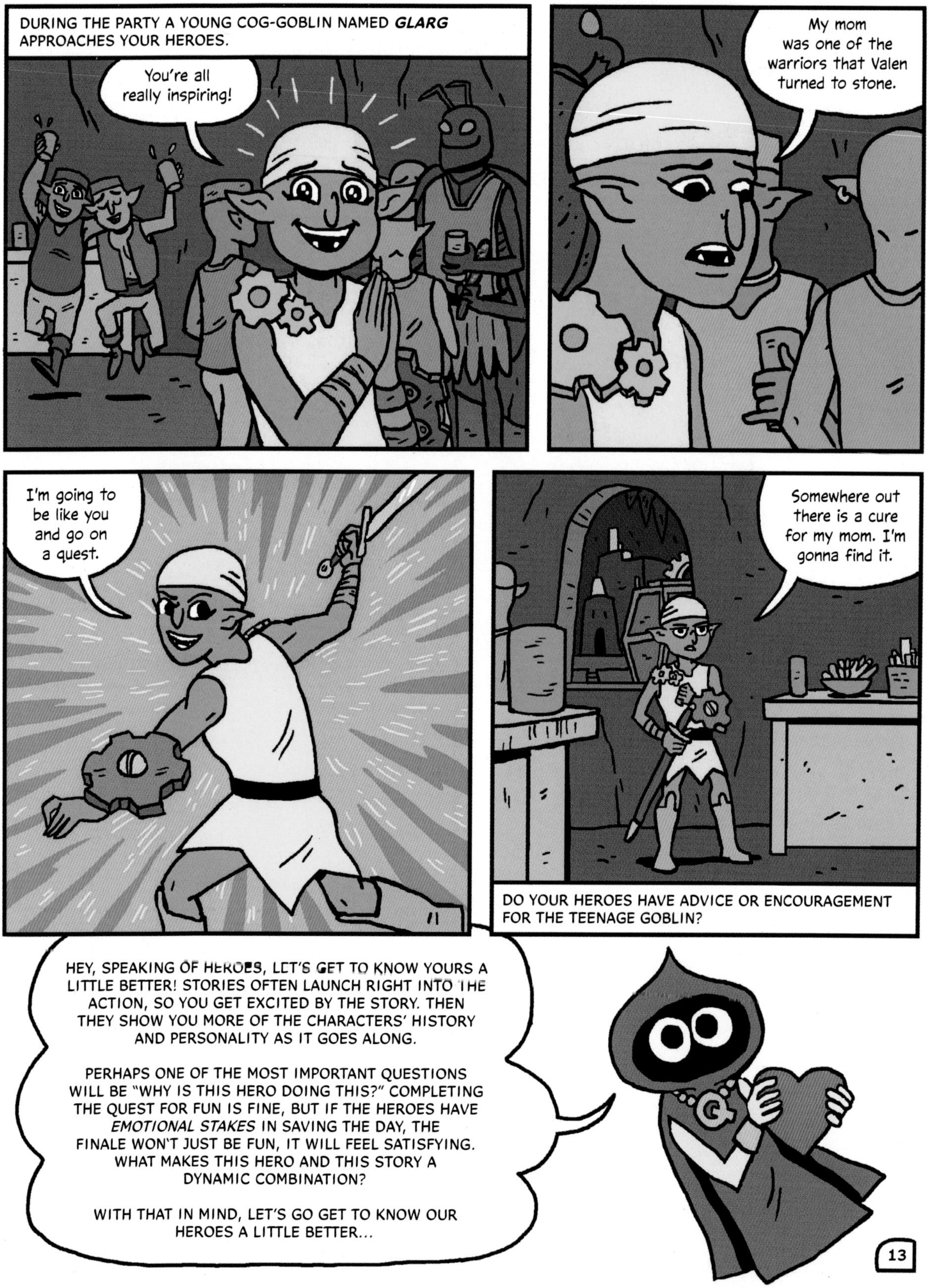
DURING THE PARTY A YOUNG COG-GOBLIN NAMED GLARG APPROACHES YOUR HEROES.
You're all really inspiring!
My mom was one of the warriors that Valen turned to stone.
I'm going to be like you and go on a quest.
Somewhere out there is a cure for my mom. I'm gonna find it.
DO YOUR HEROES HAVE ADVICE OR ENCOURAGEMENT FOR THE TEENAGE GOBLIN?
HEY, SPEAKING OF HEROES, LET'S GET TO KNOW YOURS A LITTLE BETTER! STORIES OFTEN LAUNCH RIGHT INTO THE ACTION, SO YOU GET EXCITED BY THE STORY. THEN THEY SHOW YOU MORE OF THE CHARACTERS' HISTORY AND PERSONALITY AS IT GOES ALONG.
PERHAPS ONE OF THE MOST IMPORTANT QUESTIONS WILL BE "WHY IS THIS HERO DOING THIS?" COMPLETING THE QUEST FOR FUN IS FINE, BUT IF THE HEROES HAVE EMOTIONAL STAKES IN SAVING THE DAY, THE FINALE WON'T JUST BE FUN, IT WILL FEEL SATISFYING. WHAT MAKES THIS HERO AND THIS STORY A DYNAMIC COMBINATION?
WITH THAT IN MIND, LET'S GO GET TO KNOW OUR HEROES A LITTLE BETTER...

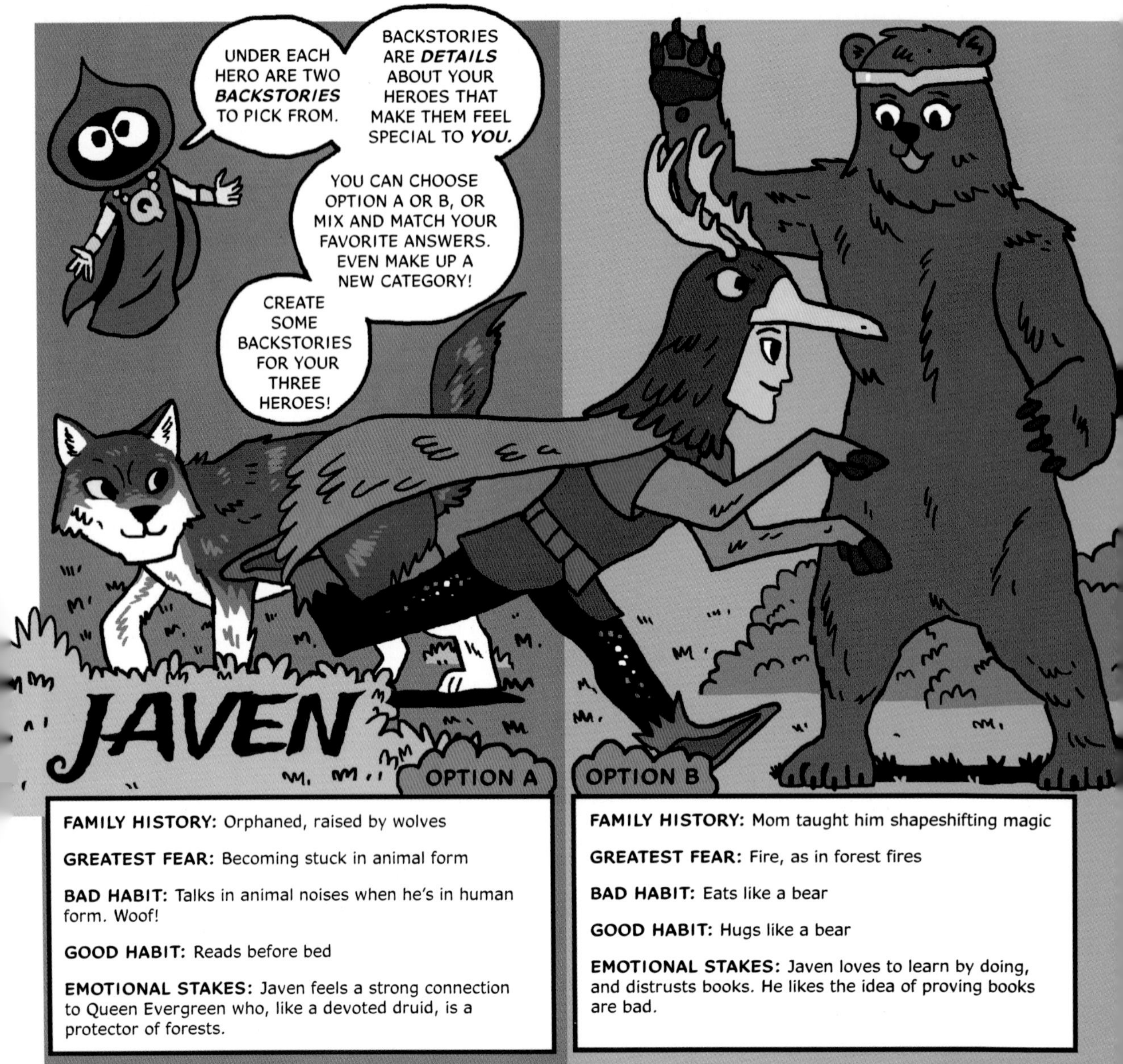
UNDER EACH HERO ARE TWO ***BACKSTORIES*** TO PICK FROM.
BACKSTORIES ARE ***DETAILS*** ABOUT YOUR HEROES THAT MAKE THEM FEEL SPECIAL TO ***YOU.***
YOU CAN CHOOSE OPTION A OR B, OR MIX AND MATCH YOUR FAVORITE ANSWERS. EVEN MAKE UP A NEW CATEGORY!
CREATE SOME BACKSTORIES FOR YOUR THREE HEROES!
JAVEN
OPTION A
OPTION B

FAMILY HISTORY: Orphaned, raised by wolves

GREATEST FEAR: Becoming stuck in animal form

BAD HABIT: Talks in animal noises when he's in human form. Woof!

GOOD HABIT: Reads before bed

EMOTIONAL STAKES: Javen feels a strong connection to Queen Evergreen who, like a devoted druid, is a protector of forests.

FAMILY HISTORY: Mom taught him shapeshifting magic

GREATEST FEAR: Fire, as in forest fires

BAD HABIT: Eats like a bear

GOOD HABIT: Hugs like a bear

EMOTIONAL STAKES: Javen loves to learn by doing, and distrusts books. He likes the idea of proving books are bad.

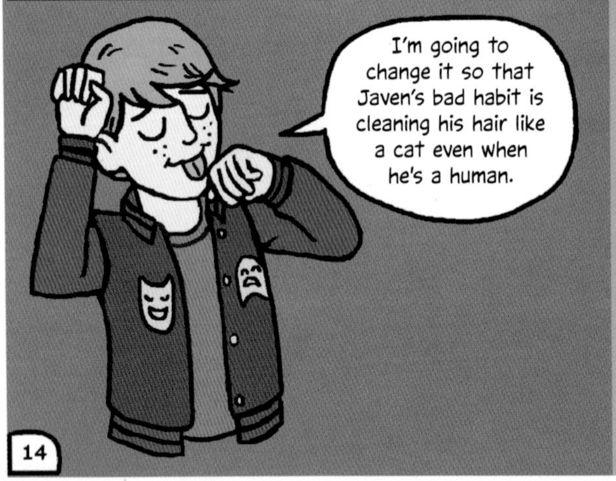
I'm going to change it so that Javen's bad habit is cleaning his hair like a cat even when he's a human.

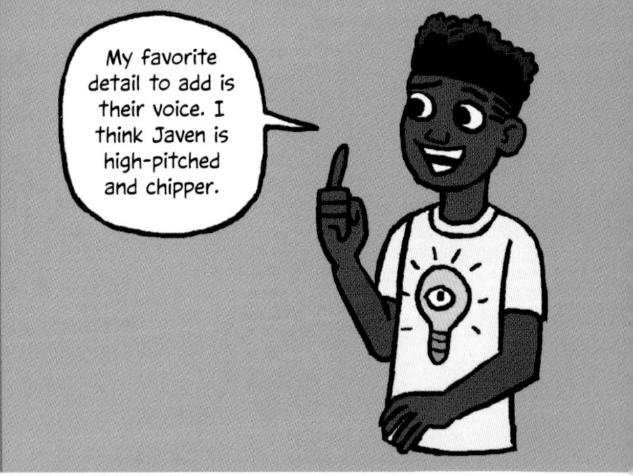
My favorite detail to add is their voice. I think Javen is high-pitched and chipper.

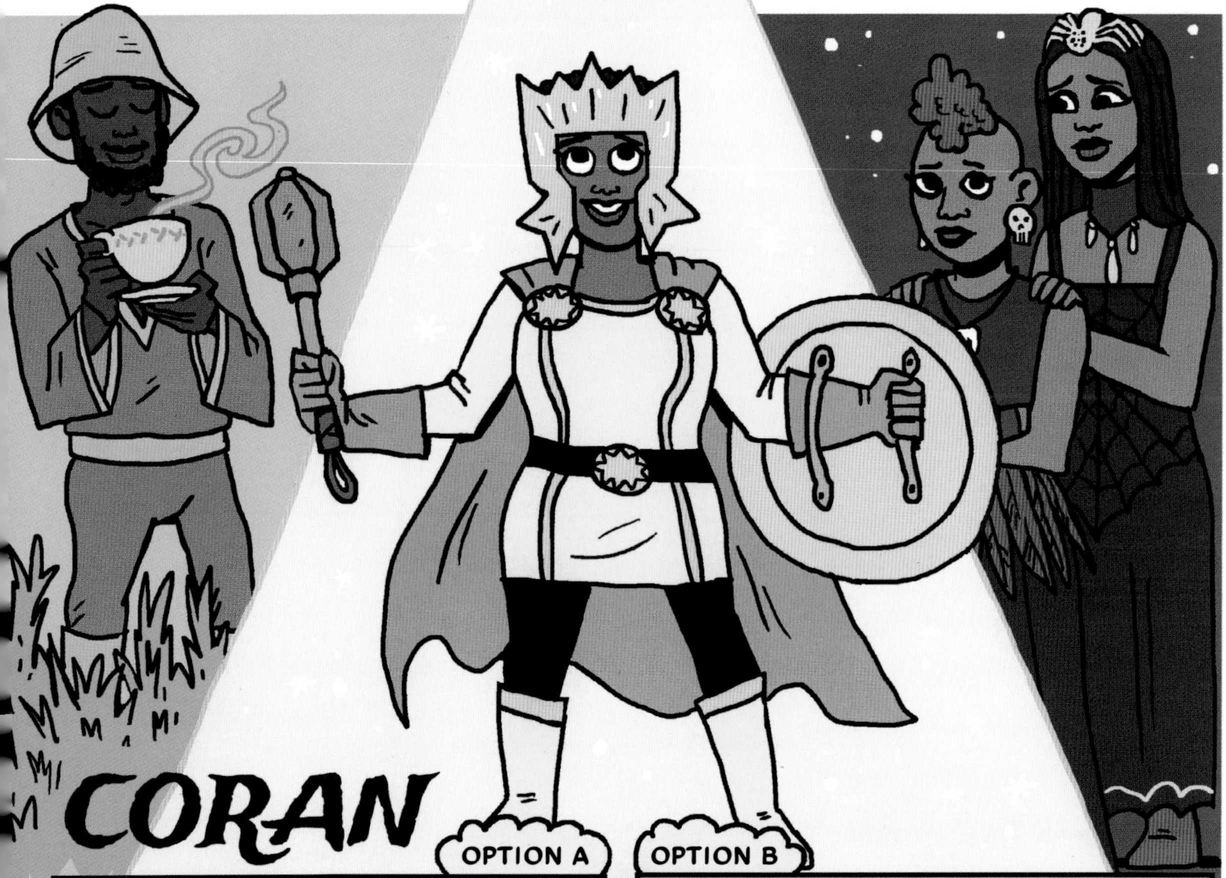
CORAN
OPTION A
OPTION B

Option A

FAMILY HISTORY: They tend a garden for unusual tea leaves that she helps grow with sunshine.

GREATEST FEAR: The dark

BAD HABIT: Hums, making it hard to sneak around

GOOD HABIT: Makes everyone tea to help them sleep

EMOTIONAL STAKES: Coran's mom got very sick and died and she couldn't do anything to stop it. Saving someone else's mom is the closest thing she'll get to being able to save hers.

Option B

FAMILY HISTORY: They're all goths who don't understand her sun worship.

GREATEST FEAR: Losing the Sun God's approval

BAD HABIT: Forgets details about quests

GOOD HABIT: Accepts people for who they are

EMOTIONAL STAKES: When Queen Evergreen was a princess, she and Coran were best friends. They'd play and talk for hours. Both of their duties sent them down different paths, but they still really care for each other.

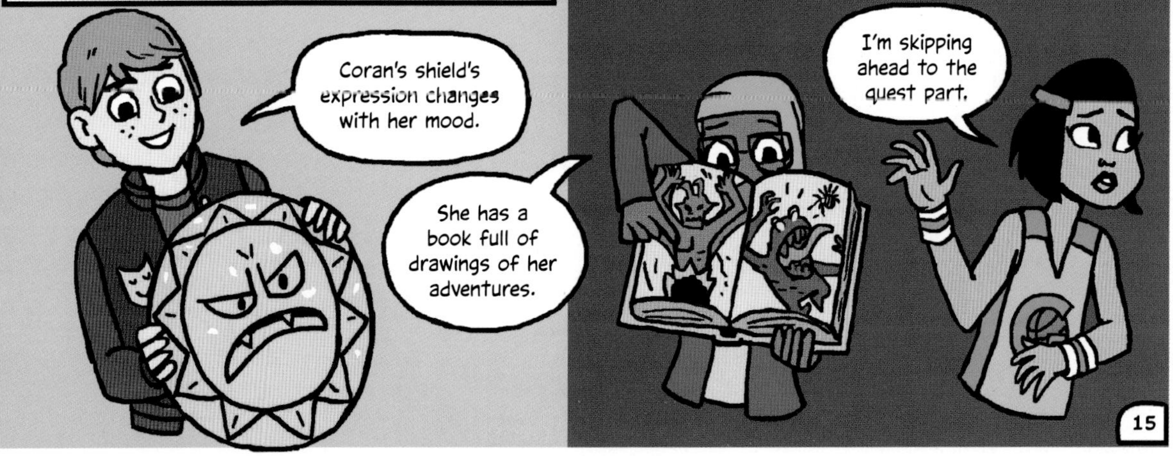
Coran's shield's expression changes with her mood.
She has a book full of drawings of her adventures.
I'm skipping ahead to the quest part.

BLADE

OPTION A	OPTION B
FAMILY HISTORY: Travelers who often change hometowns	**FAMILY HISTORY:** Big family, too many mouths to feed
GREATEST FEAR: Not making a best friend	**GREATEST FEAR:** That she won't see her family again
BAD HABIT: Asks too many questions at the wrong time	**BAD HABIT:** Eats with mouth open
GOOD HABIT: Not even a little bit gullible	**GOOD HABIT:** Pays all her debts
EMOTIONAL STAKES: Blade wants to prove that Florins and Kith can work together peacefully, even though she has had trouble with Kith in the past. Giving up on that dream means all those cruel Kith were right, that they can't live peacefully.	**EMOTIONAL STAKES:** Blade needs the reward from Marisha to pay for her parents' medical bills. Their life is in as much danger as the queen's.

Weird habit: She likes to smell everything new to her.

Her name is from a blade of grass, not a sword.

And her stakes are that she can sell one of the potion's ingredients to pay for her family's cure. Will she think about running away with the queen's cure?

ZIX

	OPTION A	OPTION B

OPTION A

FAMILY HISTORY: Supported Zix by buying them books

GREATEST FEAR: Talking in front of crowds

BAD HABIT: Mumbles when nervous

GOOD HABIT: Learns a new word every day

EMOTIONAL STAKES: Zix loves books and is furious at whoever has used them for evil. They are desperate to prove that all books are good. But are they right?

OPTION B

FAMILY HISTORY: All wizards, very powerful

GREATEST FEAR: Never being as good at magic as their family

BAD HABIT: Taps rhythms while reading

GOOD HABIT: Memorizes everyone's name

EMOTIONAL STAKES: Zix will do anything to become as powerful as their family. They will be tempted by what is in the books, and whoever sent them. Will they do the right thing?

New category: hobbies!

Zix whittles wands as they travel, to calm their nerves.

Favorite foods are important, too! Zix eats bugs and hard candy.

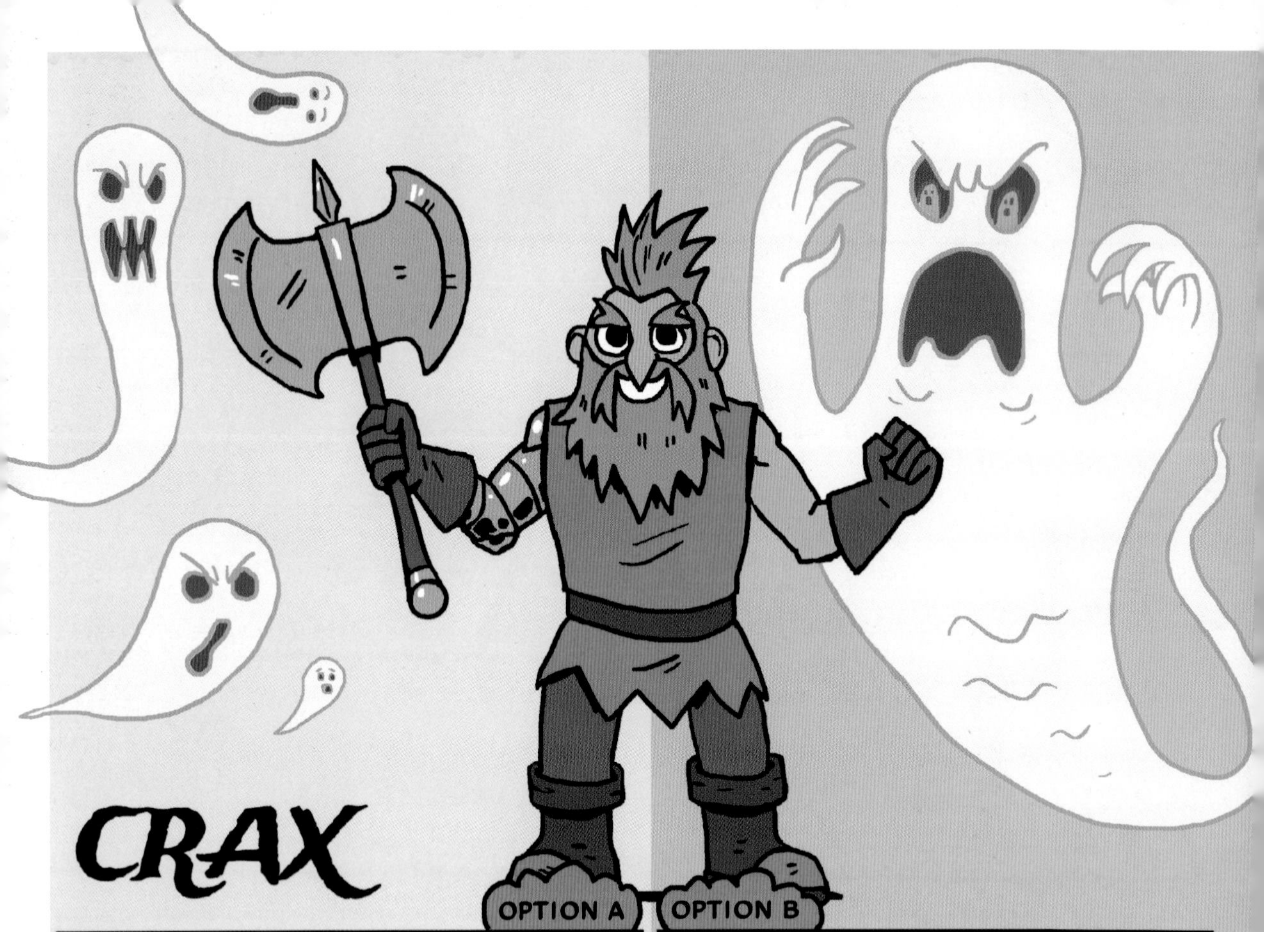

CRAX

OPTION A

FAMILY HISTORY: Has 17 other brothers and sisters he's not close with

GREATEST FEAR: Ghosts

BAD HABIT: Calls libraries "lie-buries"

GOOD HABIT: Uses libraries, loves reading

EMOTIONAL STAKES: Crax loves his brother, but is hoping to make friends with another adventurer. Can he win over the third hero without making Tonk feel left out?

OPTION B

FAMILY HISTORY: They're all jewelers, he and Tonk the only warriors.

GREATEST FEAR: No really, it's g-g-g-g-ghosts!

BAD HABIT: Doesn't clean weapons after battle

GOOD HABIT: Makes friendship bracelets for new pals

EMOTIONAL STAKES: His family said the brothers would never succeed and make a difference. He wants to prove them wrong. Or should he stop looking for their approval?

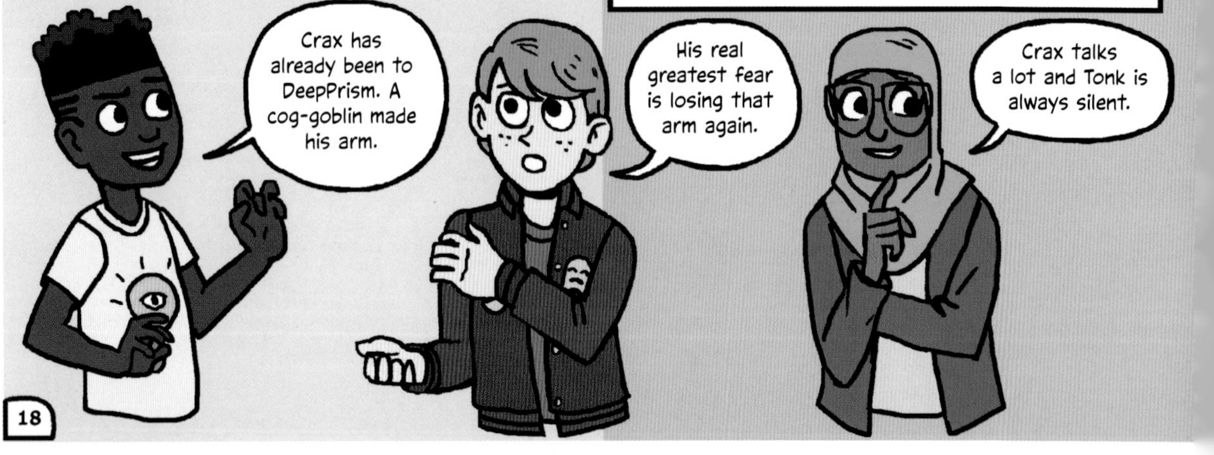
Crax has already been to DeepPrism. A cog-goblin made his arm.
His real greatest fear is losing that arm again.
Crax talks a lot and Tonk is always silent.

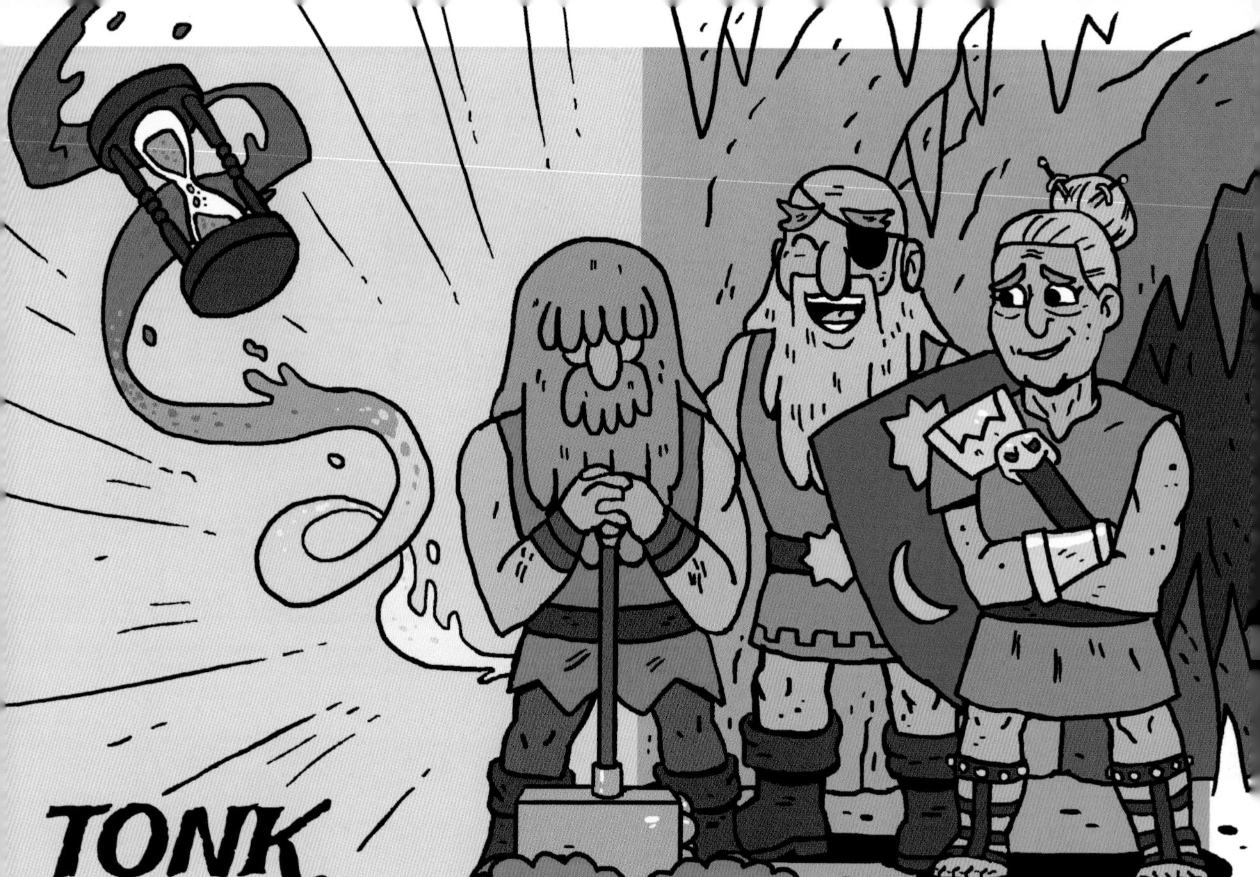

TONK

OPTION A	OPTION B
FAMILY HISTORY: Is actually Crax from the future, come back in time to help himself	**FAMILY HISTORY:** Raised by grandparent gladiators
GREATEST FEAR: Fighting the wrong person	**GREATEST FEAR:** Being separated from his brother
BAD HABIT: Snores	**BAD HABIT:** Eats food that gives him terrible breath
GOOD HABIT: Combs his beard every night before bed	**GOOD HABIT:** Tells great stories of past adventures
EMOTIONAL STAKES: Tonk failed his last quest because he didn't return with aid fast enough. Can he stay focused and not be sidetracked? Will his time-keeping bother the others? Is he still a hero?	**EMOTIONAL STAKES:** Tonk is in love with Marisha (who doesn't love him back). He would do anything for her, but needs to realize that he should move on and find someone who likes him back.

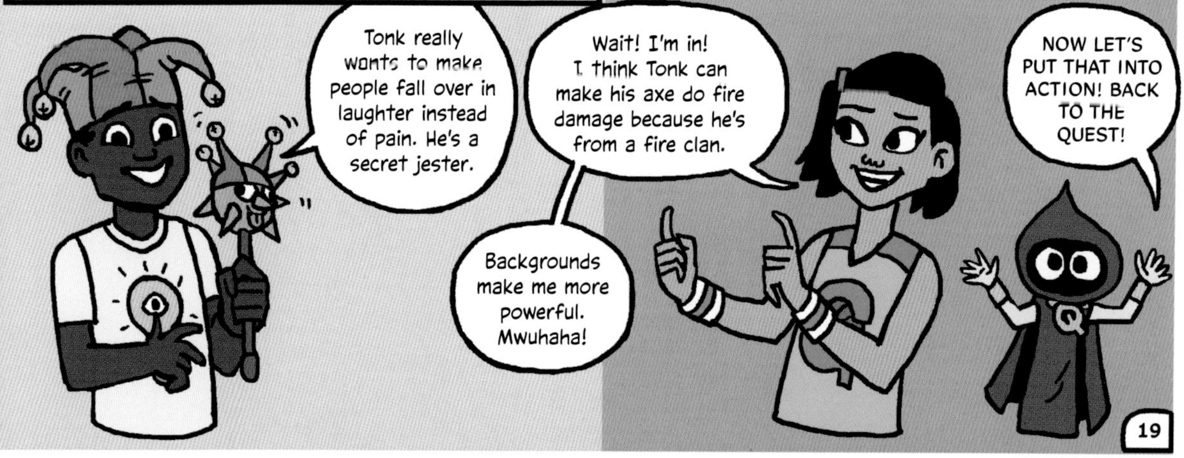
Tonk really wants to make people fall over in laughter instead of pain. He's a secret jester.
Wait! I'm in! I think Tonk can make his axe do fire damage because he's from a fire clan.
Backgrounds make me more powerful. Mwuhaha!
NOW LET'S PUT THAT INTO ACTION! BACK TO THE QUEST!

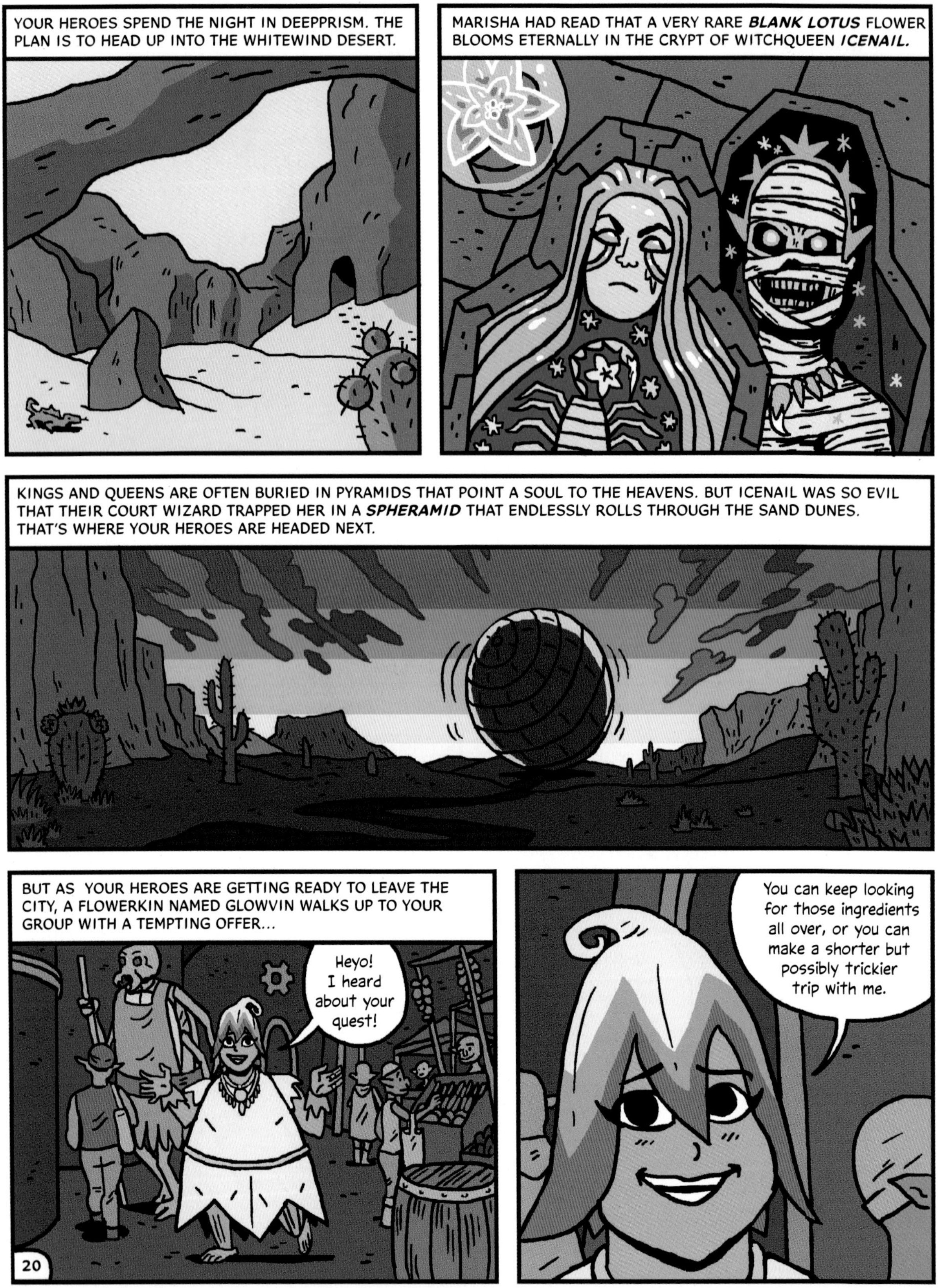
YOUR HEROES SPEND THE NIGHT IN DEEPPRISM. THE PLAN IS TO HEAD UP INTO THE WHITEWIND DESERT.
MARISHA HAD READ THAT A VERY RARE *BLANK LOTUS* FLOWER BLOOMS ETERNALLY IN THE CRYPT OF WITCHQUEEN *ICENAIL.*
KINGS AND QUEENS ARE OFTEN BURIED IN PYRAMIDS THAT POINT A SOUL TO THE HEAVENS. BUT ICENAIL WAS SO EVIL THAT THEIR COURT WIZARD TRAPPED HER IN A *SPHERAMID* THAT ENDLESSLY ROLLS THROUGH THE SAND DUNES. THAT'S WHERE YOUR HEROES ARE HEADED NEXT.
BUT AS YOUR HEROES ARE GETTING READY TO LEAVE THE CITY, A FLOWERKIN NAMED GLOWVIN WALKS UP TO YOUR GROUP WITH A TEMPTING OFFER...
Heyo! I heard about your quest!
You can keep looking for those ingredients all over, or you can make a shorter but possibly trickier trip with me.

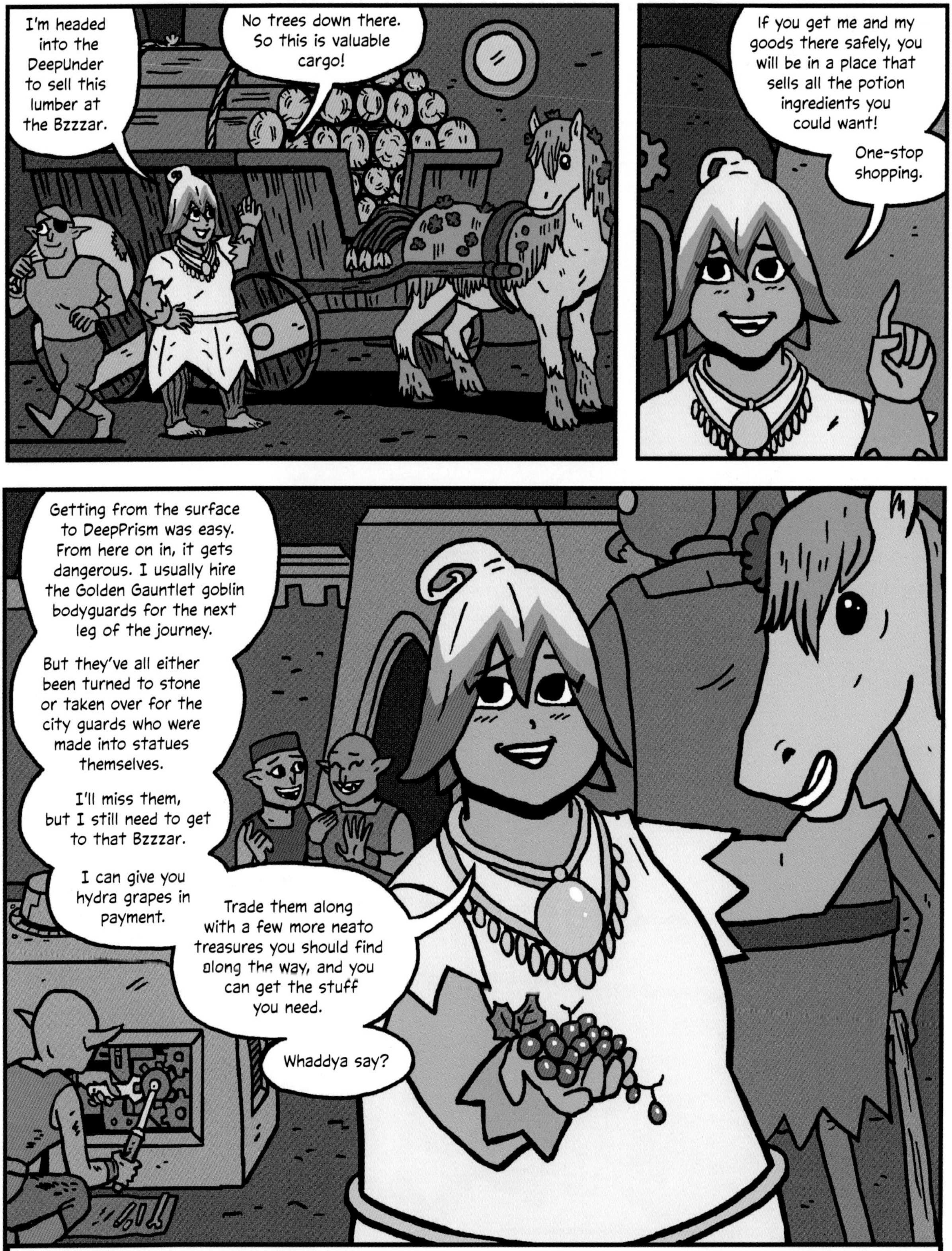
I'm headed into the DeepUnder to sell this lumber at the Bzzzar.
No trees down there. So this is valuable cargo!
If you get me and my goods there safely, you will be in a place that sells all the potion ingredients you could want!
One-stop shopping.
Getting from the surface to DeepPrism was easy. From here on in, it gets dangerous. I usually hire the Golden Gauntlet goblin bodyguards for the next leg of the journey.
But they've all either been turned to stone or taken over for the city guards who were made into statues themselves.
I'll miss them, but I still need to get to that Bzzzar.
I can give you hydra grapes in payment.
Trade them along with a few more neato treasures you should find along the way, and you can get the stuff you need.
Whaddya say?

YOU'VE GOT A CHOICE TO MAKE. YOU CAN EITHER TURN TO THE NEXT PAGE AND CONTINUE ON TO THE SPHERAMID, AS PLANNED, OR YOU CAN ***TURN TO PAGE 56*** AND ESCORT GLOWVIN THROUGH THE DEEPUNDER.

CHAPTER TWO

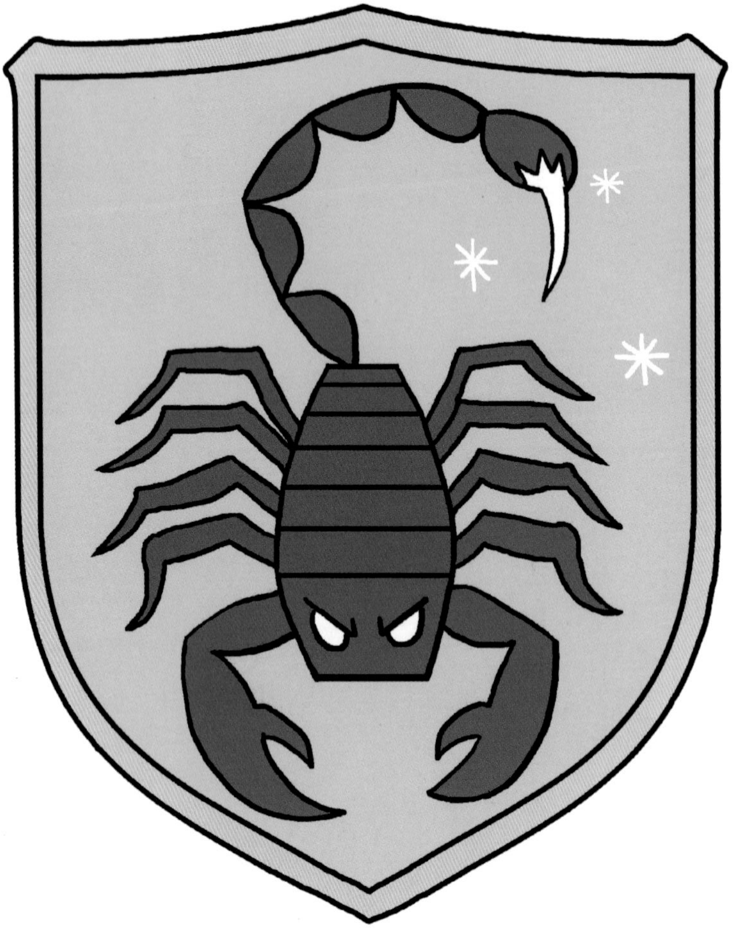

SAND HASSLE

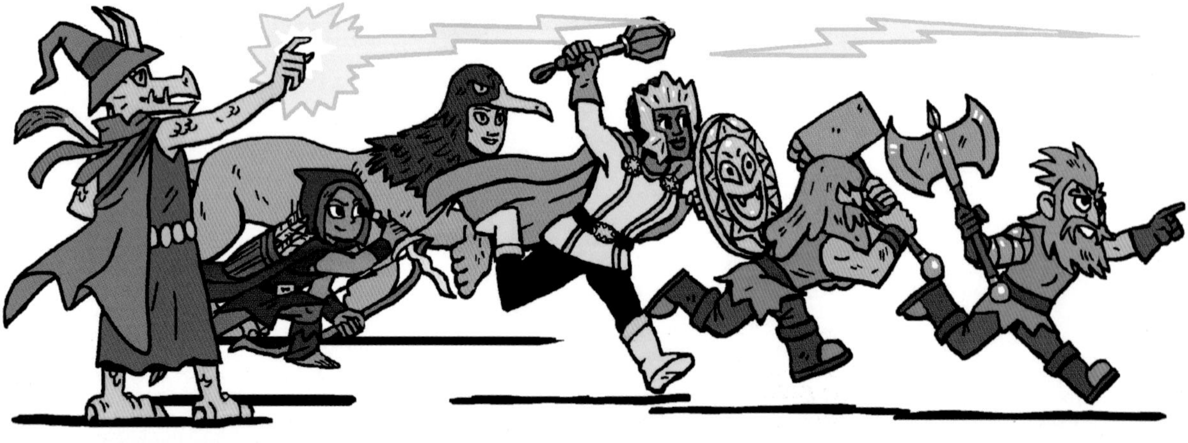

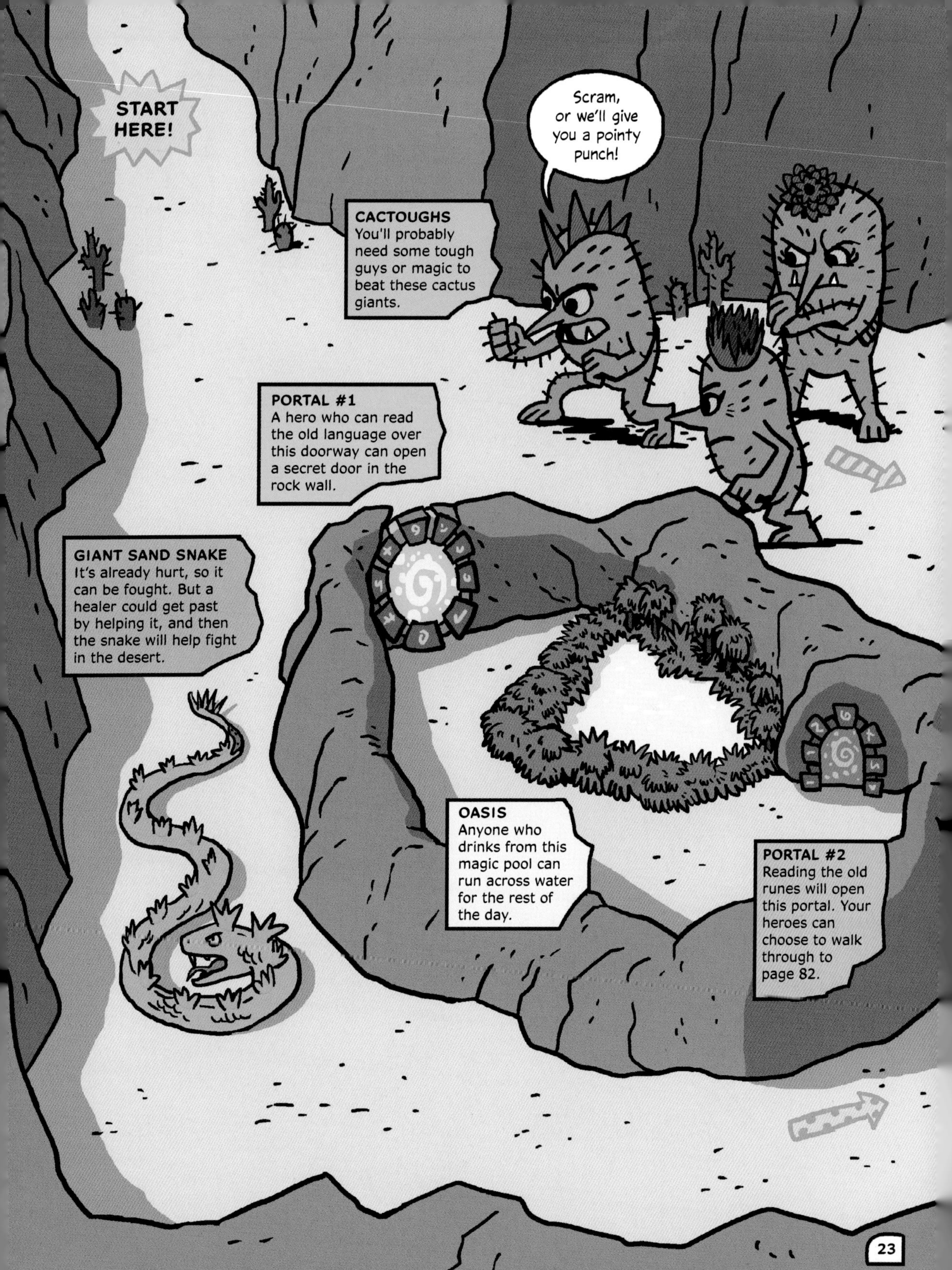
START HERE!
Scram, or we'll give you a pointy punch!
CACTOUGHS
You'll probably need some tough guys or magic to beat these cactus giants.
PORTAL #1
A hero who can read the old language over this doorway can open a secret door in the rock wall.
GIANT SAND SNAKE
It's already hurt, so it can be fought. But a healer could get past by helping it, and then the snake will help fight in the desert.
OASIS
Anyone who drinks from this magic pool can run across water for the rest of the day.
PORTAL #2
Reading the old runes will open this portal. Your heroes can choose to walk through to page 82.

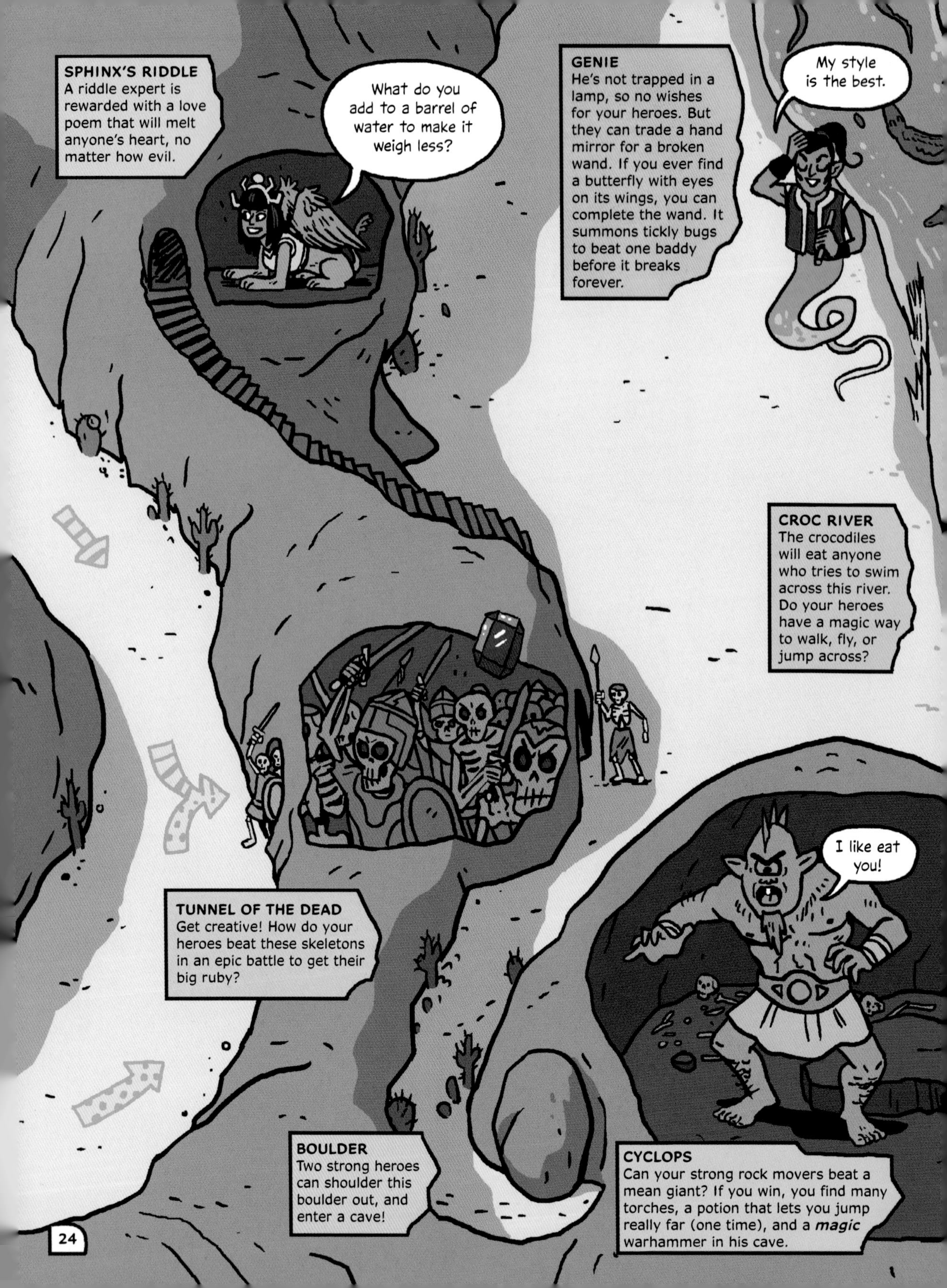
SPHINX'S RIDDLE
A riddle expert is rewarded with a love poem that will melt anyone's heart, no matter how evil.
What do you add to a barrel of water to make it weigh less?
GENIE
He's not trapped in a lamp, so no wishes for your heroes. But they can trade a hand mirror for a broken wand. If you ever find a butterfly with eyes on its wings, you can complete the wand. It summons tickly bugs to beat one baddy before it breaks forever.
My style is the best.
CROC RIVER
The crocodiles will eat anyone who tries to swim across this river. Do your heroes have a magic way to walk, fly, or jump across?
TUNNEL OF THE DEAD
Get creative! How do your heroes beat these skeletons in an epic battle to get their big ruby?
I like eat you!
BOULDER
Two strong heroes can shoulder this boulder out, and enter a cave!
CYCLOPS
Can your strong rock movers beat a mean giant? If you win, you find many torches, a potion that lets you jump really far (one time), and a *magic* warhammer in his cave.

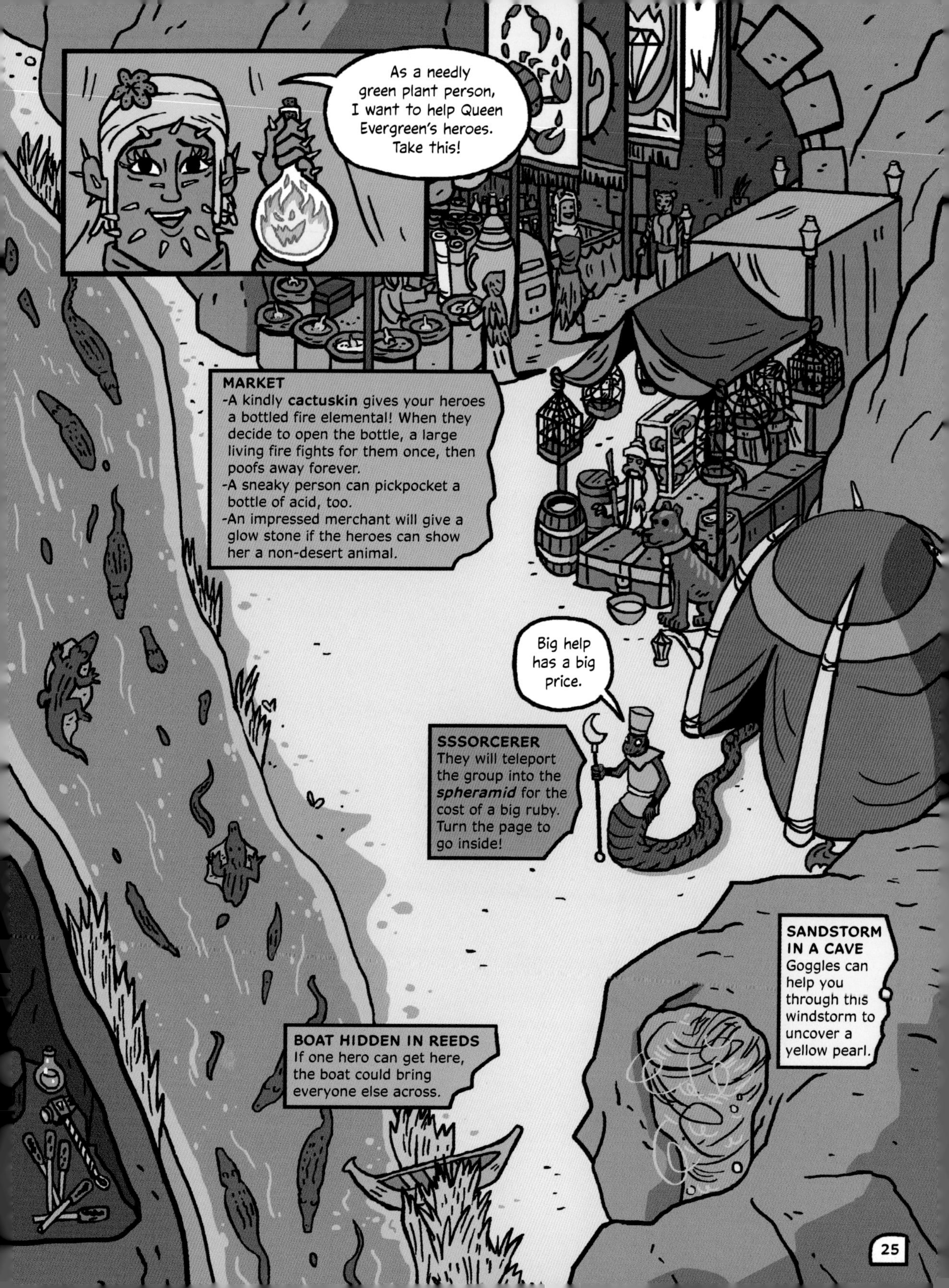
As a needly green plant person, I want to help Queen Evergreen's heroes. Take this!
MARKET
-A kindly cactuskin gives your heroes a bottled fire elemental! When they decide to open the bottle, a large living fire fights for them once, then poofs away forever.
-A sneaky person can pickpocket a bottle of acid, too.
-An impressed merchant will give a glow stone if the heroes can show her a non-desert animal.
Big help has a big price.
SSSORCERER
They will teleport the group into the spheramid for the cost of a big ruby. Turn the page to go inside!
SANDSTORM IN A CAVE
Goggles can help you through this windstorm to uncover a yellow pearl.
BOAT HIDDEN IN REEDS
If one hero can get here, the boat could bring everyone else across.

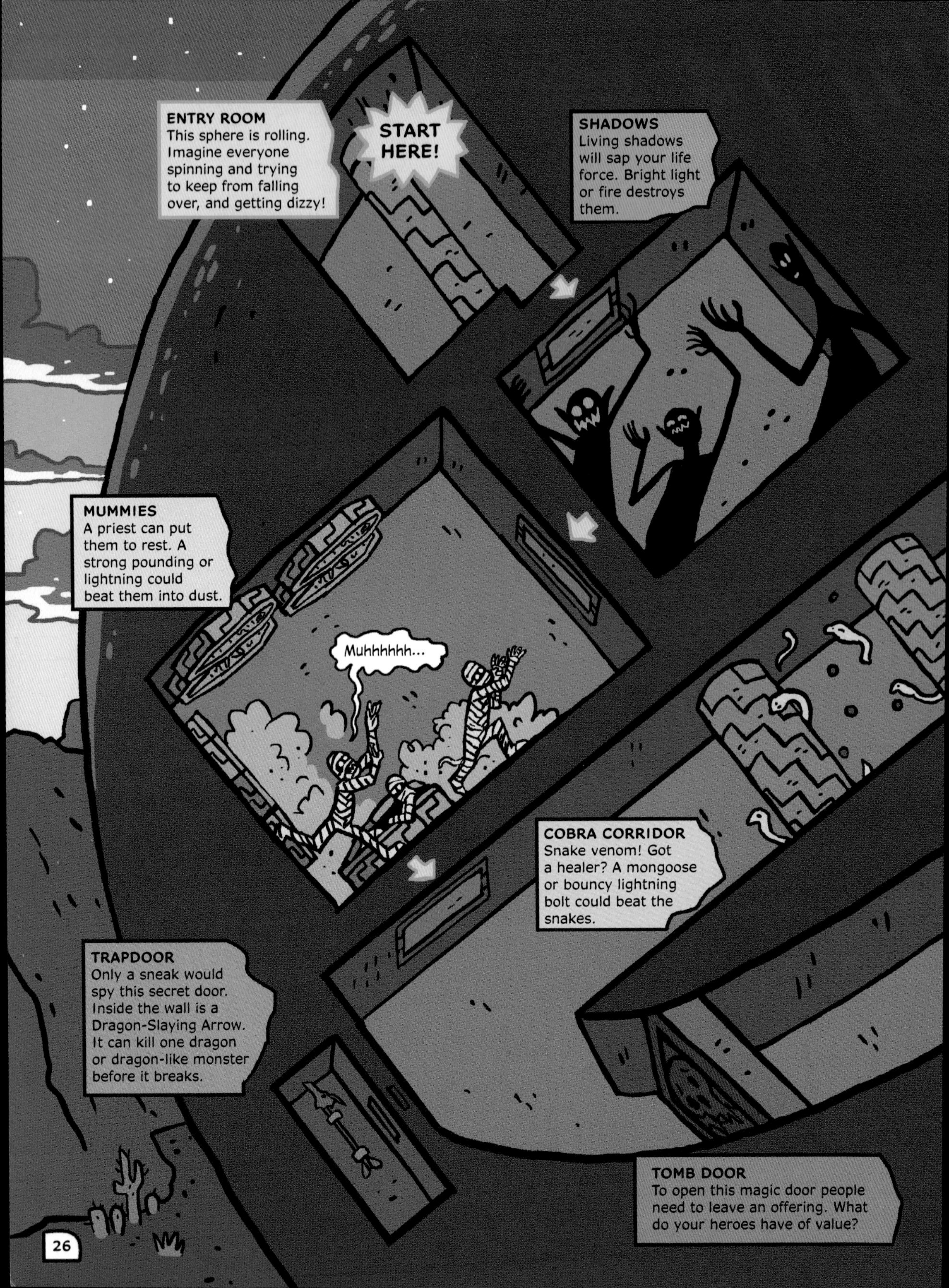
ENTRY ROOM
This sphere is rolling. Imagine everyone spinning and trying to keep from falling over, and getting dizzy!
START HERE!
SHADOWS
Living shadows will sap your life force. Bright light or fire destroys them.
MUMMIES
A priest can put them to rest. A strong pounding or lightning could beat them into dust.
Muhhhhhh...
COBRA CORRIDOR
Snake venom! Got a healer? A mongoose or bouncy lightning bolt could beat the snakes.
TRAPDOOR
Only a sneak would spy this secret door. Inside the wall is a Dragon-Slaying Arrow. It can kill one dragon or dragon-like monster before it breaks.
TOMB DOOR
To open this magic door people need to leave an offering. What do your heroes have of value?

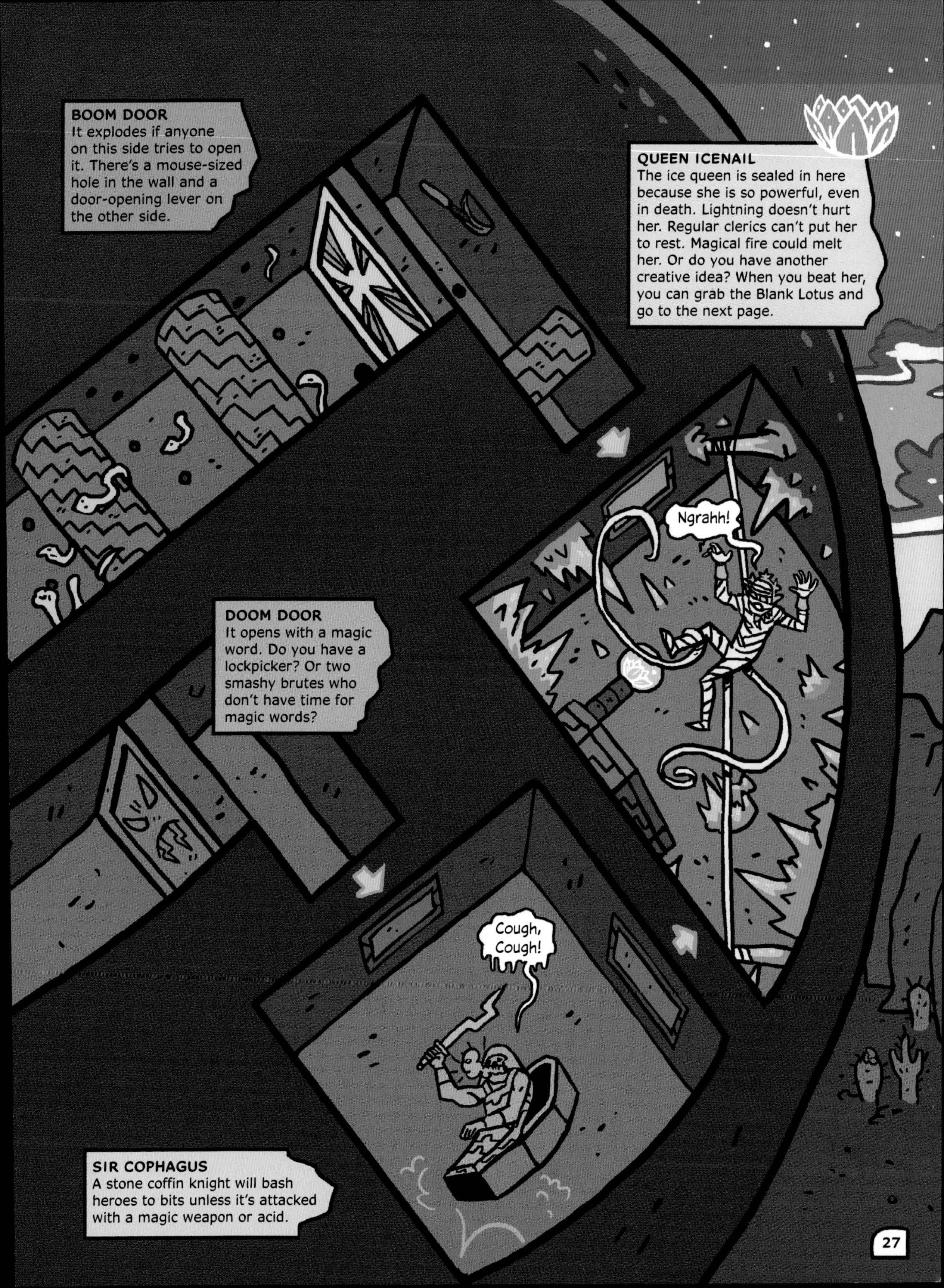
BOOM DOOR
It explodes if anyone on this side tries to open it. There's a mouse-sized hole in the wall and a door-opening lever on the other side.
QUEEN ICENAIL
The ice queen is sealed in here because she is so powerful, even in death. Lightning doesn't hurt her. Regular clerics can't put her to rest. Magical fire could melt her. Or do you have another creative idea? When you beat her, you can grab the Blank Lotus and go to the next page.
Ngrahh!
DOOM DOOR
It opens with a magic word. Do you have a lockpicker? Or two smashy brutes who don't have time for magic words?
Cough, Cough!
SIR COPHAGUS
A stone coffin knight will bash heroes to bits unless it's attacked with a magic weapon or acid.

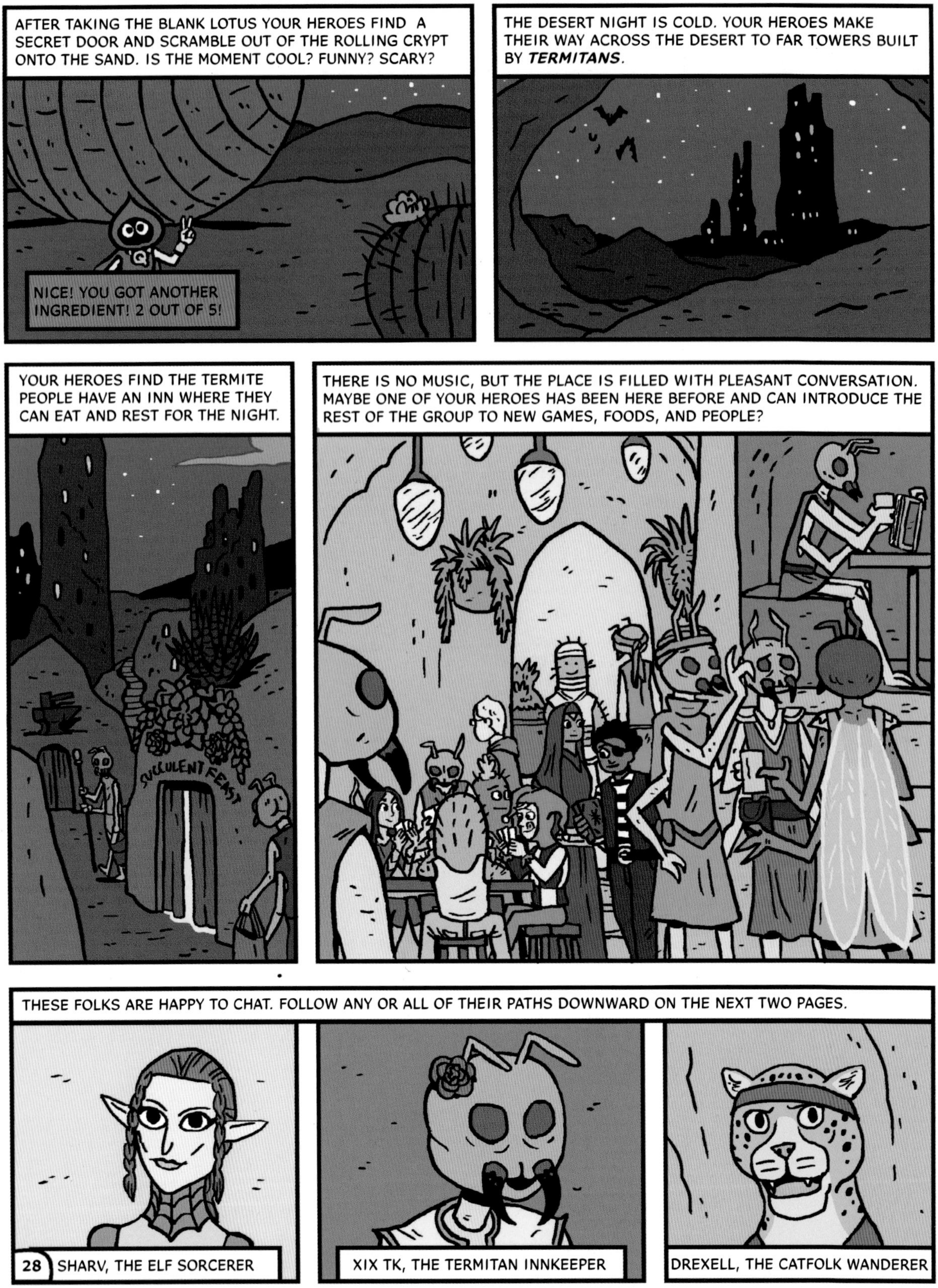
AFTER TAKING THE BLANK LOTUS YOUR HEROES FIND A SECRET DOOR AND SCRAMBLE OUT OF THE ROLLING CRYPT ONTO THE SAND. IS THE MOMENT COOL? FUNNY? SCARY?
NICE! YOU GOT ANOTHER INGREDIENT! 2 OUT OF 5!
THE DESERT NIGHT IS COLD. YOUR HEROES MAKE THEIR WAY ACROSS THE DESERT TO FAR TOWERS BUILT BY ***TERMITANS***.
YOUR HEROES FIND THE TERMITE PEOPLE HAVE AN INN WHERE THEY CAN EAT AND REST FOR THE NIGHT.
SUCCULENT FEAST
THERE IS NO MUSIC, BUT THE PLACE IS FILLED WITH PLEASANT CONVERSATION. MAYBE ONE OF YOUR HEROES HAS BEEN HERE BEFORE AND CAN INTRODUCE THE REST OF THE GROUP TO NEW GAMES, FOODS, AND PEOPLE?
THESE FOLKS ARE HAPPY TO CHAT. FOLLOW ANY OR ALL OF THEIR PATHS DOWNWARD ON THE NEXT TWO PAGES.
SHARV, THE ELF SORCERER
XIX TK, THE TERMITAN INNKEEPER
DREXELL, THE CATFOLK WANDERER

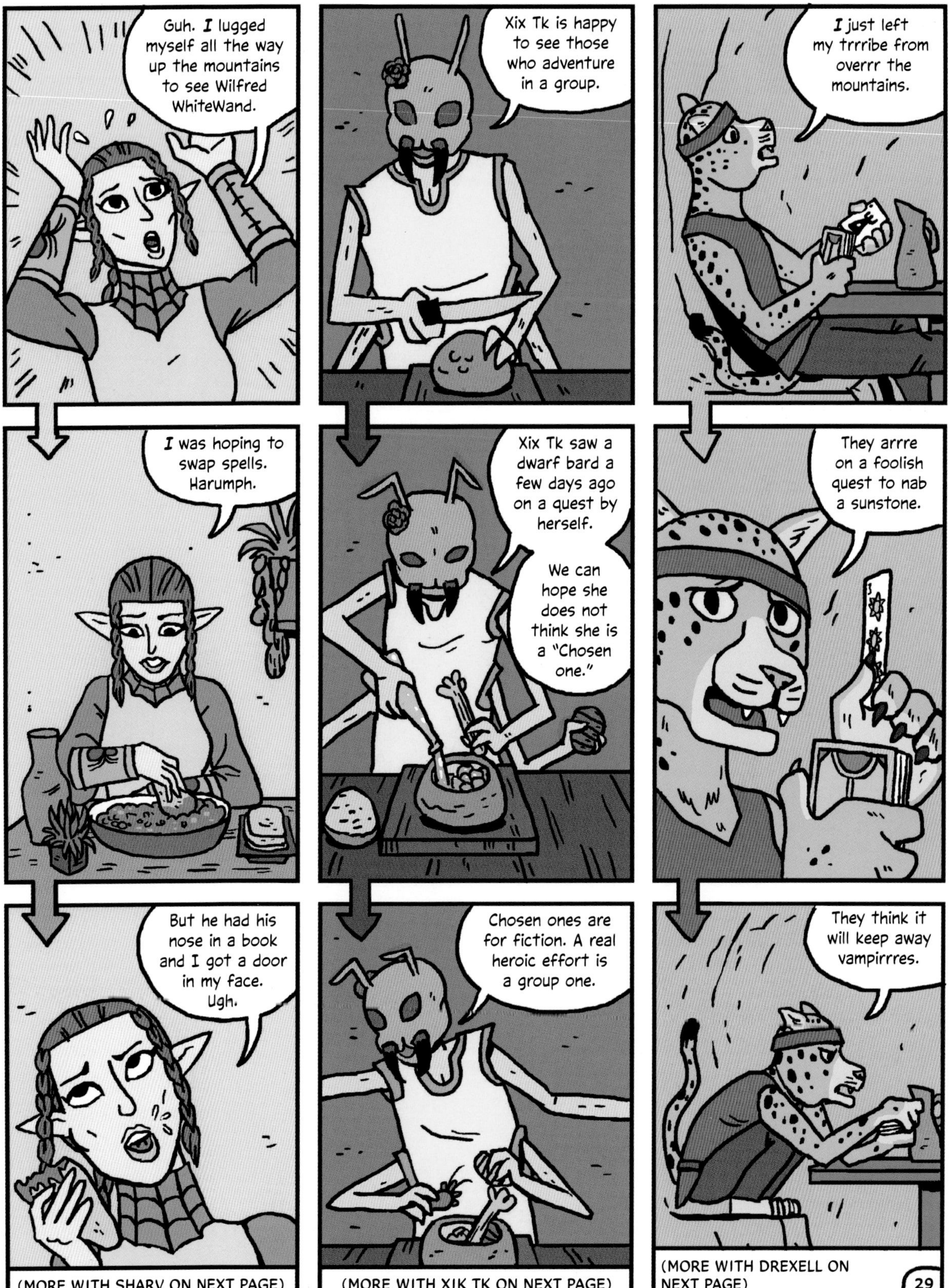
Guh. I lugged myself all the way up the mountains to see Wilfred WhiteWand.
I was hoping to swap spells. Harumph.
But he had his nose in a book and I got a door in my face. Ugh.
(MORE WITH SHARV ON NEXT PAGE)
Xix Tk is happy to see those who adventure in a group.
Xix Tk saw a dwarf bard a few days ago on a quest by herself.
We can hope she does not think she is a "Chosen one."
Chosen ones are for fiction. A real heroic effort is a group one.
(MORE WITH XIK TK ON NEXT PAGE)
I just left my trrribe from overrr the mountains.
They arrre on a foolish quest to nab a sunstone.
They think it will keep away vampirrres.
(MORE WITH DREXELL ON NEXT PAGE)

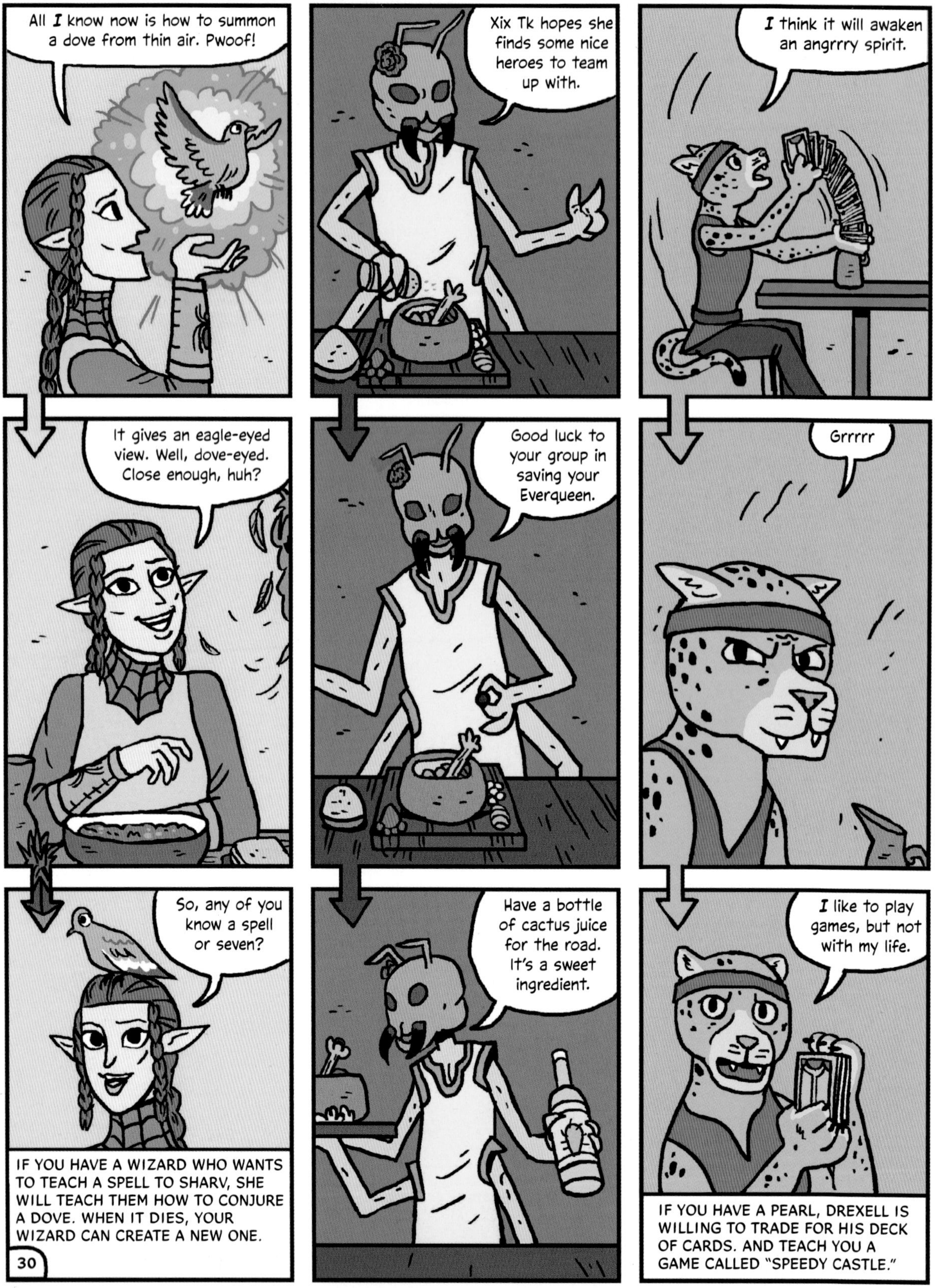
All *I* know now is how to summon a dove from thin air. Pwoof!
It gives an eagle-eyed view. Well, dove-eyed. Close enough, huh?
So, any of you know a spell or seven?
IF YOU HAVE A WIZARD WHO WANTS TO TEACH A SPELL TO SHARV, SHE WILL TEACH THEM HOW TO CONJURE A DOVE. WHEN IT DIES, YOUR WIZARD CAN CREATE A NEW ONE.
Xix Tk hopes she finds some nice heroes to team up with.
Good luck to your group in saving your Everqueen.
Have a bottle of cactus juice for the road. It's a sweet ingredient.
I think it will awaken an angrrry spirit.
Grrrrr
I like to play games, but not with my life.
IF YOU HAVE A PEARL, DREXELL IS WILLING TO TRADE FOR HIS DECK OF CARDS. AND TEACH YOU A GAME CALLED "SPEEDY CASTLE."

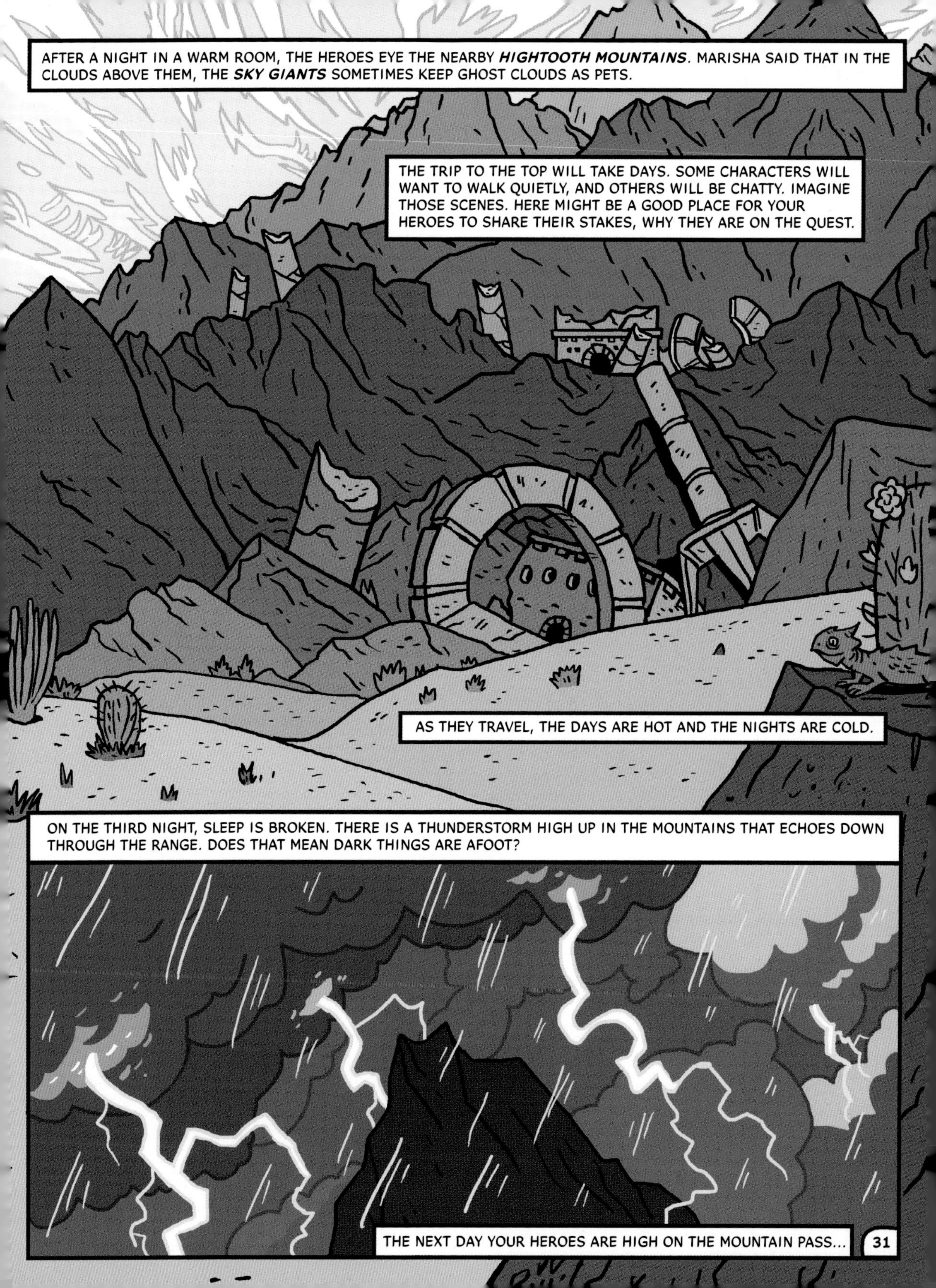
AFTER A NIGHT IN A WARM ROOM, THE HEROES EYE THE NEARBY HIGHTOOTH MOUNTAINS. MARISHA SAID THAT IN THE CLOUDS ABOVE THEM, THE SKY GIANTS SOMETIMES KEEP GHOST CLOUDS AS PETS.
THE TRIP TO THE TOP WILL TAKE DAYS. SOME CHARACTERS WILL WANT TO WALK QUIETLY, AND OTHERS WILL BE CHATTY. IMAGINE THOSE SCENES. HERE MIGHT BE A GOOD PLACE FOR YOUR HEROES TO SHARE THEIR STAKES, WHY THEY ARE ON THE QUEST.
AS THEY TRAVEL, THE DAYS ARE HOT AND THE NIGHTS ARE COLD.
ON THE THIRD NIGHT, SLEEP IS BROKEN. THERE IS A THUNDERSTORM HIGH UP IN THE MOUNTAINS THAT ECHOES DOWN THROUGH THE RANGE. DOES THAT MEAN DARK THINGS ARE AFOOT?
THE NEXT DAY YOUR HEROES ARE HIGH ON THE MOUNTAIN PASS...

CHAPTER THREE

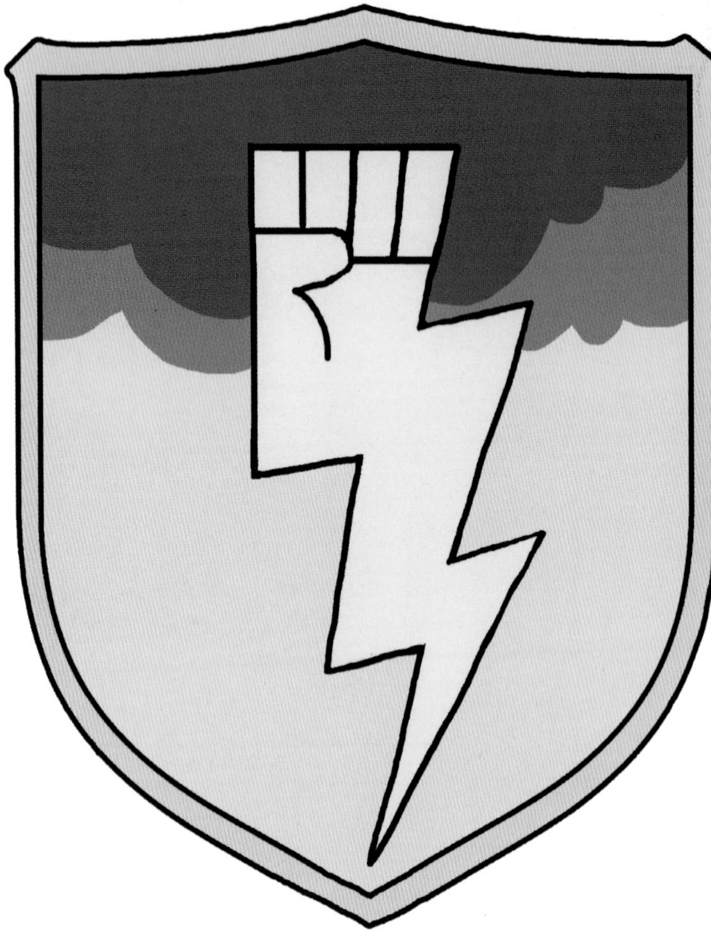

THUNDERTAKER

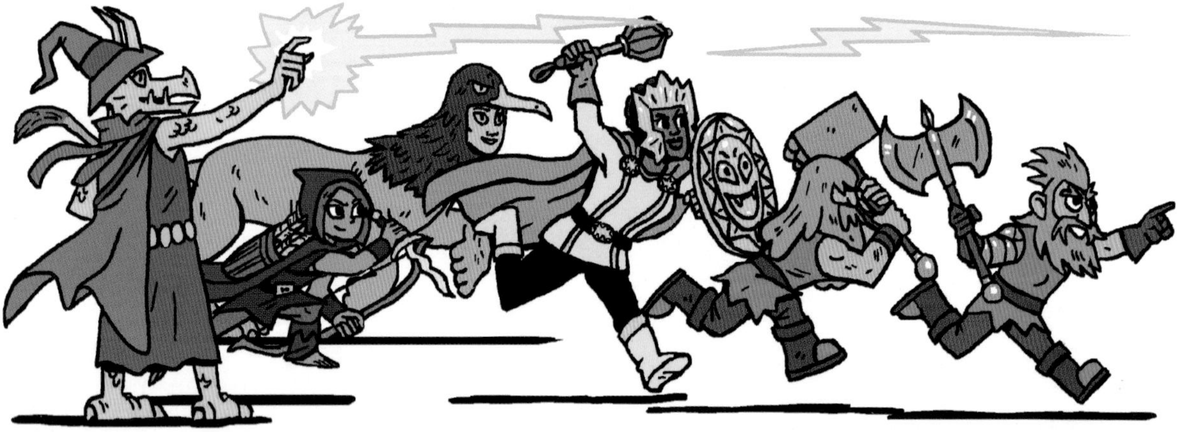

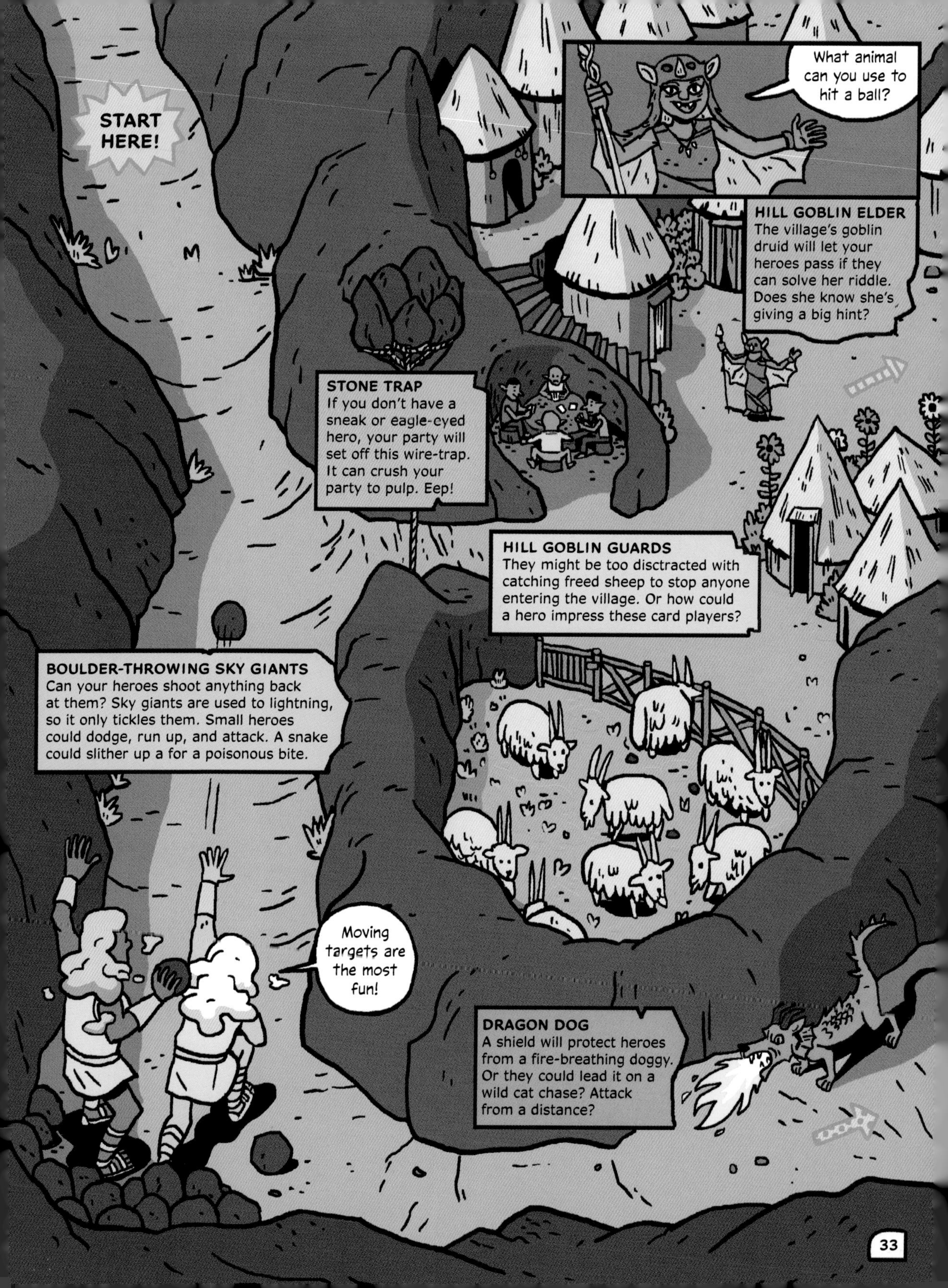
START HERE!
What animal can you use to hit a ball?
HILL GOBLIN ELDER
The village's goblin druid will let your heroes pass if they can solve her riddle. Does she know she's giving a big hint?
STONE TRAP
If you don't have a sneak or eagle-eyed hero, your party will set off this wire-trap. It can crush your party to pulp. Eep!
HILL GOBLIN GUARDS
They might be too disctracted with catching freed sheep to stop anyone entering the village. Or how could a hero impress these card players?
BOULDER-THROWING SKY GIANTS
Can your heroes shoot anything back at them? Sky giants are used to lightning, so it only tickles them. Small heroes could dodge, run up, and attack. A snake could slither up a for a poisonous bite.
Moving targets are the most fun!
DRAGON DOG
A shield will protect heroes from a fire-breathing doggy. Or they could lead it on a wild cat chase? Attack from a distance?

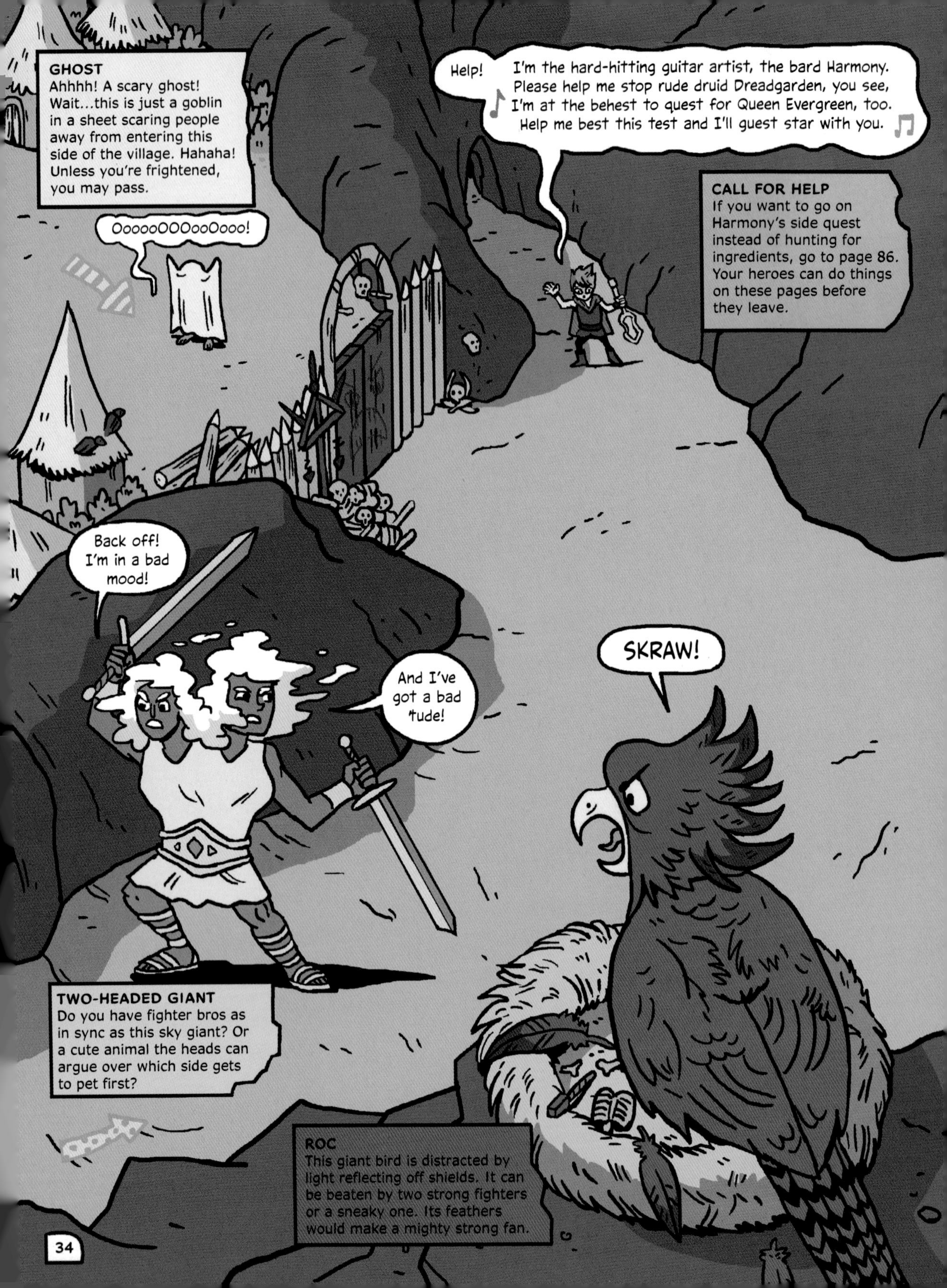
GHOST
Ahhhh! A scary ghost! Wait...this is just a goblin in a sheet scaring people away from entering this side of the village. Hahaha! Unless you're frightened, you may pass.
OooooOOOooOooo!
Help!
I'm the hard-hitting guitar artist, the bard Harmony. Please help me stop rude druid Dreadgarden, you see, I'm at the behest to quest for Queen Evergreen, too. Help me best this test and I'll guest star with you.
CALL FOR HELP
If you want to go on Harmony's side quest instead of hunting for ingredients, go to page 86. Your heroes can do things on these pages before they leave.
Back off! I'm in a bad mood!
And I've got a bad 'tude!
SKRAW!
TWO-HEADED GIANT
Do you have fighter bros as in sync as this sky giant? Or a cute animal the heads can argue over which side gets to pet first?
ROC
This giant bird is distracted by light reflecting off shields. It can be beaten by two strong fighters or a sneaky one. Its feathers would make a mighty strong fan.

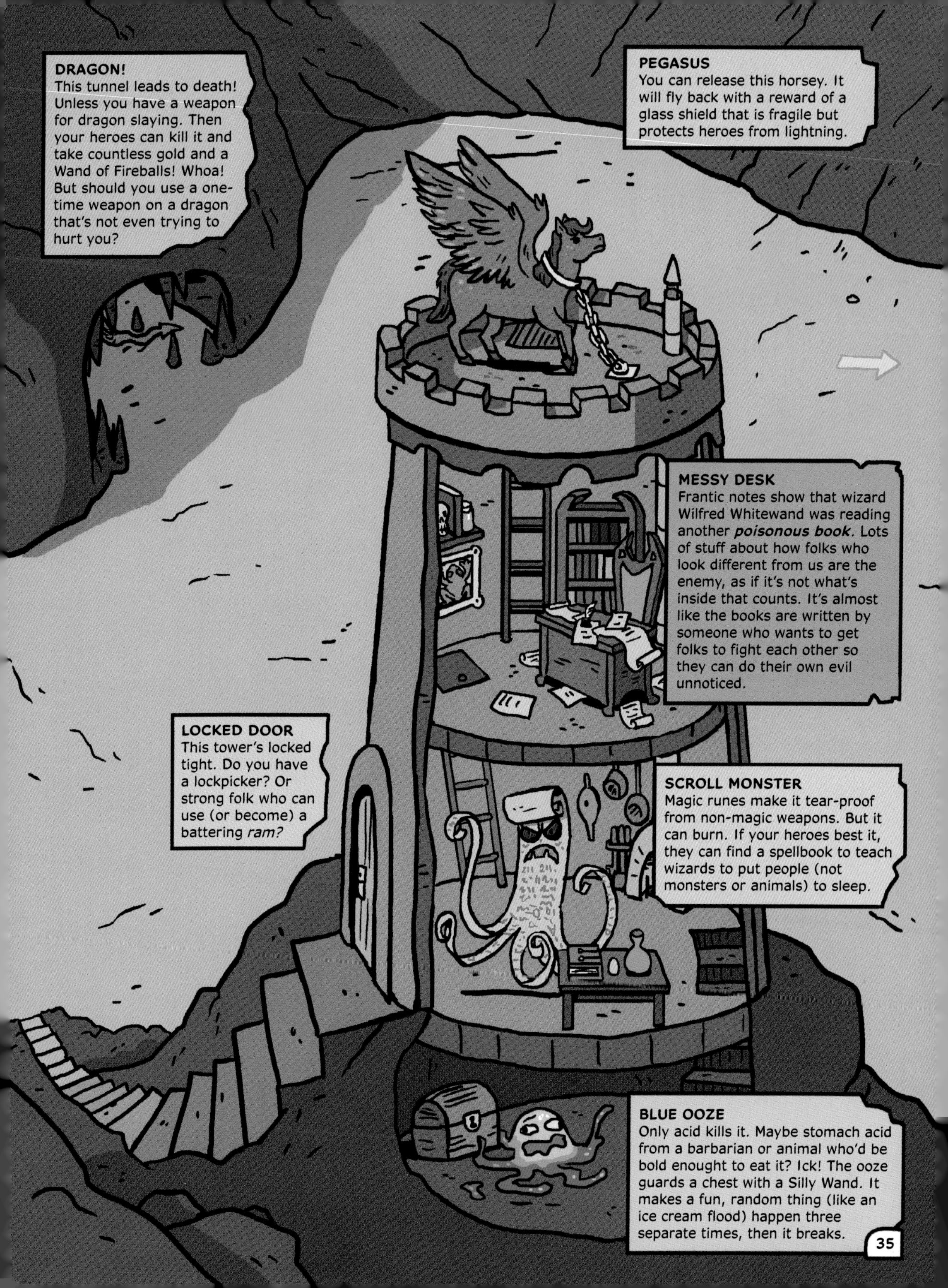
DRAGON!
This tunnel leads to death! Unless you have a weapon for dragon slaying. Then your heroes can kill it and take countless gold and a Wand of Fireballs! Whoa! But should you use a one-time weapon on a dragon that's not even trying to hurt you?
PEGASUS
You can release this horsey. It will fly back with a reward of a glass shield that is fragile but protects heroes from lightning.
MESSY DESK
Frantic notes show that wizard Wilfred Whitewand was reading another *poisonous book.* Lots of stuff about how folks who look different from us are the enemy, as if it's not what's inside that counts. It's almost like the books are written by someone who wants to get folks to fight each other so they can do their own evil unnoticed.
LOCKED DOOR
This tower's locked tight. Do you have a lockpicker? Or strong folk who can use (or become) a battering *ram?*
SCROLL MONSTER
Magic runes make it tear-proof from non-magic weapons. But it can burn. If your heroes best it, they can find a spellbook to teach wizards to put people (not monsters or animals) to sleep.
BLUE OOZE
Only acid kills it. Maybe stomach acid from a barbarian or animal who'd be bold enought to eat it? Ick! The ooze guards a chest with a Silly Wand. It makes a fun, random thing (like an ice cream flood) happen three separate times, then it breaks.

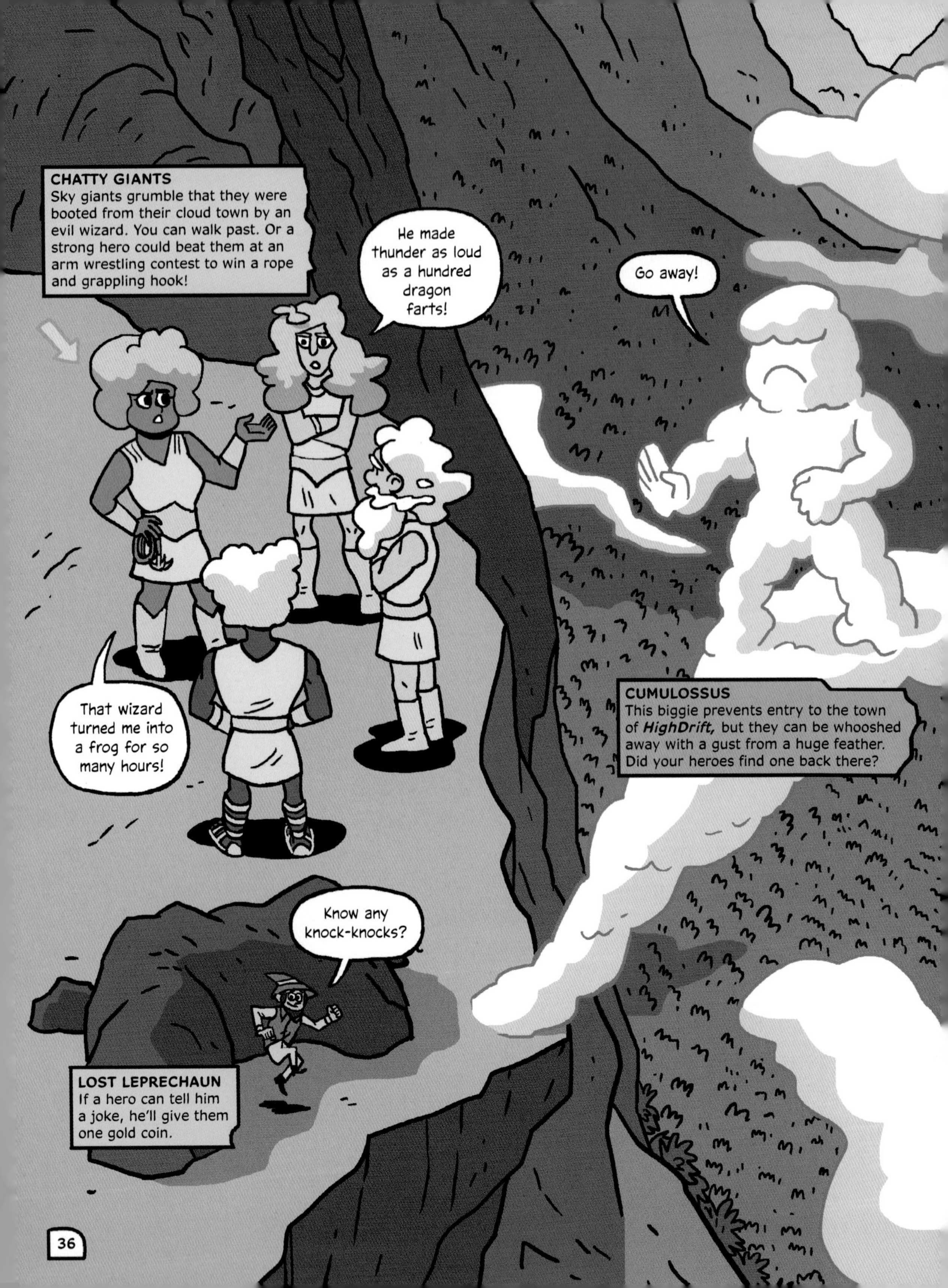
CHATTY GIANTS
Sky giants grumble that they were booted from their cloud town by an evil wizard. You can walk past. Or a strong hero could beat them at an arm wrestling contest to win a rope and grappling hook!
He made thunder as loud as a hundred dragon farts!
Go away!
That wizard turned me into a frog for so many hours!
CUMULOSSUS
This biggie prevents entry to the town of HighDrift, but they can be whooshed away with a gust from a huge feather. Did your heroes find one back there?
Know any knock-knocks?
LOST LEPRECHAUN
If a hero can tell him a joke, he'll give them one gold coin.

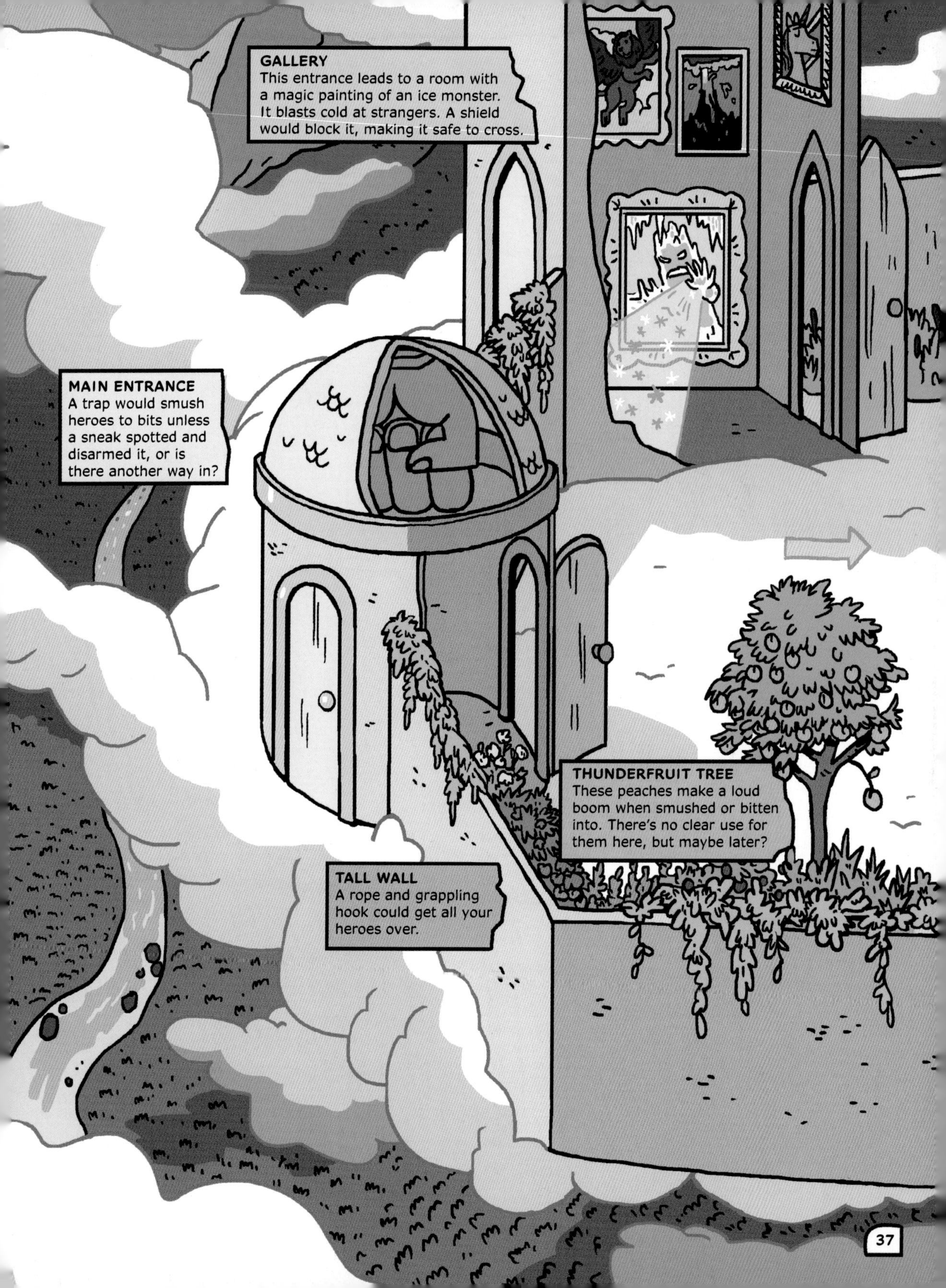
GALLERY
This entrance leads to a room with a magic painting of an ice monster. It blasts cold at strangers. A shield would block it, making it safe to cross.
MAIN ENTRANCE
A trap would smush heroes to bits unless a sneak spotted and disarmed it, or is there another way in?
THUNDERFRUIT TREE
These peaches make a loud boom when smushed or bitten into. There's no clear use for them here, but maybe later?
TALL WALL
A rope and grappling hook could get all your heroes over.

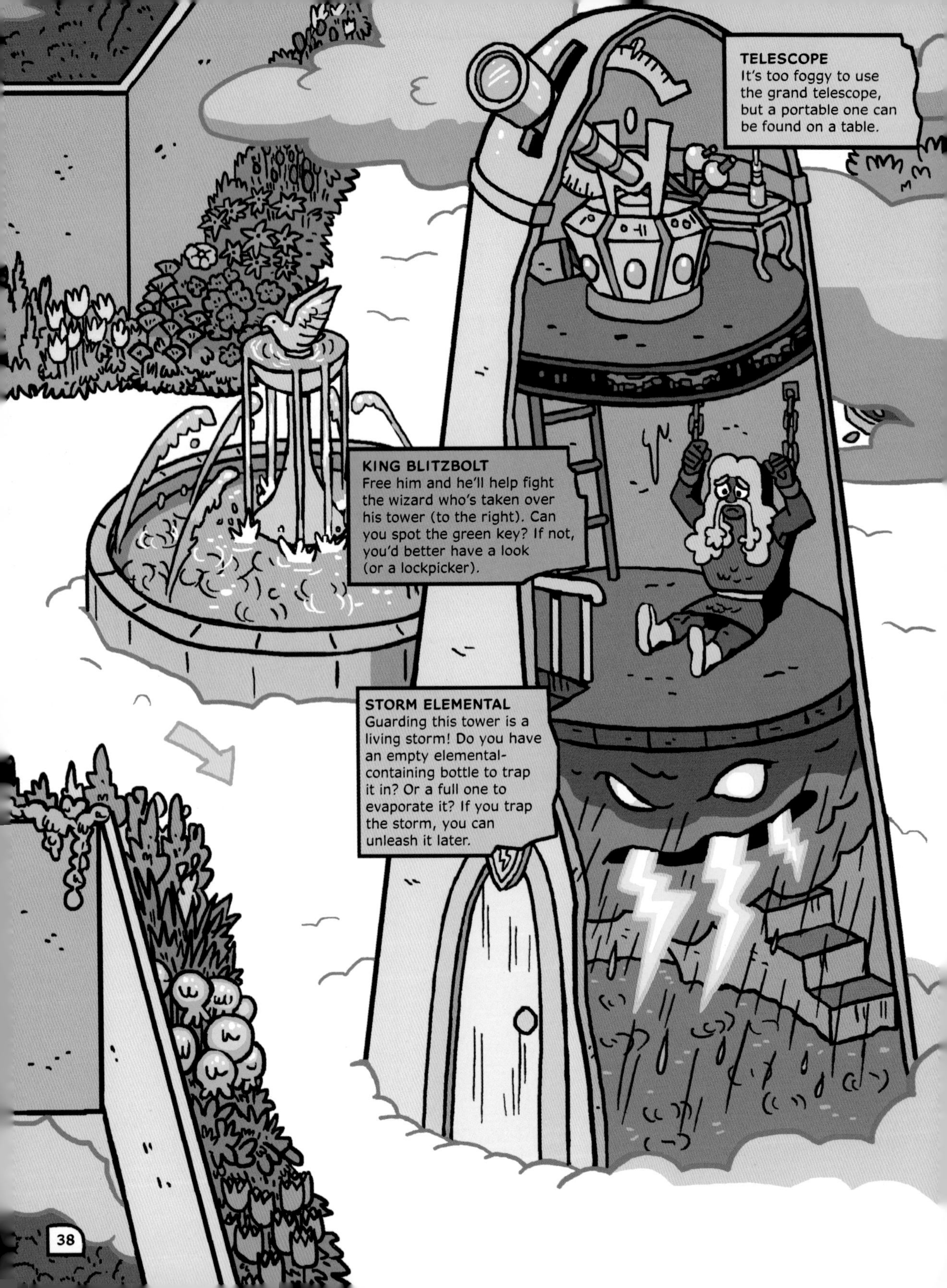
TELESCOPE
It's too foggy to use the grand telescope, but a portable one can be found on a table.
KING BLITZBOLT
Free him and he'll help fight the wizard who's taken over his tower (to the right). Can you spot the green key? If not, you'd better have a look (or a lockpicker).
STORM ELEMENTAL
Guarding this tower is a living storm! Do you have an empty elemental-containing bottle to trap it in? Or a full one to evaporate it? If you trap the storm, you can unleash it later.

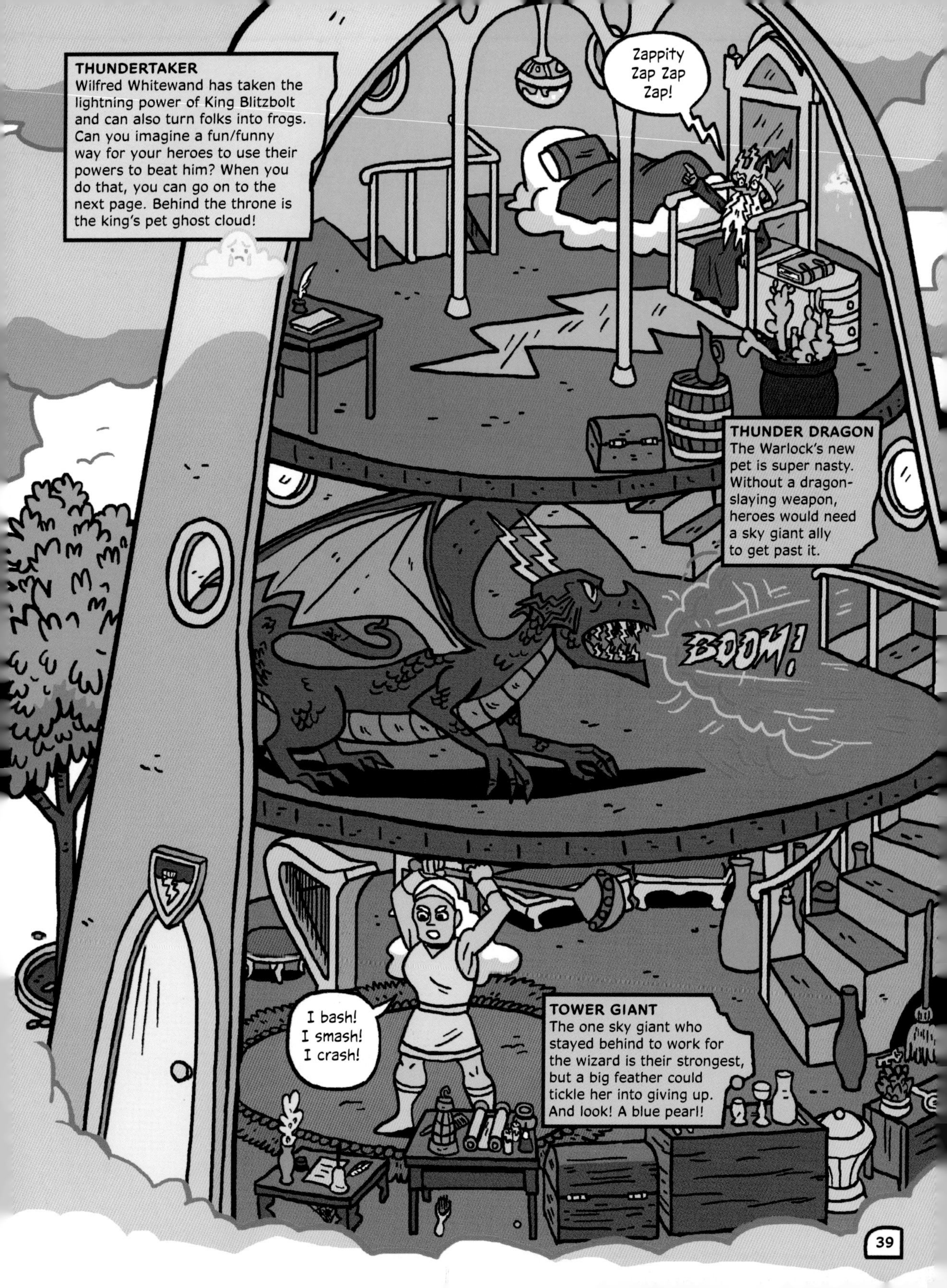
THUNDERTAKER
Wilfred Whitewand has taken the lightning power of King Blitzbolt and can also turn folks into frogs. Can you imagine a fun/funny way for your heroes to use their powers to beat him? When you do that, you can go on to the next page. Behind the throne is the king's pet ghost cloud!
Zappity Zap Zap Zap!
THUNDER DRAGON
The Warlock's new pet is super nasty. Without a dragon-slaying weapon, heroes would need a sky giant ally to get past it.
BOOM!
I bash! I smash! I crash!
TOWER GIANT
The one sky giant who stayed behind to work for the wizard is their strongest, but a big feather could tickle her into giving up. And look! A blue pearl!

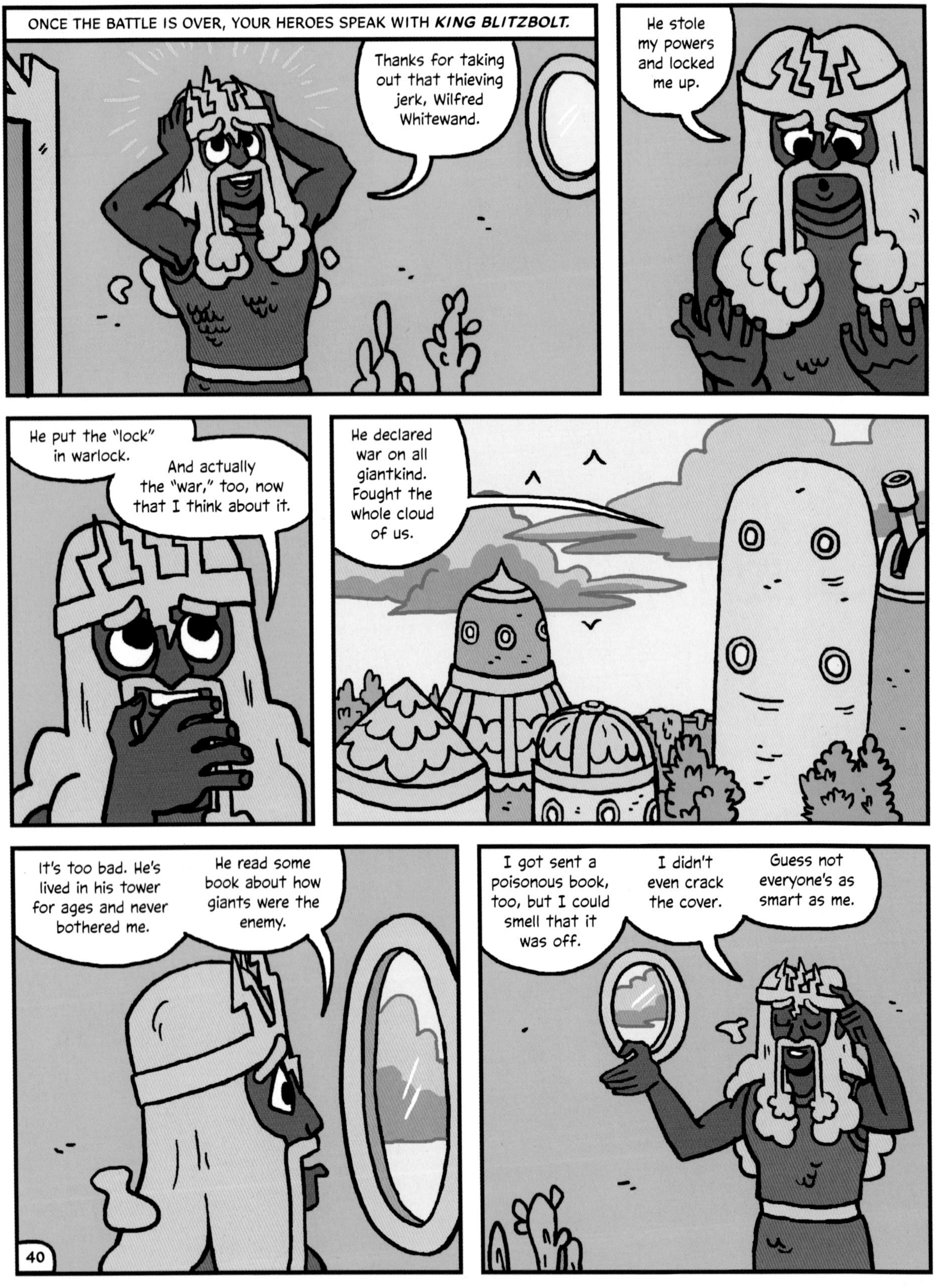
ONCE THE BATTLE IS OVER, YOUR HEROES SPEAK WITH *KING BLITZBOLT.*
Thanks for taking out that thieving jerk, Wilfred Whitewand.
He stole my powers and locked me up.
He put the "lock" in warlock.
And actually the "war," too, now that I think about it.
He declared war on all giantkind. Fought the whole cloud of us.
It's too bad. He's lived in his tower for ages and never bothered me.
He read some book about how giants were the enemy.
I got sent a poisonous book, too, but I could smell that it was off.
I didn't even crack the cover.
Guess not everyone's as smart as me.

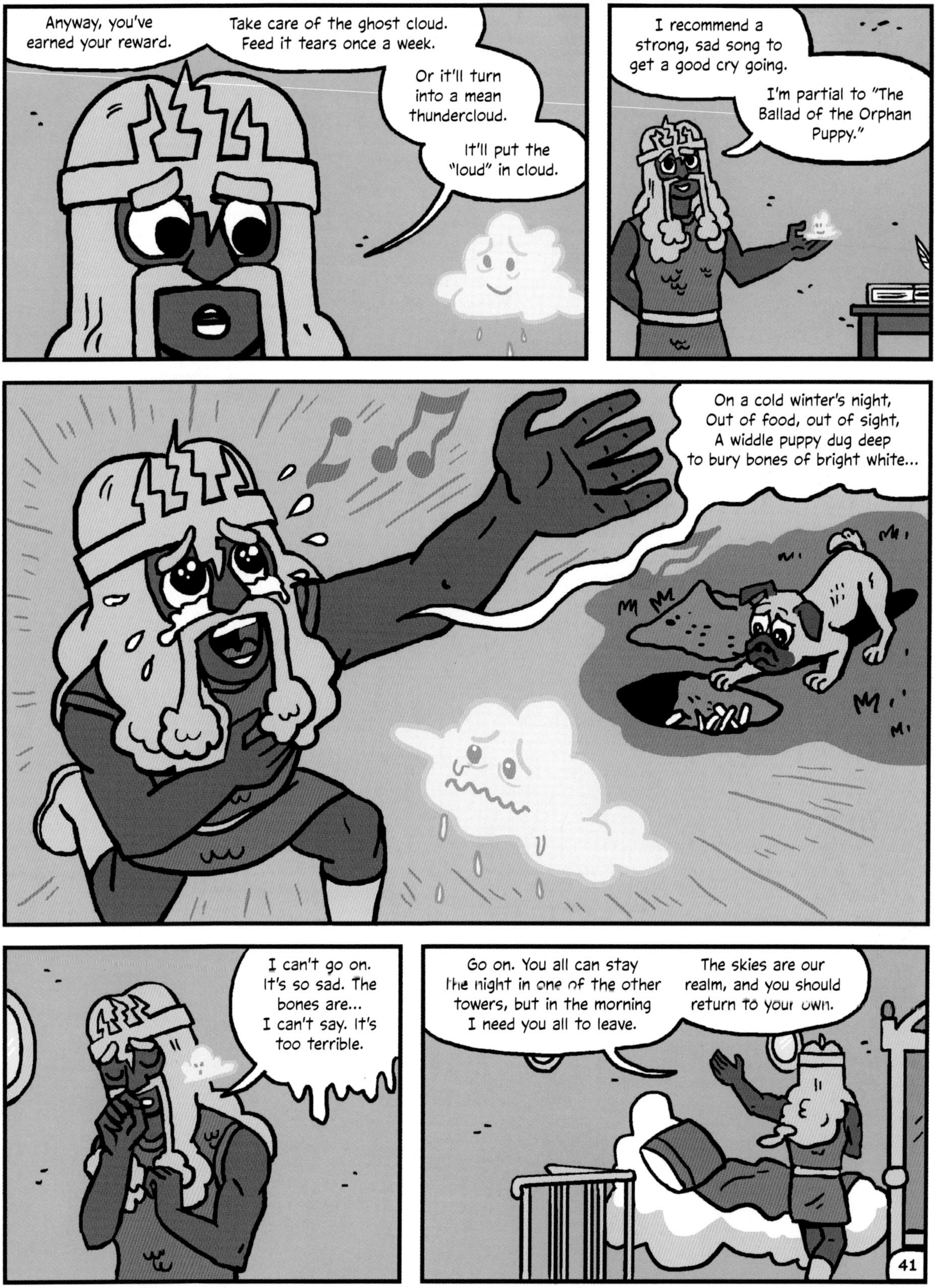
Anyway, you've earned your reward.
Take care of the ghost cloud. Feed it tears once a week.
Or it'll turn into a mean thundercloud.
It'll put the "loud" in cloud.
I recommend a strong, sad song to get a good cry going.
I'm partial to "The Ballad of the Orphan Puppy."
On a cold winter's night, Out of food, out of sight, A widdle puppy dug deep to bury bones of bright white...
I can't go on. It's so sad. The bones are... I can't say. It's too terrible.
Go on. You all can stay the night in one of the other towers, but in the morning I need you all to leave.
The skies are our realm, and you should return to your own.

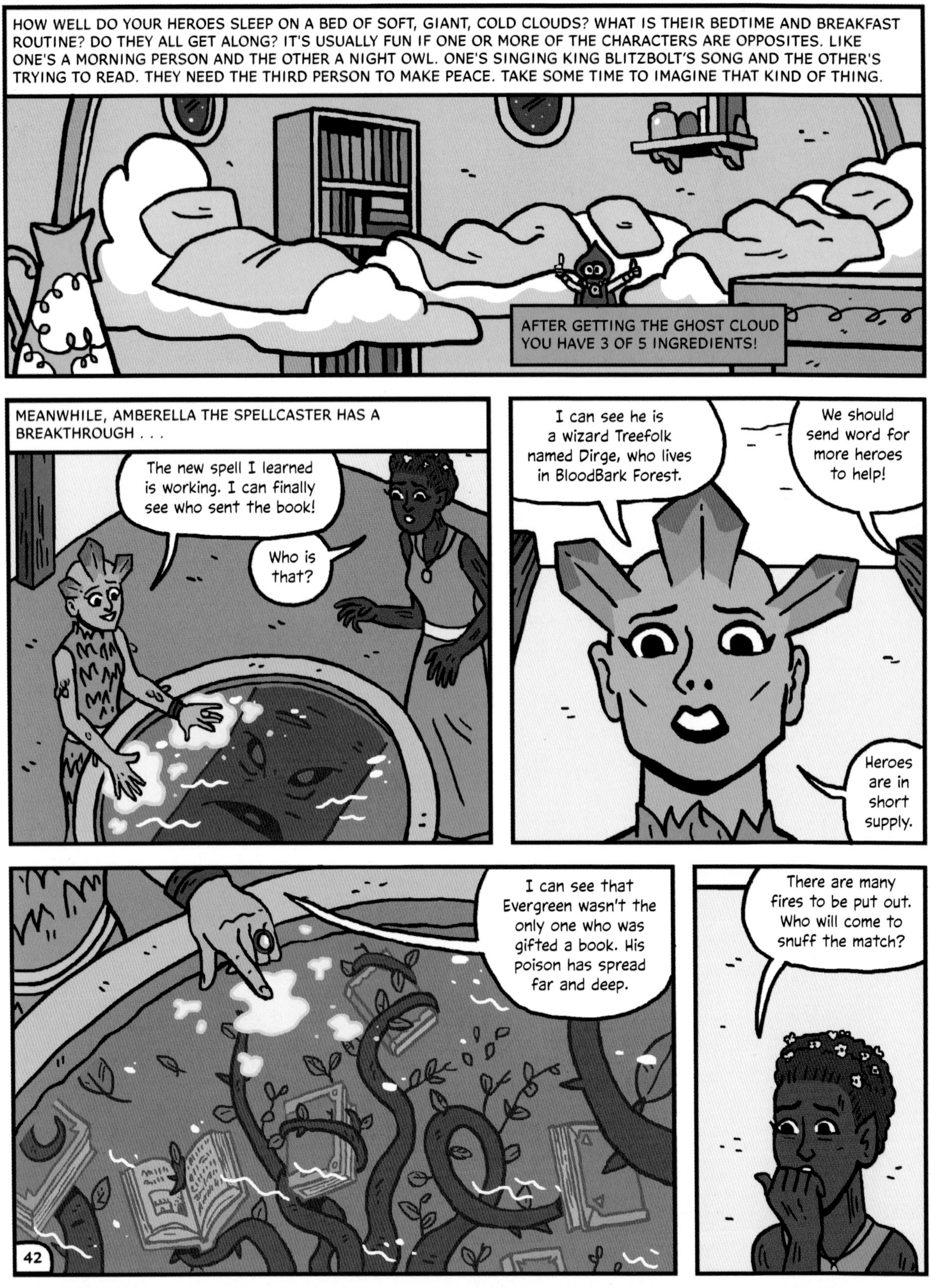
HOW WELL DO YOUR HEROES SLEEP ON A BED OF SOFT, GIANT, COLD CLOUDS? WHAT IS THEIR BEDTIME AND BREAKFAST ROUTINE? DO THEY ALL GET ALONG? IT'S USUALLY FUN IF ONE OR MORE OF THE CHARACTERS ARE OPPOSITES. LIKE ONE'S A MORNING PERSON AND THE OTHER A NIGHT OWL. ONE'S SINGING KING BLITZBOLT'S SONG AND THE OTHER'S TRYING TO READ. THEY NEED THE THIRD PERSON TO MAKE PEACE. TAKE SOME TIME TO IMAGINE THAT KIND OF THING.
AFTER GETTING THE GHOST CLOUD YOU HAVE 3 OF 5 INGREDIENTS!
MEANWHILE, AMBERELLA THE SPELLCASTER HAS A BREAKTHROUGH . . .
The new spell I learned is working. I can finally see who sent the book!
Who is that?
I can see he is a wizard Treefolk named Dirge, who lives in BloodBark Forest.
We should send word for more heroes to help!
Heroes are in short supply.
I can see that Evergreen wasn't the only one who was gifted a book. His poison has spread far and deep.
There are many fires to be put out. Who will come to snuff the match?

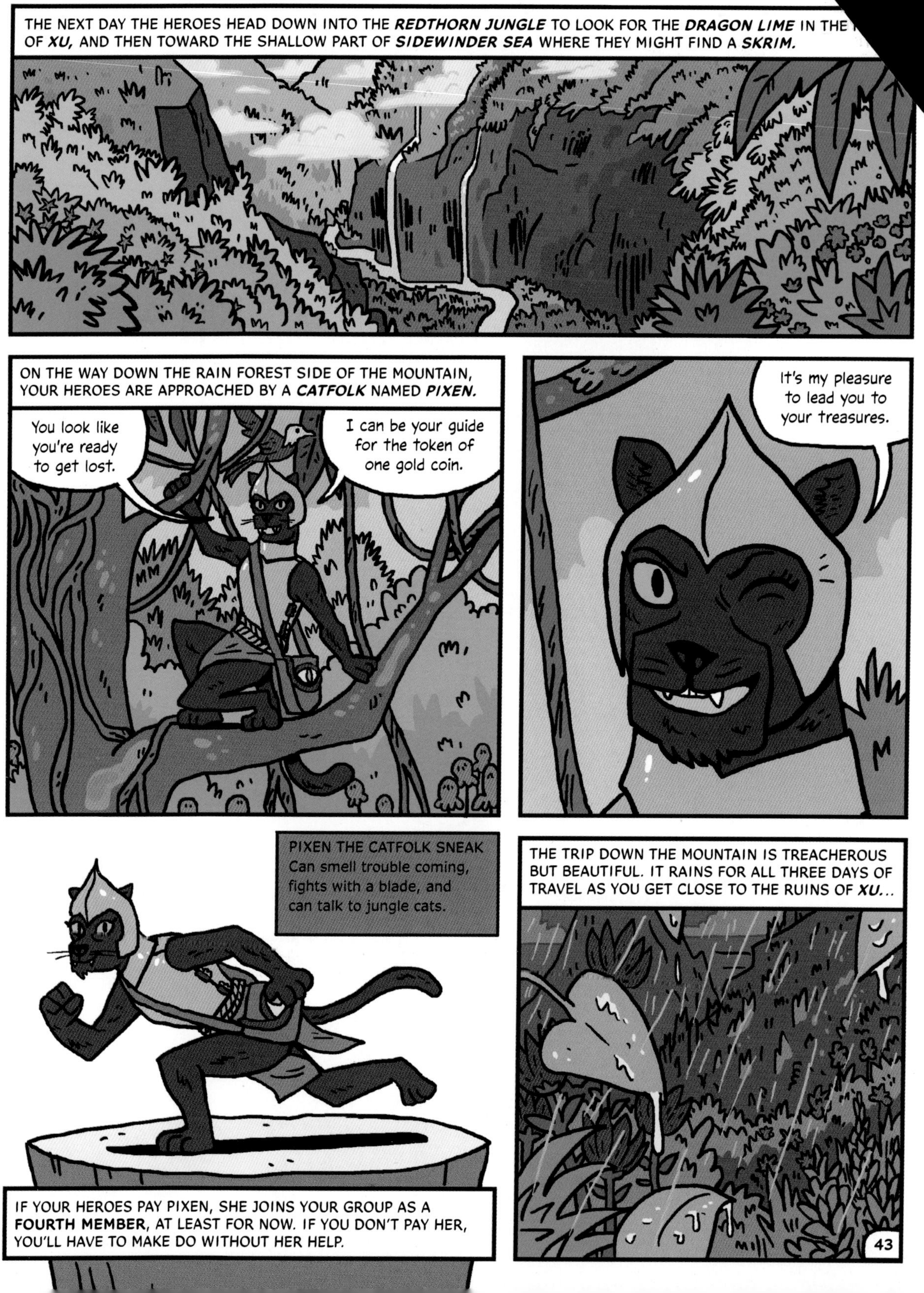
THE NEXT DAY THE HEROES HEAD DOWN INTO THE REDTHORN JUNGLE TO LOOK FOR THE DRAGON LIME IN THE
OF XU, AND THEN TOWARD THE SHALLOW PART OF SIDEWINDER SEA WHERE THEY MIGHT FIND A SKRIM.
ON THE WAY DOWN THE RAIN FOREST SIDE OF THE MOUNTAIN, YOUR HEROES ARE APPROACHED BY A CATFOLK NAMED PIXEN.
You look like you're ready to get lost.
I can be your guide for the token of one gold coin.
It's my pleasure to lead you to your treasures.
PIXEN THE CATFOLK SNEAK Can smell trouble coming, fights with a blade, and can talk to jungle cats.
IF YOUR HEROES PAY PIXEN, SHE JOINS YOUR GROUP AS A FOURTH MEMBER, AT LEAST FOR NOW. IF YOU DON'T PAY HER, YOU'LL HAVE TO MAKE DO WITHOUT HER HELP.
THE TRIP DOWN THE MOUNTAIN IS TREACHEROUS BUT BEAUTIFUL. IT RAINS FOR ALL THREE DAYS OF TRAVEL AS YOU GET CLOSE TO THE RUINS OF XU...

CHAPTER FOUR

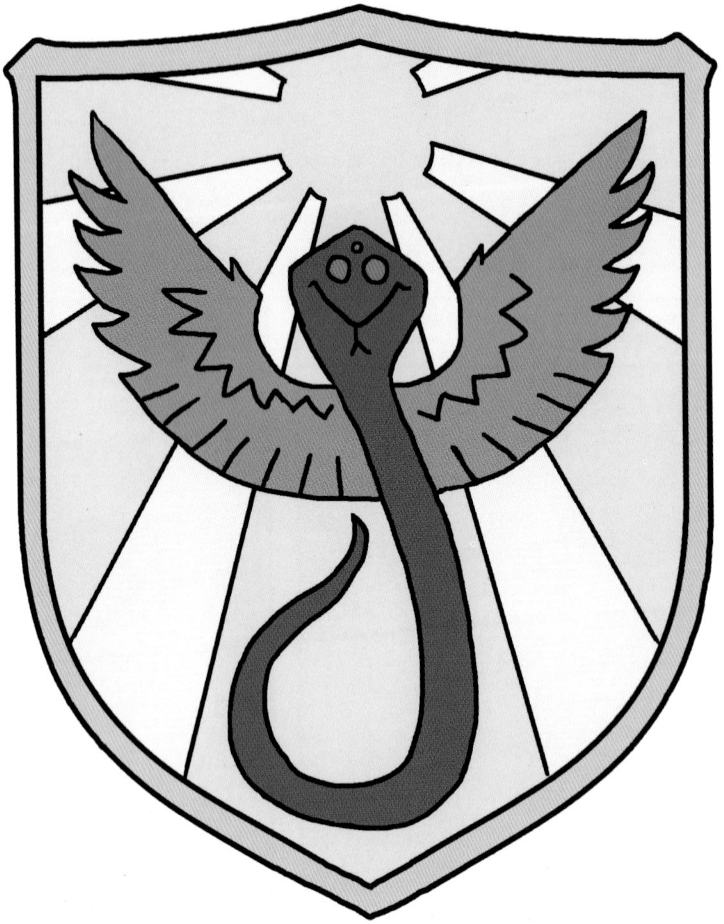

STING OF THE JUNGLE

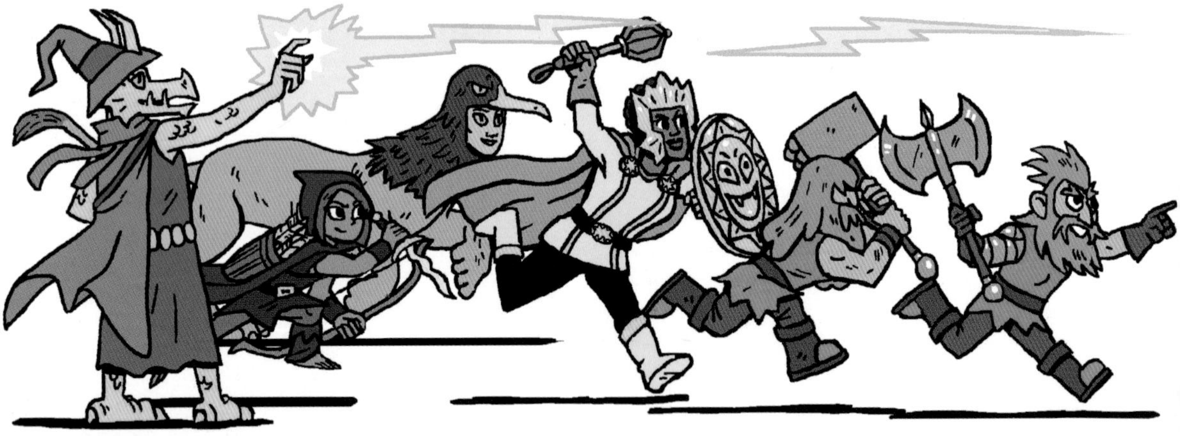

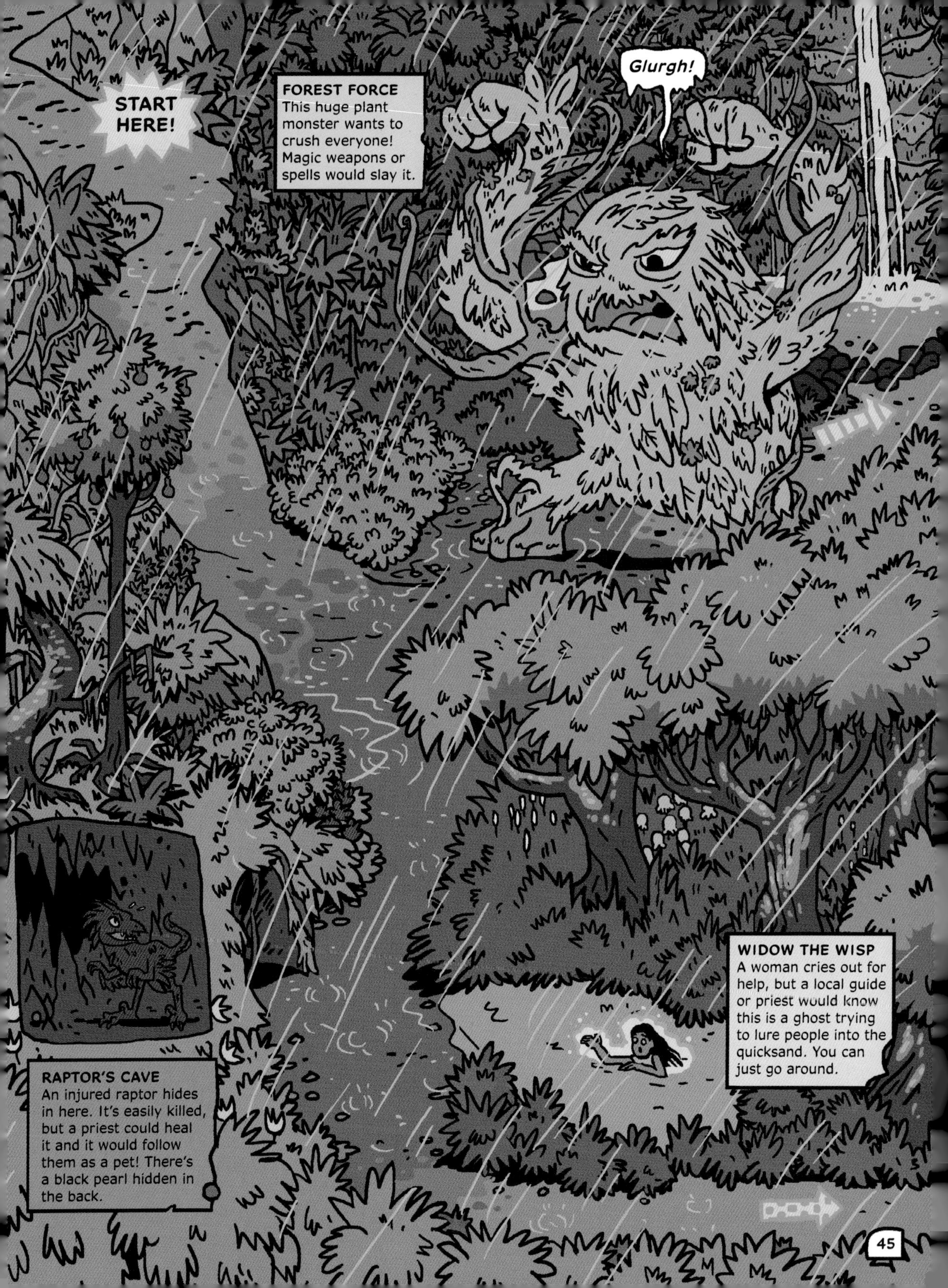

START HERE!
FOREST FORCE
This huge plant monster wants to crush everyone! Magic weapons or spells would slay it.
Glurgh!
RAPTOR'S CAVE
An injured raptor hides in here. It's easily killed, but a priest could heal it and it would follow them as a pet! There's a black pearl hidden in the back.
WIDOW THE WISP
A woman cries out for help, but a local guide or priest would know this is a ghost trying to lure people into the quicksand. You can just go around.

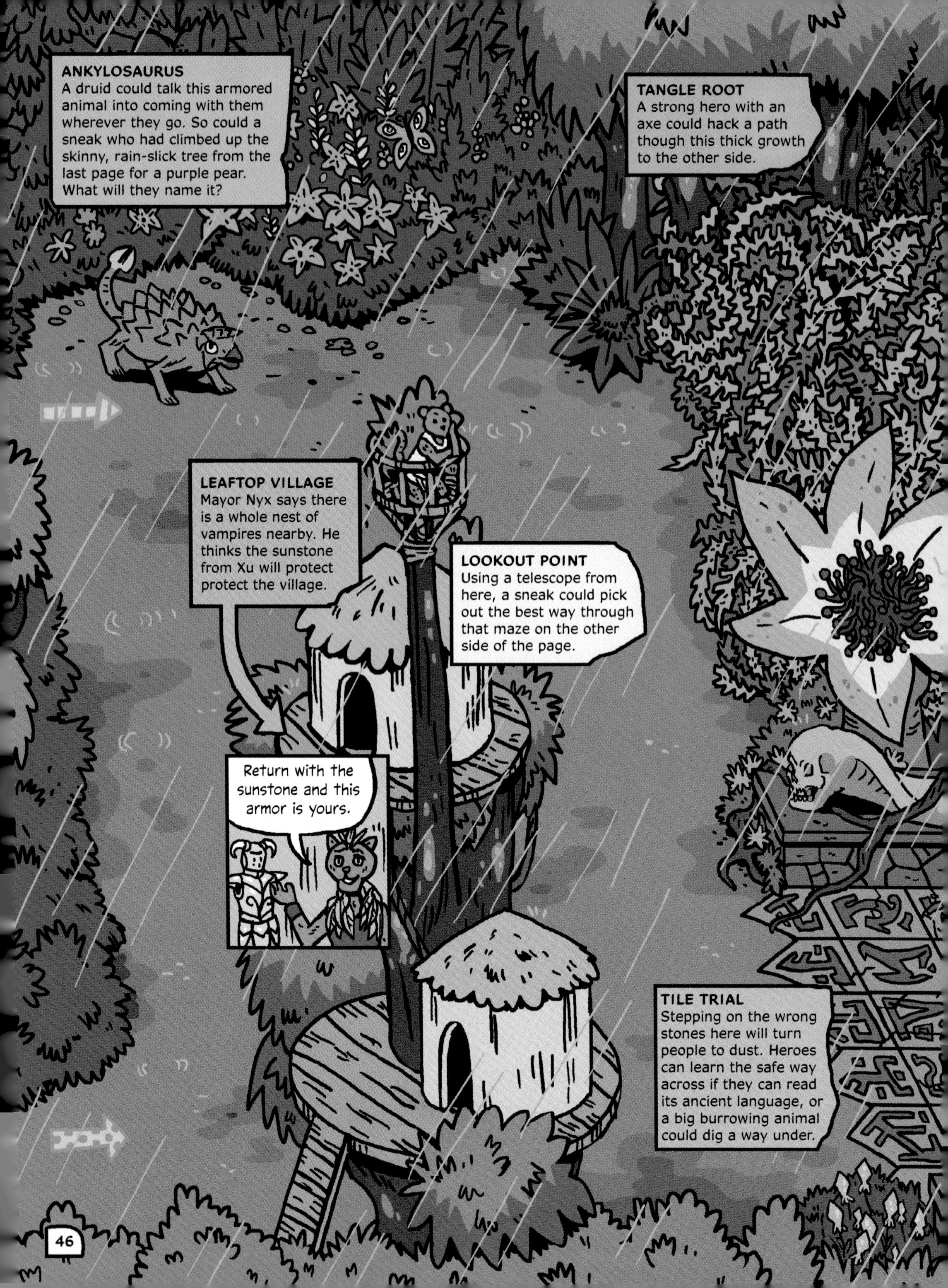
ANKYLOSAURUS
A druid could talk this armored animal into coming with them wherever they go. So could a sneak who had climbed up the skinny, rain-slick tree from the last page for a purple pear. What will they name it?
TANGLE ROOT
A strong hero with an axe could hack a path though this thick growth to the other side.
LEAFTOP VILLAGE
Mayor Nyx says there is a whole nest of vampires nearby. He thinks the sunstone from Xu will protect protect the village.
LOOKOUT POINT
Using a telescope from here, a sneak could pick out the best way through that maze on the other side of the page.
Return with the sunstone and this armor is yours.
TILE TRIAL
Stepping on the wrong stones here will turn people to dust. Heroes can learn the safe way across if they can read its ancient language, or a big burrowing animal could dig a way under.

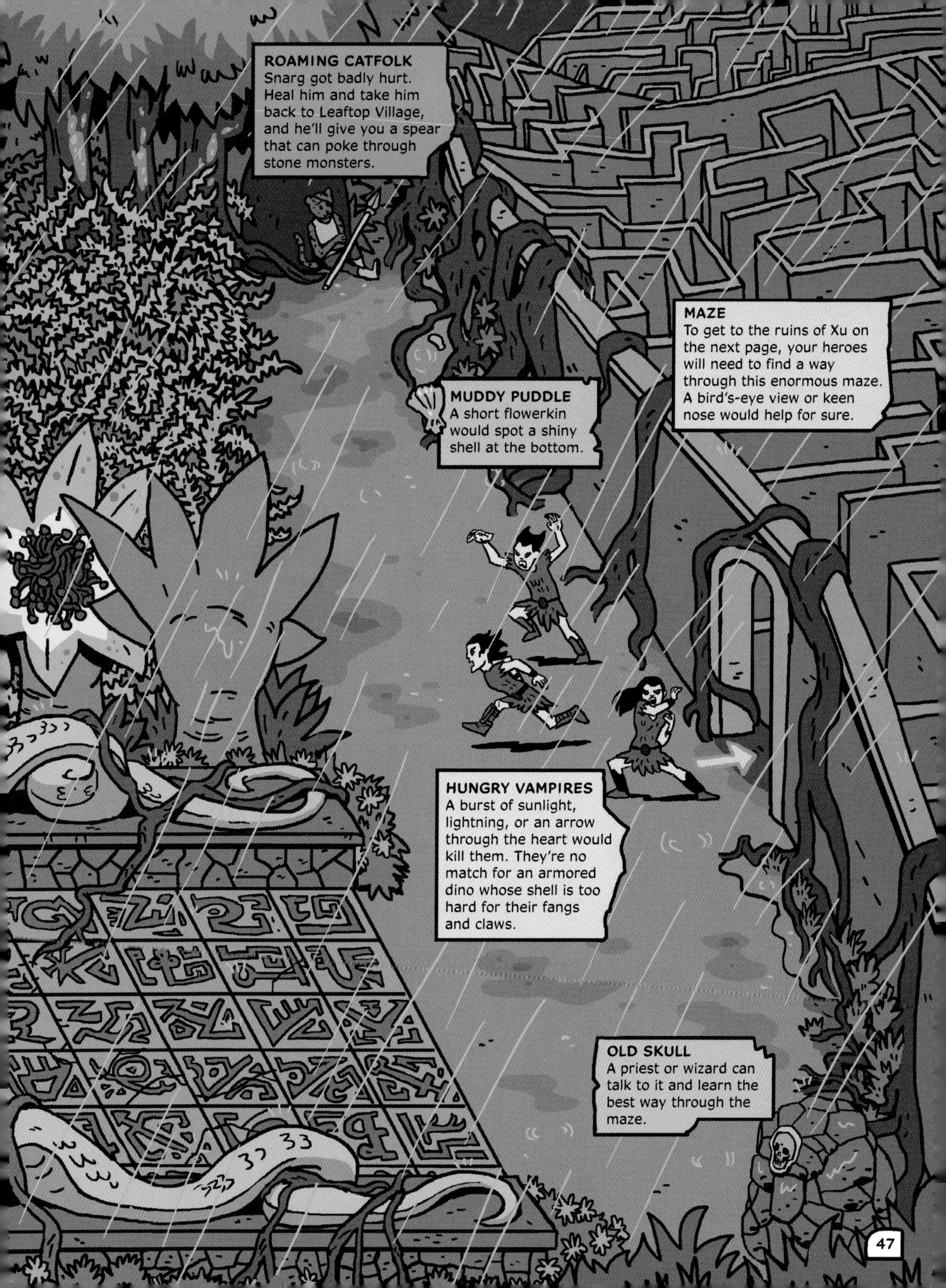
ROAMING CATFOLK
Snarg got badly hurt. Heal him and take him back to Leaftop Village, and he'll give you a spear that can poke through stone monsters.
MAZE
To get to the ruins of Xu on the next page, your heroes will need to find a way through this enormous maze. A bird's-eye view or keen nose would help for sure.
MUDDY PUDDLE
A short flowerkin would spot a shiny shell at the bottom.
HUNGRY VAMPIRES
A burst of sunlight, lightning, or an arrow through the heart would kill them. They're no match for an armored dino whose shell is too hard for their fangs and claws.
OLD SKULL
A priest or wizard can talk to it and learn the best way through the maze.

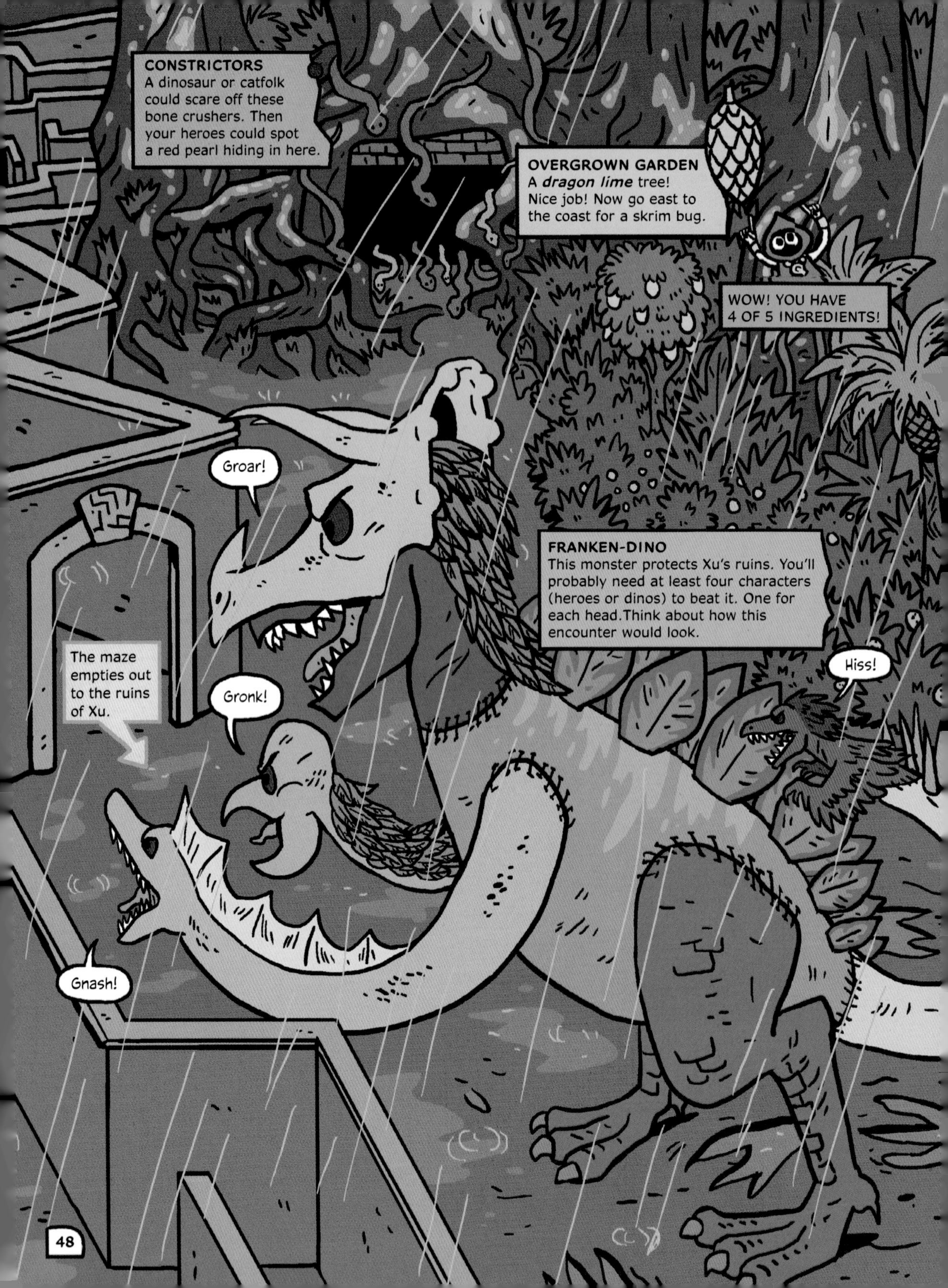
CONSTRICTORS
A dinosaur or catfolk could scare off these bone crushers. Then your heroes could spot a red pearl hiding in here.
OVERGROWN GARDEN
A *dragon lime* tree! Nice job! Now go east to the coast for a skrim bug.
WOW! YOU HAVE 4 OF 5 INGREDIENTS!
Groar!
FRANKEN-DINO
This monster protects Xu's ruins. You'll probably need at least four characters (heroes or dinos) to beat it. One for each head.Think about how this encounter would look.
The maze empties out to the ruins of Xu.
Gronk!
Hiss!
Gnash!

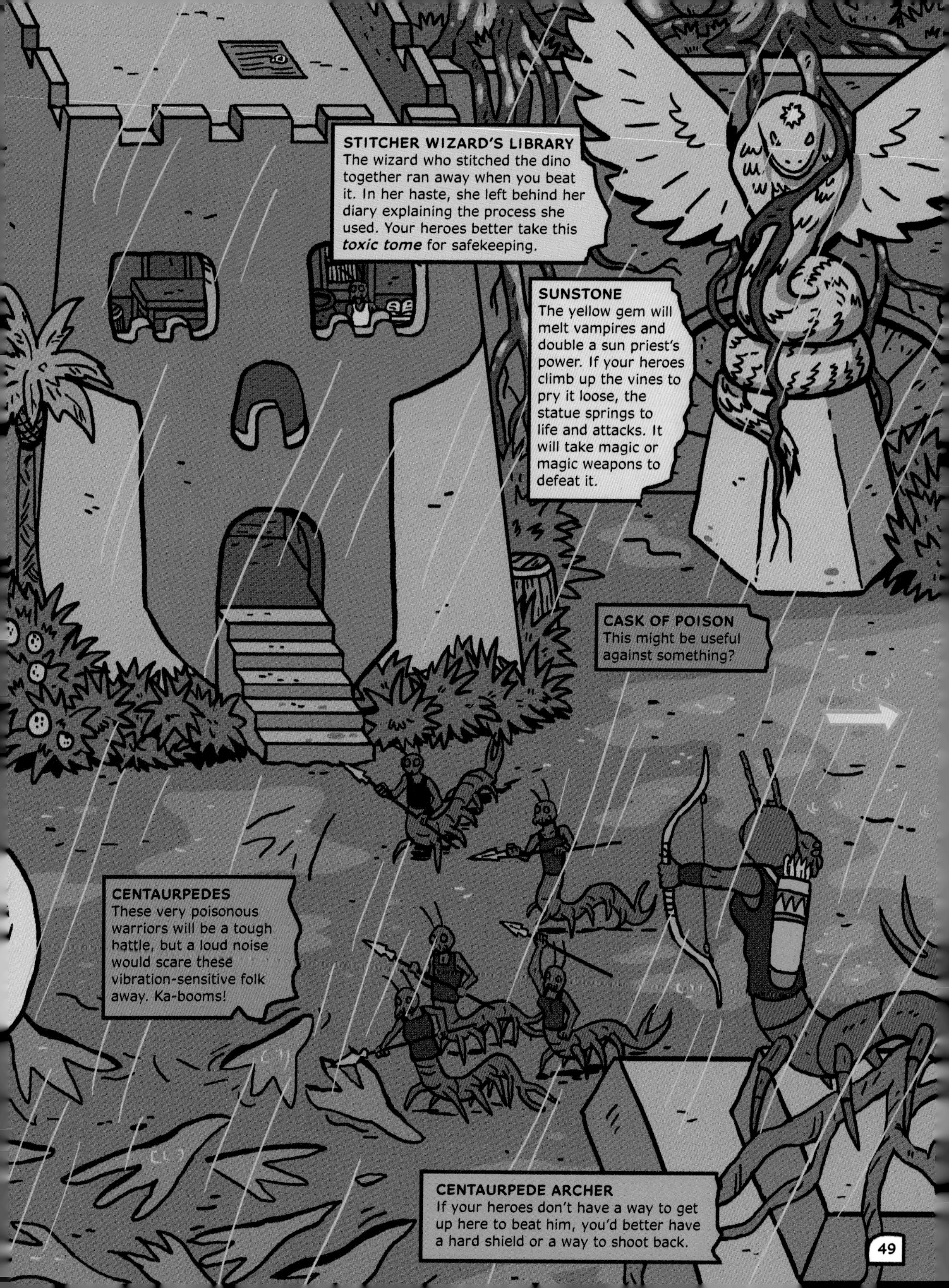
STITCHER WIZARD'S LIBRARY
The wizard who stitched the dino together ran away when you beat it. In her haste, she left behind her diary explaining the process she used. Your heroes better take this *toxic tome* for safekeeping.
SUNSTONE
The yellow gem will melt vampires and double a sun priest's power. If your heroes climb up the vines to pry it loose, the statue springs to life and attacks. It will take magic or magic weapons to defeat it.
CASK OF POISON
This might be useful against something?
CENTAURPEDES
These very poisonous warriors will be a tough battle, but a loud noise would scare these vibration-sensitive folk away. Ka-booms!
CENTAURPEDE ARCHER
If your heroes don't have a way to get up here to beat him, you'd better have a hard shield or a way to shoot back.

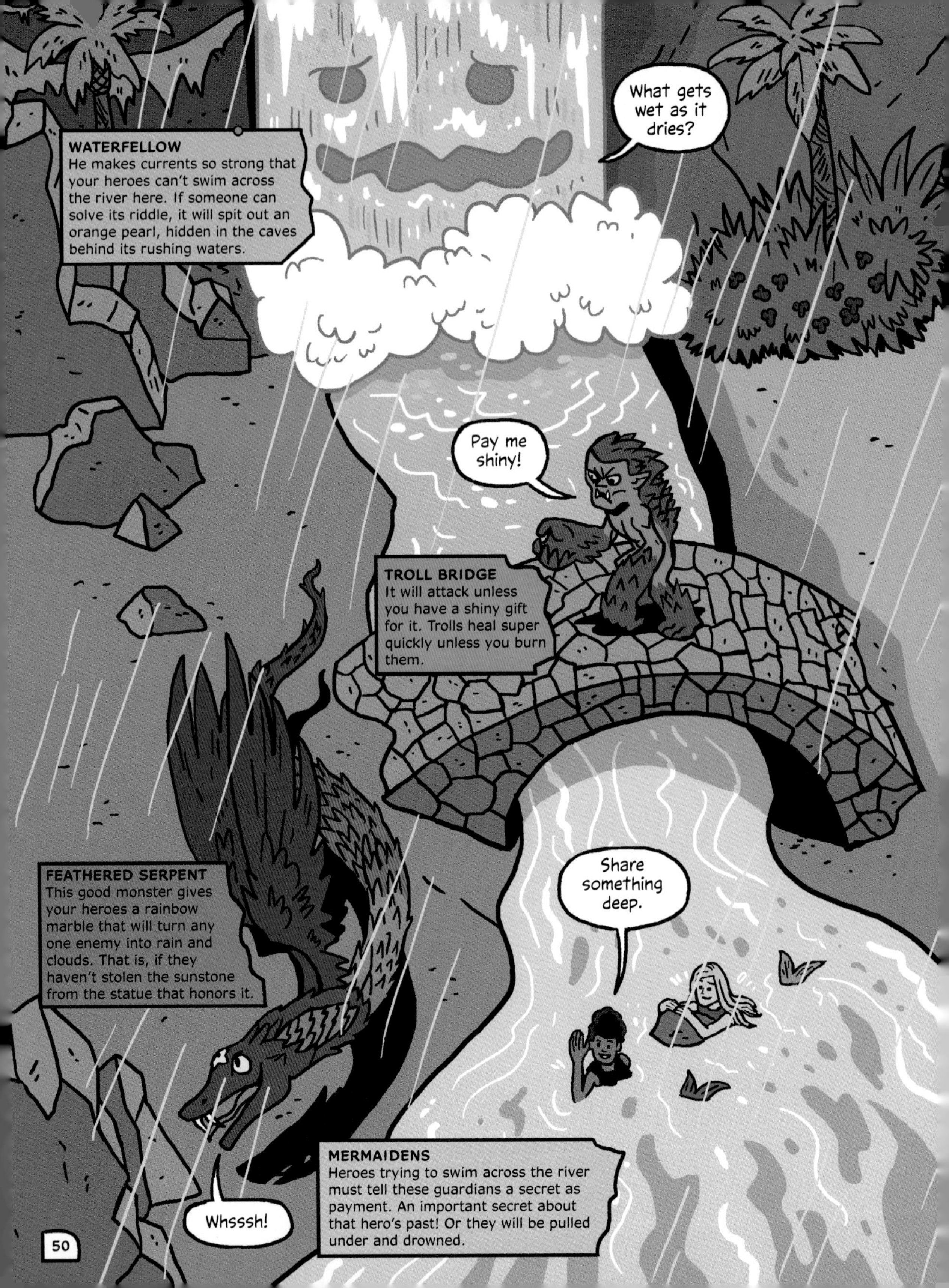
WATERFELLOW
He makes currents so strong that your heroes can't swim across the river here. If someone can solve its riddle, it will spit out an orange pearl, hidden in the caves behind its rushing waters.
What gets wet as it dries?
Pay me shiny!
TROLL BRIDGE
It will attack unless you have a shiny gift for it. Trolls heal super quickly unless you burn them.
FEATHERED SERPENT
This good monster gives your heroes a rainbow marble that will turn any one enemy into rain and clouds. That is, if they haven't stolen the sunstone from the statue that honors it.
Share something deep.
Whsssh!
MERMAIDENS
Heroes trying to swim across the river must tell these guardians a secret as payment. An important secret about that hero's past! Or they will be pulled under and drowned.

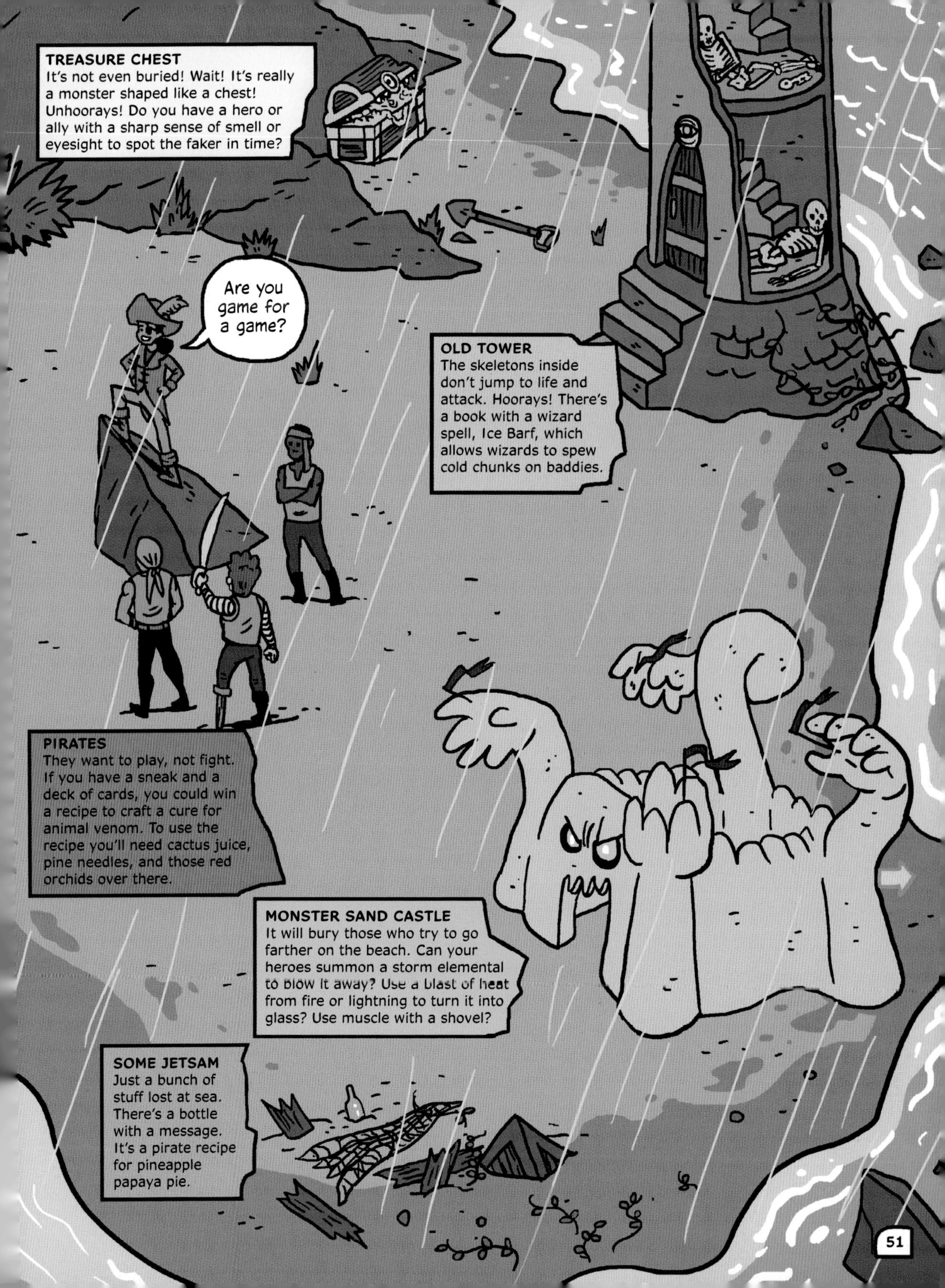
TREASURE CHEST
It's not even buried! Wait! It's really a monster shaped like a chest! Unhoorays! Do you have a hero or ally with a sharp sense of smell or eyesight to spot the faker in time?
Are you game for a game?
OLD TOWER
The skeletons inside don't jump to life and attack. Hoorays! There's a book with a wizard spell, Ice Barf, which allows wizards to spew cold chunks on baddies.
PIRATES
They want to play, not fight. If you have a sneak and a deck of cards, you could win a recipe to craft a cure for animal venom. To use the recipe you'll need cactus juice, pine needles, and those red orchids over there.
MONSTER SAND CASTLE
It will bury those who try to go farther on the beach. Can your heroes summon a storm elemental to blow it away? Use a blast of heat from fire or lightning to turn it into glass? Use muscle with a shovel?
SOME JETSAM
Just a bunch of stuff lost at sea. There's a bottle with a message. It's a pirate recipe for pineapple papaya pie.

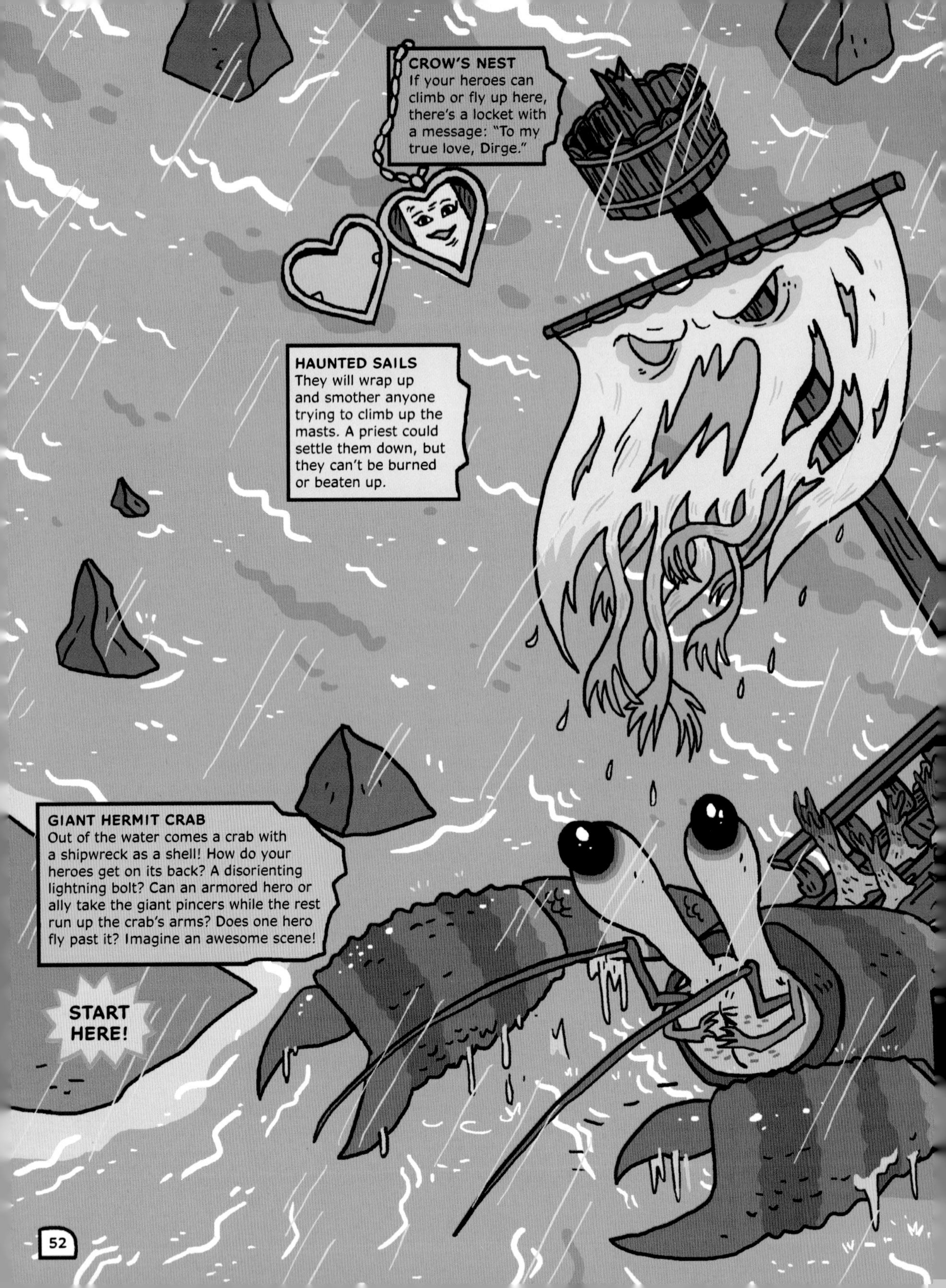
CROW'S NEST
If your heroes can climb or fly up here, there's a locket with a message: "To my true love, Dirge."
HAUNTED SAILS
They will wrap up and smother anyone trying to climb up the masts. A priest could settle them down, but they can't be burned or beaten up.
GIANT HERMIT CRAB
Out of the water comes a crab with a shipwreck as a shell! How do your heroes get on its back? A disorienting lightning bolt? Can an armored hero or ally take the giant pincers while the rest run up the crab's arms? Does one hero fly past it? Imagine an awesome scene!
START HERE!

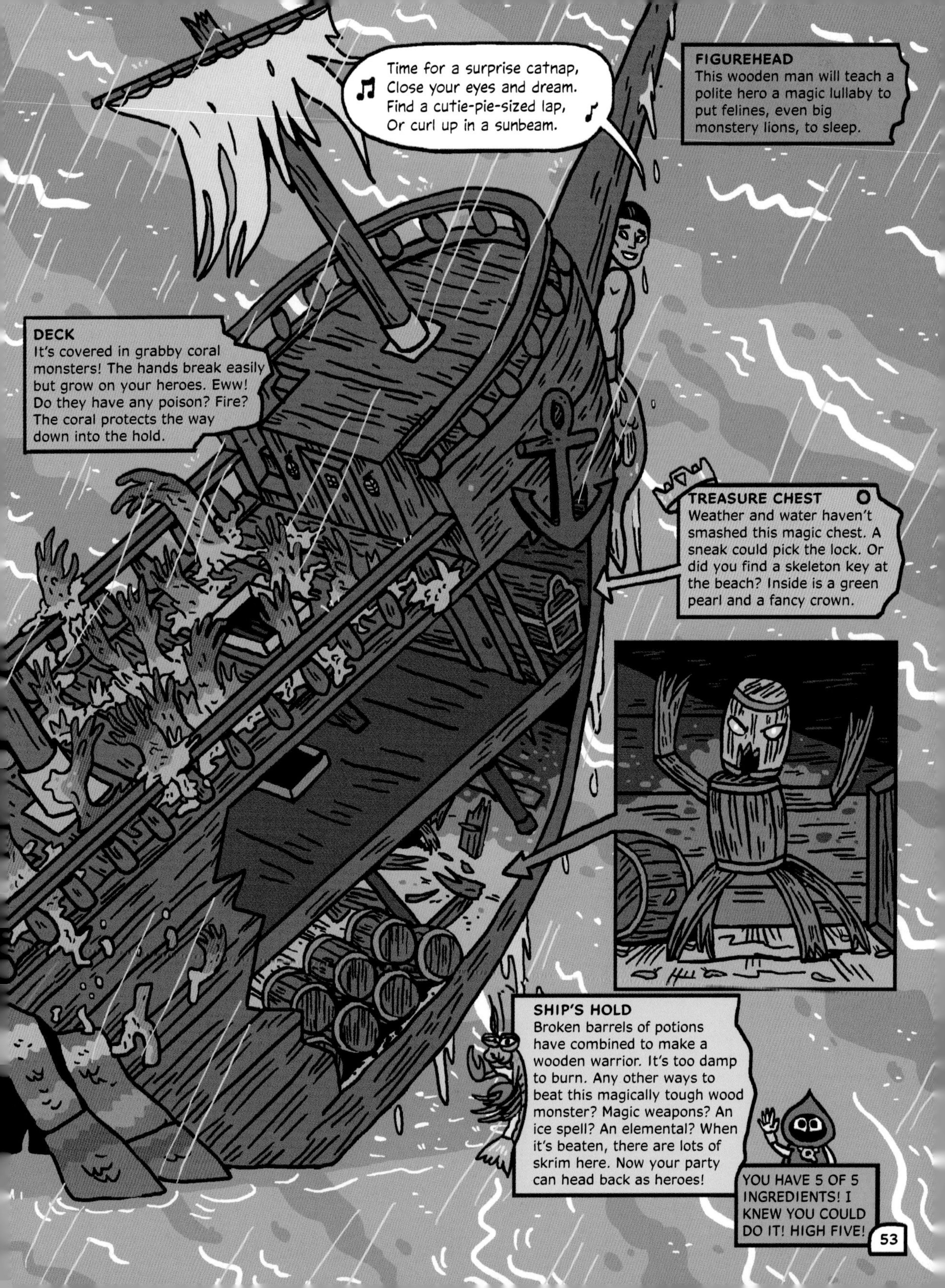

Time for a surprise catnap, Close your eyes and dream. Find a cutie-pie-sized lap, Or curl up in a sunbeam.
FIGUREHEAD
This wooden man will teach a polite hero a magic lullaby to put felines, even big monstery lions, to sleep.
DECK
It's covered in grabby coral monsters! The hands break easily but grow on your heroes. Eww! Do they have any poison? Fire? The coral protects the way down into the hold.
TREASURE CHEST
Weather and water haven't smashed this magic chest. A sneak could pick the lock. Or did you find a skeleton key at the beach? Inside is a green pearl and a fancy crown.
SHIP'S HOLD
Broken barrels of potions have combined to make a wooden warrior. It's too damp to burn. Any other ways to beat this magically tough wood monster? Magic weapons? An ice spell? An elemental? When it's beaten, there are lots of skrim here. Now your party can head back as heroes!
YOU HAVE 5 OF 5 INGREDIENTS! I KNEW YOU COULD DO IT! HIGH FIVE!

RIDING HIGH ON THEIR SUCCESS, YOUR HEROES MAKE THEIR WAY UP THE COAST TO THE PORT CITY, ***COBALT COVE.***

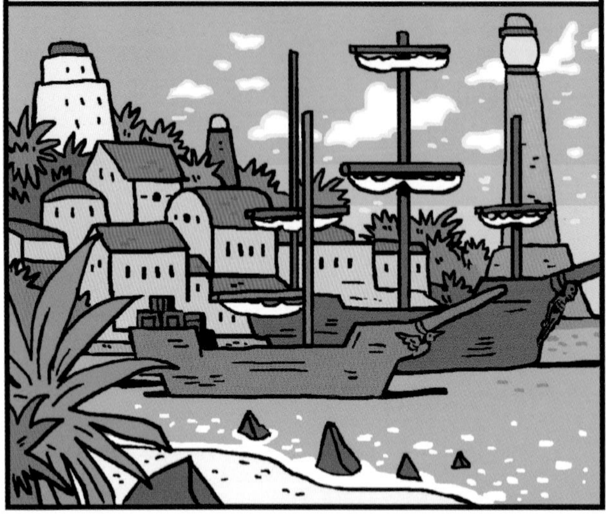

IF YOUR HEROES ARE TRAVELING WITH PIXEN, SHE WISHES THEM GOOD LUCK AND SLIPS AWAY.

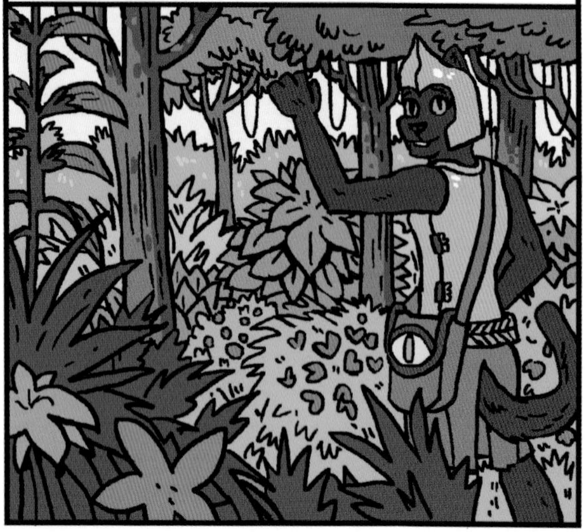

GETTING A RIDE ON A SHIP TO CASTLE EVERGREEN ISN'T HARD. ARE THEY BRINGING DINOSAURS? HOW DO THEY FEEL AT THIS STAGE IN THE JOURNEY? DO ANY OF THEM HAVE A CRUSH ON EACH OTHER? WHEN A READER WANTS CHARACTERS TO HAVE A ROMANTIC RELATIONSHIP WITH EACH OTHER IT'S CALLED ***SHIPPING.*** ARE YOU SHIPPING ANYONE ON THE SHIP?

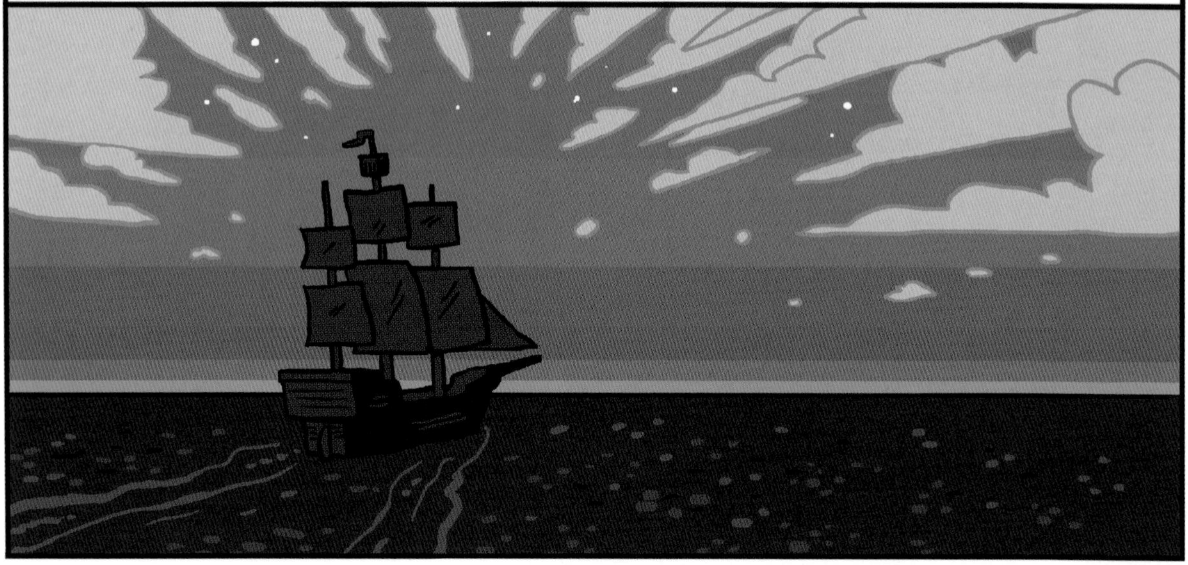

WHEN YOUR HEROES ARRIVE, THE HEALERS GRAB THE ***STAR DIAMOND*** TO FOCUS SUNLIGHT AT THE MAGIC POISON. THEY FEED THE EVER-SLEEPING QUEEN THE D***RAGON LIME*** JUICE TO BURN AWAY THE POISON INSIDE. THE ***SKRIM*** IS SHRUNK AND PUT INTO HER BLOODSTREAM. IT EATS UP THE POISON'S DEEPEST PARTS. AS THE EVIL MAGIC LEAVES, IT IS CAUGHT IN THE ***BLANK LOTUS.*** FINALLY, THE ***GHOST CLOUD*** SINGS A SONG TO COAX THE QUEEN'S SOUL BACK TO HER BODY.

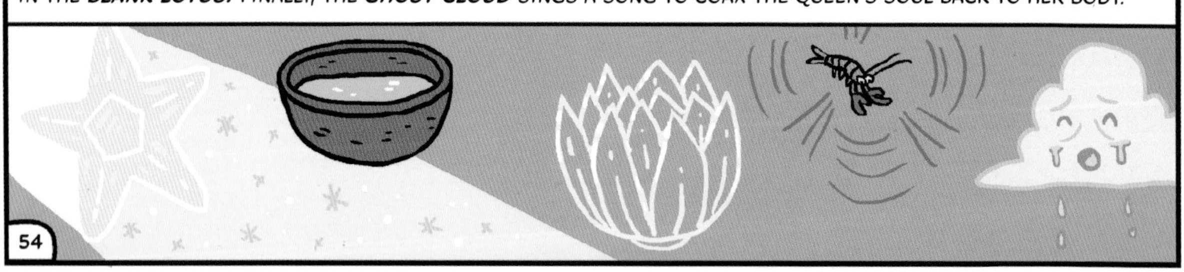

THEN MARISHA SAYS, "IT DIDN'T WORK! THERE IS NO SAVING HER." BUT, JUST AS THE LAST PERSON HAS ***GIVEN UP ALL HOPE,*** SOBBING DEEP IN THEIR CHEST, THE QUEEN SPUTTERS AWAKE. EVERYONE HUGS AND CRIES WITH RELIEF.

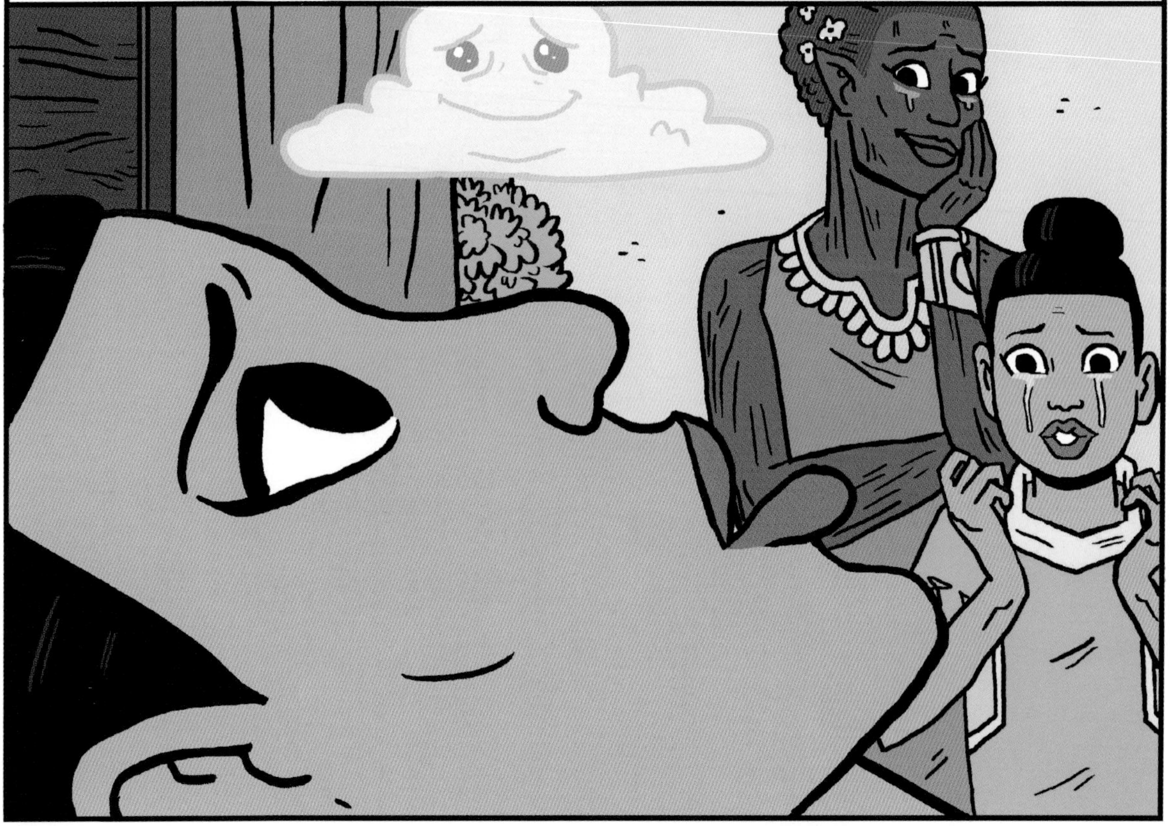

YOU'RE WRITING THIS STORY, TOO. MAYBE YOU THINK IT'S BETTER IF YOUR HEROES ***ARE*** TOO LATE TO SAVE THE QUEEN. YOU COULD IMAGINE THE HEROES DO THE NEXT PART OF THE QUEST FOR MARISHA AND THE NEW QUEEN, VIOLET EVERGREEN. WE MET HER BRIEFLY IN THE OPENING CHAPTER. IF SHE IS TAKING OVER, IT WOULD HAVE BEEN BETTER TO GIVE HER MORE SCENES SO WE GET TO KNOW HER. CAST YOUR MIND BACK AND IMAGINE HOW VIOLET WOULD HAVE FELT THROUGHOUT THE STORY. WHAT WORDS OF WISDOM DID HER MOTHER GIVE HER THAT ARE HELPING HER NOW?

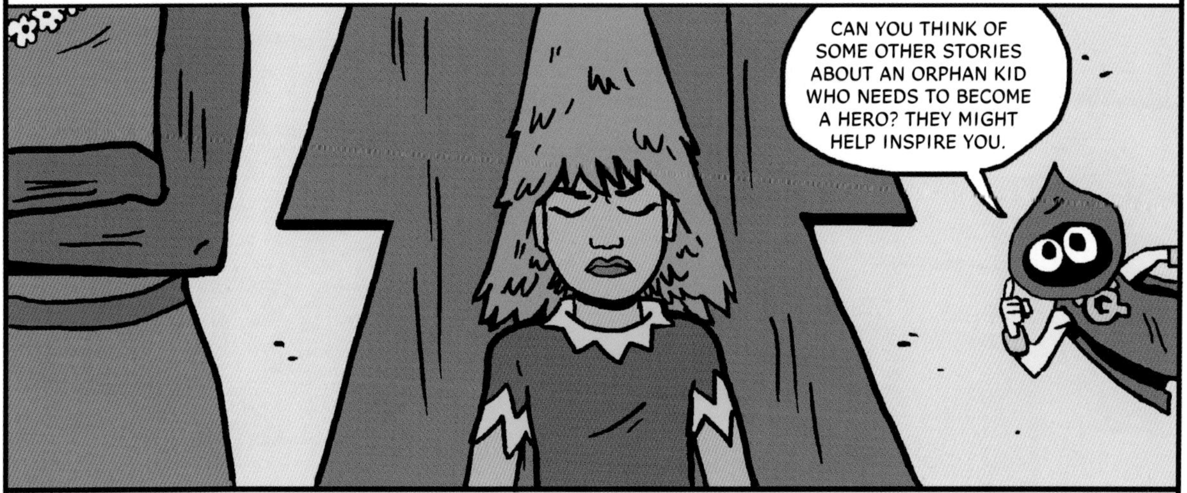
CAN YOU THINK OF SOME OTHER STORIES ABOUT AN ORPHAN KID WHO NEEDS TO BECOME A HERO? THEY MIGHT HELP INSPIRE YOU.

NOW SKIP AHEAD TO ***PAGE 100*** TO BEGIN THE FINAL CHAPTER. IF YOU WANT VIOLET TO BE THE NEW QUEEN, YOU'LL HAVE TO IMAGINE THAT. THE PAGES ARE MADE AS IF QUEEN EVERGREEN WAS SAVED, BUT IT'S UP TO YOU.

CHAPTER TWO

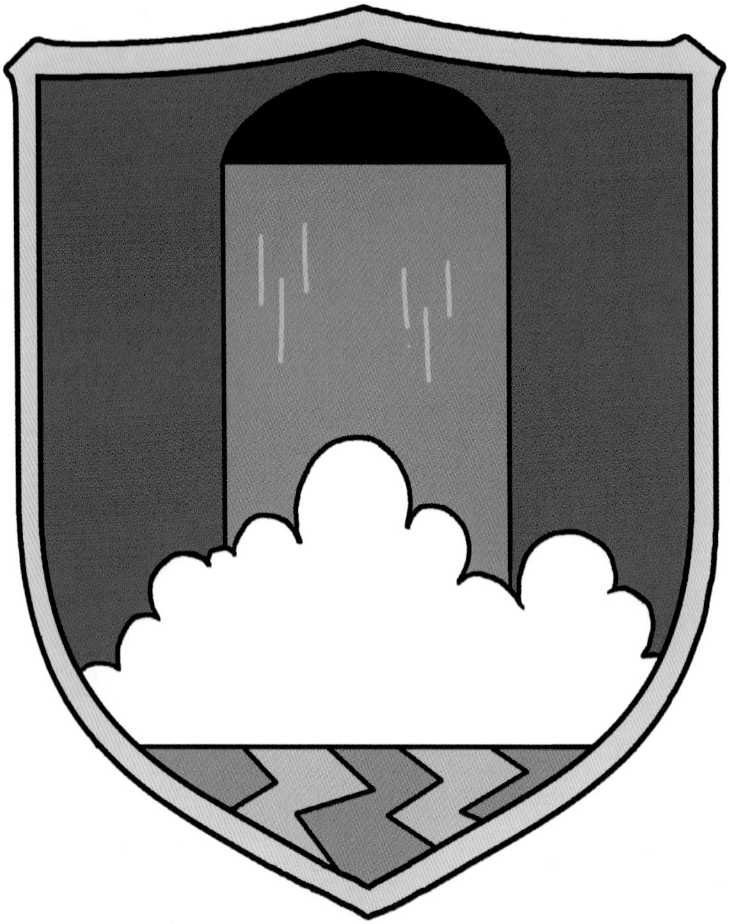

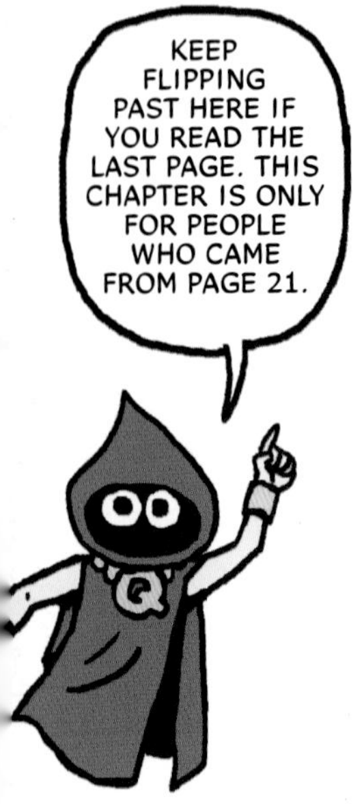
KEEP FLIPPING PAST HERE IF YOU READ THE LAST PAGE. THIS CHAPTER IS ONLY FOR PEOPLE WHO CAME FROM PAGE 21.

MINE OR MUSH

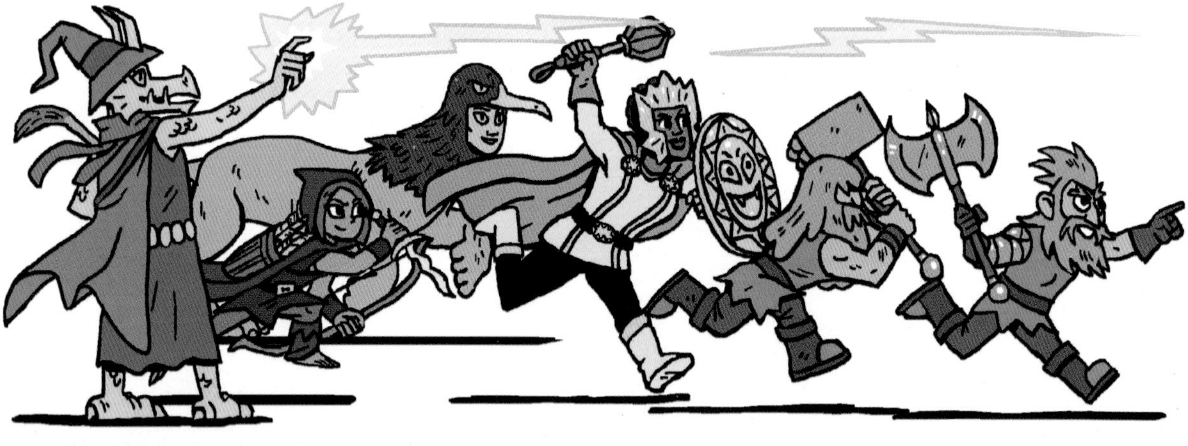

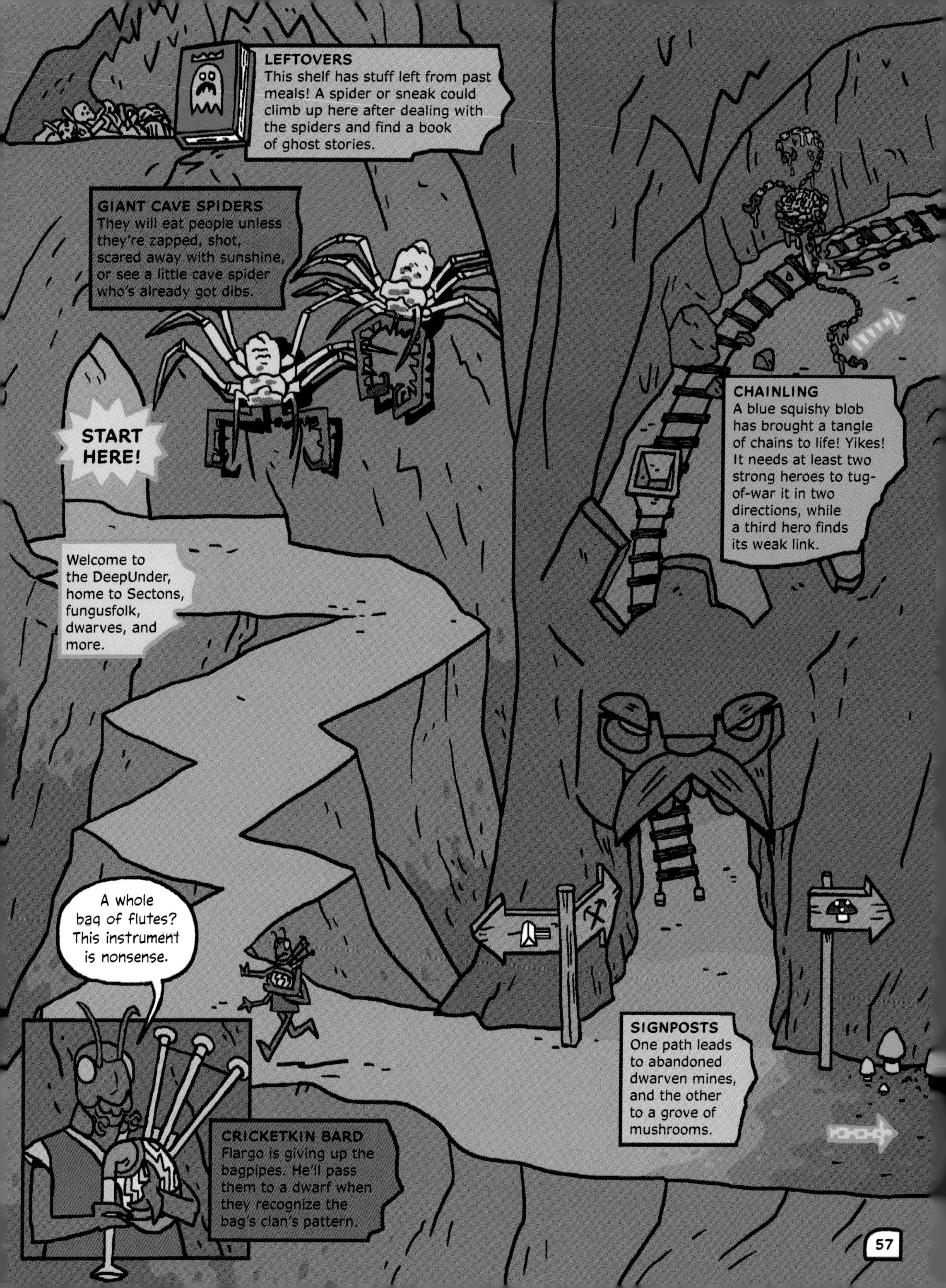
LEFTOVERS
This shelf has stuff left from past meals! A spider or sneak could climb up here after dealing with the spiders and find a book of ghost stories.
GIANT CAVE SPIDERS
They will eat people unless they're zapped, shot, scared away with sunshine, or see a little cave spider who's already got dibs.
CHAINLING
A blue squishy blob has brought a tangle of chains to life! Yikes! It needs at least two strong heroes to tug-of-war it in two directions, while a third hero finds its weak link.
START HERE!
Welcome to the DeepUnder, home to Sectons, fungusfolk, dwarves, and more.
A whole bag of flutes? This instrument is nonsense.
SIGNPOSTS
One path leads to abandoned dwarven mines, and the other to a grove of mushrooms.
CRICKETKIN BARD
Flargo is giving up the bagpipes. He'll pass them to a dwarf when they recognize the bag's clan's pattern.

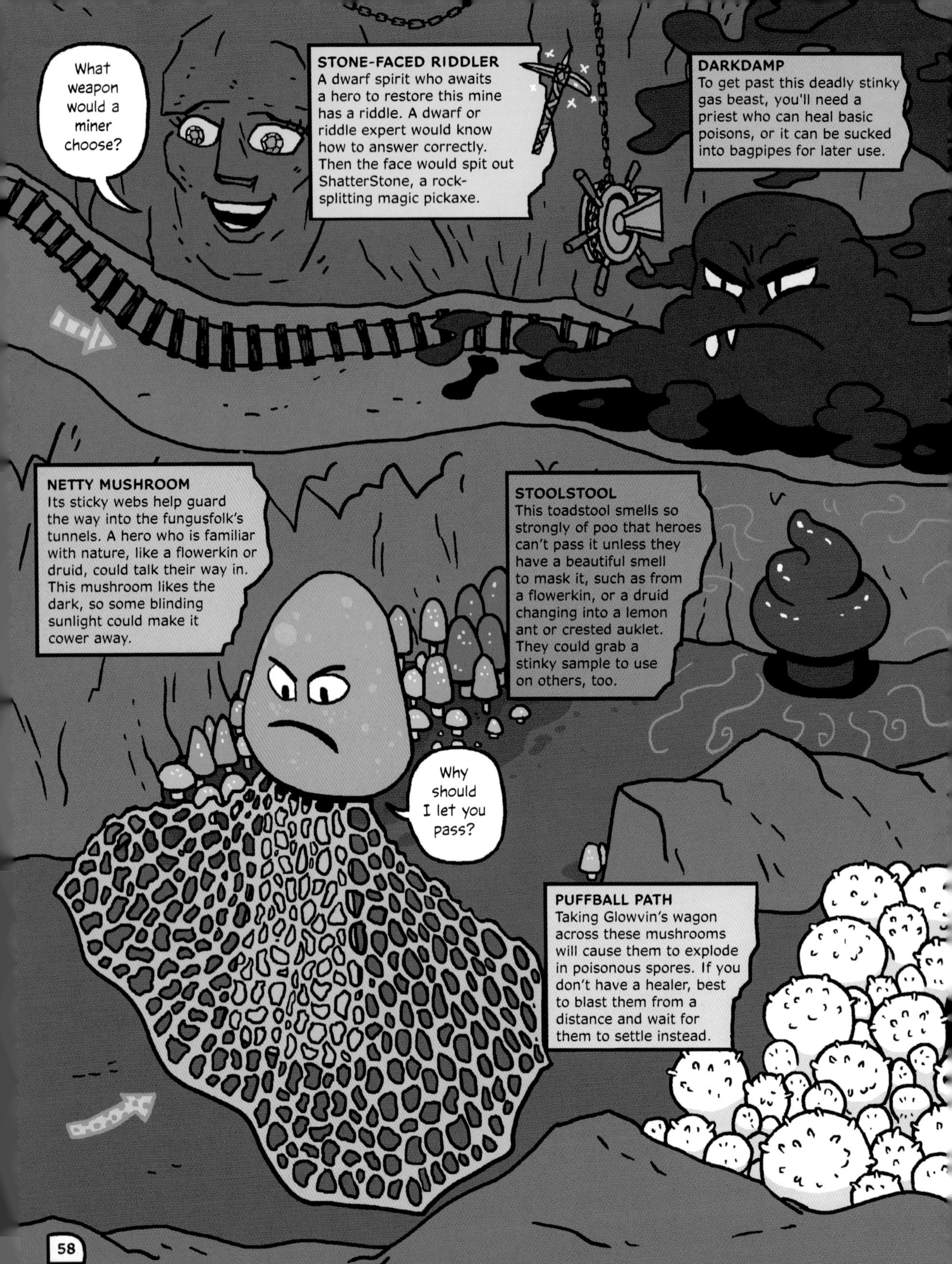
What weapon would a miner choose?
STONE-FACED RIDDLER
A dwarf spirit who awaits a hero to restore this mine has a riddle. A dwarf or riddle expert would know how to answer correctly. Then the face would spit out ShatterStone, a rock-splitting magic pickaxe.
DARKDAMP
To get past this deadly stinky gas beast, you'll need a priest who can heal basic poisons, or it can be sucked into bagpipes for later use.
NETTY MUSHROOM
Its sticky webs help guard the way into the fungusfolk's tunnels. A hero who is familiar with nature, like a flowerkin or druid, could talk their way in. This mushroom likes the dark, so some blinding sunlight could make it cower away.
STOOLSTOOL
This toadstool smells so strongly of poo that heroes can't pass it unless they have a beautiful smell to mask it, such as from a flowerkin, or a druid changing into a lemon ant or crested auklet. They could grab a stinky sample to use on others, too.
Why should I let you pass?
PUFFBALL PATH
Taking Glowvin's wagon across these mushrooms will cause them to explode in poisonous spores. If you don't have a healer, best to blast them from a distance and wait for them to settle instead.

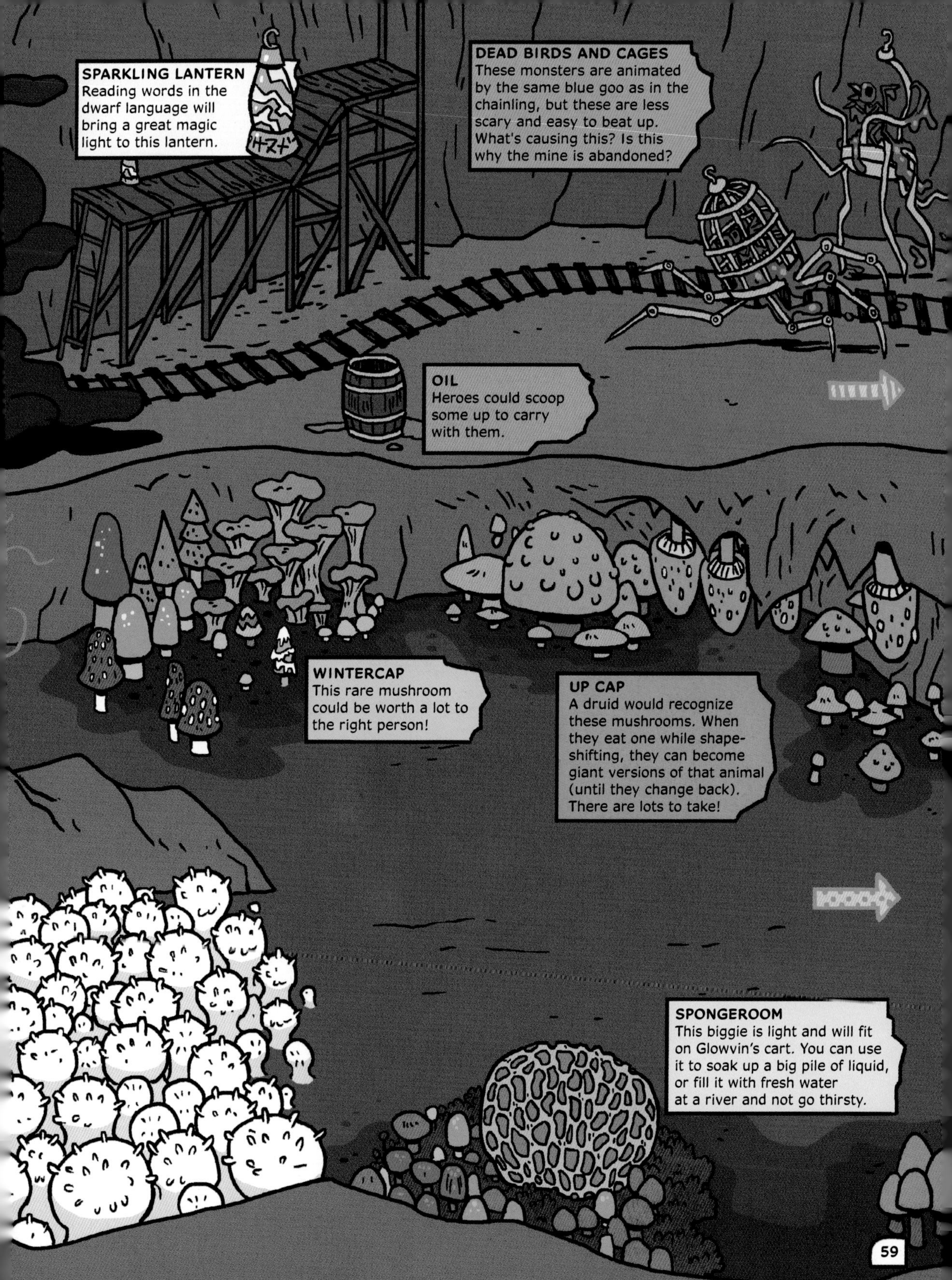
SPARKLING LANTERN
Reading words in the dwarf language will bring a great magic light to this lantern.
DEAD BIRDS AND CAGES
These monsters are animated by the same blue goo as in the chainling, but these are less scary and easy to beat up. What's causing this? Is this why the mine is abandoned?
OIL
Heroes could scoop some up to carry with them.
WINTERCAP
This rare mushroom could be worth a lot to the right person!
UP CAP
A druid would recognize these mushrooms. When they eat one while shape-shifting, they can become giant versions of that animal (until they change back). There are lots to take!
SPONGEROOM
This biggie is light and will fit on Glowvin's cart. You can use it to soak up a big pile of liquid, or fill it with fresh water at a river and not go thirsty.

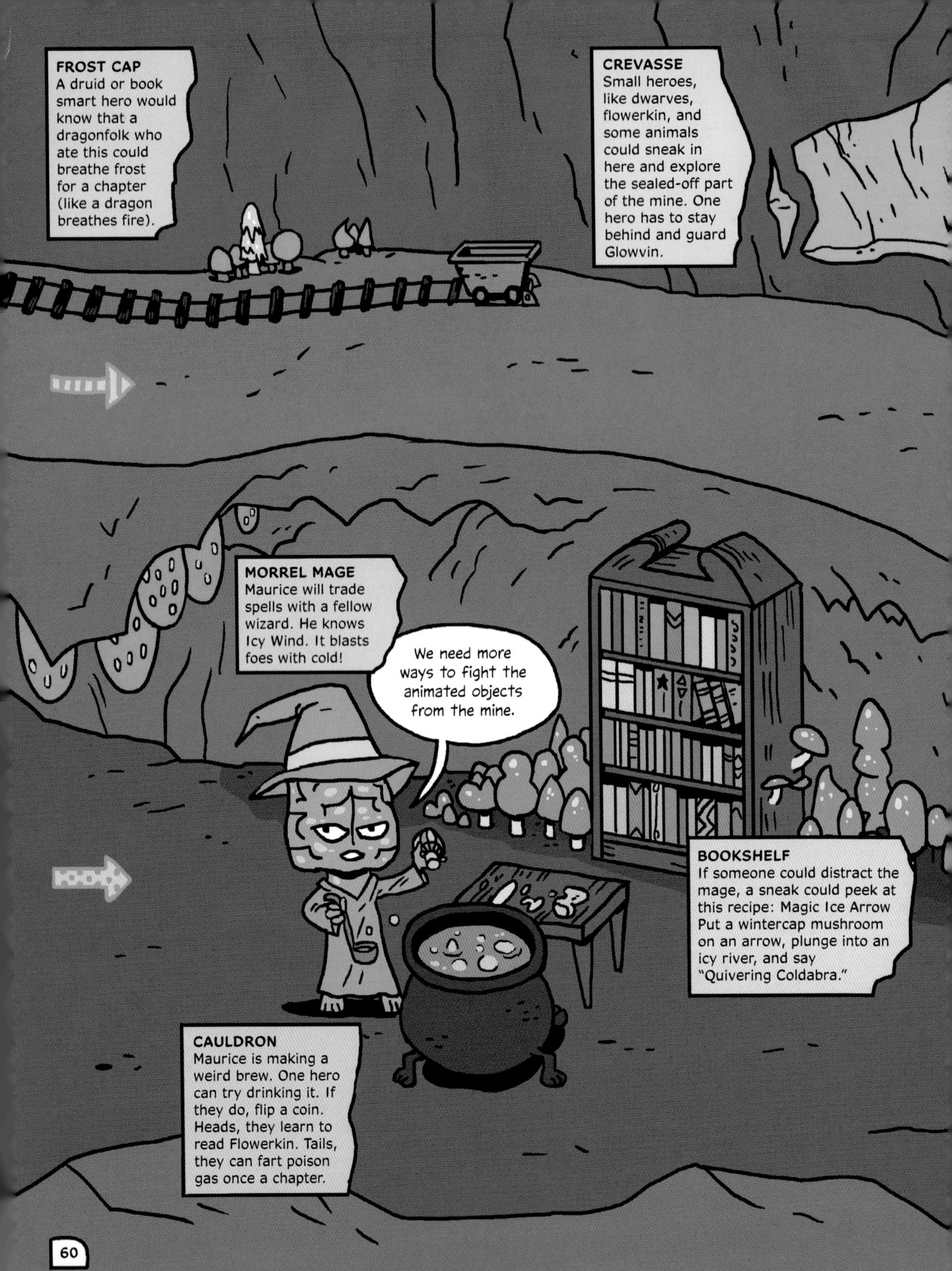
FROST CAP
A druid or book smart hero would know that a dragonfolk who ate this could breathe frost for a chapter (like a dragon breathes fire).
CREVASSE
Small heroes, like dwarves, flowerkin, and some animals could sneak in here and explore the sealed-off part of the mine. One hero has to stay behind and guard Glowvin.
MORREL MAGE
Maurice will trade spells with a fellow wizard. He knows Icy Wind. It blasts foes with cold!
We need more ways to fight the animated objects from the mine.
BOOKSHELF
If someone could distract the mage, a sneak could peek at this recipe: Magic Ice Arrow Put a wintercap mushroom on an arrow, plunge into an icy river, and say "Quivering Coldabra."
CAULDRON
Maurice is making a weird brew. One hero can try drinking it. If they do, flip a coin. Heads, they learn to read Flowerkin. Tails, they can fart poison gas once a chapter.

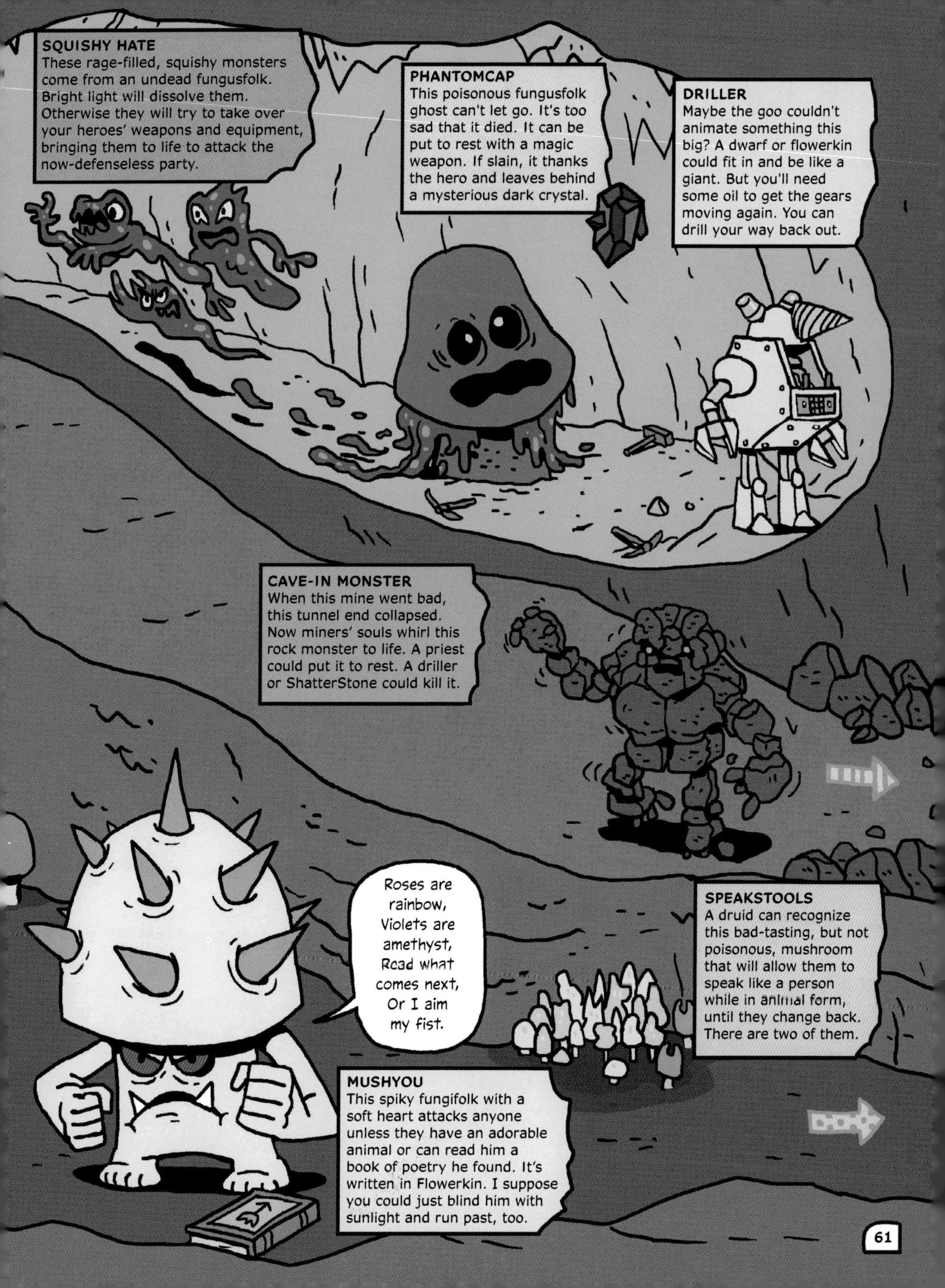
SQUISHY HATE
These rage-filled, squishy monsters come from an undead fungusfolk. Bright light will dissolve them. Otherwise they will try to take over your heroes' weapons and equipment, bringing them to life to attack the now-defenseless party.
PHANTOMCAP
This poisonous fungusfolk ghost can't let go. It's too sad that it died. It can be put to rest with a magic weapon. If slain, it thanks the hero and leaves behind a mysterious dark crystal.
DRILLER
Maybe the goo couldn't animate something this big? A dwarf or flowerkin could fit in and be like a giant. But you'll need some oil to get the gears moving again. You can drill your way back out.
CAVE-IN MONSTER
When this mine went bad, this tunnel end collapsed. Now miners' souls whirl this rock monster to life. A priest could put it to rest. A driller or ShatterStone could kill it.
Roses are rainbow, Violets are amethyst, Read what comes next, Or I aim my fist.
SPEAKSTOOLS
A druid can recognize this bad-tasting, but not poisonous, mushroom that will allow them to speak like a person while in animal form, until they change back. There are two of them.
MUSHYOU
This spiky fungifolk with a soft heart attacks anyone unless they have an adorable animal or can read him a book of poetry he found. It's written in Flowerkin. I suppose you could just blind him with sunlight and run past, too.

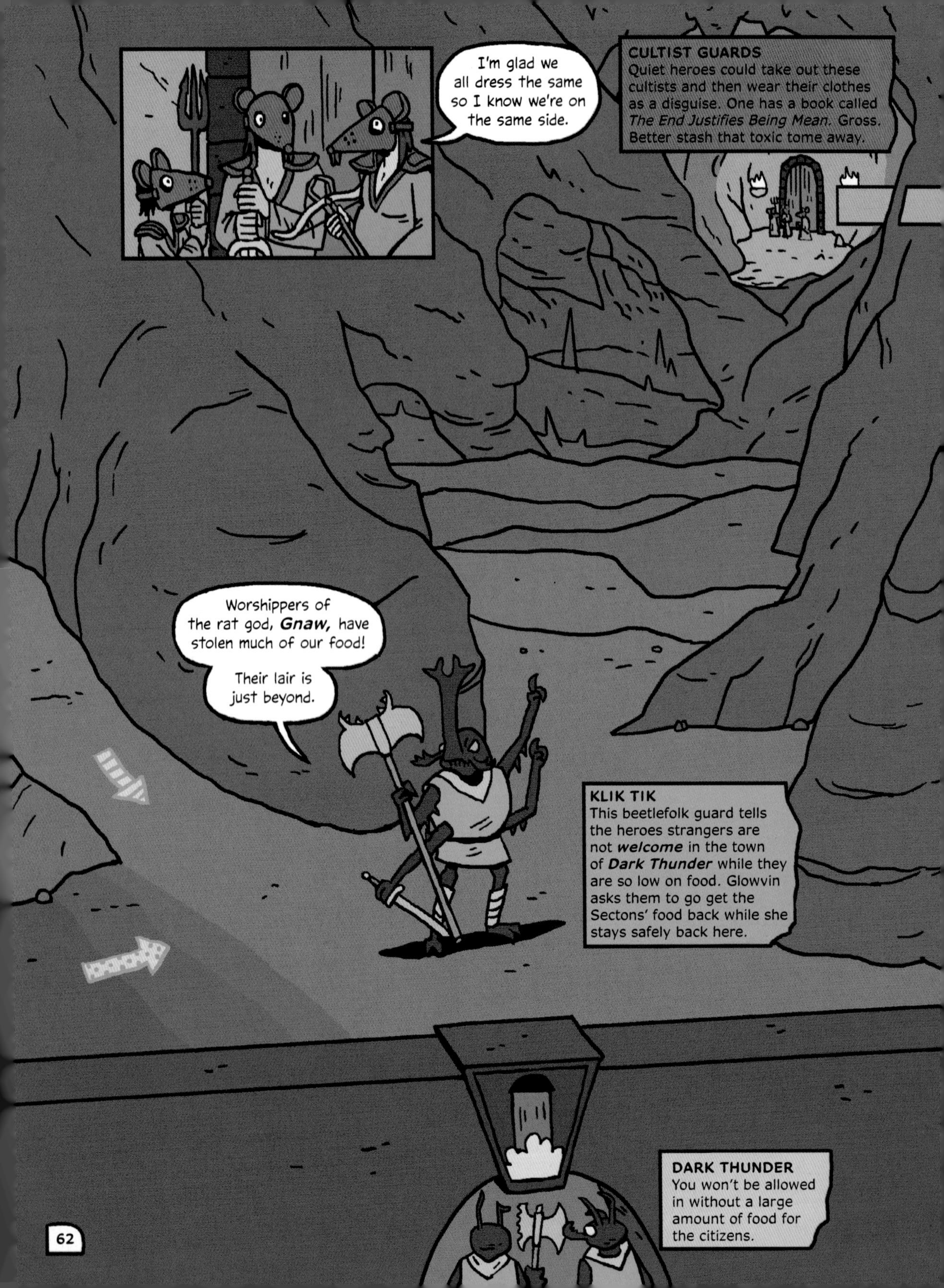

I'm glad we all dress the same so I know we're on the same side.
CULTIST GUARDS
Quiet heroes could take out these cultists and then wear their clothes as a disguise. One has a book called *The End Justifies Being Mean.* Gross. Better stash that toxic tome away.
Worshippers of the rat god, ***Gnaw,*** have stolen much of our food!
Their lair is just beyond.
KLIK TIK
This beetlefolk guard tells the heroes strangers are not ***welcome*** in the town of ***Dark Thunder*** while they are so low on food. Glowvin asks them to go get the Sectons' food back while she stays safely back here.
DARK THUNDER
You won't be allowed in without a large amount of food for the citizens.

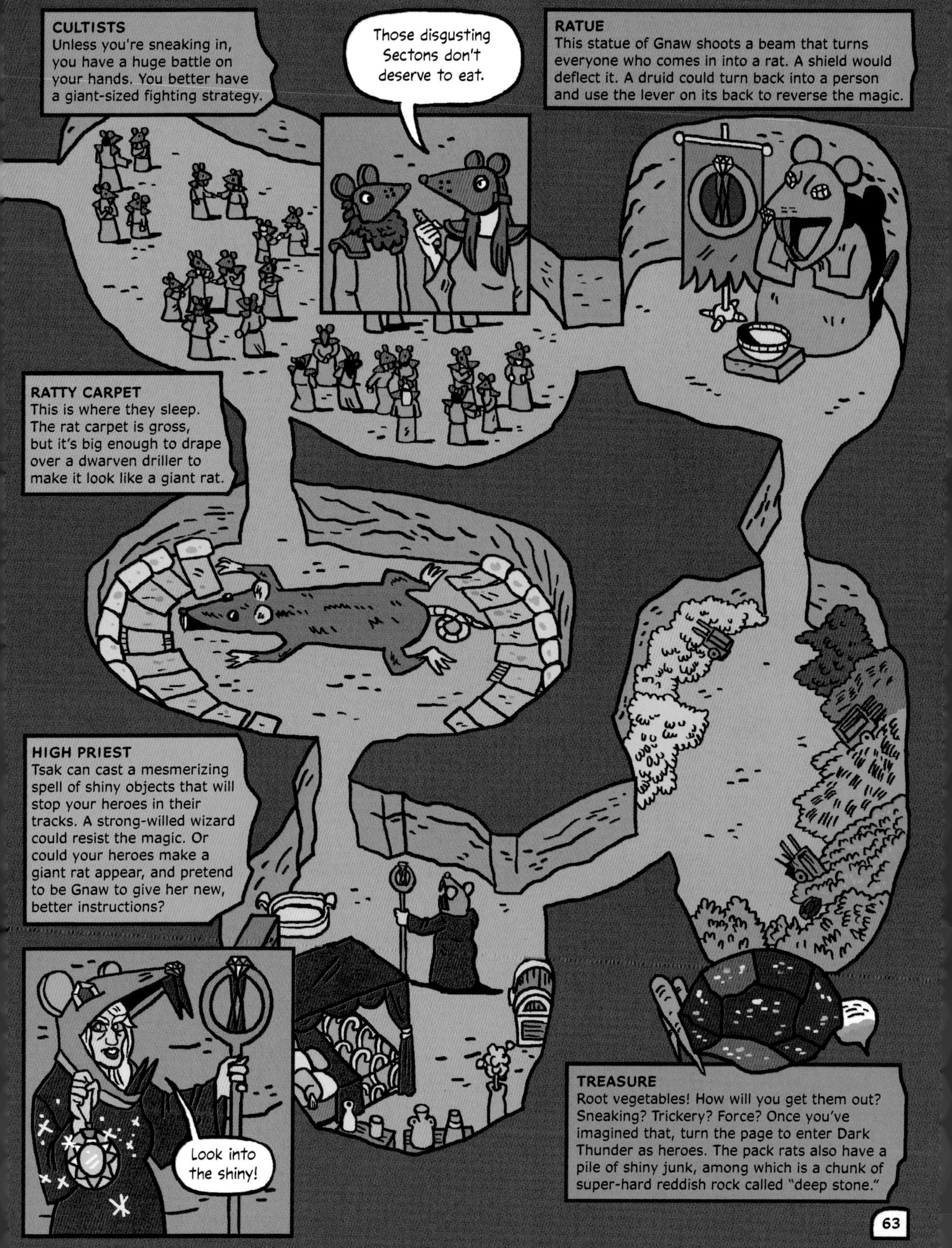
CULTISTS
Unless you're sneaking in, you have a huge battle on your hands. You better have a giant-sized fighting strategy.
Those disgusting Sectons don't deserve to eat.
RATUE
This statue of Gnaw shoots a beam that turns everyone who comes in into a rat. A shield would deflect it. A druid could turn back into a person and use the lever on its back to reverse the magic.
RATTY CARPET
This is where they sleep. The rat carpet is gross, but it's big enough to drape over a dwarven driller to make it look like a giant rat.
HIGH PRIEST
Tsak can cast a mesmerizing spell of shiny objects that will stop your heroes in their tracks. A strong-willed wizard could resist the magic. Or could your heroes make a giant rat appear, and pretend to be Gnaw to give her new, better instructions?
Look into the shiny!
TREASURE
Root vegetables! How will you get them out? Sneaking? Trickery? Force? Once you've imagined that, turn the page to enter Dark Thunder as heroes. The pack rats also have a pile of shiny junk, among which is a chunk of super-hard reddish rock called "deep stone."

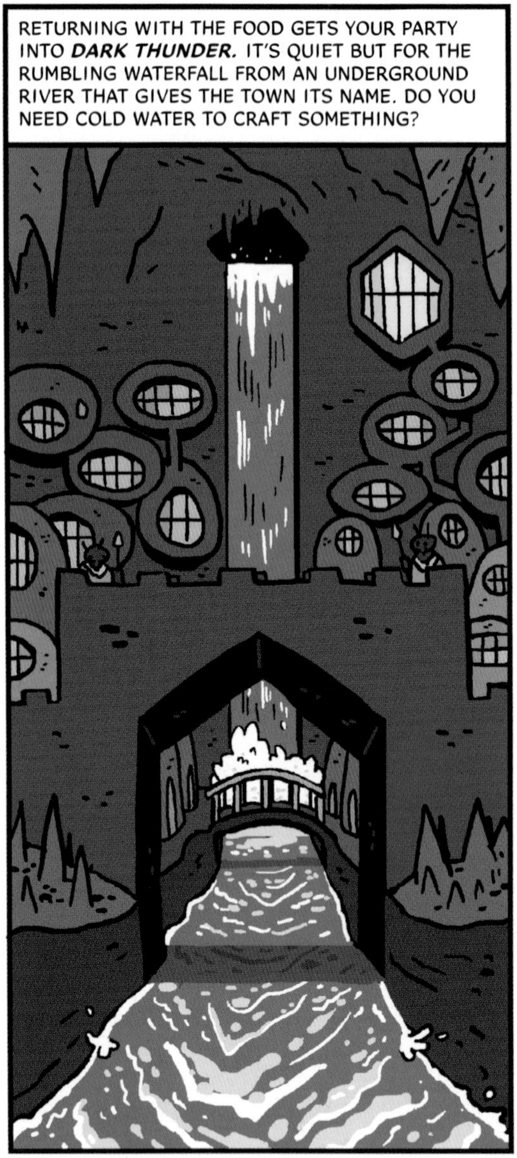
RETURNING WITH THE FOOD GETS YOUR PARTY INTO ***DARK THUNDER.*** IT'S QUIET BUT FOR THE RUMBLING WATERFALL FROM AN UNDERGROUND RIVER THAT GIVES THE TOWN ITS NAME. DO YOU NEED COLD WATER TO CRAFT SOMETHING?

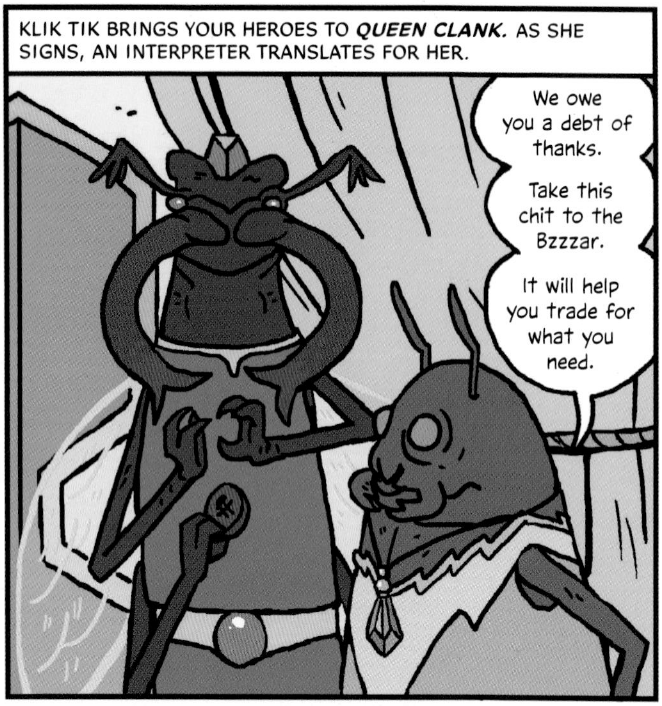
KLIK TIK BRINGS YOUR HEROES TO ***QUEEN CLANK.*** AS SHE SIGNS, AN INTERPRETER TRANSLATES FOR HER.
We owe you a debt of thanks.
Take this chit to the Bzzzar.
It will help you trade for what you need.

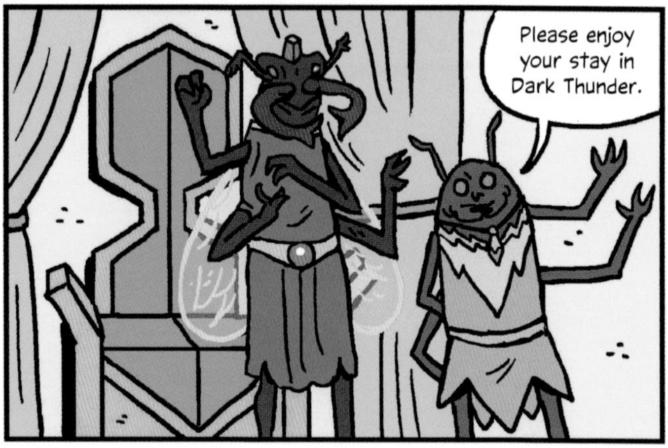
Please enjoy your stay in Dark Thunder.

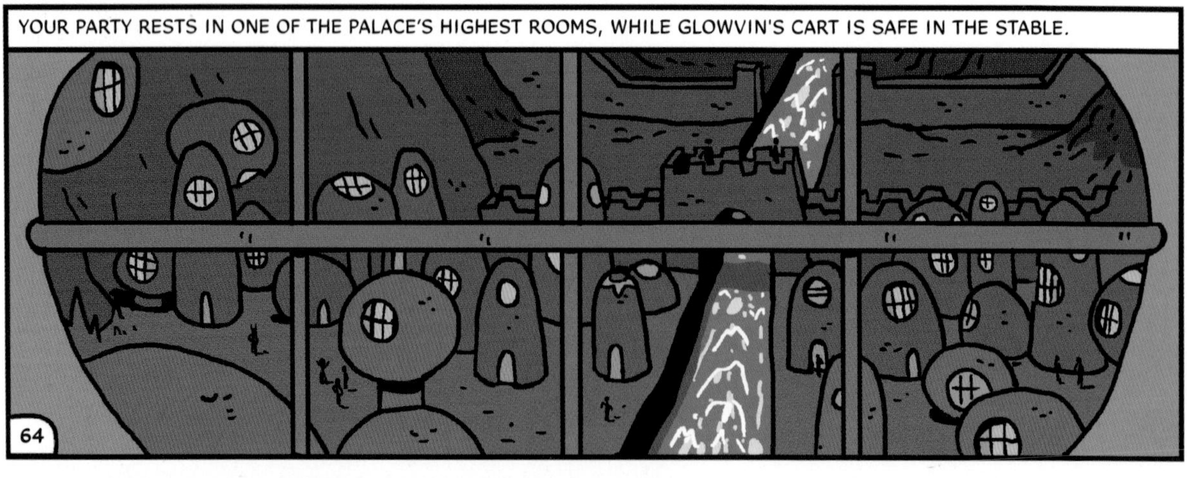
YOUR PARTY RESTS IN ONE OF THE PALACE'S HIGHEST ROOMS, WHILE GLOWVIN'S CART IS SAFE IN THE STABLE.

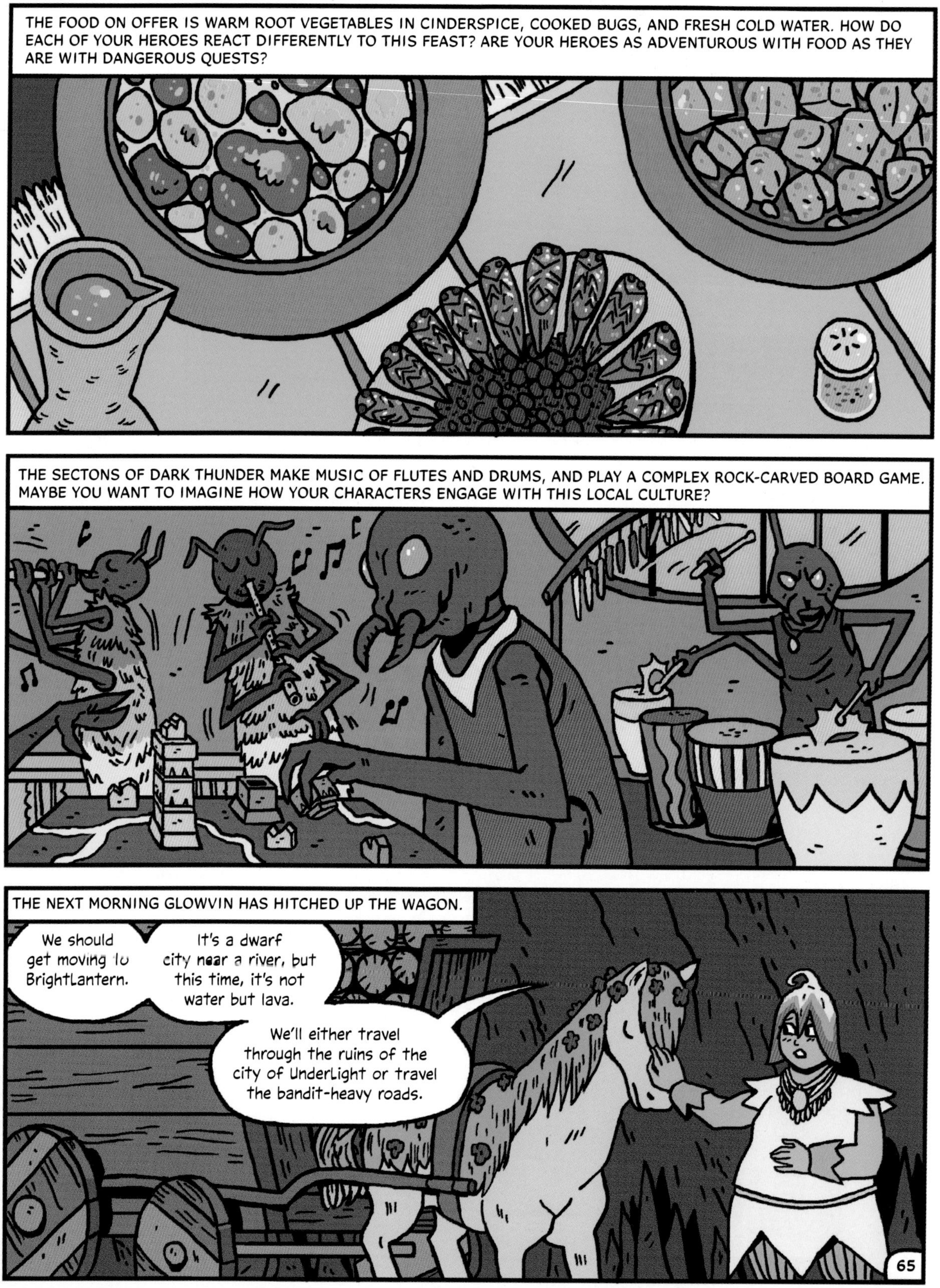
THE FOOD ON OFFER IS WARM ROOT VEGETABLES IN CINDERSPICE, COOKED BUGS, AND FRESH COLD WATER. HOW DO EACH OF YOUR HEROES REACT DIFFERENTLY TO THIS FEAST? ARE YOUR HEROES AS ADVENTUROUS WITH FOOD AS THEY ARE WITH DANGEROUS QUESTS?
THE SECTONS OF DARK THUNDER MAKE MUSIC OF FLUTES AND DRUMS, AND PLAY A COMPLEX ROCK-CARVED BOARD GAME. MAYBE YOU WANT TO IMAGINE HOW YOUR CHARACTERS ENGAGE WITH THIS LOCAL CULTURE?
THE NEXT MORNING GLOWVIN HAS HITCHED UP THE WAGON.
We should get moving to BrightLantern.
It's a dwarf city near a river, but this time, it's not water but lava.
We'll either travel through the ruins of the city of UnderLight or travel the bandit-heavy roads.

CHAPTER THREE

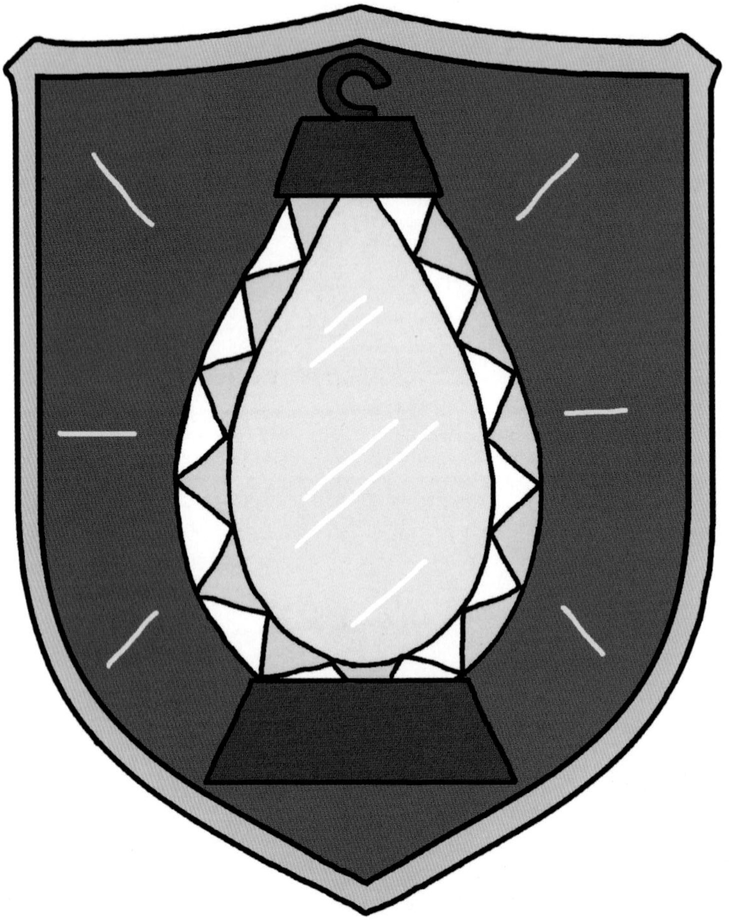

WARM UNWELCOME

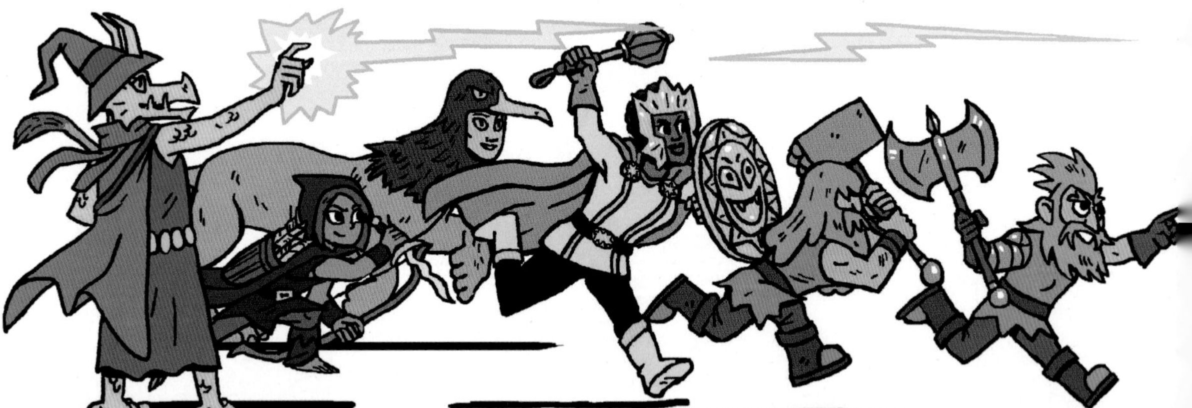

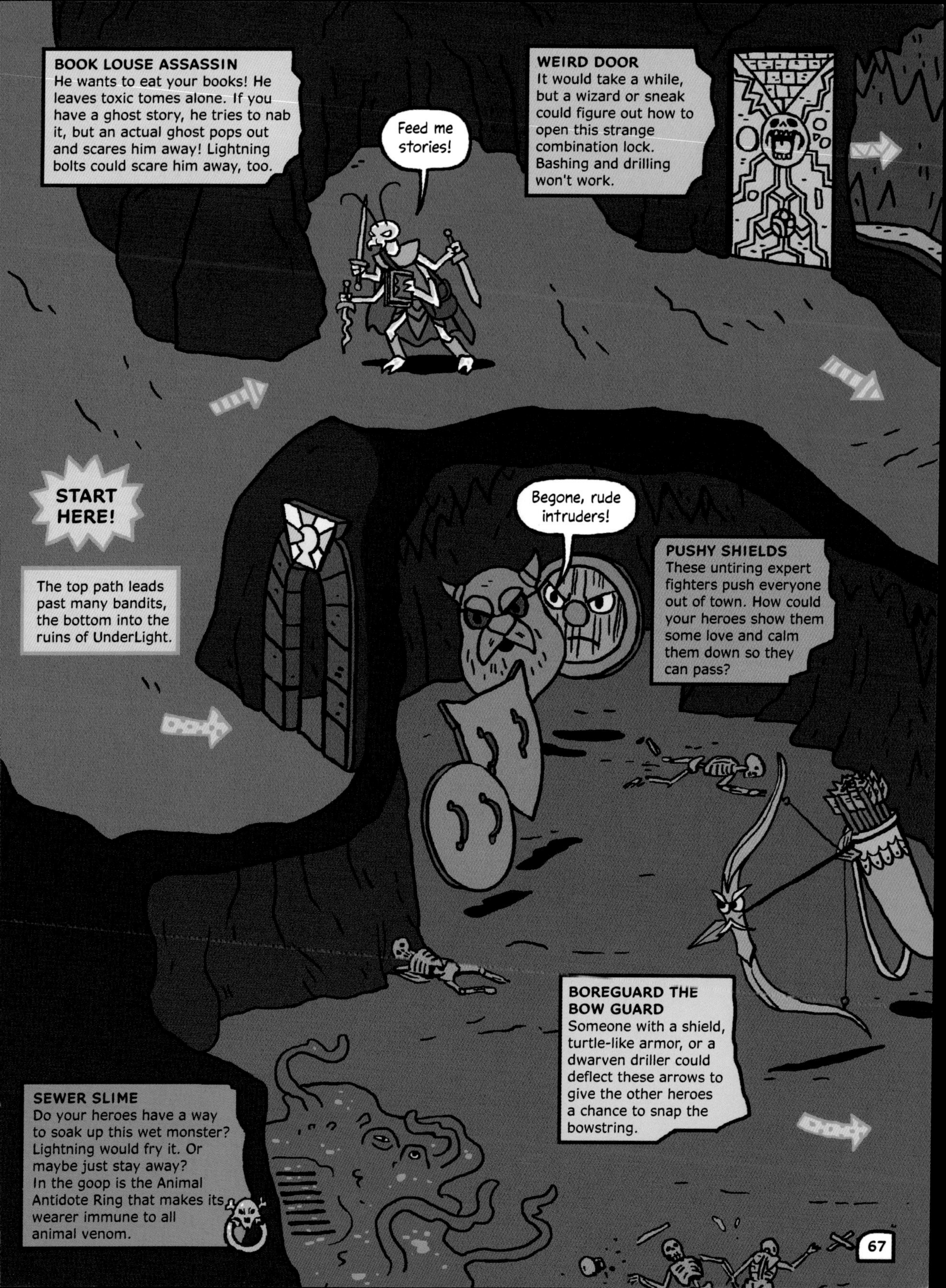
BOOK LOUSE ASSASSIN
He wants to eat your books! He leaves toxic tomes alone. If you have a ghost story, he tries to nab it, but an actual ghost pops out and scares him away! Lightning bolts could scare him away, too.
Feed me stories!
WEIRD DOOR
It would take a while, but a wizard or sneak could figure out how to open this strange combination lock. Bashing and drilling won't work.
START HERE!
The top path leads past many bandits, the bottom into the ruins of UnderLight.
Begone, rude intruders!
PUSHY SHIELDS
These untiring expert fighters push everyone out of town. How could your heroes show them some love and calm them down so they can pass?
BOREGUARD THE BOW GUARD
Someone with a shield, turtle-like armor, or a dwarven driller could deflect these arrows to give the other heroes a chance to snap the bowstring.
SEWER SLIME
Do your heroes have a way to soak up this wet monster? Lightning would fry it. Or maybe just stay away?
In the goop is the Animal Antidote Ring that makes its wearer immune to all animal venom.

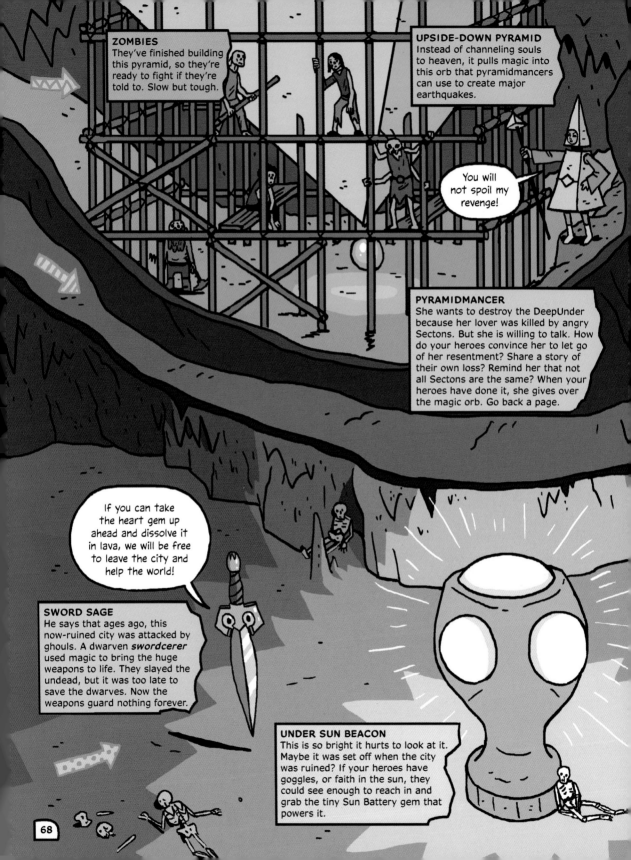

ZOMBIES
They've finished building this pyramid, so they're ready to fight if they're told to. Slow but tough.

UPSIDE-DOWN PYRAMID
Instead of channeling souls to heaven, it pulls magic into this orb that pyramidmancers can use to create major earthquakes.

You will not spoil my revenge!

PYRAMIDMANCER
She wants to destroy the DeepUnder because her lover was killed by angry Sectons. But she is willing to talk. How do your heroes convince her to let go of her resentment? Share a story of their own loss? Remind her that not all Sectons are the same? When your heroes have done it, she gives over the magic orb. Go back a page.

If you can take the heart gem up ahead and dissolve it in lava, we will be free to leave the city and help the world!

SWORD SAGE
He says that ages ago, this now-ruined city was attacked by ghouls. A dwarven *swordcerer* used magic to bring the huge weapons to life. They slayed the undead, but it was too late to save the dwarves. Now the weapons guard nothing forever.

UNDER SUN BEACON
This is so bright it hurts to look at it. Maybe it was set off when the city was ruined? If your heroes have goggles, or faith in the sun, they could see enough to reach in and grab the tiny Sun Battery gem that powers it.

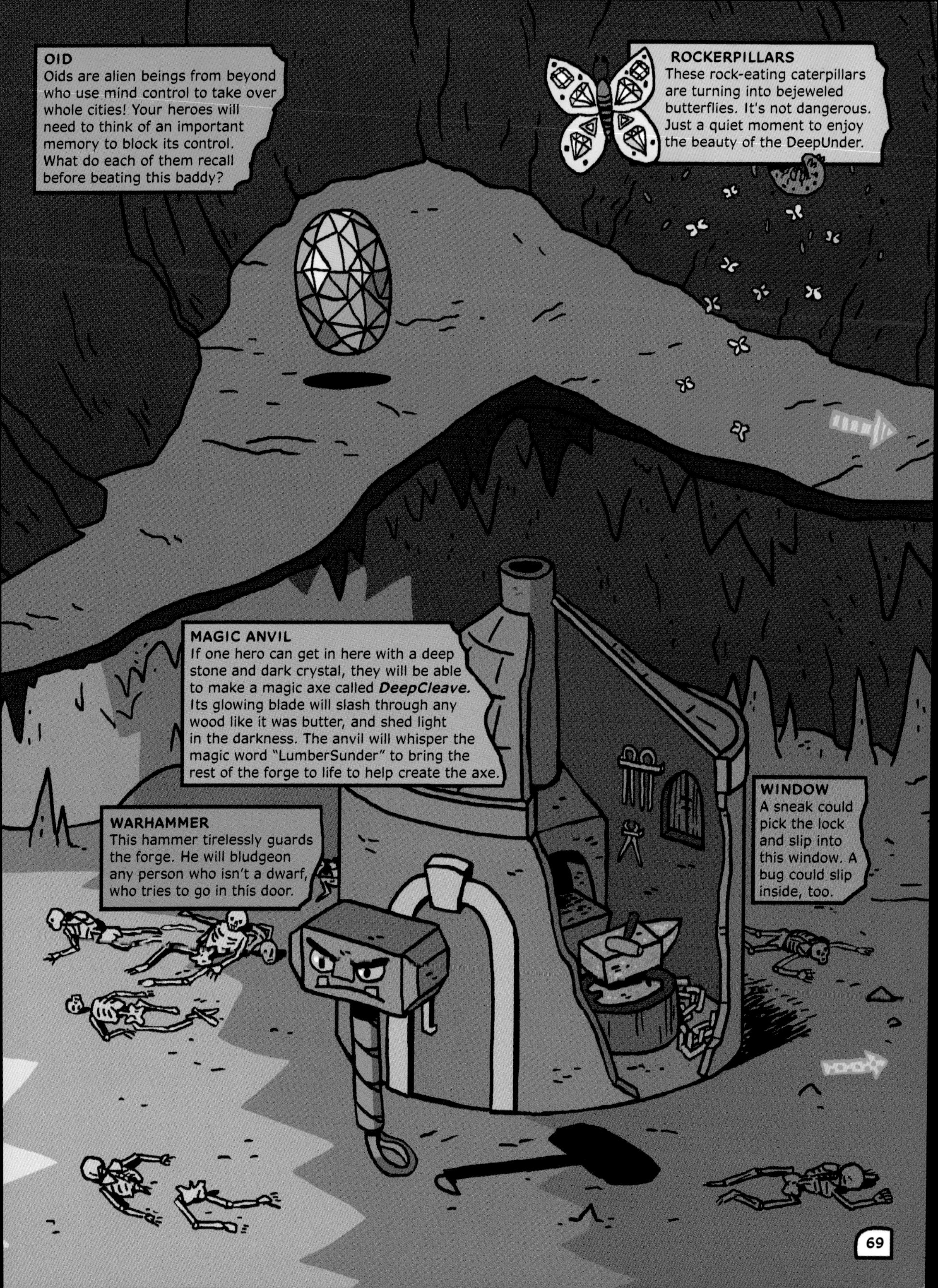
OID
Oids are alien beings from beyond who use mind control to take over whole cities! Your heroes will need to think of an important memory to block its control. What do each of them recall before beating this baddy?
ROCKERPILLARS
These rock-eating caterpillars are turning into bejeweled butterflies. It's not dangerous. Just a quiet moment to enjoy the beauty of the DeepUnder.
MAGIC ANVIL
If one hero can get in here with a deep stone and dark crystal, they will be able to make a magic axe called *DeepCleave.* Its glowing blade will slash through any wood like it was butter, and shed light in the darkness. The anvil will whisper the magic word "LumberSunder" to bring the rest of the forge to life to help create the axe.
WARHAMMER
This hammer tirelessly guards the forge. He will bludgeon any person who isn't a dwarf, who tries to go in this door.
WINDOW
A sneak could pick the lock and slip into this window. A bug could slip inside, too.

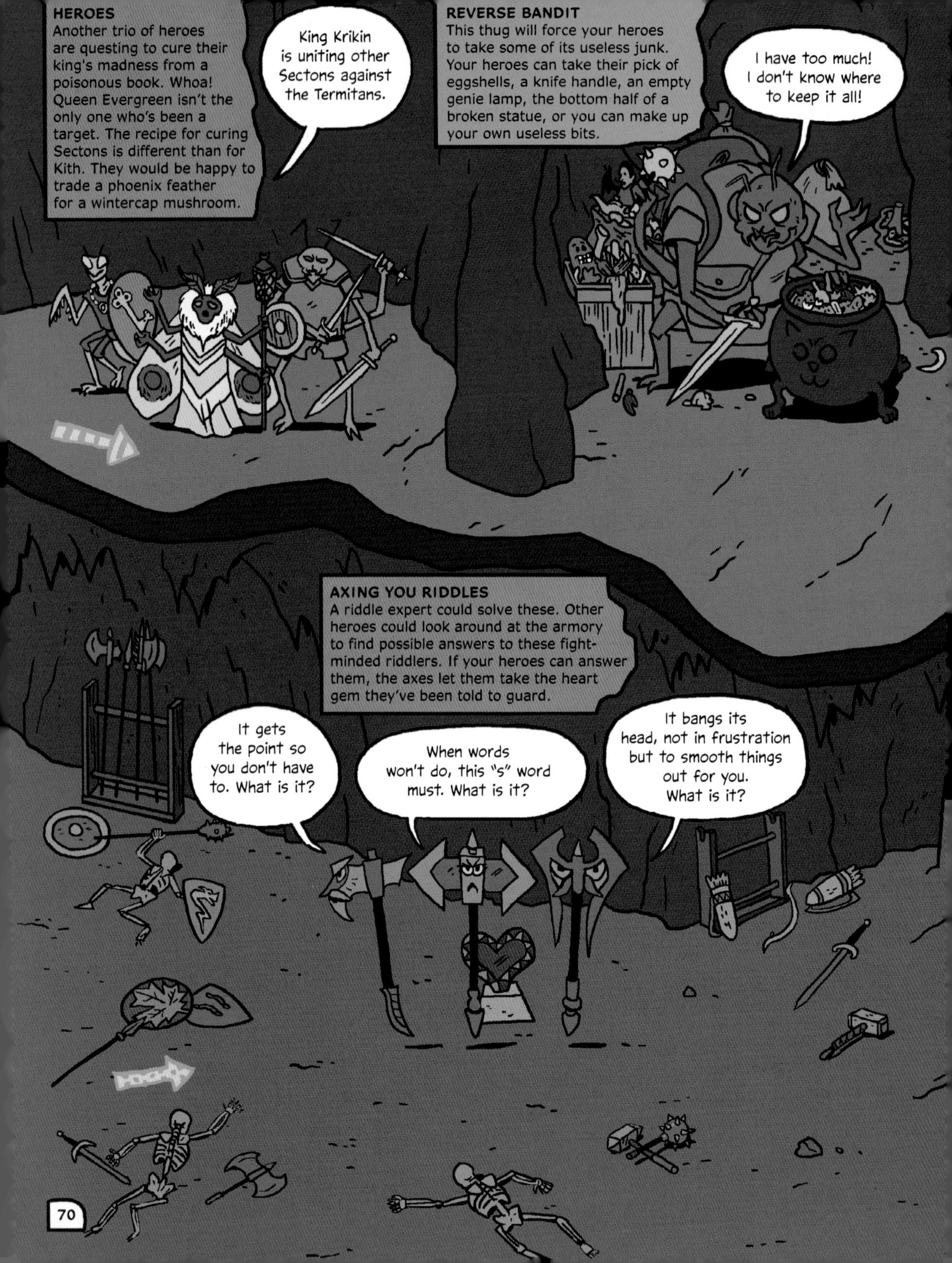
HEROES
Another trio of heroes are questing to cure their king's madness from a poisonous book. Whoa! Queen Evergreen isn't the only one who's been a target. The recipe for curing Sectons is different than for Kith. They would be happy to trade a phoenix feather for a wintercap mushroom.
King Krikin is uniting other Sectons against the Termitans.
REVERSE BANDIT
This thug will force your heroes to take some of its useless junk. Your heroes can take their pick of eggshells, a knife handle, an empty genie lamp, the bottom half of a broken statue, or you can make up your own useless bits.
I have too much! I don't know where to keep it all!
AXING YOU RIDDLES
A riddle expert could solve these. Other heroes could look around at the armory to find possible answers to these fight-minded riddlers. If your heroes can answer them, the axes let them take the heart gem they've been told to guard.
It gets the point so you don't have to. What is it?
When words won't do, this "s" word must. What is it?
It bangs its head, not in frustration but to smooth things out for you. What is it?

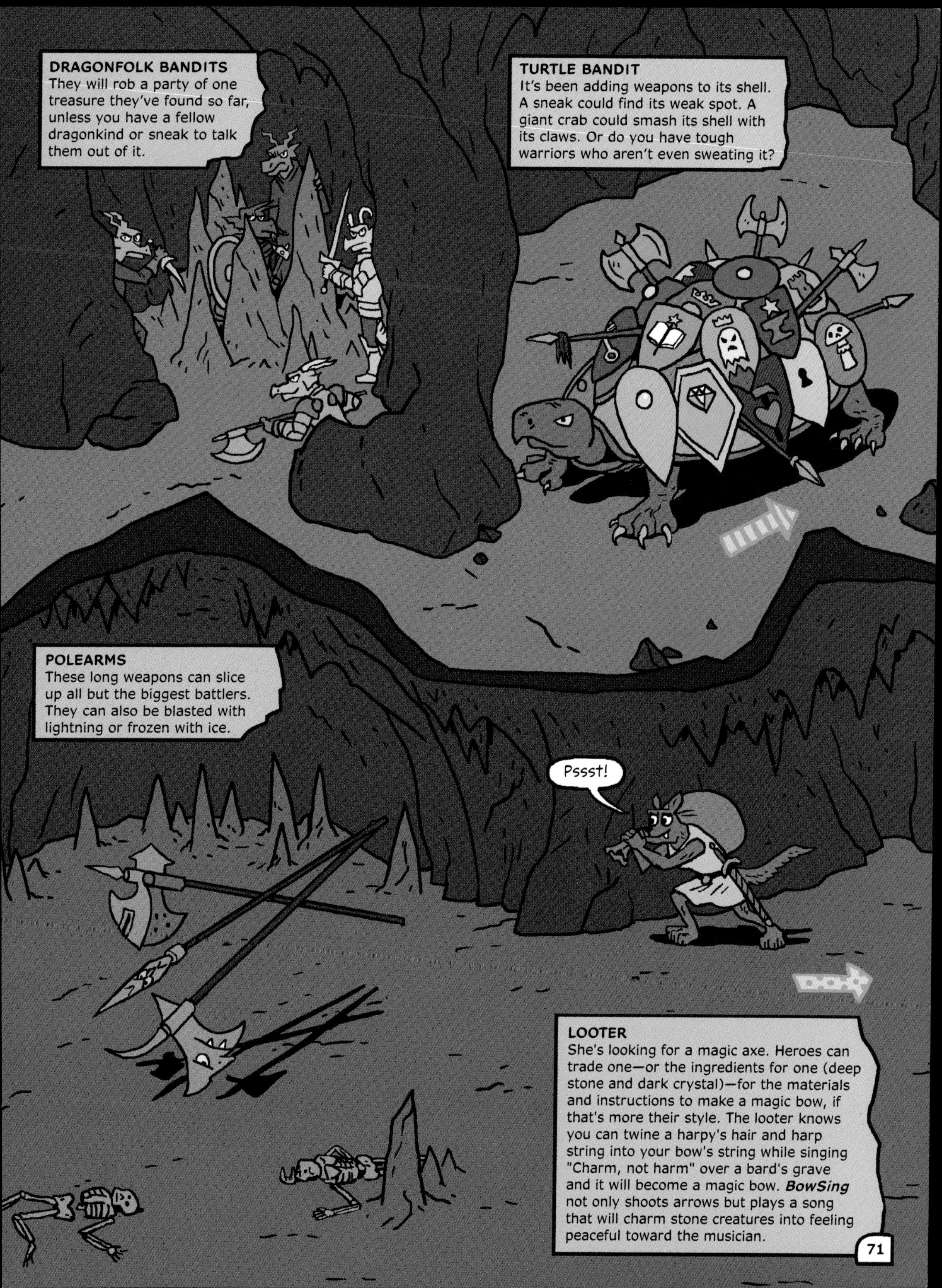
DRAGONFOLK BANDITS
They will rob a party of one treasure they've found so far, unless you have a fellow dragonkind or sneak to talk them out of it.
TURTLE BANDIT
It's been adding weapons to its shell. A sneak could find its weak spot. A giant crab could smash its shell with its claws. Or do you have tough warriors who aren't even sweating it?
POLEARMS
These long weapons can slice up all but the biggest battlers. They can also be blasted with lightning or frozen with ice.
Pssst!
LOOTER
She's looking for a magic axe. Heroes can trade one—or the ingredients for one (deep stone and dark crystal)—for the materials and instructions to make a magic bow, if that's more their style. The looter knows you can twine a harpy's hair and harp string into your bow's string while singing "Charm, not harm" over a bard's grave and it will become a magic bow. *BowSing* not only shoots arrows but plays a song that will charm stone creatures into feeling peaceful toward the musician.

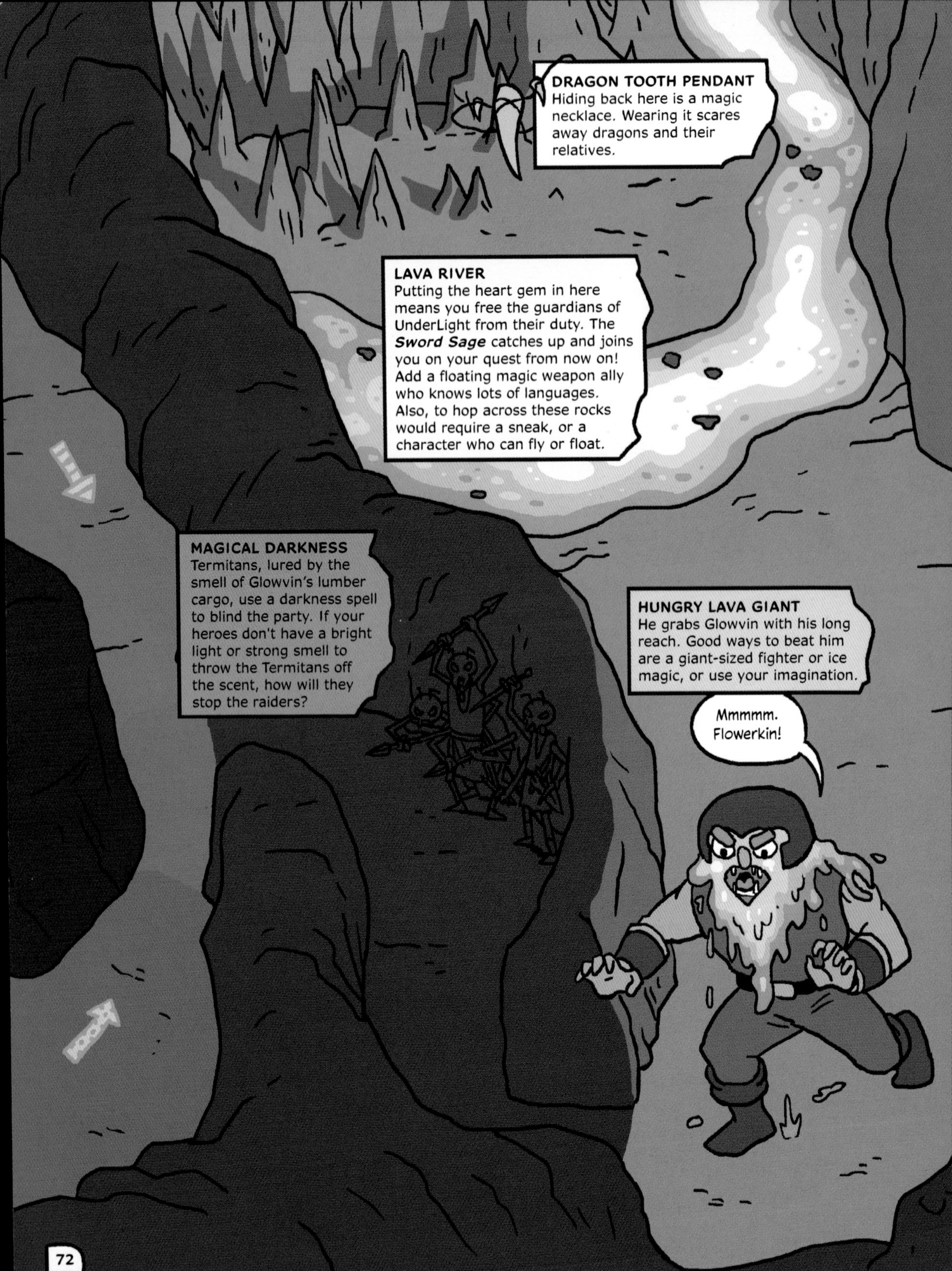
DRAGON TOOTH PENDANT
Hiding back here is a magic necklace. Wearing it scares away dragons and their relatives.
LAVA RIVER
Putting the heart gem in here means you free the guardians of UnderLight from their duty. The *Sword Sage* catches up and joins you on your quest from now on! Add a floating magic weapon ally who knows lots of languages. Also, to hop across these rocks would require a sneak, or a character who can fly or float.
MAGICAL DARKNESS
Termitans, lured by the smell of Glowvin's lumber cargo, use a darkness spell to blind the party. If your heroes don't have a bright light or strong smell to throw the Termitans off the scent, how will they stop the raiders?
HUNGRY LAVA GIANT
He grabs Glowvin with his long reach. Good ways to beat him are a giant-sized fighter or ice magic, or use your imagination.
Mmmmm. Flowerkin!

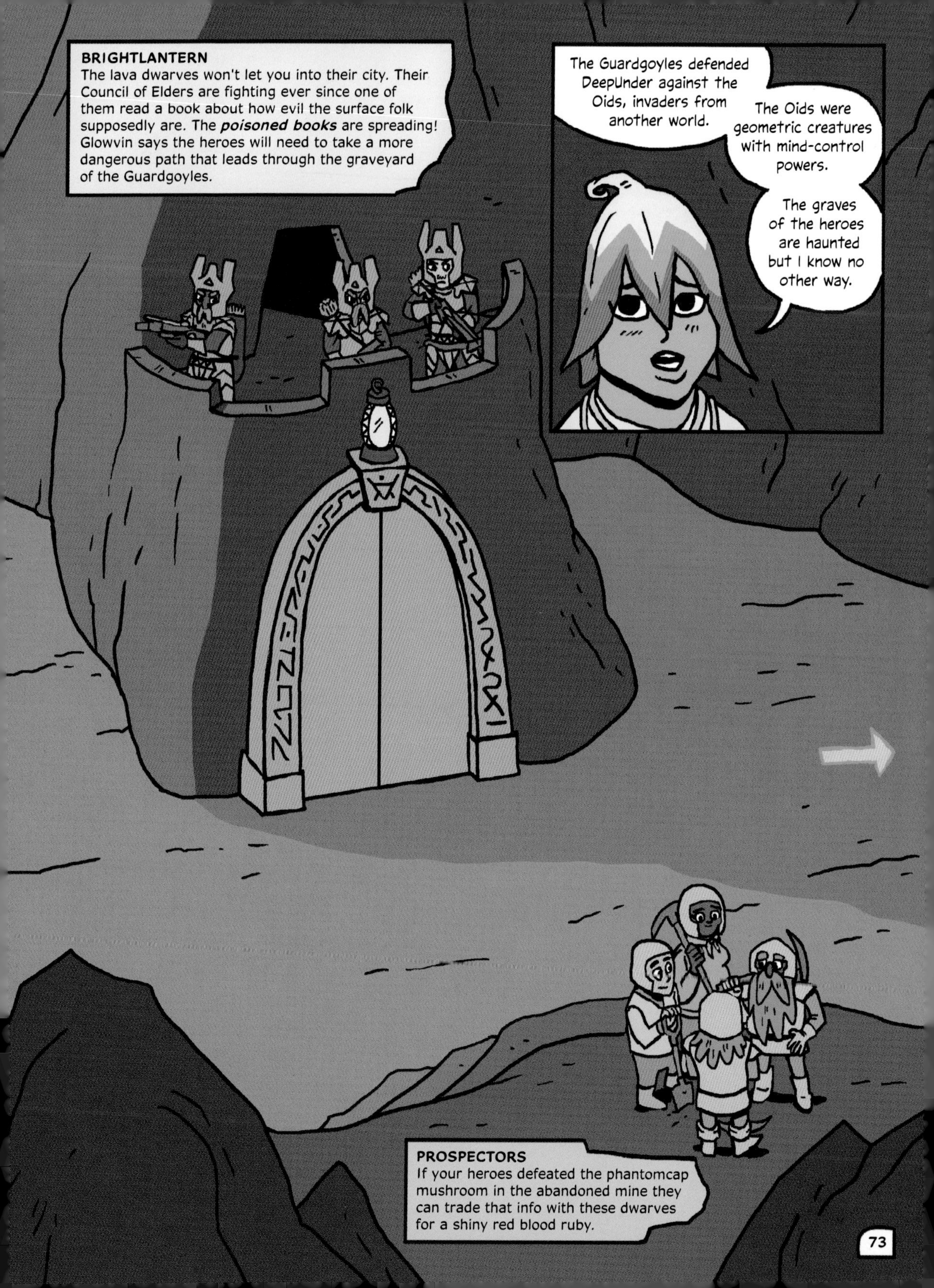
BRIGHTLANTERN
The lava dwarves won't let you into their city. Their Council of Elders are fighting ever since one of them read a book about how evil the surface folk supposedly are. The poisoned books are spreading! Glowvin says the heroes will need to take a more dangerous path that leads through the graveyard of the Guardgoyles.
The Guardgoyles defended DeepUnder against the Oids, invaders from another world.
The Oids were geometric creatures with mind-control powers.
The graves of the heroes are haunted but I know no other way.
PROSPECTORS
If your heroes defeated the phantomcap mushroom in the abandoned mine they can trade that info with these dwarves for a shiny red blood ruby.

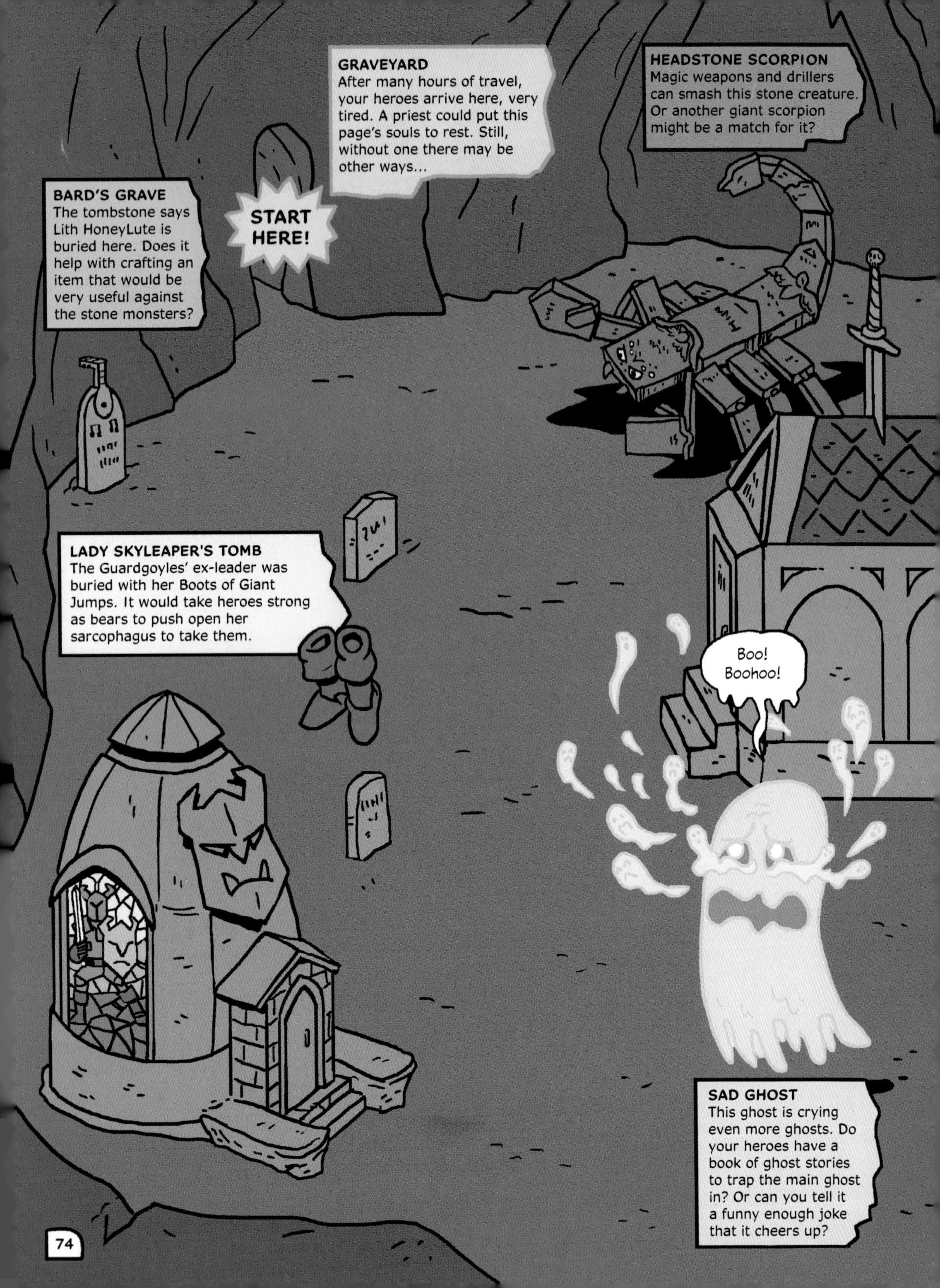
GRAVEYARD
After many hours of travel, your heroes arrive here, very tired. A priest could put this page's souls to rest. Still, without one there may be other ways...
START HERE!
BARD'S GRAVE
The tombstone says Lith HoneyLute is buried here. Does it help with crafting an item that would be very useful against the stone monsters?
HEADSTONE SCORPION
Magic weapons and drillers can smash this stone creature. Or another giant scorpion might be a match for it?
LADY SKYLEAPER'S TOMB
The Guardgoyles' ex-leader was buried with her Boots of Giant Jumps. It would take heroes strong as bears to push open her sarcophagus to take them.
Boo! Boohoo!
SAD GHOST
This ghost is crying even more ghosts. Do your heroes have a book of ghost stories to trap the main ghost in? Or can you tell it a funny enough joke that it cheers up?

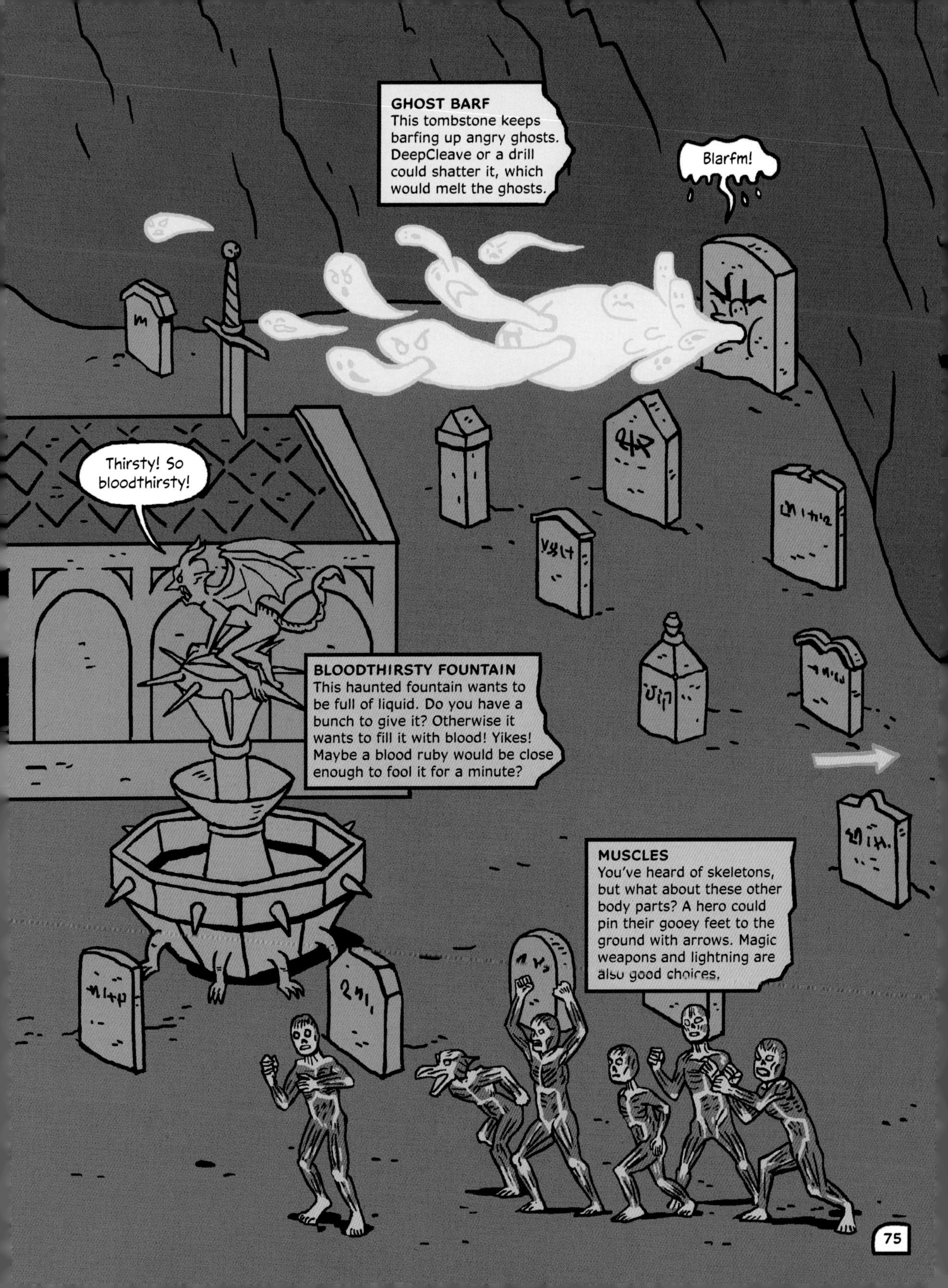
GHOST BARF
This tombstone keeps barfing up angry ghosts. DeepCleave or a drill could shatter it, which would melt the ghosts.
Blarfm!
Thirsty! So bloodthirsty!
BLOODTHIRSTY FOUNTAIN
This haunted fountain wants to be full of liquid. Do you have a bunch to give it? Otherwise it wants to fill it with blood! Yikes! Maybe a blood ruby would be close enough to fool it for a minute?
MUSCLES
You've heard of skeletons, but what about these other body parts? A hero could pin their gooey feet to the ground with arrows. Magic weapons and lightning are also good choices.

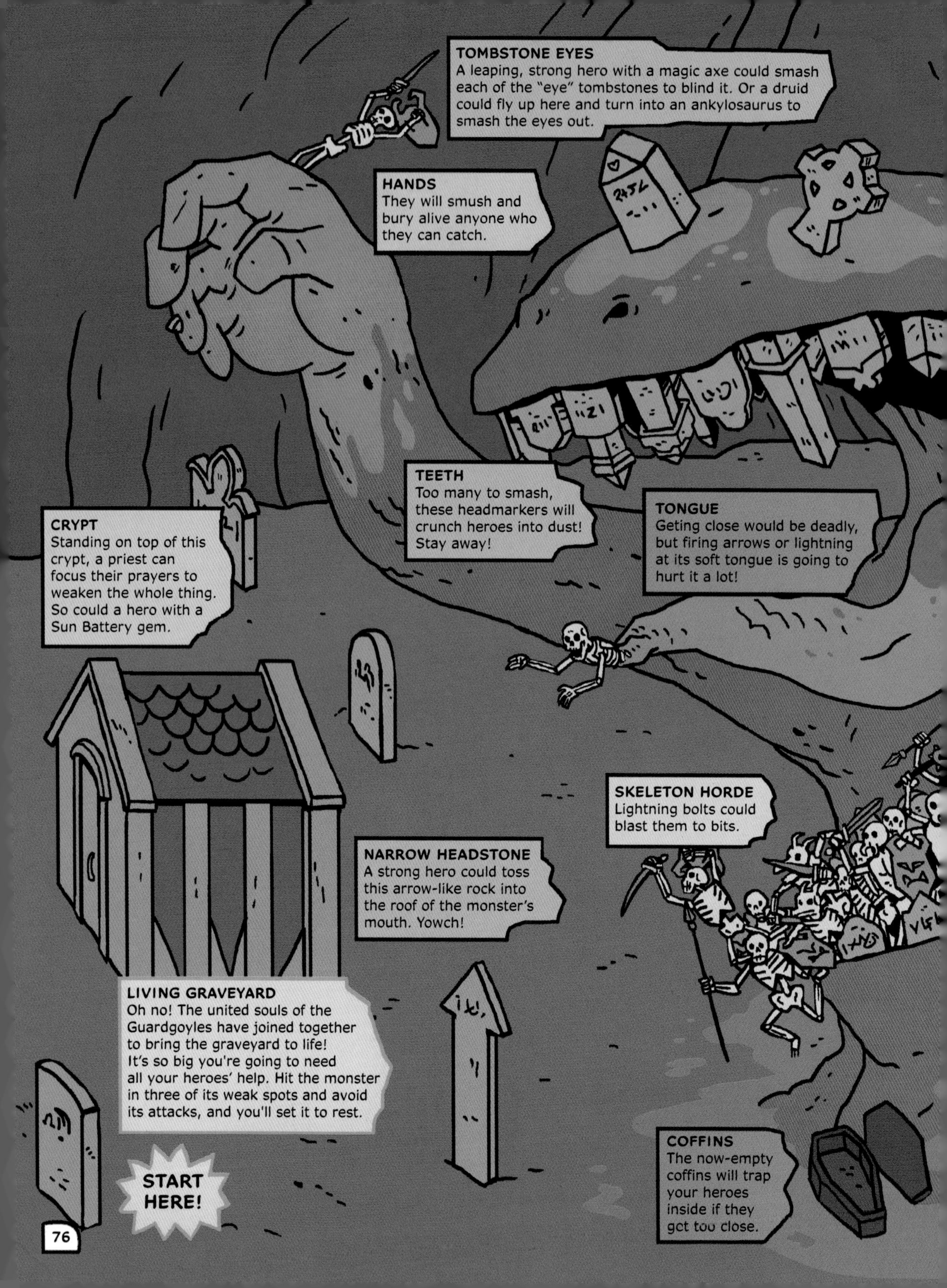
TOMBSTONE EYES
A leaping, strong hero with a magic axe could smash each of the "eye" tombstones to blind it. Or a druid could fly up here and turn into an ankylosaurus to smash the eyes out.
HANDS
They will smush and bury alive anyone who they can catch.
TEETH
Too many to smash, these headmarkers will crunch heroes into dust! Stay away!
CRYPT
Standing on top of this crypt, a priest can focus their prayers to weaken the whole thing. So could a hero with a Sun Battery gem.
TONGUE
Geting close would be deadly, but firing arrows or lightning at its soft tongue is going to hurt it a lot!
SKELETON HORDE
Lightning bolts could blast them to bits.
NARROW HEADSTONE
A strong hero could toss this arrow-like rock into the roof of the monster's mouth. Yowch!
LIVING GRAVEYARD
Oh no! The united souls of the Guardgoyles have joined together to bring the graveyard to life! It's so big you're going to need all your heroes' help. Hit the monster in three of its weak spots and avoid its attacks, and you'll set it to rest.
COFFINS
The now-empty coffins will trap your heroes inside if they get too close.
START HERE!

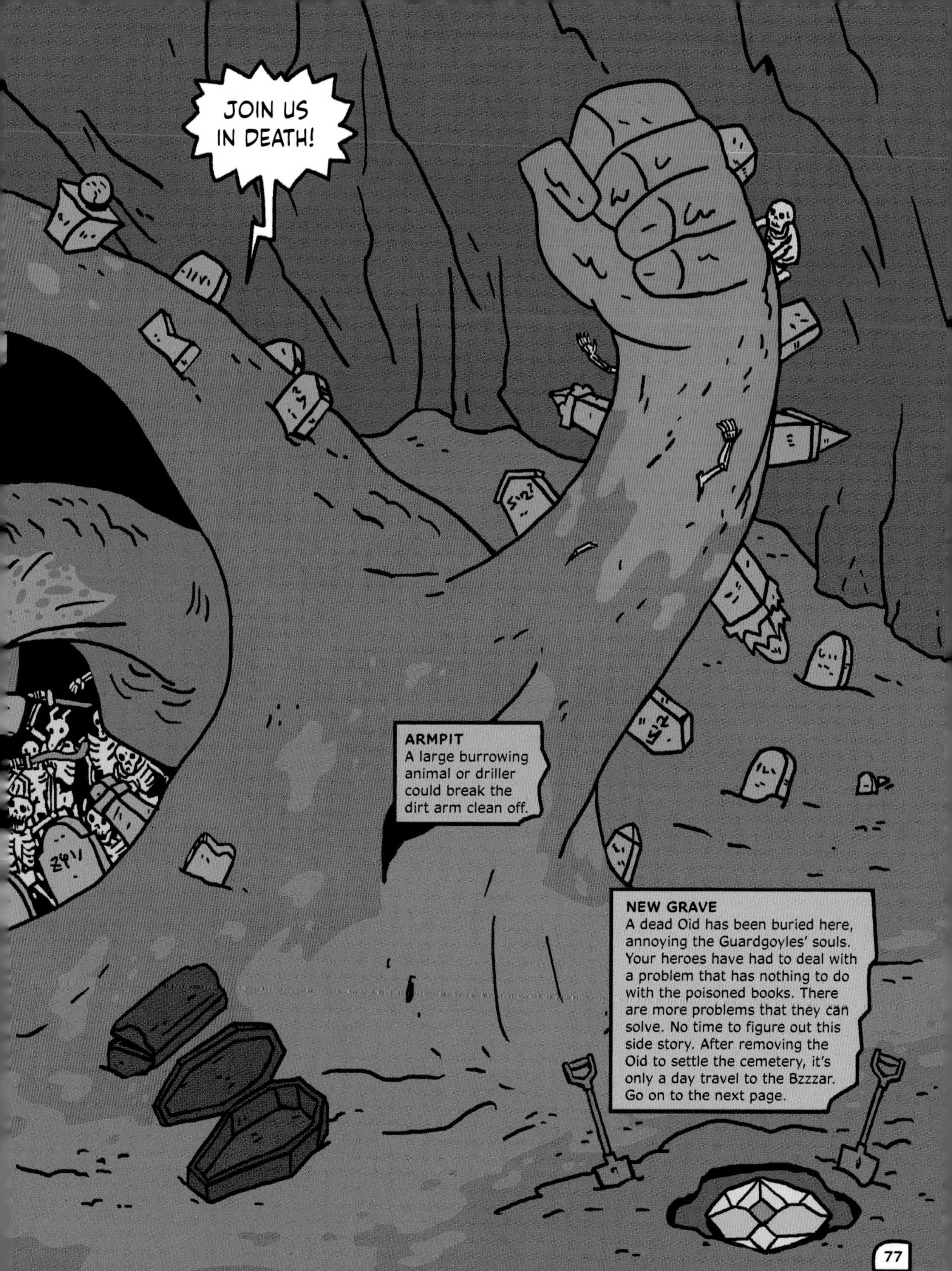
JOIN US IN DEATH!
ARMPIT
A large burrowing animal or driller could break the dirt arm clean off.
NEW GRAVE
A dead Oid has been buried here, annoying the Guardgoyles' souls. Your heroes have had to deal with a problem that has nothing to do with the poisoned books. There are more problems that they can solve. No time to figure out this side story. After removing the Oid to settle the cemetery, it's only a day travel to the Bzzzar. Go on to the next page.

AFTER A LONG, STRANGE JOURNEY, YOUR HEROES HAVE ESCORTED GLOWVIN TO THE ***BZZZAR.*** THE SECTONS, DWARVES, AND OTHER DEEPUNDER FOLK SWARM HER CART WITH OFFERS FOR HER TIMBER.

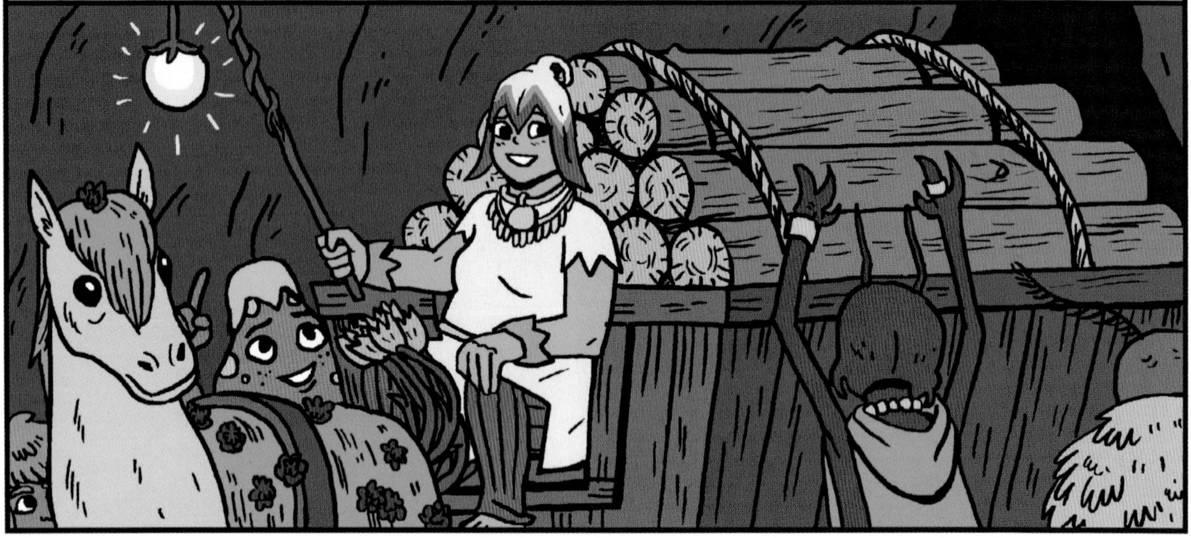

GLOWVIN THANKS YOUR HEROES AND GIVES THEM THEIR REWARD OF HYDRA GRAPES, WHICH SLOWLY REGROW AFTER A FRUIT IS PLUCKED FROM ITS STEM. YOUR HEROES RUSH OFF TO BUY AND SELL! THEY ENCOUNTER A STORM TO THE SENSES OF UNUSUAL THINGS TO SEE, SMELL, HEAR, TOUCH, AND TASTE. HOW DO YOUR HEROES REACT TO THE CROWDS?

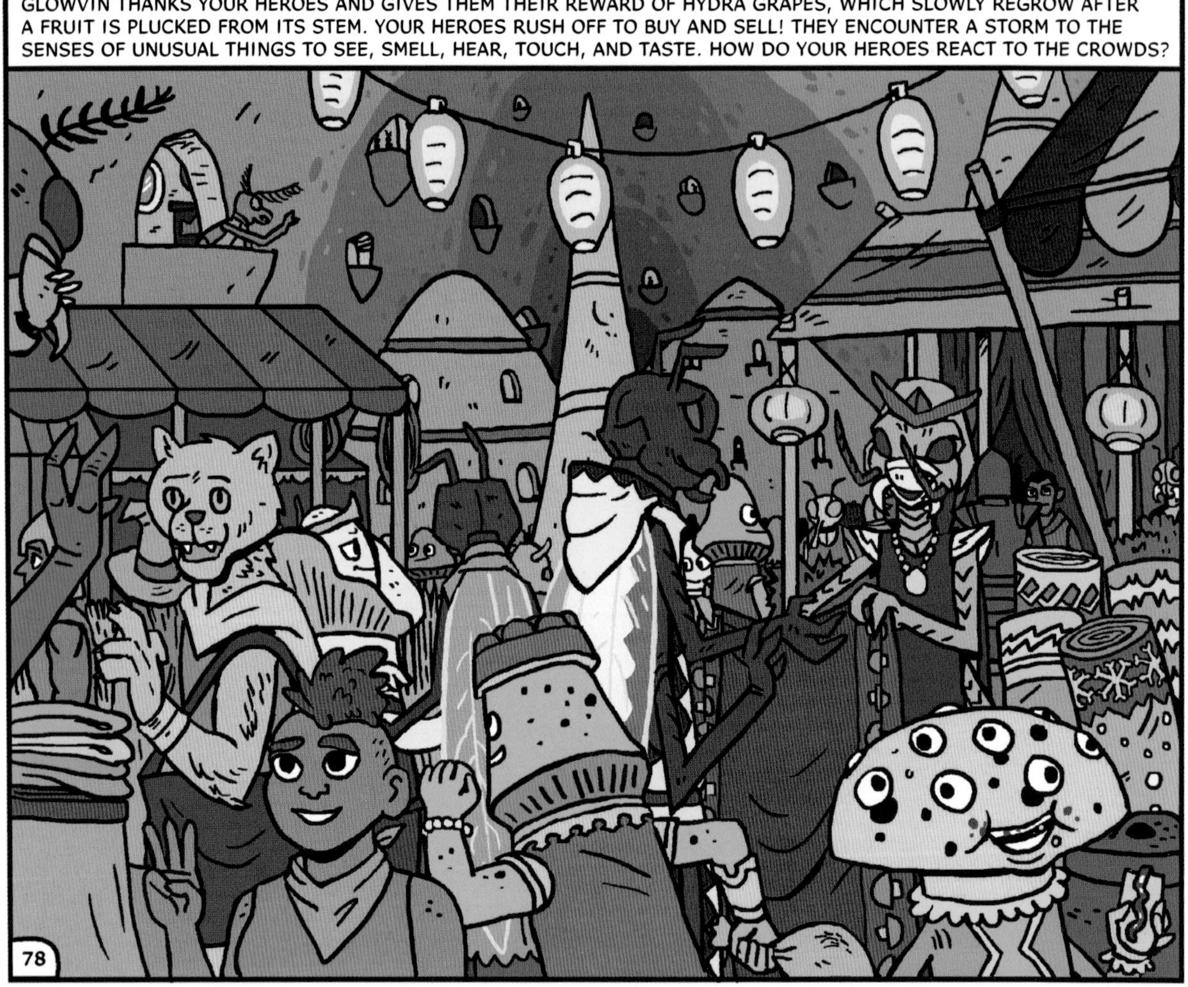

SOON ENOUGH, YOUR HEROES FIND A ***DRAGON LIME, A SKRIM,*** A ***GHOST CLOUD,*** AND A ***BLANK LOTUS.*** TO GET THEM, THEY HAVE TO TRADE IN ***100 GOLD*** WORTH OF TREASURES. IF THEY HAVE MORE THAN THEY NEED, THEY CAN CAN BUY SOME THINGS THAT MIGHT CATCH THEIR ADVENTURING EYES. WHO DOES THE TALKING AND BARGAINING? DOES THE PARTY ARGUE ABOUT WHAT TO BUY AND SELL?

ITEMS TO SELL
10 gold
Bagpipes
Stolen Book of Flowerkin Poetry
Winter Cap Mushroom

20 gold
Hydra Grapes
Sparkling Lantern

30 gold
Bagpipes Full of Poison
Book of Ghost Stories
Dark Crystal
Deep Stone
Ice Arrow
Sun Battery Gem

40 gold
Boots of Giant Jumps
Chit from Dark Thunder
Phoenix Feather
Shiny Blood Ruby

60 gold
Animal Antidote Ring
BowSing
DeepCleave
Dragon Tooth Pendant
Dwarven Driller

100 gold
Magical Orb

ITEMS TO BUY
20 gold
Rust Potion

50 gold
Fireball Spell
Elemental Bottle

80 gold
SapSucker

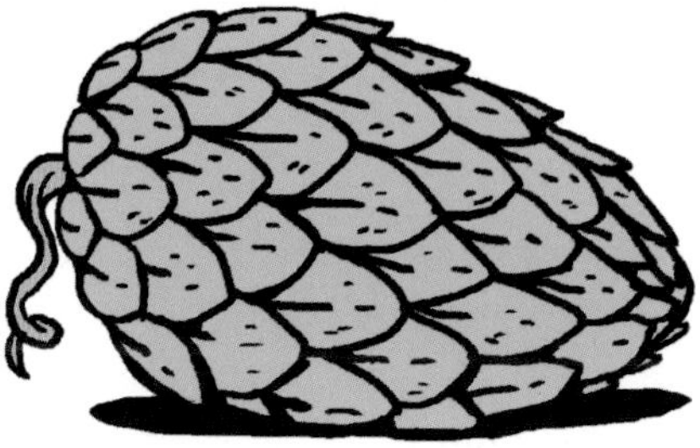

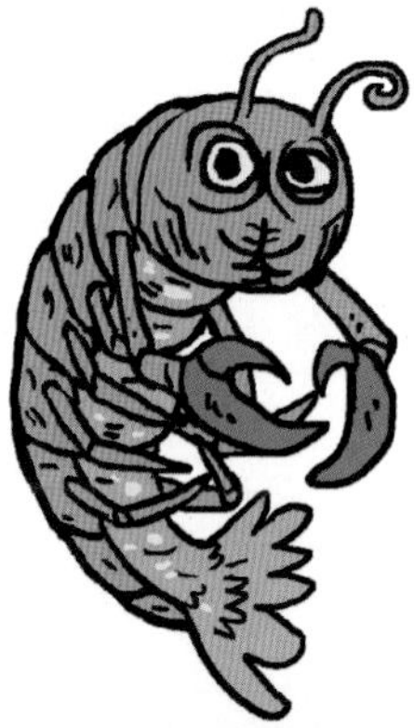

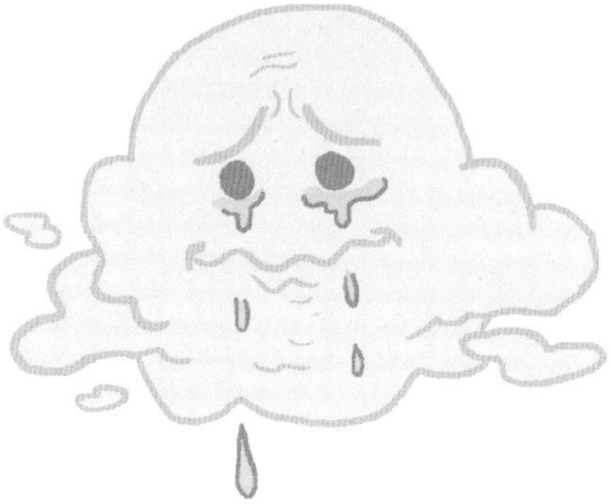

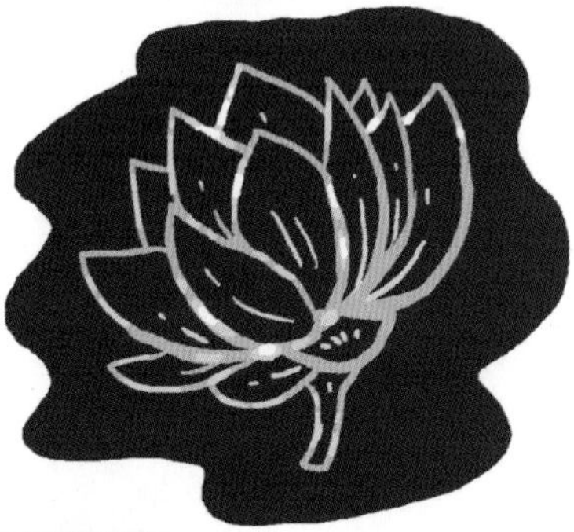

RUST POTION
Throwing this potion at someone in armor or made of metal will rust them so bad that the metal crumbles.

ELEMENTAL BOTTLE
It's empty, but it can suck an elemental into it. Then it can be released at a later time to fight on the bottle owner's behalf.

FIREBALL SPELL
A wizard can learn how to make this large fiery explosion.

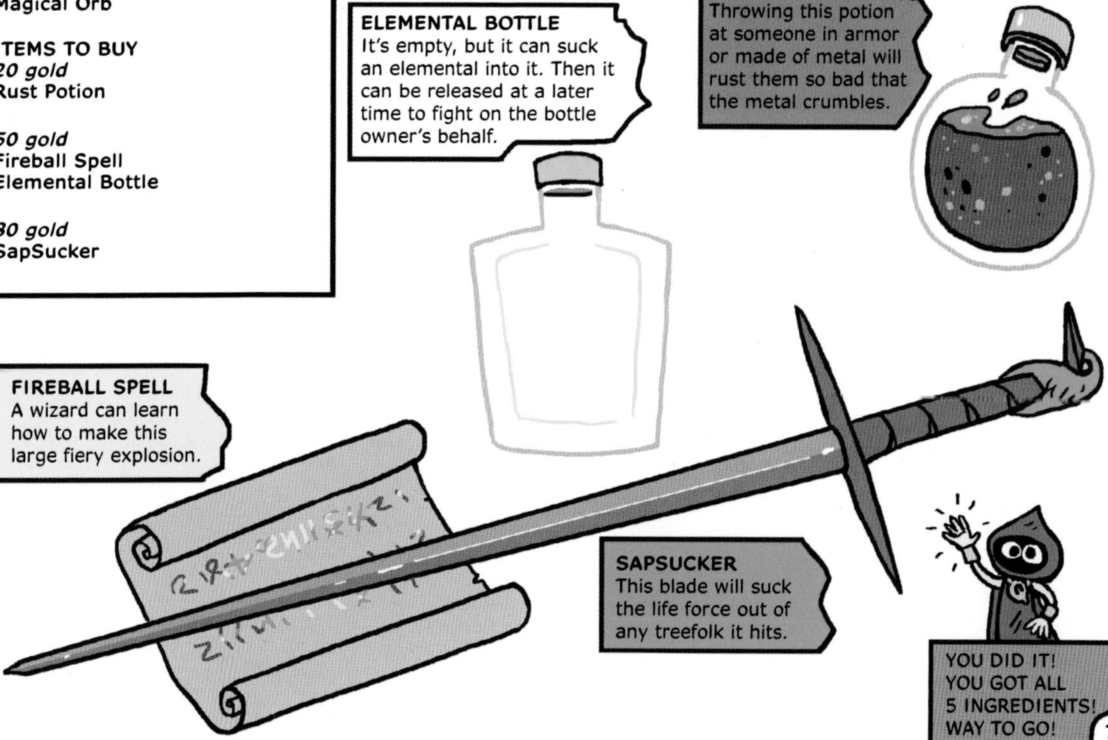

SAPSUCKER
This blade will suck the life force out of any treefolk it hits.

YOU DID IT!
YOU GOT ALL
5 INGREDIENTS!
WAY TO GO!

AMAZING! YOU GOT EVERYTHING YOU NEEDED! YOUR HEROES ARE GOING TO SAVE THE QUEEN! FIRST, THOUGH, THEY TAKE A MOMENT TO FIND ANOTHER ***ADVENTURING GROUP*** AND TELL THEM ABOUT THE DEAD OID IN THE GUARDGOYLE GRAVEYARD. THAT PARTY DECIDES TO LOOK INTO IT. YOUR SMALL GROUP CAN'T SOLVE EVERY PROBLEM, BUT THEY CAN HELP SPREAD THE WORD TO GET OTHERS OUT THERE TO HELP. GOOD THING, TOO. THOSE HEROES WILL STOP ANOTHER OID INVASION, BUT THAT'S A STORY FOR YOU TO MAKE UP.

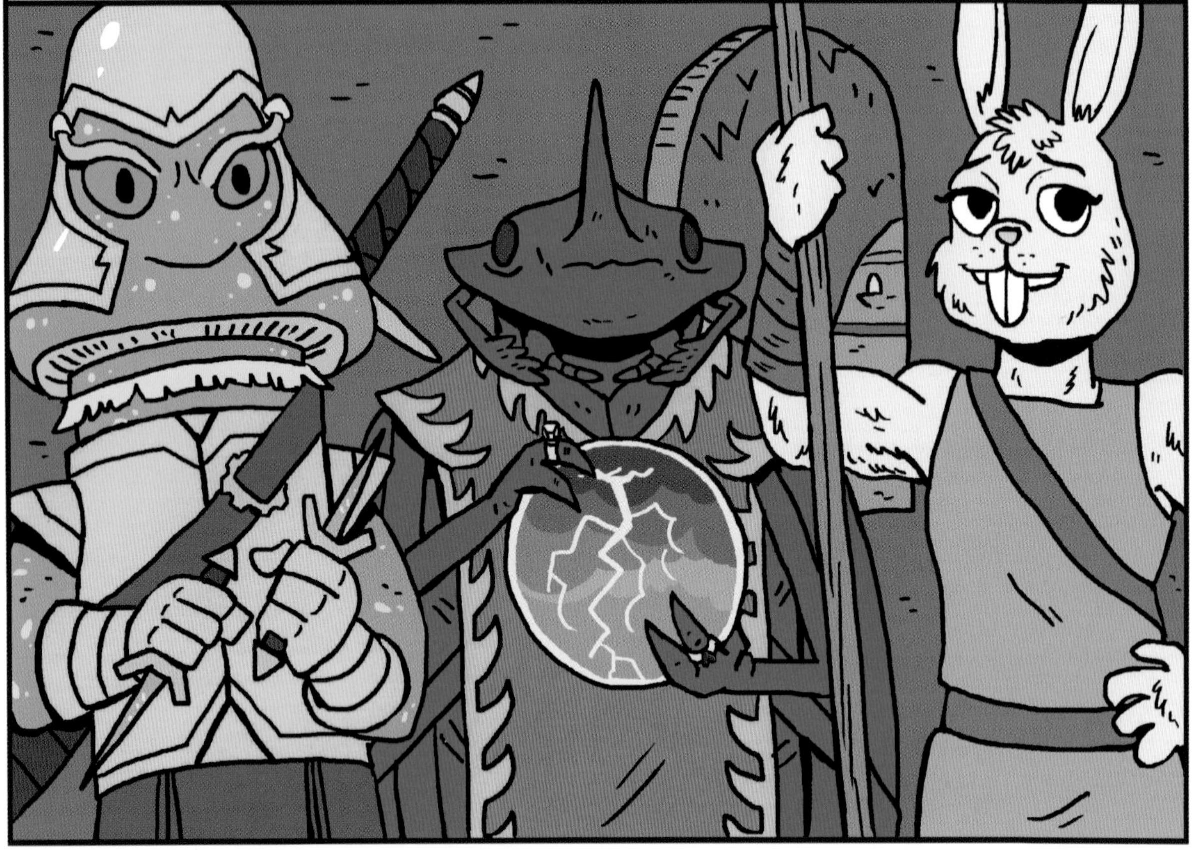

HOW ARE YOUR PARTY FEELING NOW? ARE THEY DESPERATELY MISSING THE SUN? THEY'VE BEEN IN CRAMPED, DARK SPACES FOR DAYS. IT'S OFTEN AT THIS POINT IN A STORY THAT TWO OF THE HEROES GET IN AN ARGUMENT AND ONE STORMS OFF. THINGS SEEM BLEAK. BUT AT THE END BATTLE, THEY COME IN AT THE LAST MINUTE, HAVING CHANGED THEIR MIND, AND SURPRISE THE VILLAIN AND THE AUDIENCE. MAYBE YOU WANT TO IMAGINE THAT.

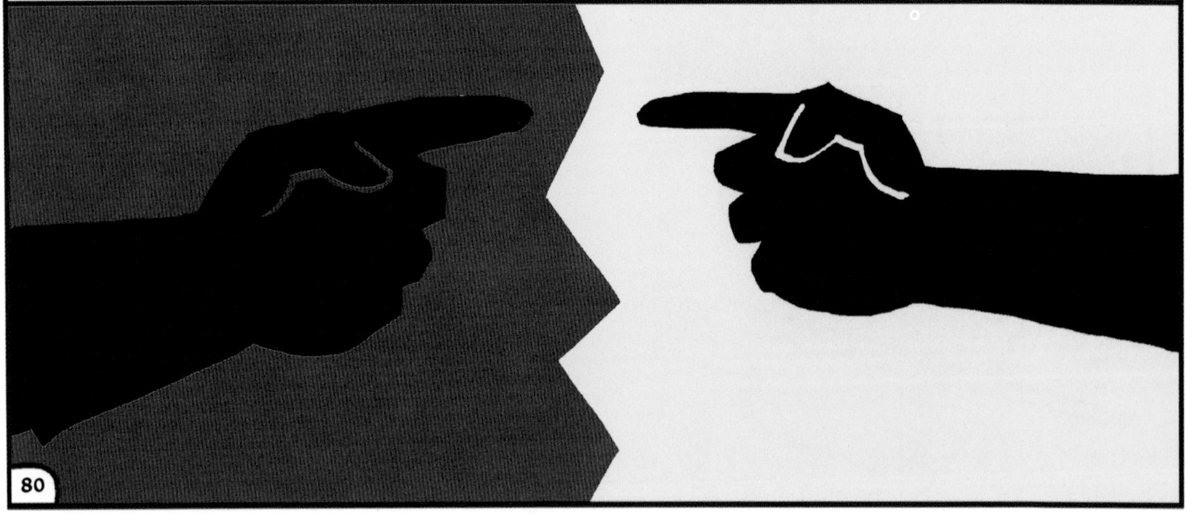

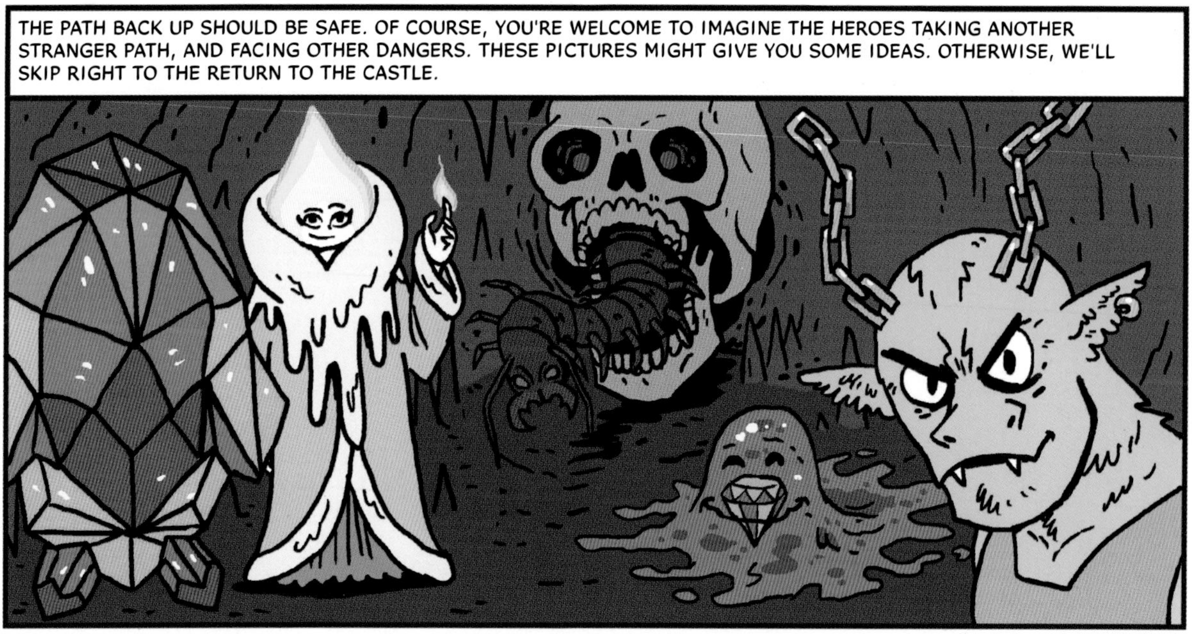
THE PATH BACK UP SHOULD BE SAFE. OF COURSE, YOU'RE WELCOME TO IMAGINE THE HEROES TAKING ANOTHER STRANGER PATH, AND FACING OTHER DANGERS. THESE PICTURES MIGHT GIVE YOU SOME IDEAS. OTHERWISE, WE'LL SKIP RIGHT TO THE RETURN TO THE CASTLE.

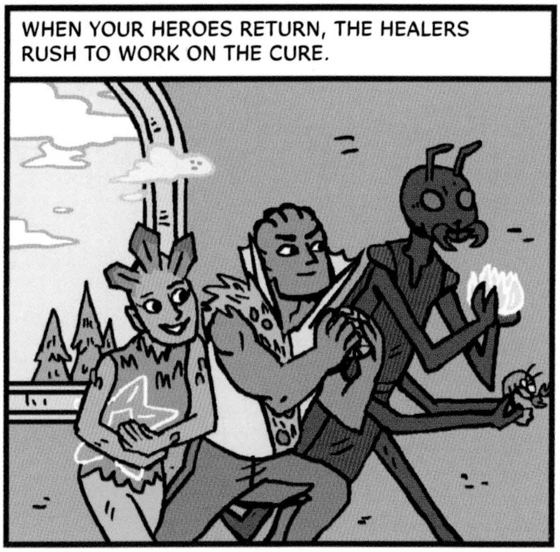
WHEN YOUR HEROES RETURN, THE HEALERS RUSH TO WORK ON THE CURE.

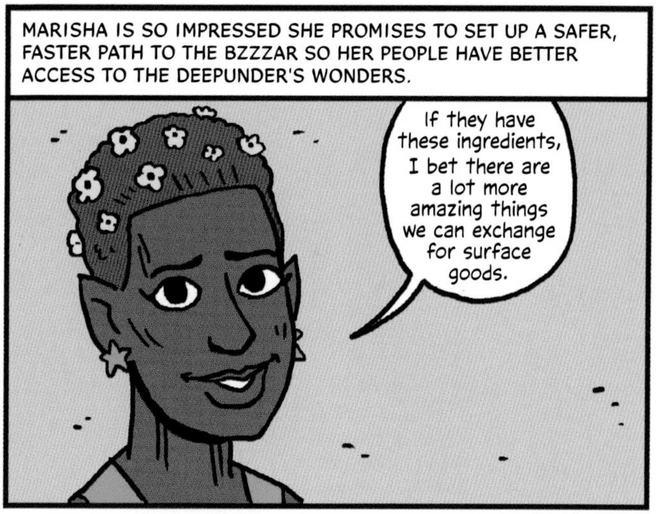
MARISHA IS SO IMPRESSED SHE PROMISES TO SET UP A SAFER, FASTER PATH TO THE BZZZAR SO HER PEOPLE HAVE BETTER ACCESS TO THE DEEPUNDER'S WONDERS.
If they have these ingredients, I bet there are a lot more amazing things we can exchange for surface goods.

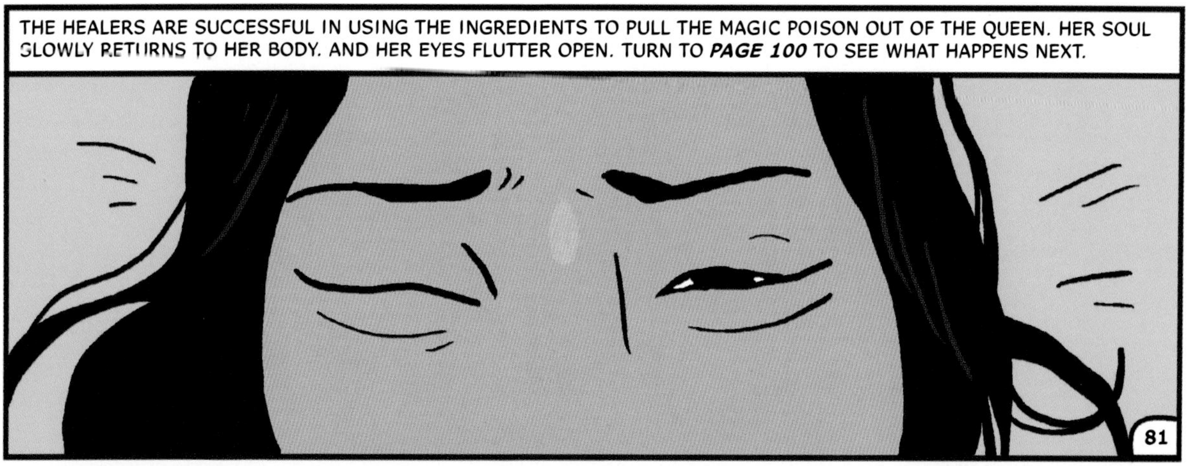
THE HEALERS ARE SUCCESSFUL IN USING THE INGREDIENTS TO PULL THE MAGIC POISON OUT OF THE QUEEN. HER SOUL SLOWLY RETURNS TO HER BODY. AND HER EYES FLUTTER OPEN. TURN TO ***PAGE 100*** TO SEE WHAT HAPPENS NEXT.

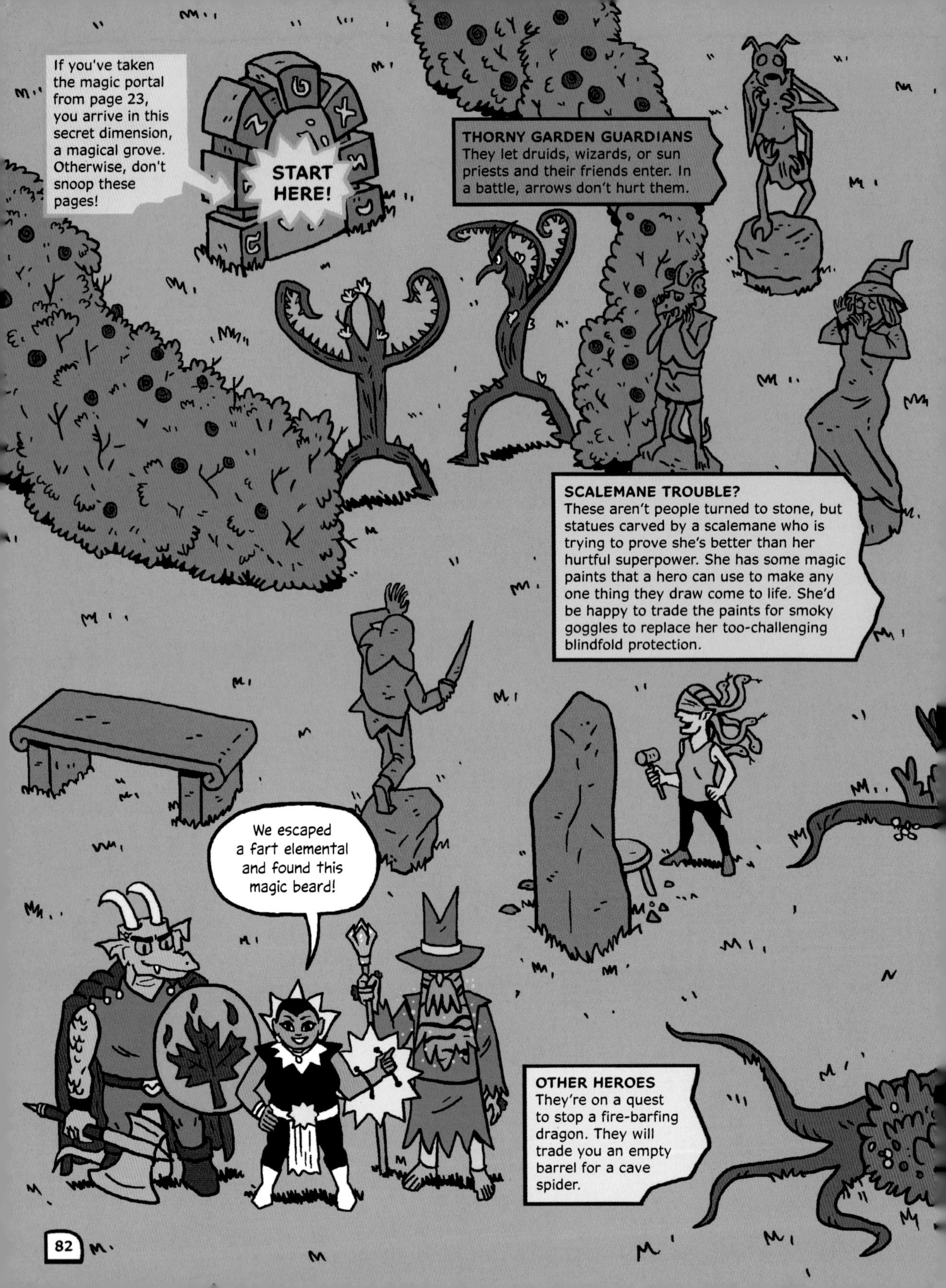
If you've taken the magic portal from page 23, you arrive in this secret dimension, a magical grove. Otherwise, don't snoop these pages!
START HERE!
THORNY GARDEN GUARDIANS
They let druids, wizards, or sun priests and their friends enter. In a battle, arrows don't hurt them.
SCALEMANE TROUBLE?
These aren't people turned to stone, but statues carved by a scalemane who is trying to prove she's better than her hurtful superpower. She has some magic paints that a hero can use to make any one thing they draw come to life. She'd be happy to trade the paints for smoky goggles to replace her too-challenging blindfold protection.
We escaped a fart elemental and found this magic beard!
OTHER HEROES
They're on a quest to stop a fire-barfing dragon. They will trade you an empty barrel for a cave spider.

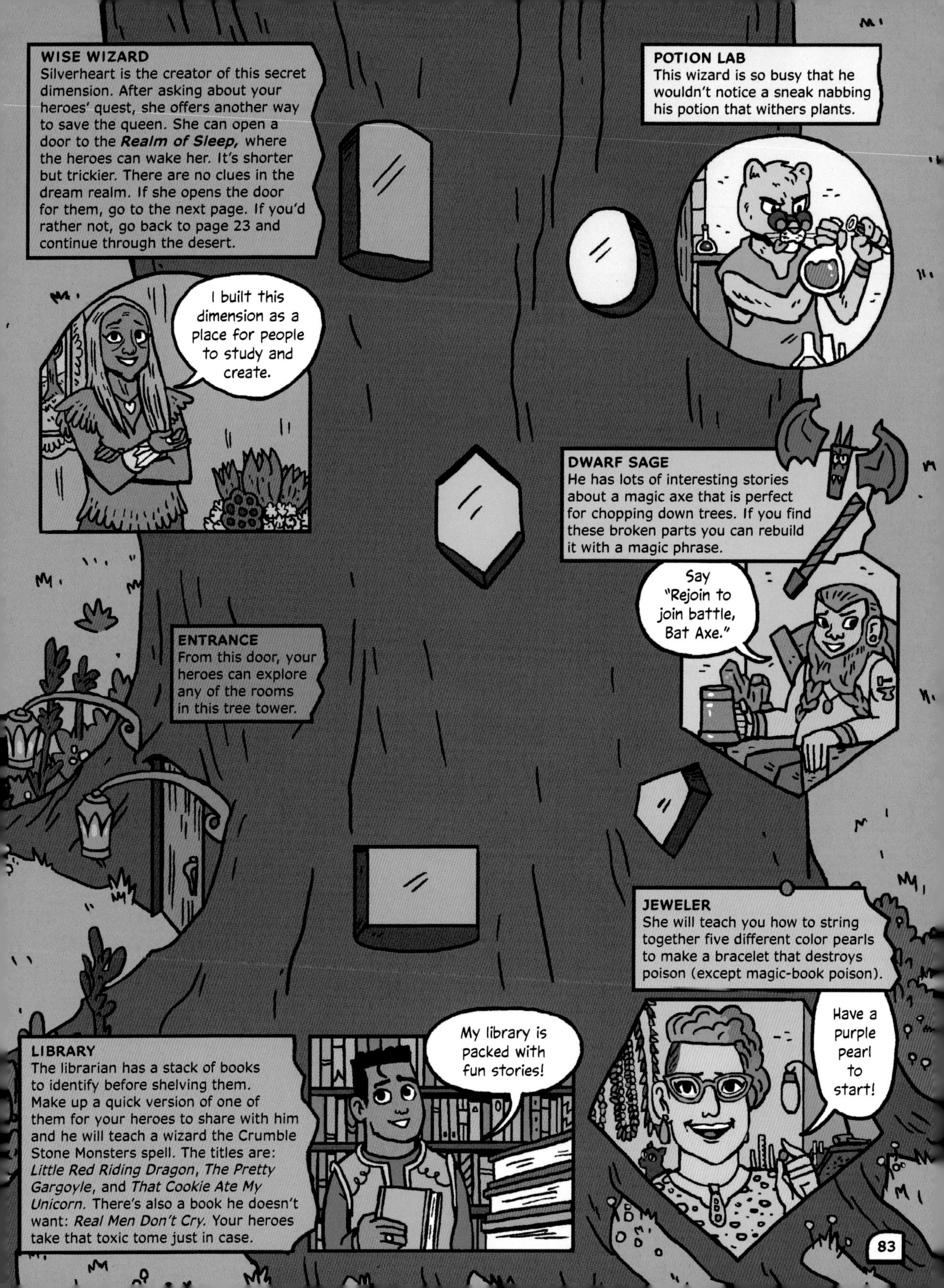
WISE WIZARD
Silverheart is the creator of this secret dimension. After asking about your heroes' quest, she offers another way to save the queen. She can open a door to the *Realm of Sleep,* where the heroes can wake her. It's shorter but trickier. There are no clues in the dream realm. If she opens the door for them, go to the next page. If you'd rather not, go back to page 23 and continue through the desert.
POTION LAB
This wizard is so busy that he wouldn't notice a sneak nabbing his potion that withers plants.
I built this dimension as a place for people to study and create.
DWARF SAGE
He has lots of interesting stories about a magic axe that is perfect for chopping down trees. If you find these broken parts you can rebuild it with a magic phrase.
Say "Rejoin to join battle, Bat Axe."
ENTRANCE
From this door, your heroes can explore any of the rooms in this tree tower.
JEWELER
She will teach you how to string together five different color pearls to make a bracelet that destroys poison (except magic-book poison).
LIBRARY
The librarian has a stack of books to identify before shelving them. Make up a quick version of one of them for your heroes to share with him and he will teach a wizard the Crumble Stone Monsters spell. The titles are: *Little Red Riding Dragon*, *The Pretty Gargoyle*, and *That Cookie Ate My Unicorn.* There's also a book he doesn't want: *Real Men Don't Cry.* Your heroes take that toxic tome just in case.
My library is packed with fun stories!
Have a purple pearl to start!

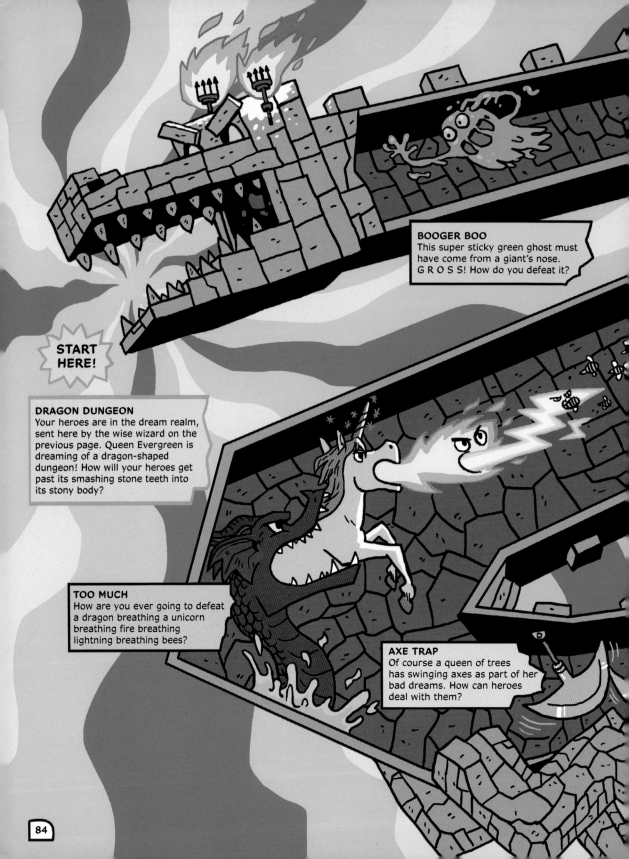

BOOGER BOO
This super sticky green ghost must have come from a giant's nose. G R O S S! How do you defeat it?

START HERE!

DRAGON DUNGEON
Your heroes are in the dream realm, sent here by the wise wizard on the previous page. Queen Evergreen is dreaming of a dragon-shaped dungeon! How will your heroes get past its smashing stone teeth into its stony body?

TOO MUCH
How are you ever going to defeat a dragon breathing a unicorn breathing fire breathing lightning breathing bees?

AXE TRAP
Of course a queen of trees has swinging axes as part of her bad dreams. How can heroes deal with them?

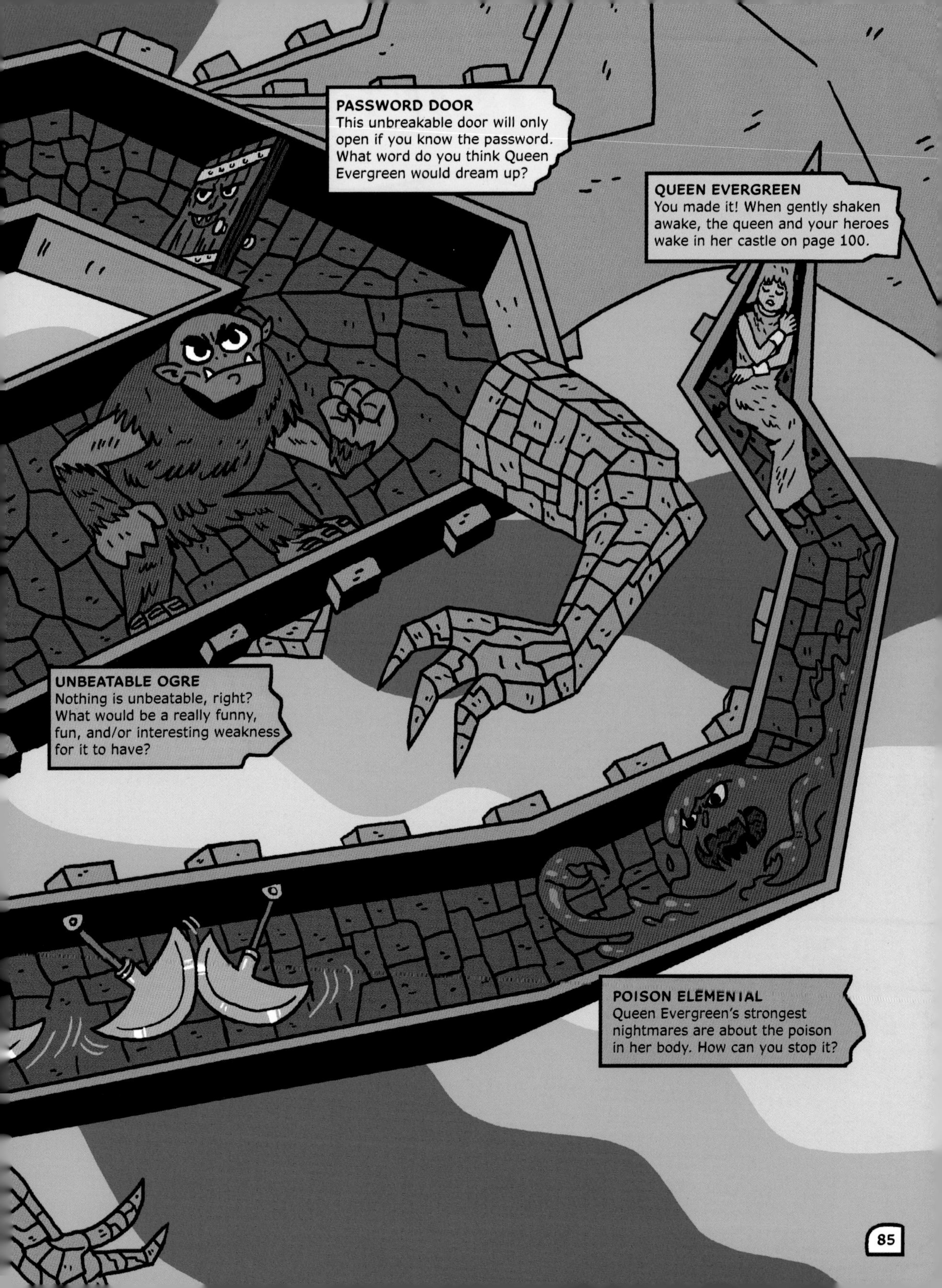
PASSWORD DOOR
This unbreakable door will only open if you know the password. What word do you think Queen Evergreen would dream up?
QUEEN EVERGREEN
You made it! When gently shaken awake, the queen and your heroes wake in her castle on page 100.
UNBEATABLE OGRE
Nothing is unbeatable, right? What would be a really funny, fun, and/or interesting weakness for it to have?
POISON ELEMENTAL
Queen Evergreen's strongest nightmares are about the poison in her body. How can you stop it?

CHAPTER FOUR

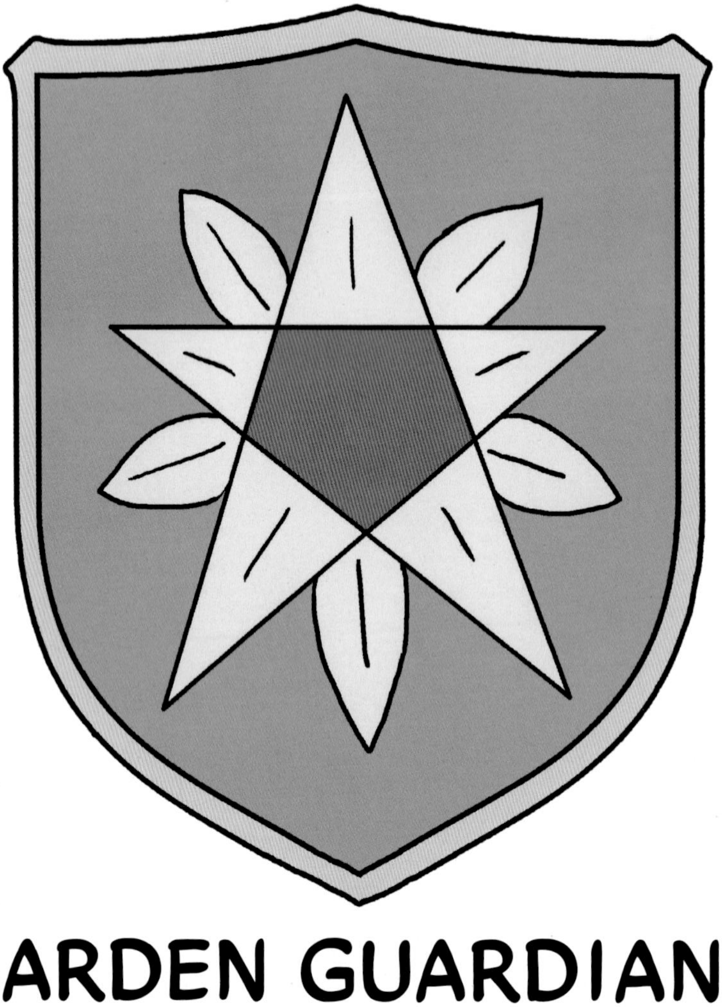

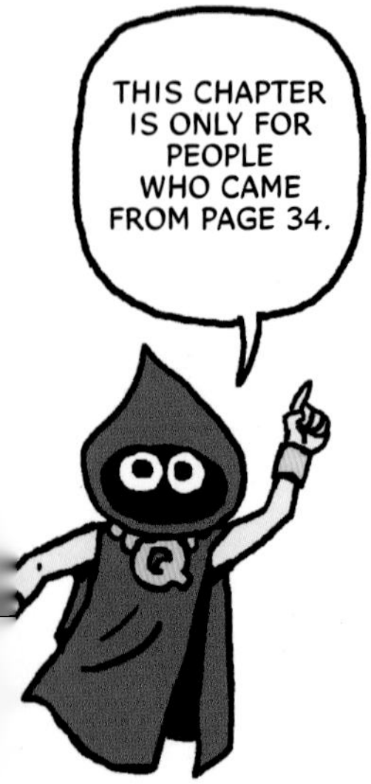
THIS CHAPTER IS ONLY FOR PEOPLE WHO CAME FROM PAGE 34.

GARDEN GUARDIANS

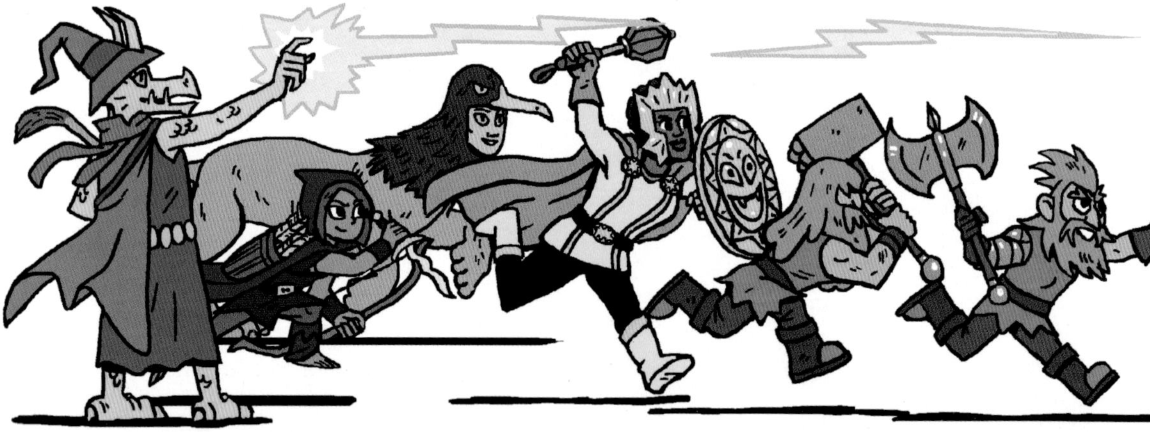

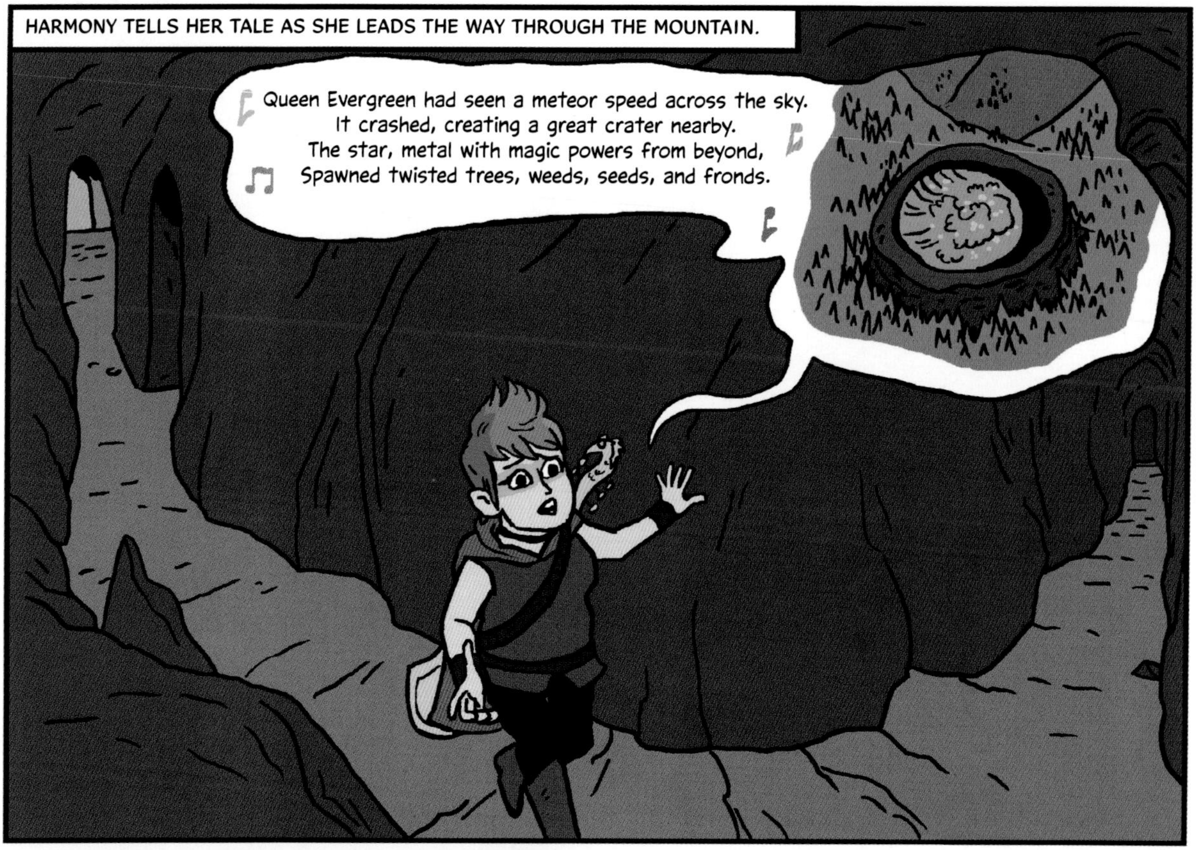
HARMONY TELLS HER TALE AS SHE LEADS THE WAY THROUGH THE MOUNTAIN.
Queen Evergreen had seen a meteor speed across the sky. It crashed, creating a great crater nearby. The star, metal with magic powers from beyond, Spawned twisted trees, weeds, seeds, and fronds.

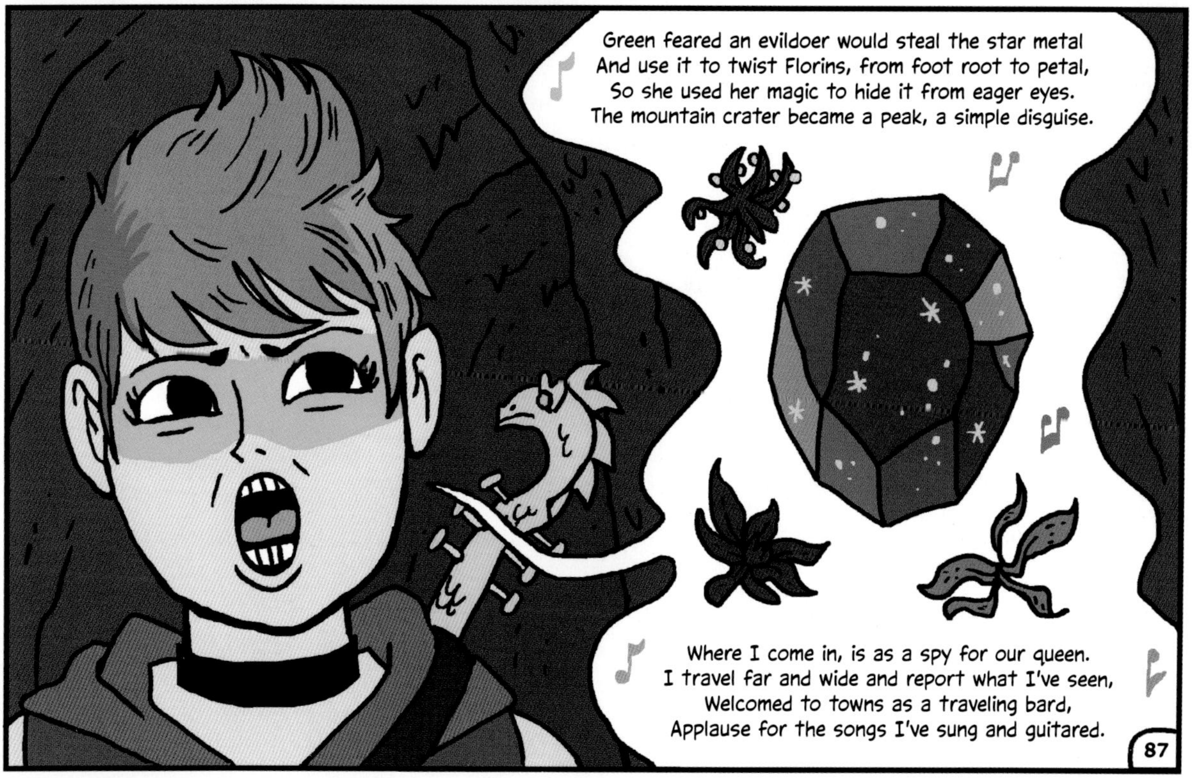
Green feared an evildoer would steal the star metal And use it to twist Florins, from foot root to petal, So she used her magic to hide it from eager eyes. The mountain crater became a peak, a simple disguise.
Where I come in, is as a spy for our queen. I travel far and wide and report what I've seen, Welcomed to towns as a traveling bard, Applause for the songs I've sung and guitared.

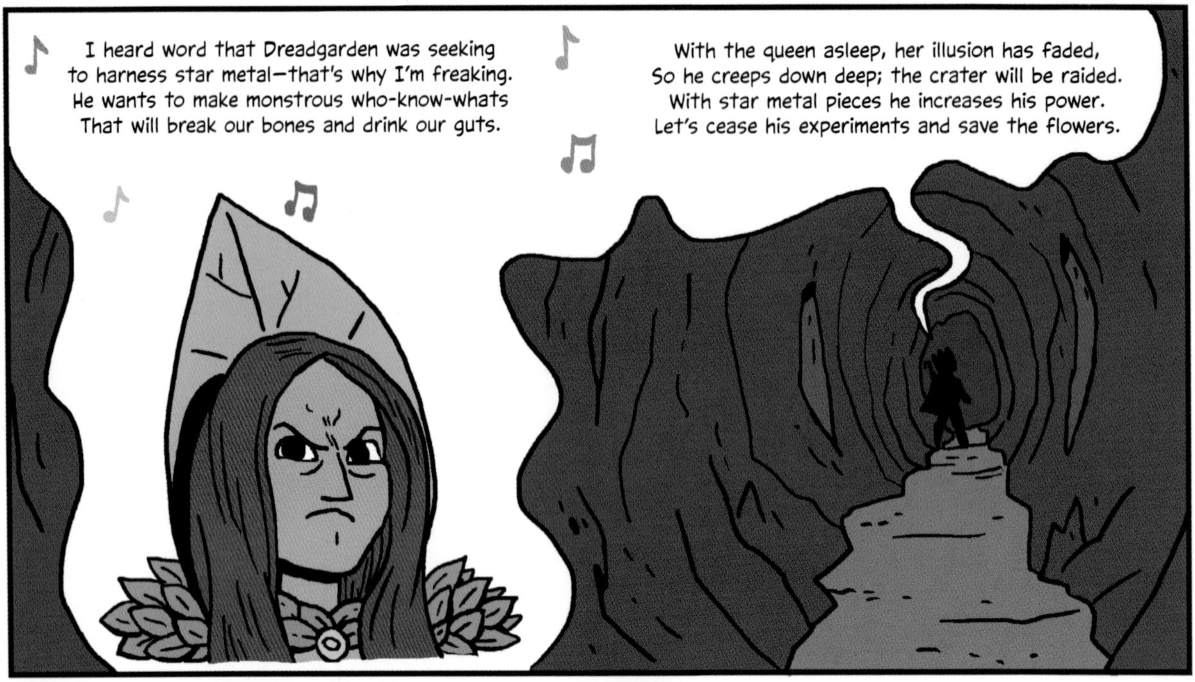
I heard word that Dreadgarden was seeking to harness star metal—that's why I'm freaking. He wants to make monstrous who-know-whats That will break our bones and drink our guts.
With the queen asleep, her illusion has faded, So he creeps down deep; the crater will be raided. With star metal pieces he increases his power. Let's cease his experiments and save the flowers.

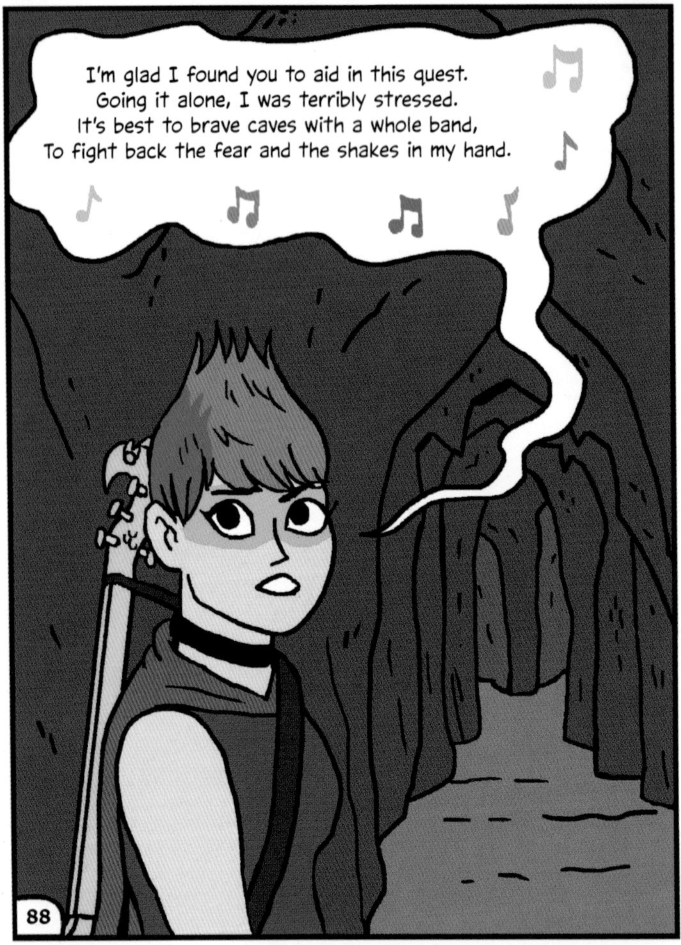
I'm glad I found you to aid in this quest. Going it alone, I was terribly stressed. It's best to brave caves with a whole band, To fight back the fear and the shakes in my hand.

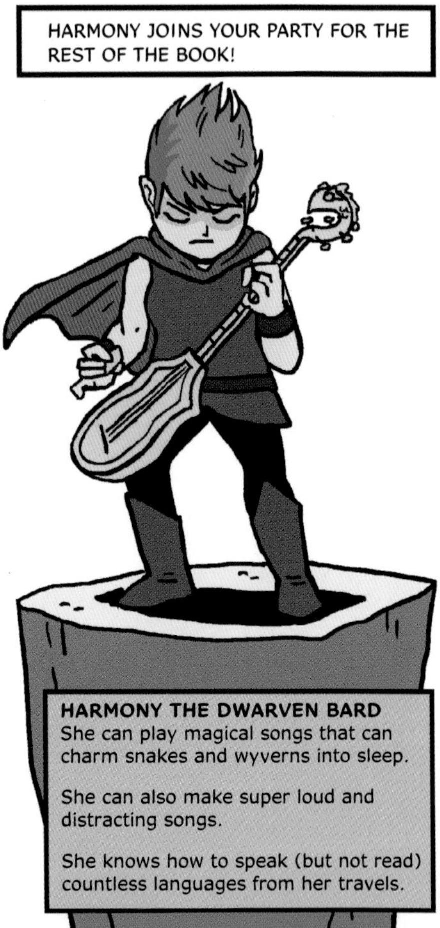
HARMONY JOINS YOUR PARTY FOR THE REST OF THE BOOK!
HARMONY THE DWARVEN BARD
She can play magical songs that can charm snakes and wyverns into sleep.
She can also make super loud and distracting songs.
She knows how to speak (but not read) countless languages from her travels.

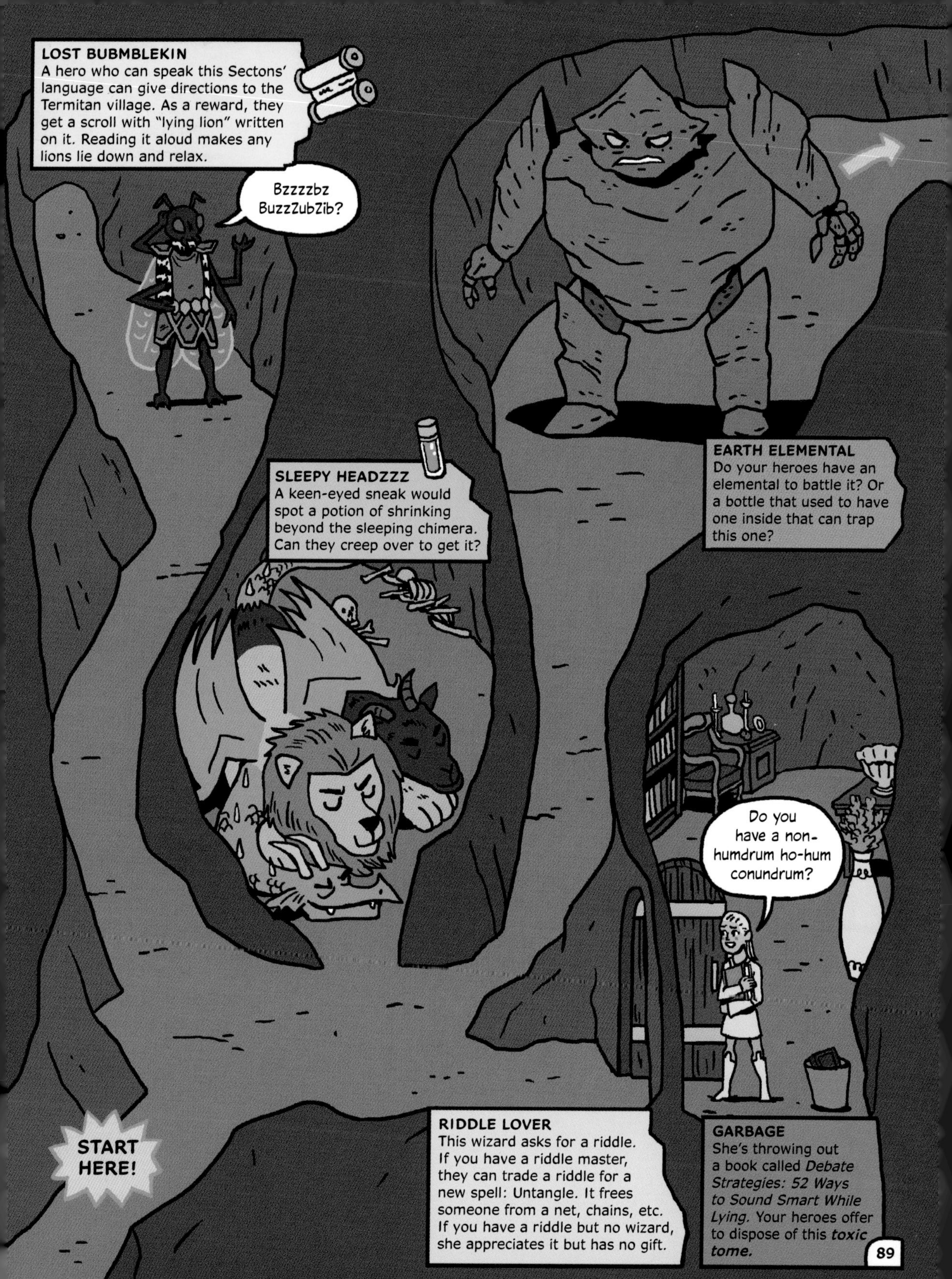
LOST BUBMBLEKIN
A hero who can speak this Sectons' language can give directions to the Termitan village. As a reward, they get a scroll with "lying lion" written on it. Reading it aloud makes any lions lie down and relax.
Bzzzzbz BuzzZubZib?
SLEEPY HEADZZZ
A keen-eyed sneak would spot a potion of shrinking beyond the sleeping chimera. Can they creep over to get it?
EARTH ELEMENTAL
Do your heroes have an elemental to battle it? Or a bottle that used to have one inside that can trap this one?
Do you have a non-humdrum ho-hum conundrum?
START HERE!
RIDDLE LOVER
This wizard asks for a riddle. If you have a riddle master, they can trade a riddle for a new spell: Untangle. It frees someone from a net, chains, etc. If you have a riddle but no wizard, she appreciates it but has no gift.
GARBAGE
She's throwing out a book called *Debate Strategies: 52 Ways to Sound Smart While Lying.* Your heroes offer to dispose of this *toxic tome.*

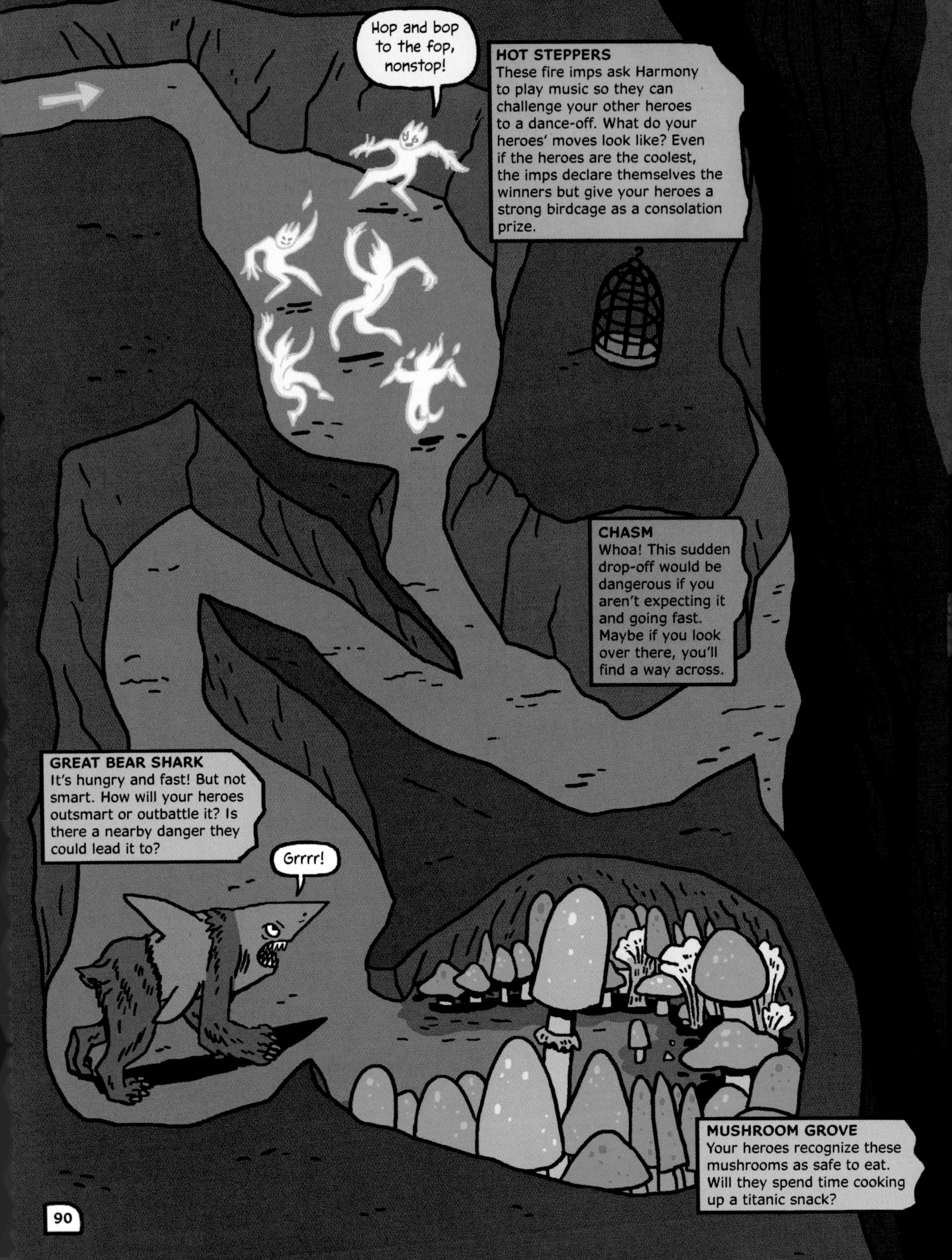
Hop and bop to the fop, nonstop!
HOT STEPPERS
These fire imps ask Harmony to play music so they can challenge your other heroes to a dance-off. What do your heroes' moves look like? Even if the heroes are the coolest, the imps declare themselves the winners but give your heroes a strong birdcage as a consolation prize.
CHASM
Whoa! This sudden drop-off would be dangerous if you aren't expecting it and going fast. Maybe if you look over there, you'll find a way across.
GREAT BEAR SHARK
It's hungry and fast! But not smart. How will your heroes outsmart or outbattle it? Is there a nearby danger they could lead it to?
Grrrr!
MUSHROOM GROVE
Your heroes recognize these mushrooms as safe to eat. Will they spend time cooking up a titanic snack?

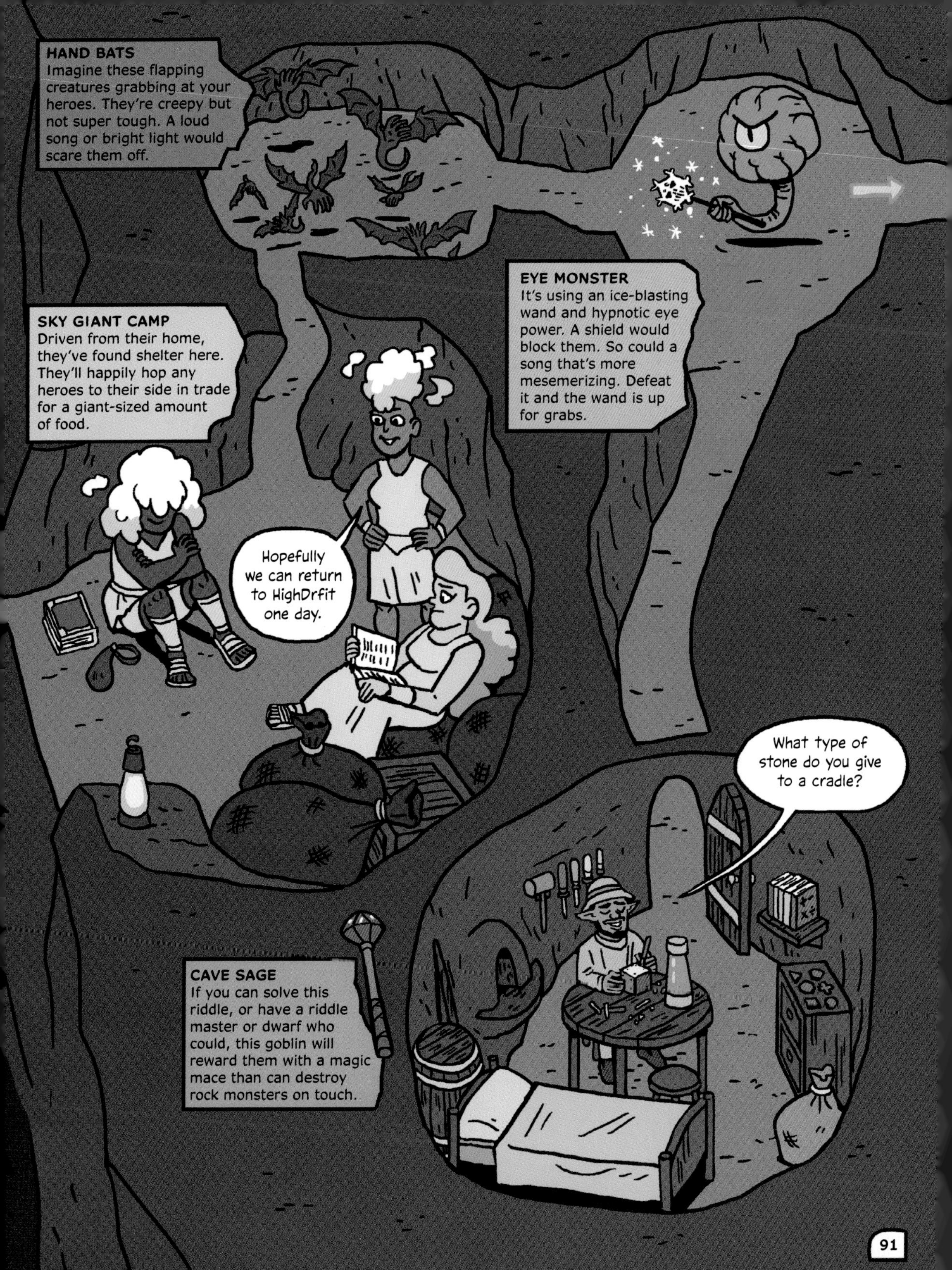
HAND BATS
Imagine these flapping creatures grabbing at your heroes. They're creepy but not super tough. A loud song or bright light would scare them off.
EYE MONSTER
It's using an ice-blasting wand and hypnotic eye power. A shield would block them. So could a song that's more mesemerizing. Defeat it and the wand is up for grabs.
SKY GIANT CAMP
Driven from their home, they've found shelter here. They'll happily hop any heroes to their side in trade for a giant-sized amount of food.
Hopefully we can return to HighDrfit one day.
What type of stone do you give to a cradle?
CAVE SAGE
If you can solve this riddle, or have a riddle master or dwarf who could, this goblin will reward them with a magic mace than can destroy rock monsters on touch.

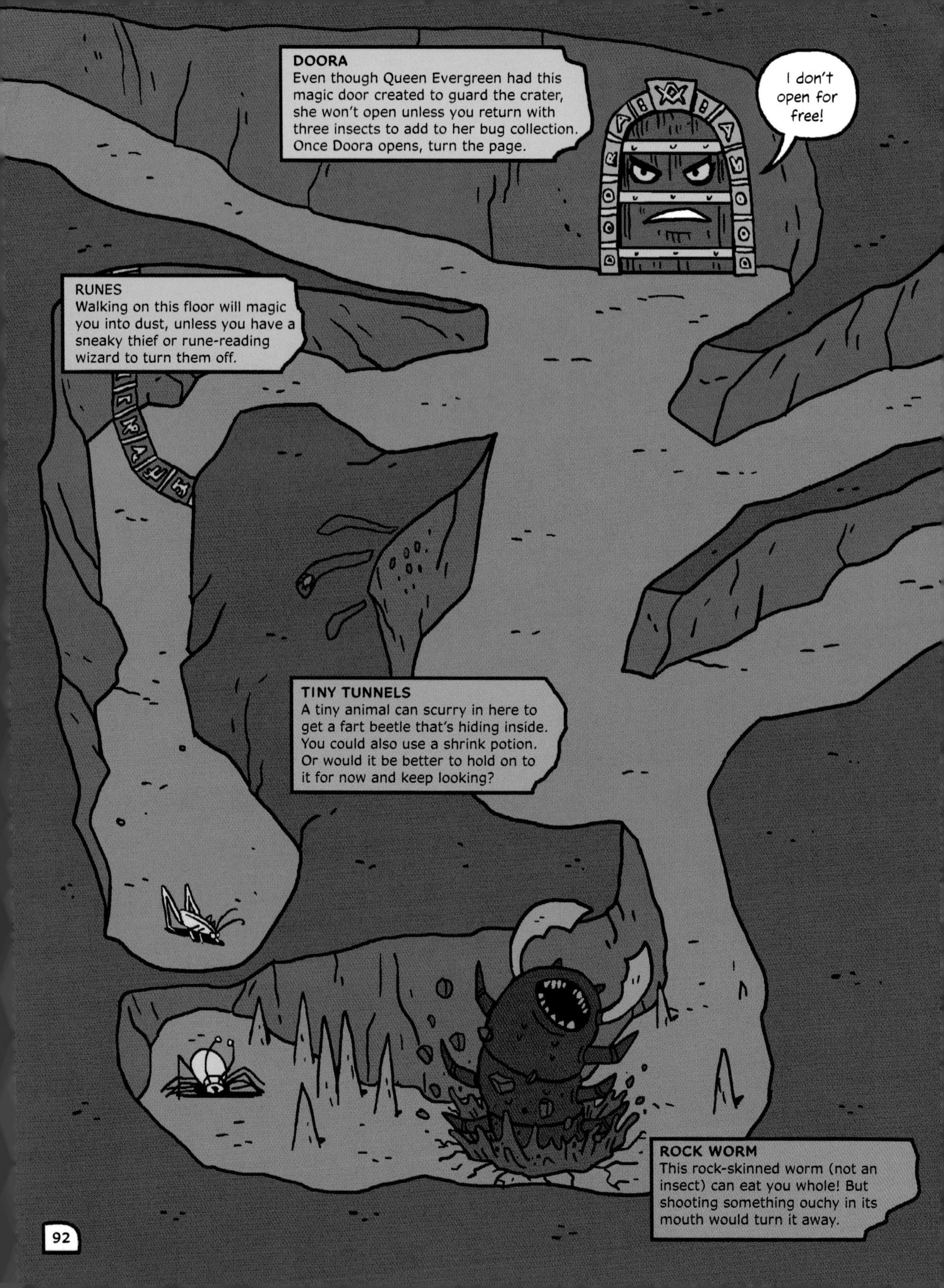
DOORA
Even though Queen Evergreen had this magic door created to guard the crater, she won't open unless you return with three insects to add to her bug collection. Once Doora opens, turn the page.
I don't open for free!
RUNES
Walking on this floor will magic you into dust, unless you have a sneaky thief or rune-reading wizard to turn them off.
TINY TUNNELS
A tiny animal can scurry in here to get a fart beetle that's hiding inside. You could also use a shrink potion. Or would it be better to hold on to it for now and keep looking?
ROCK WORM
This rock-skinned worm (not an insect) can eat you whole! But shooting something ouchy in its mouth would turn it away.

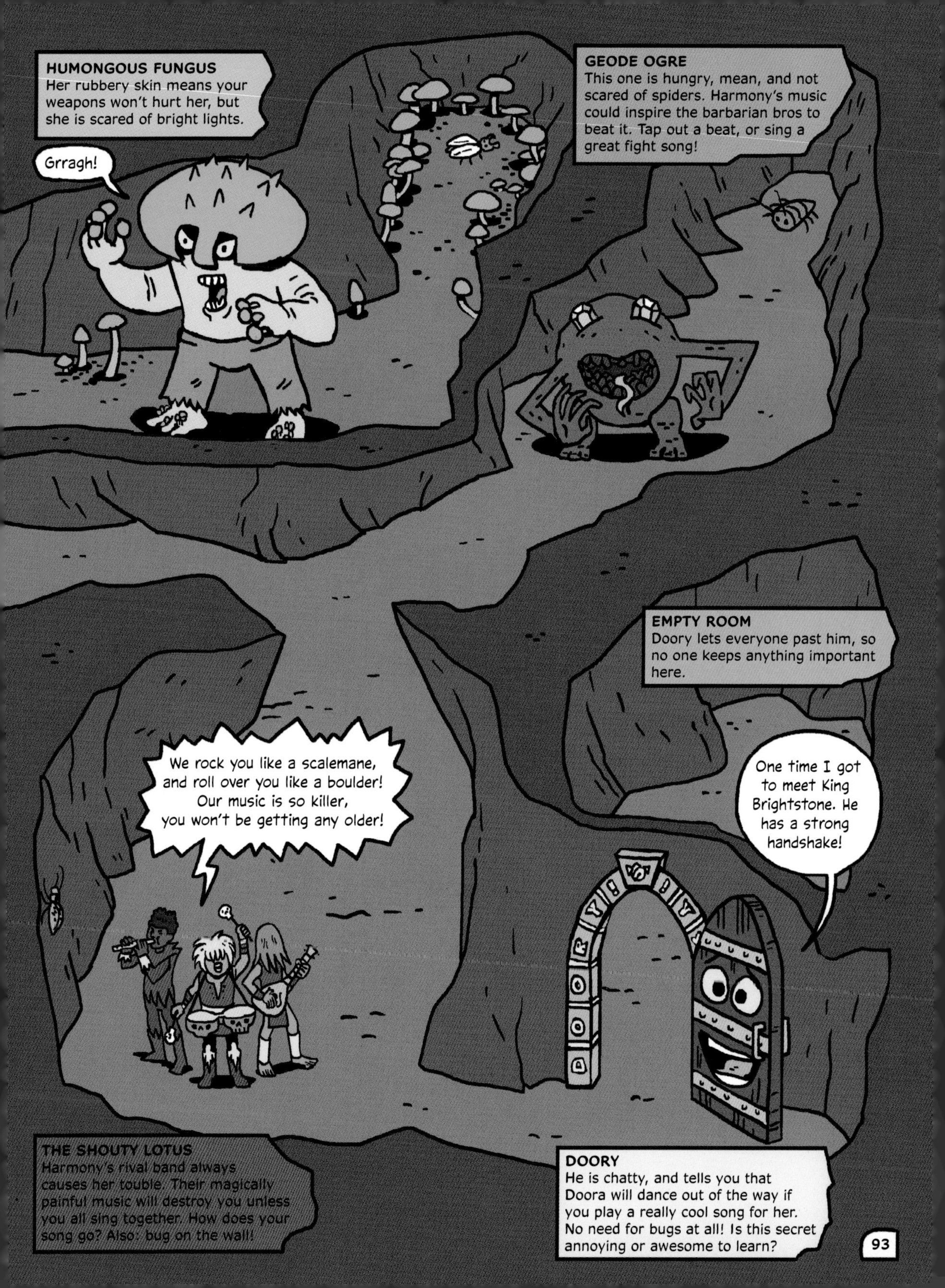
HUMONGOUS FUNGUS
Her rubbery skin means your weapons won't hurt her, but she is scared of bright lights.
Grragh!
GEODE OGRE
This one is hungry, mean, and not scared of spiders. Harmony's music could inspire the barbarian bros to beat it. Tap out a beat, or sing a great fight song!
EMPTY ROOM
Doory lets everyone past him, so no one keeps anything important here.
We rock you like a scalemane, and roll over you like a boulder! Our music is so killer, you won't be getting any older!
One time I got to meet King Brightstone. He has a strong handshake!
DOORY
THE SHOUTY LOTUS
Harmony's rival band always causes her touble. Their magically painful music will destroy you unless you all sing together. How does your song go? Also: bug on the wall!
DOORY
He is chatty, and tells you that Doora will dance out of the way if you play a really cool song for her. No need for bugs at all! Is this secret annoying or awesome to learn?

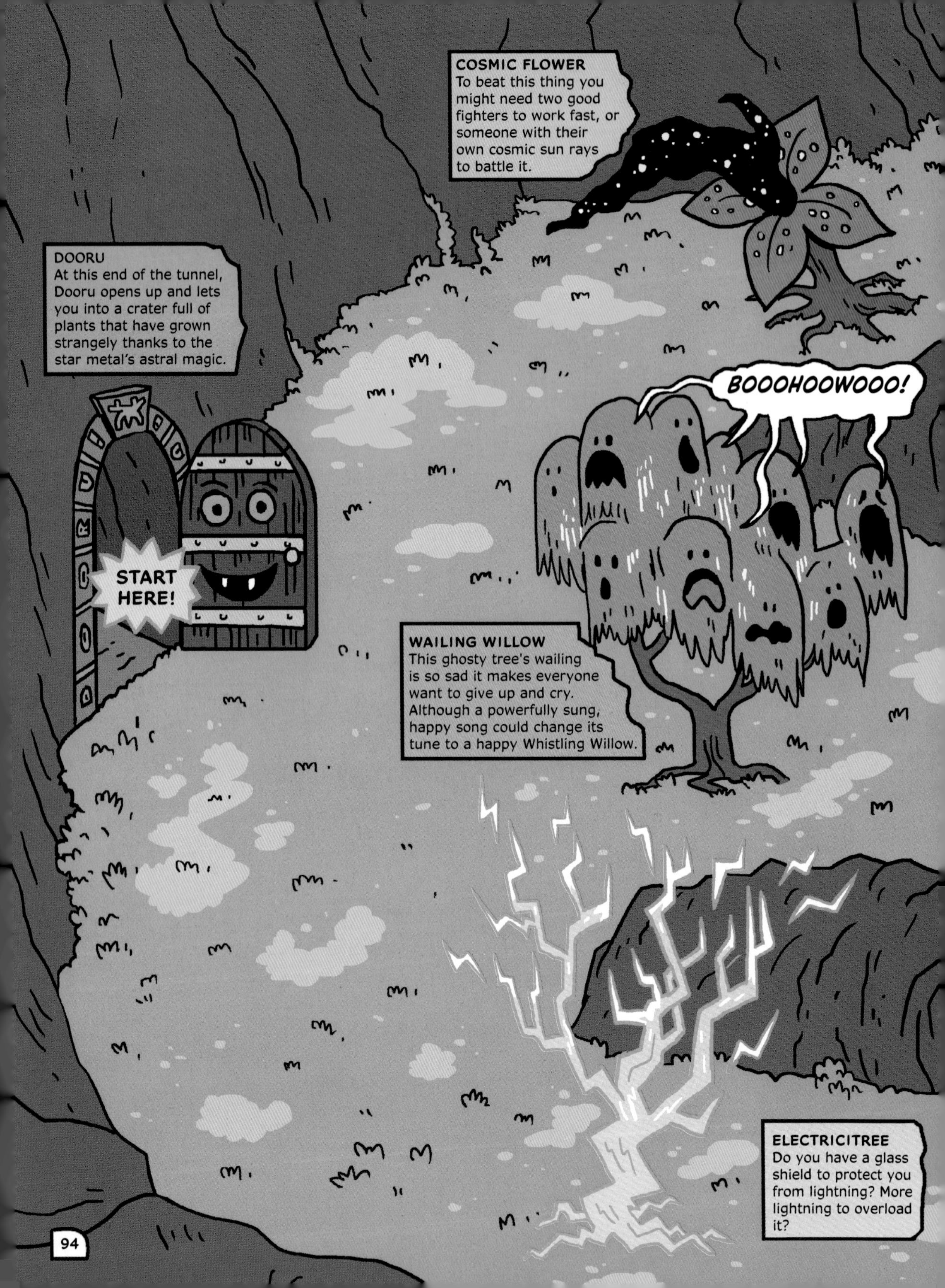
DOORU
At this end of the tunnel, Dooru opens up and lets you into a crater full of plants that have grown strangely thanks to the star metal's astral magic.
START HERE!
COSMIC FLOWER
To beat this thing you might need two good fighters to work fast, or someone with their own cosmic sun rays to battle it.
BOOOHOOWOOO!
WAILING WILLOW
This ghosty tree's wailing is so sad it makes everyone want to give up and cry. Although a powerfully sung, happy song could change its tune to a happy Whistling Willow.
ELECTRICITREE
Do you have a glass shield to protect you from lightning? More lightning to overload it?

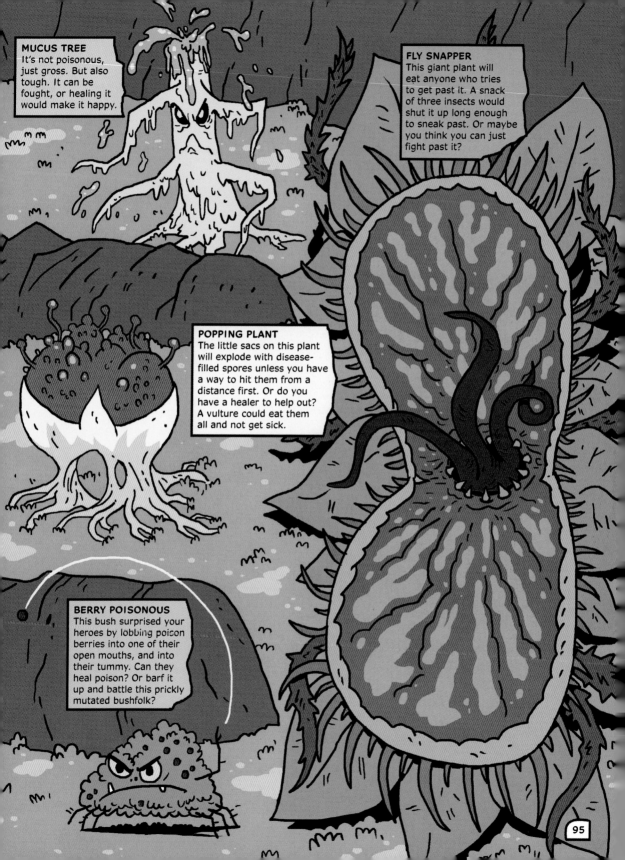

MUCUS TREE
It's not poisonous, just gross. But also tough. It can be fought, or healing it would make it happy.

FLY SNAPPER
This giant plant will eat anyone who tries to get past it. A snack of three insects would shut it up long enough to sneak past. Or maybe you think you can just fight past it?

POPPING PLANT
The little sacs on this plant will explode with disease-filled spores unless you have a way to hit them from a distance first. Or do you have a healer to help out? A vulture could eat them all and not get sick.

BERRY POISONOUS
This bush surprised your heroes by lobbing poison berries into one of their open mouths, and into their tummy. Can they heal poison? Or barf it up and battle this prickly mutated bushfolk?

MONSTROSITREE

Dreadgarden lured some Florins to this crater with lies of it being a paradise. When they got here, he used his magic to attach the star metal to this dead tree. This tree monster is twisting the Florins into something new and terrible like itself, so long as they are held captive. Your heroes must rescue them before tackling the tree. Harmony will distract it with a loud song. Once the Florins are free (see below), your heroes might get the star metal free using sun rays, a magic weapon, a ram's headbutt, or something else. If you have Blade, she will have to stay back or risk turning on her group as some sort of terrible monster.

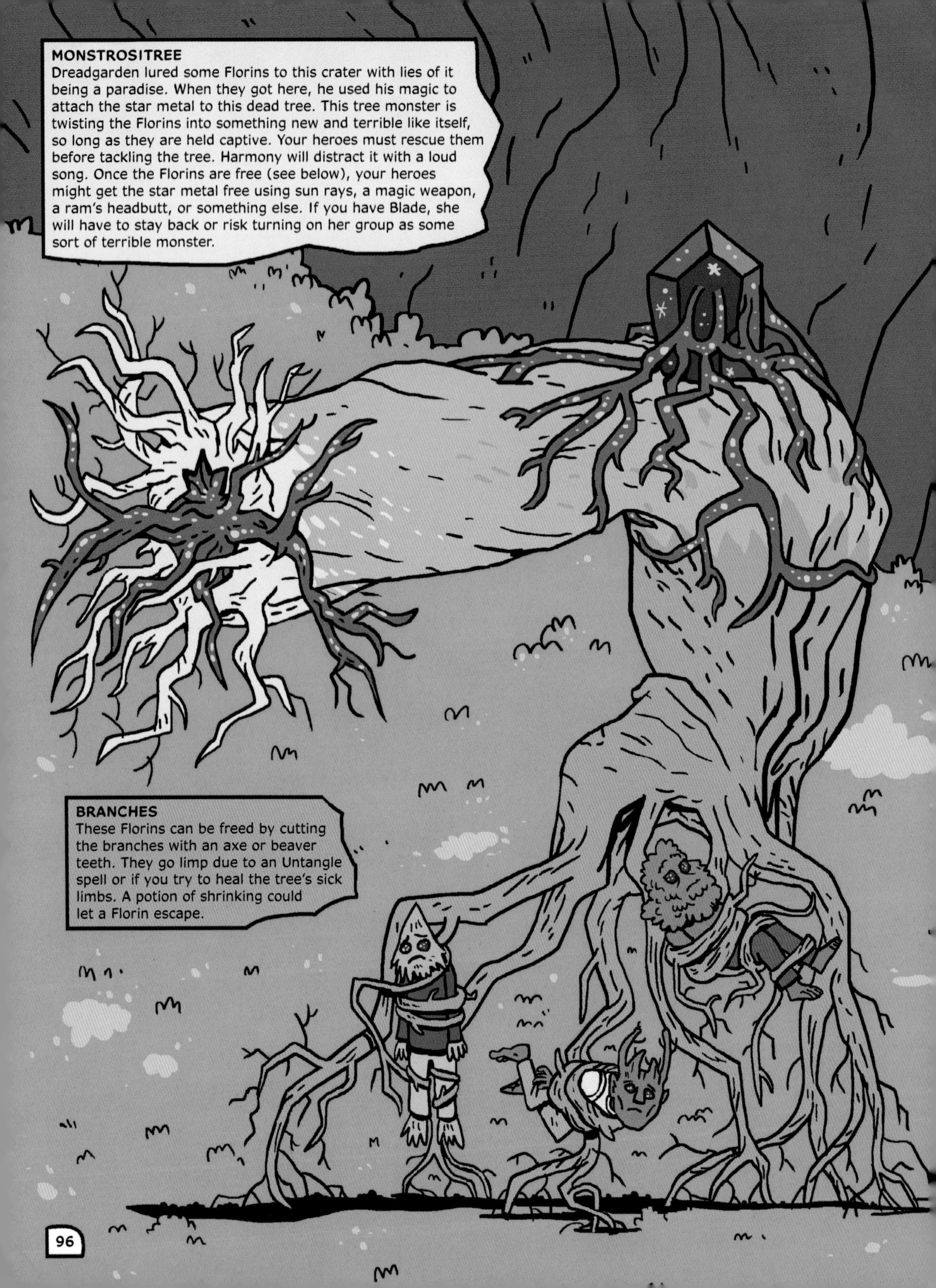

BRANCHES

These Florins can be freed by cutting the branches with an axe or beaver teeth. They go limp due to an Untangle spell or if you try to heal the tree's sick limbs. A potion of shrinking could let a Florin escape.

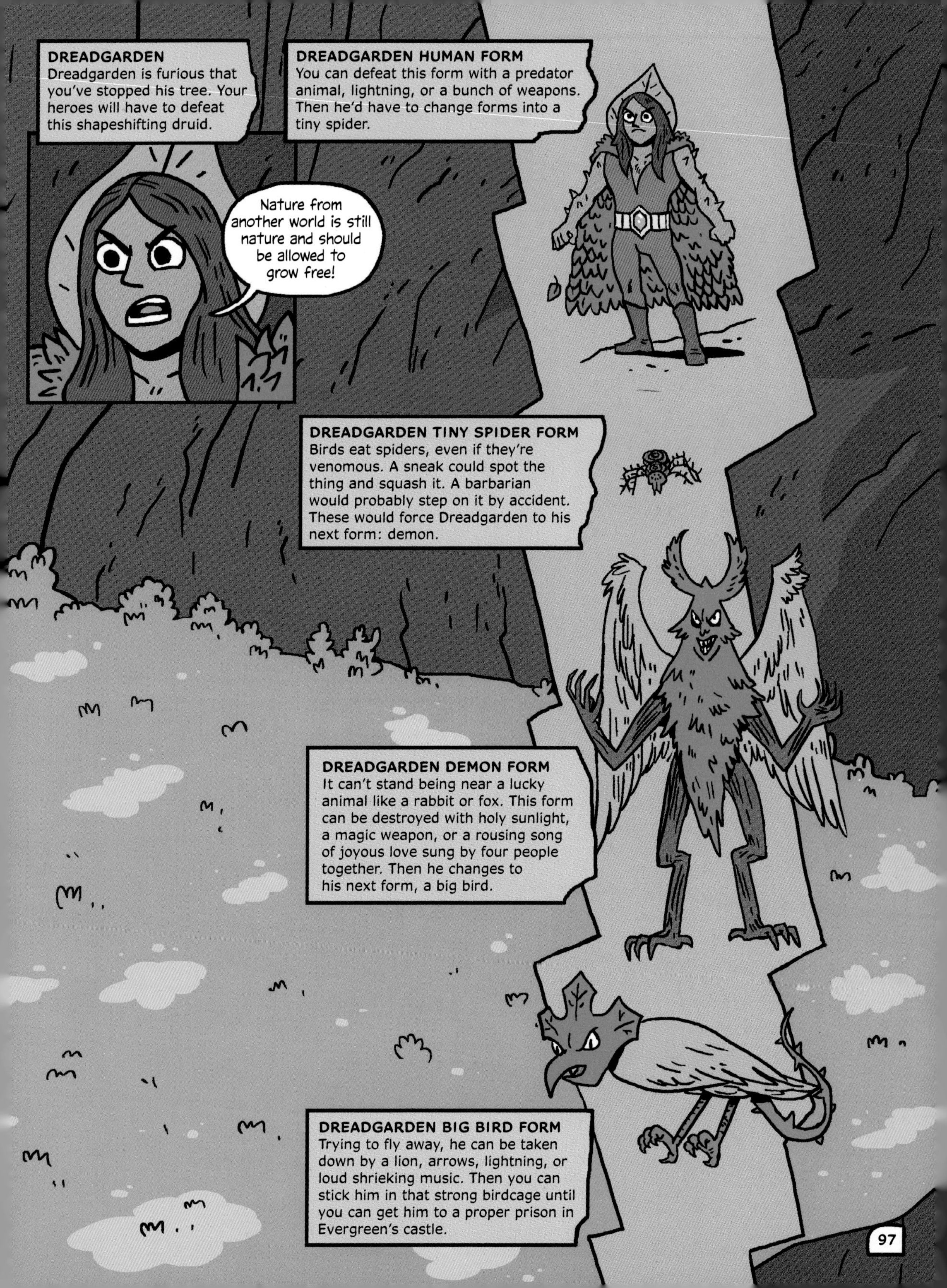
DREADGARDEN
Dreadgarden is furious that you've stopped his tree. Your heroes will have to defeat this shapeshifting druid.
DREADGARDEN HUMAN FORM
You can defeat this form with a predator animal, lightning, or a bunch of weapons. Then he'd have to change forms into a tiny spider.
Nature from another world is still nature and should be allowed to grow free!
DREADGARDEN TINY SPIDER FORM
Birds eat spiders, even if they're venomous. A sneak could spot the thing and squash it. A barbarian would probably step on it by accident. These would force Dreadgarden to his next form: demon.
DREADGARDEN DEMON FORM
It can't stand being near a lucky animal like a rabbit or fox. This form can be destroyed with holy sunlight, a magic weapon, or a rousing song of joyous love sung by four people together. Then he changes to his next form, a big bird.
DREADGARDEN BIG BIRD FORM
Trying to fly away, he can be taken down by a lion, arrows, lightning, or loud shrieking music. Then you can stick him in that strong birdcage until you can get him to a proper prison in Evergreen's castle.

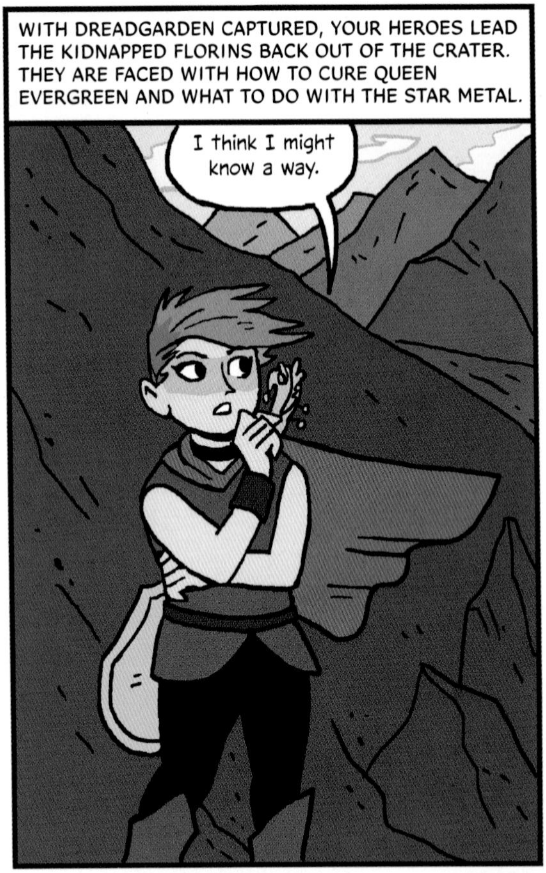
WITH DREADGARDEN CAPTURED, YOUR HEROES LEAD THE KIDNAPPED FLORINS BACK OUT OF THE CRATER. THEY ARE FACED WITH HOW TO CURE QUEEN EVERGREEN AND WHAT TO DO WITH THE STAR METAL.
I think I might know a way.

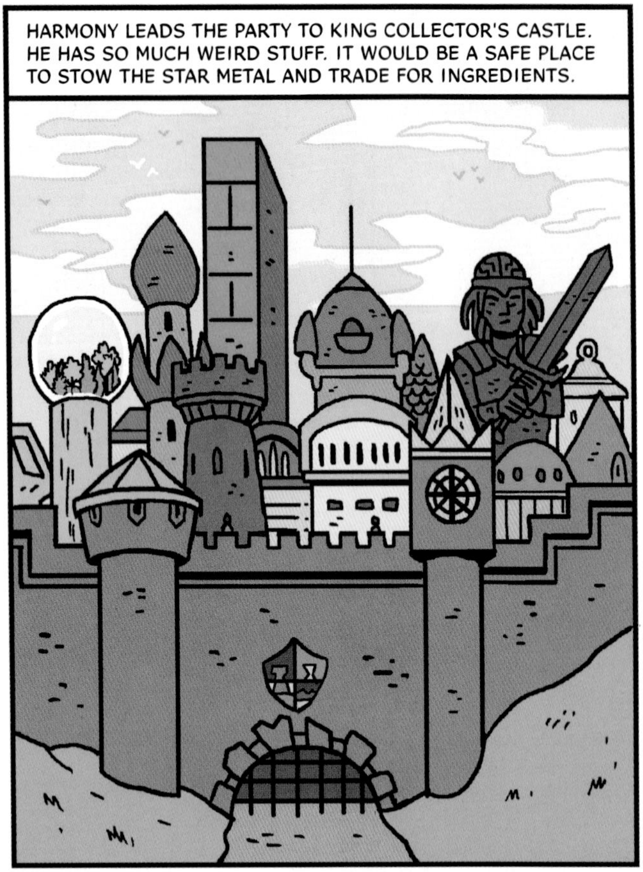
HARMONY LEADS THE PARTY TO KING COLLECTOR'S CASTLE. HE HAS SO MUCH WEIRD STUFF. IT WOULD BE A SAFE PLACE TO STOW THE STAR METAL AND TRADE FOR INGREDIENTS.

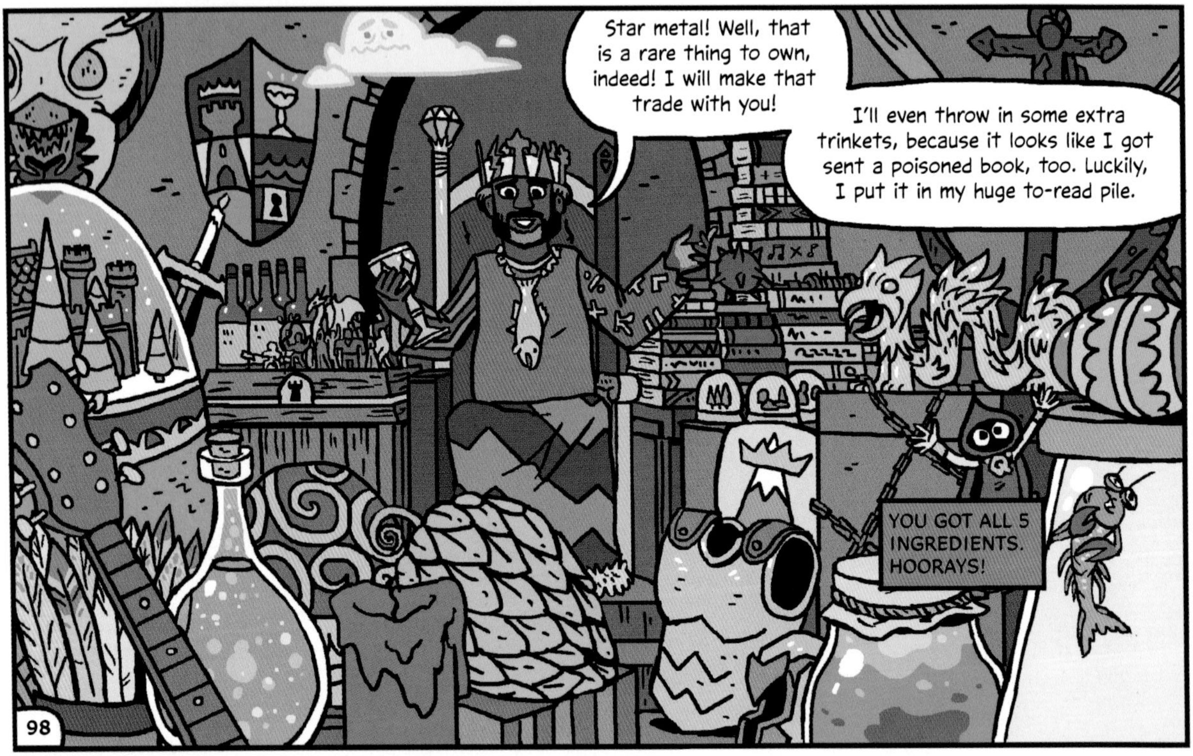
Star metal! Well, that is a rare thing to own, indeed! I will make that trade with you!
I'll even throw in some extra trinkets, because it looks like I got sent a poisoned book, too. Luckily, I put it in my huge to-read pile.
YOU GOT ALL 5 INGREDIENTS. HOORAYS!

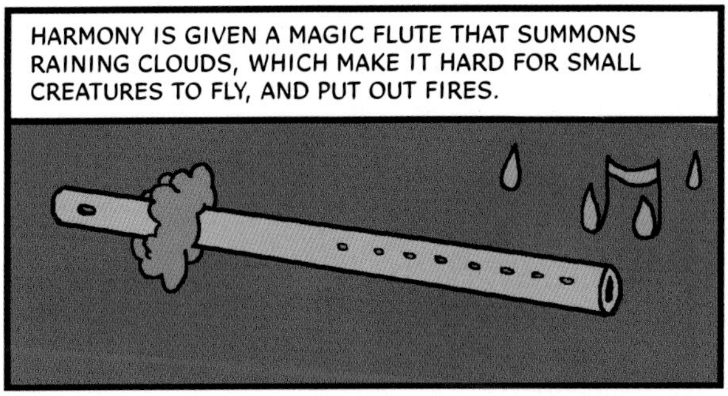
HARMONY IS GIVEN A MAGIC FLUTE THAT SUMMONS RAINING CLOUDS, WHICH MAKE IT HARD FOR SMALL CREATURES TO FLY, AND PUT OUT FIRES.

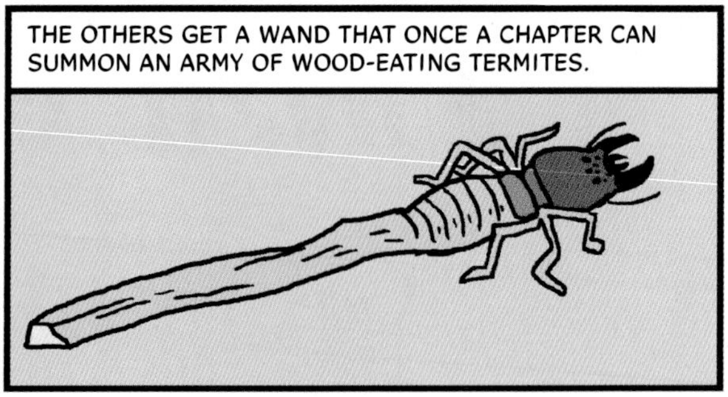
THE OTHERS GET A WAND THAT ONCE A CHAPTER CAN SUMMON AN ARMY OF WOOD-EATING TERMITES.

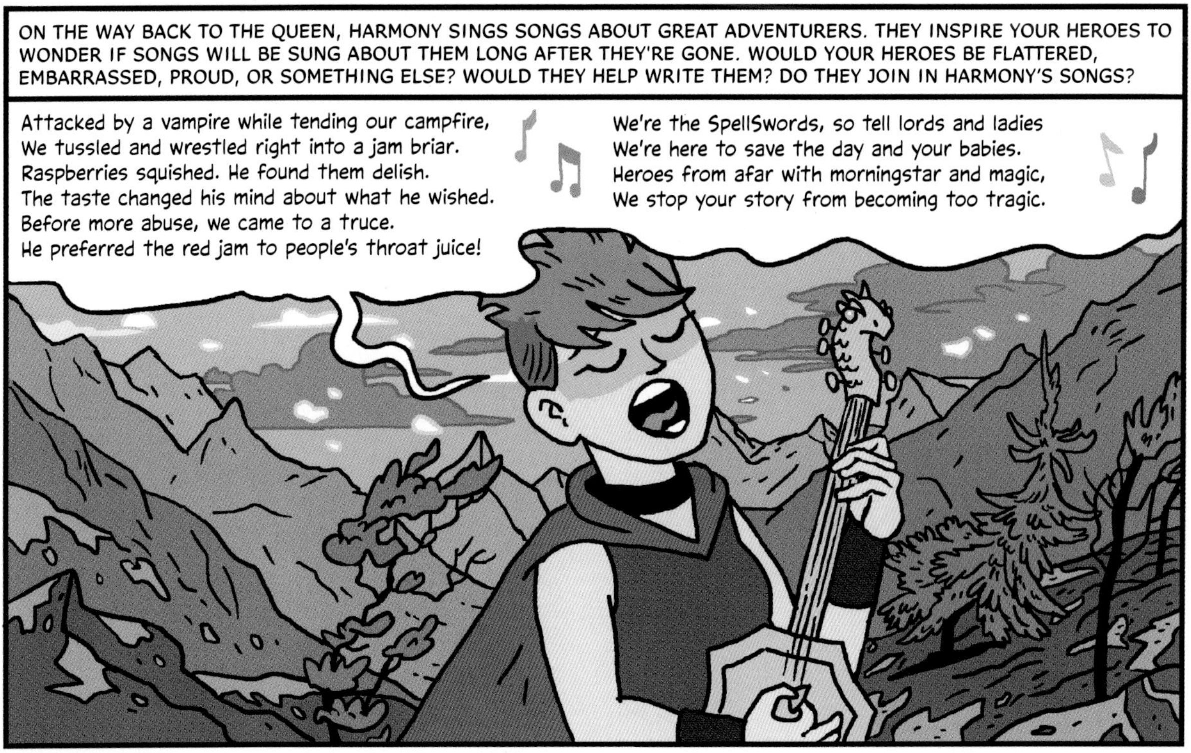
ON THE WAY BACK TO THE QUEEN, HARMONY SINGS SONGS ABOUT GREAT ADVENTURERS. THEY INSPIRE YOUR HEROES TO WONDER IF SONGS WILL BE SUNG ABOUT THEM LONG AFTER THEY'RE GONE. WOULD YOUR HEROES BE FLATTERED, EMBARRASSED, PROUD, OR SOMETHING ELSE? WOULD THEY HELP WRITE THEM? DO THEY JOIN IN HARMONY'S SONGS?
Attacked by a vampire while tending our campfire,
We tussled and wrestled right into a jam briar.
Raspberries squished. He found them delish.
The taste changed his mind about what he wished.
Before more abuse, we came to a truce.
He preferred the red jam to people's throat juice!
We're the SpellSwords, so tell lords and ladies
We're here to save the day and your babies.
Heroes from afar with morningstar and magic,
We stop your story from becoming too tragic.

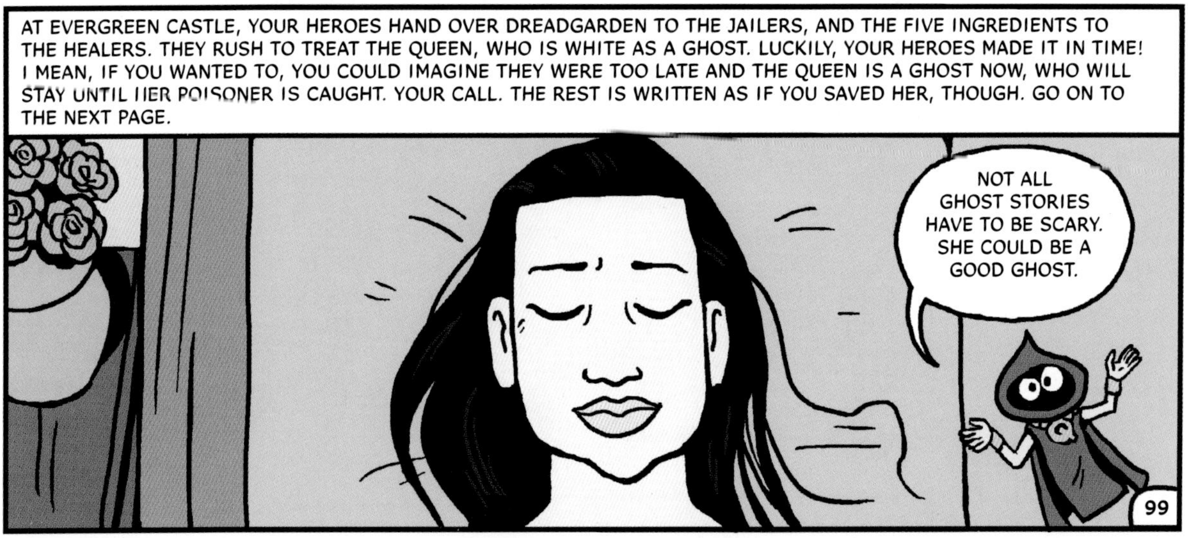
AT EVERGREEN CASTLE, YOUR HEROES HAND OVER DREADGARDEN TO THE JAILERS, AND THE FIVE INGREDIENTS TO THE HEALERS. THEY RUSH TO TREAT THE QUEEN, WHO IS WHITE AS A GHOST. LUCKILY, YOUR HEROES MADE IT IN TIME! I MEAN, IF YOU WANTED TO, YOU COULD IMAGINE THEY WERE TOO LATE AND THE QUEEN IS A GHOST NOW, WHO WILL STAY UNTIL HER POISONER IS CAUGHT. YOUR CALL. THE REST IS WRITTEN AS IF YOU SAVED HER, THOUGH. GO ON TO THE NEXT PAGE.
NOT ALL GHOST STORIES HAVE TO BE SCARY. SHE COULD BE A GOOD GHOST.

FINAL CHAPTER

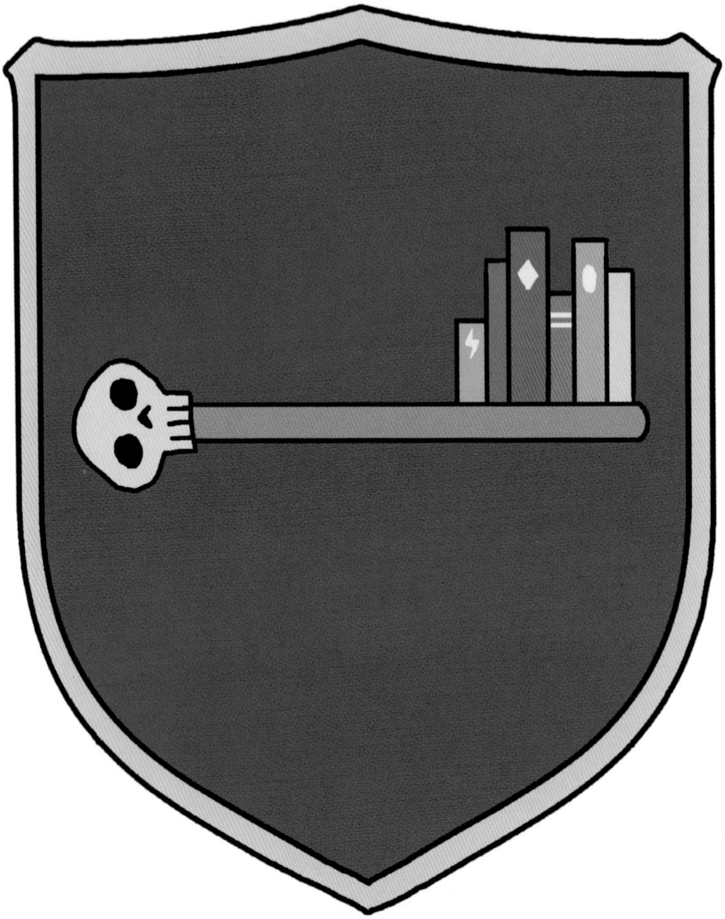

LIES BURIED IN THE LIBRARY

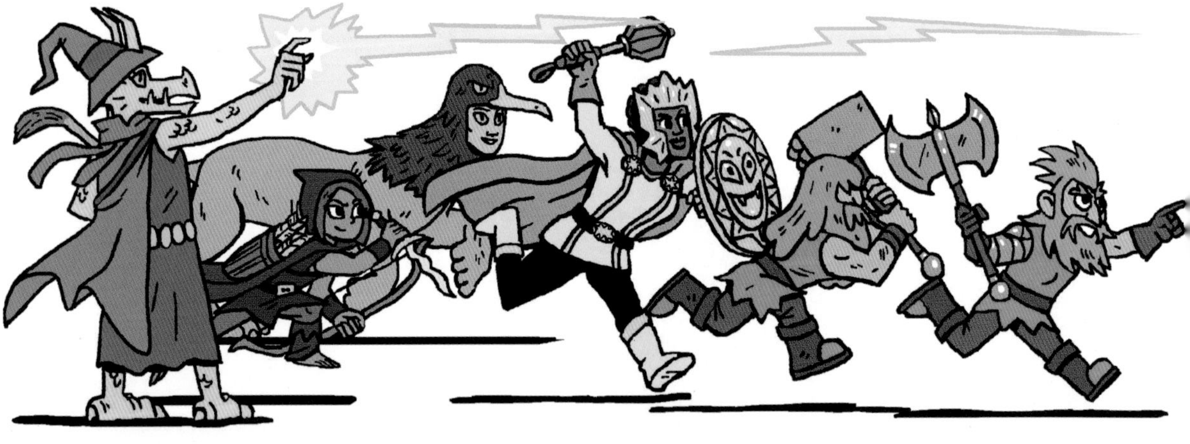

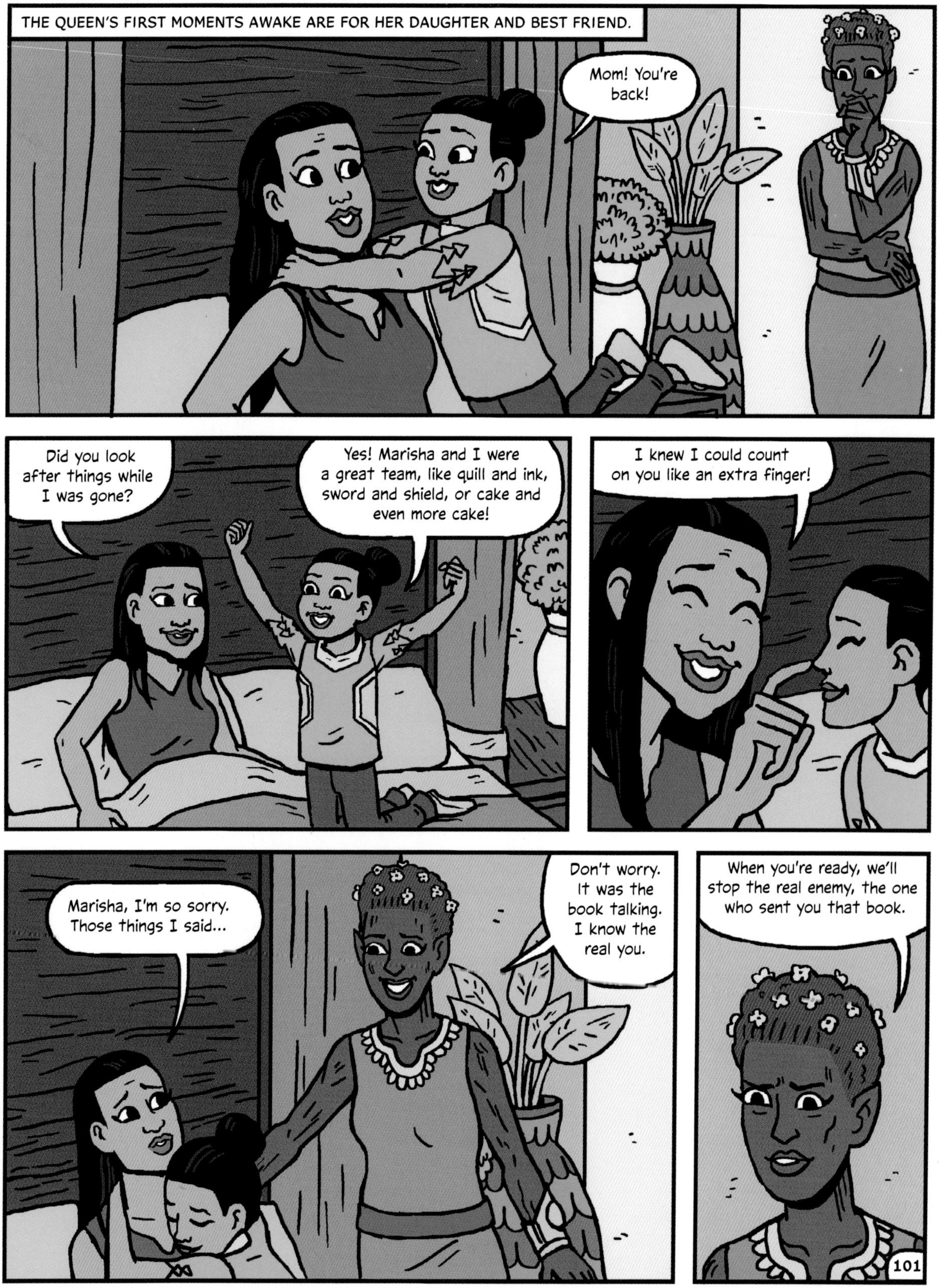
THE QUEEN'S FIRST MOMENTS AWAKE ARE FOR HER DAUGHTER AND BEST FRIEND.
Mom! You're back!
Did you look after things while I was gone?
Yes! Marisha and I were a great team, like quill and ink, sword and shield, or cake and even more cake!
I knew I could count on you like an extra finger!
Marisha, I'm so sorry. Those things I said...
Don't worry. It was the book talking. I know the real you.
When you're ready, we'll stop the real enemy, the one who sent you that book.

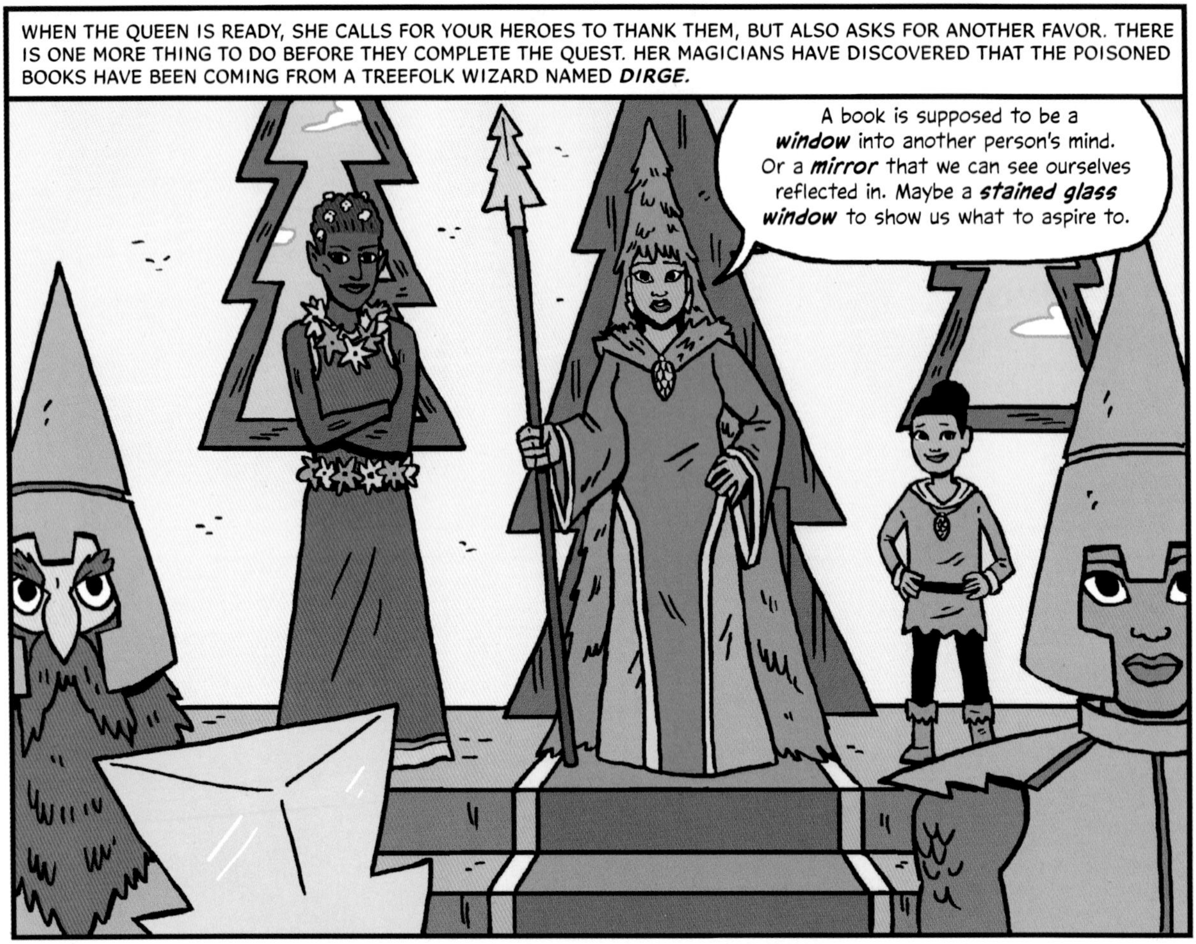
WHEN THE QUEEN IS READY, SHE CALLS FOR YOUR HEROES TO THANK THEM, BUT ALSO ASKS FOR ANOTHER FAVOR. THERE IS ONE MORE THING TO DO BEFORE THEY COMPLETE THE QUEST. HER MAGICIANS HAVE DISCOVERED THAT THE POISONED BOOKS HAVE BEEN COMING FROM A TREEFOLK WIZARD NAMED ***DIRGE.***
A book is supposed to be a ***window*** into another person's mind. Or a ***mirror*** that we can see ourselves reflected in. Maybe a ***stained glass window*** to show us what to aspire to.

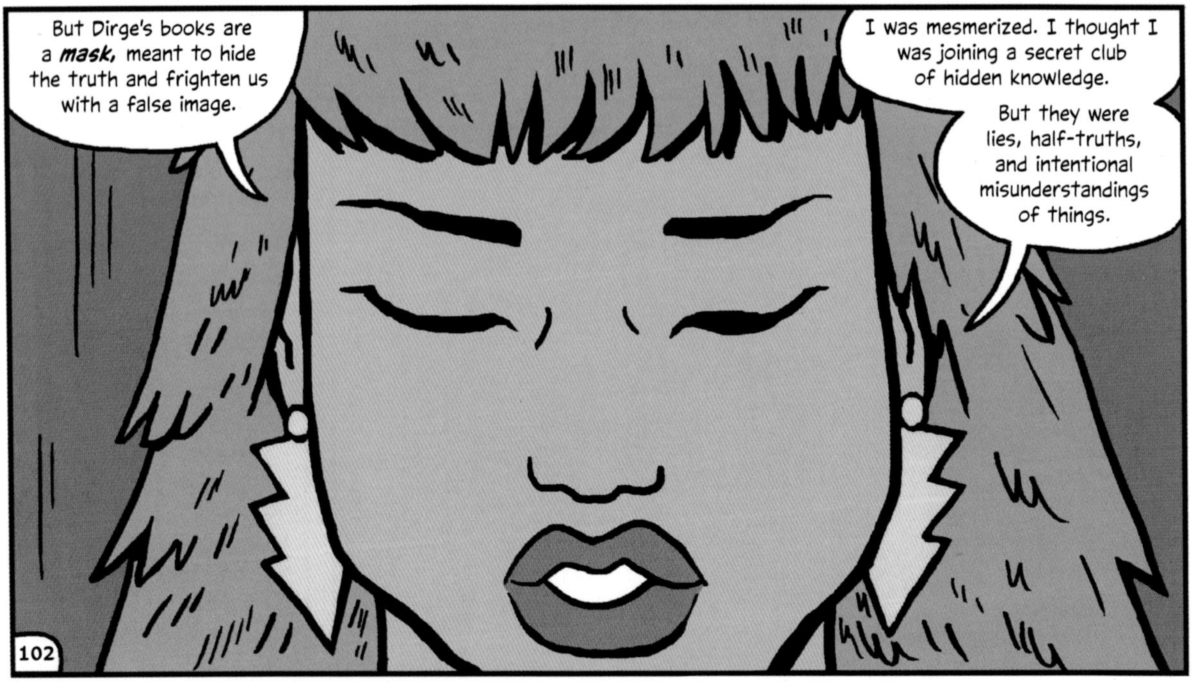
But Dirge's books are a ***mask,*** meant to hide the truth and frighten us with a false image.
I was mesmerized. I thought I was joining a secret club of hidden knowledge.
But they were lies, half-truths, and intentional misunderstandings of things.

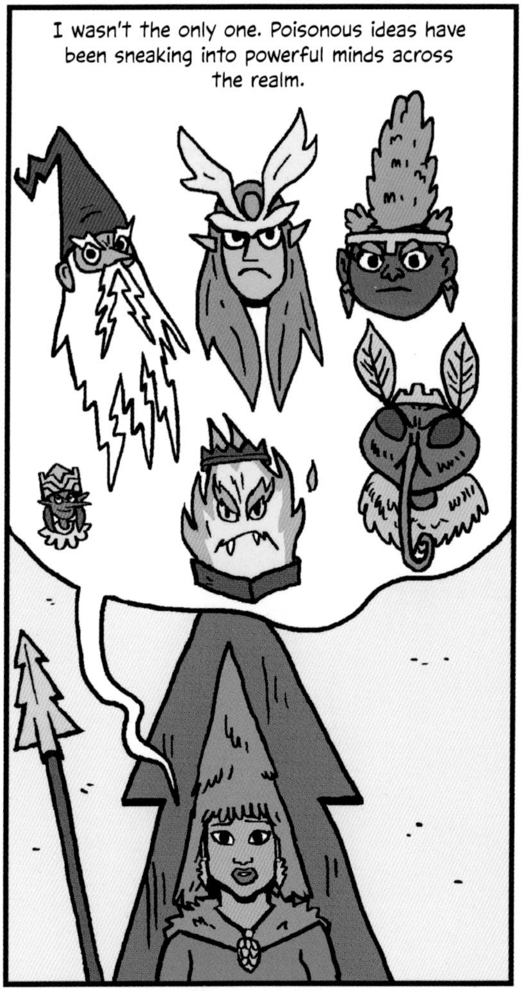
I wasn't the only one. Poisonous ideas have been sneaking into powerful minds across the realm.

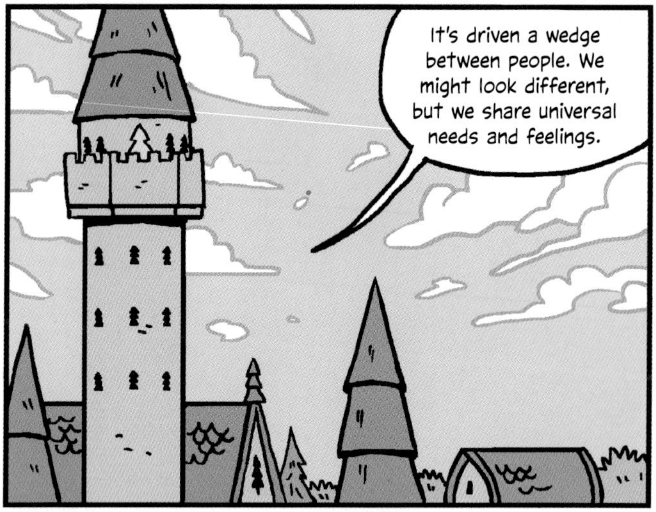
It's driven a wedge between people. We might look different, but we share universal needs and feelings.

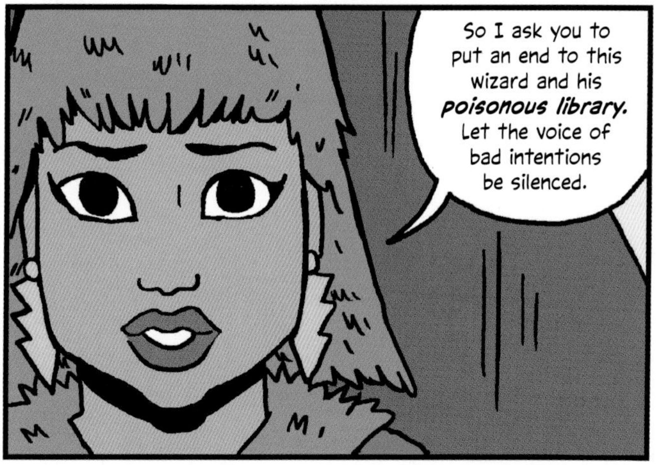
So I ask you to put an end to this wizard and his ***poisonous library.*** Let the voice of bad intentions be silenced.

THE QUEEN'S GUARDS ESCORT YOUR HEROES (INCLUDING ANY ALLIES YOU MAY HAVE) DEEP INTO THE ***BLOODBARK FOREST,*** WHERE THE POISONER HAS HIDDEN HIMSELF AWAY. ONE OR MORE OF YOUR HEROES MAY NOT MAKE IT BACK ALIVE. WHAT ARE THEY SAYING TO EACH OTHER AS THEY WALK THE WINDING TRAILS TO FACE THEIR GREATEST FOE?

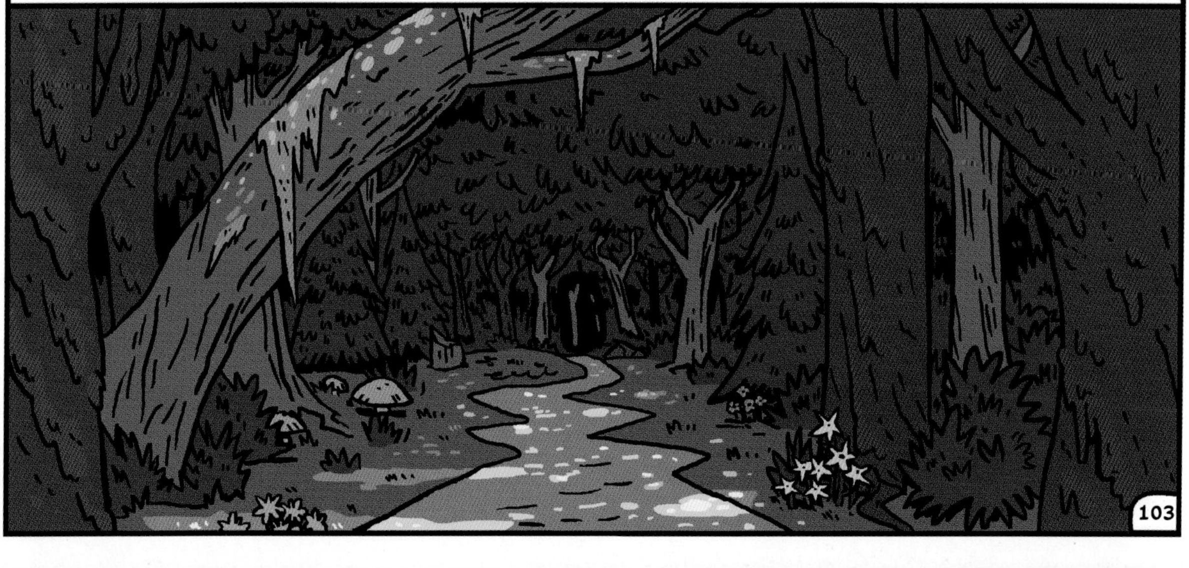

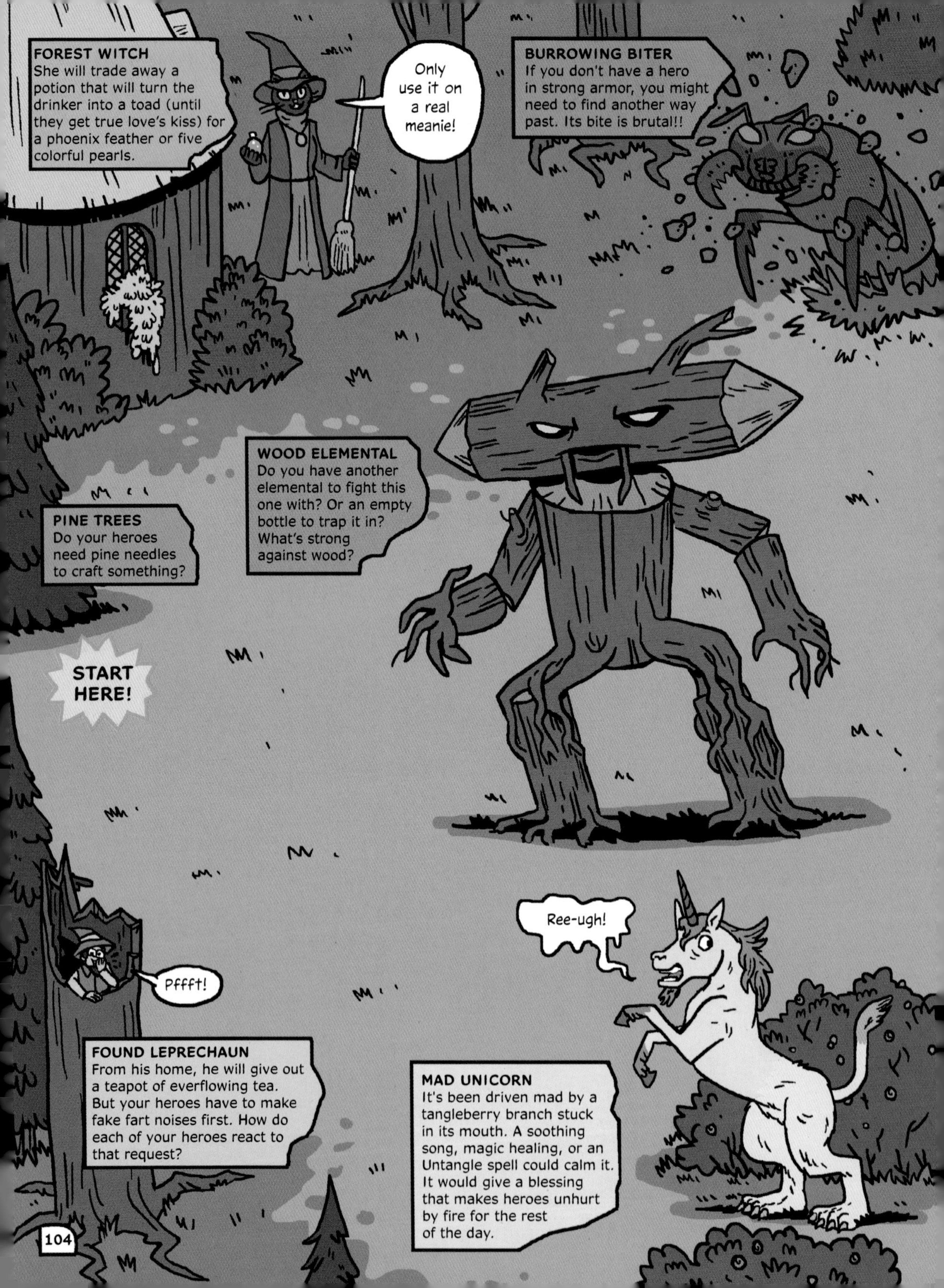
FOREST WITCH
She will trade away a potion that will turn the drinker into a toad (until they get true love's kiss) for a phoenix feather or five colorful pearls.
Only use it on a real meanie!
BURROWING BITER
If you don't have a hero in strong armor, you might need to find another way past. Its bite is brutal!!
WOOD ELEMENTAL
Do you have another elemental to fight this one with? Or an empty bottle to trap it in? What's strong against wood?
PINE TREES
Do your heroes need pine needles to craft something?
START HERE!
Pffft!
FOUND LEPRECHAUN
From his home, he will give out a teapot of everflowing tea. But your heroes have to make fake fart noises first. How do each of your heroes react to that request?
Ree-ugh!
MAD UNICORN
It's been driven mad by a tangleberry branch stuck in its mouth. A soothing song, magic healing, or an Untangle spell could calm it. It would give a blessing that makes heroes unhurt by fire for the rest of the day.

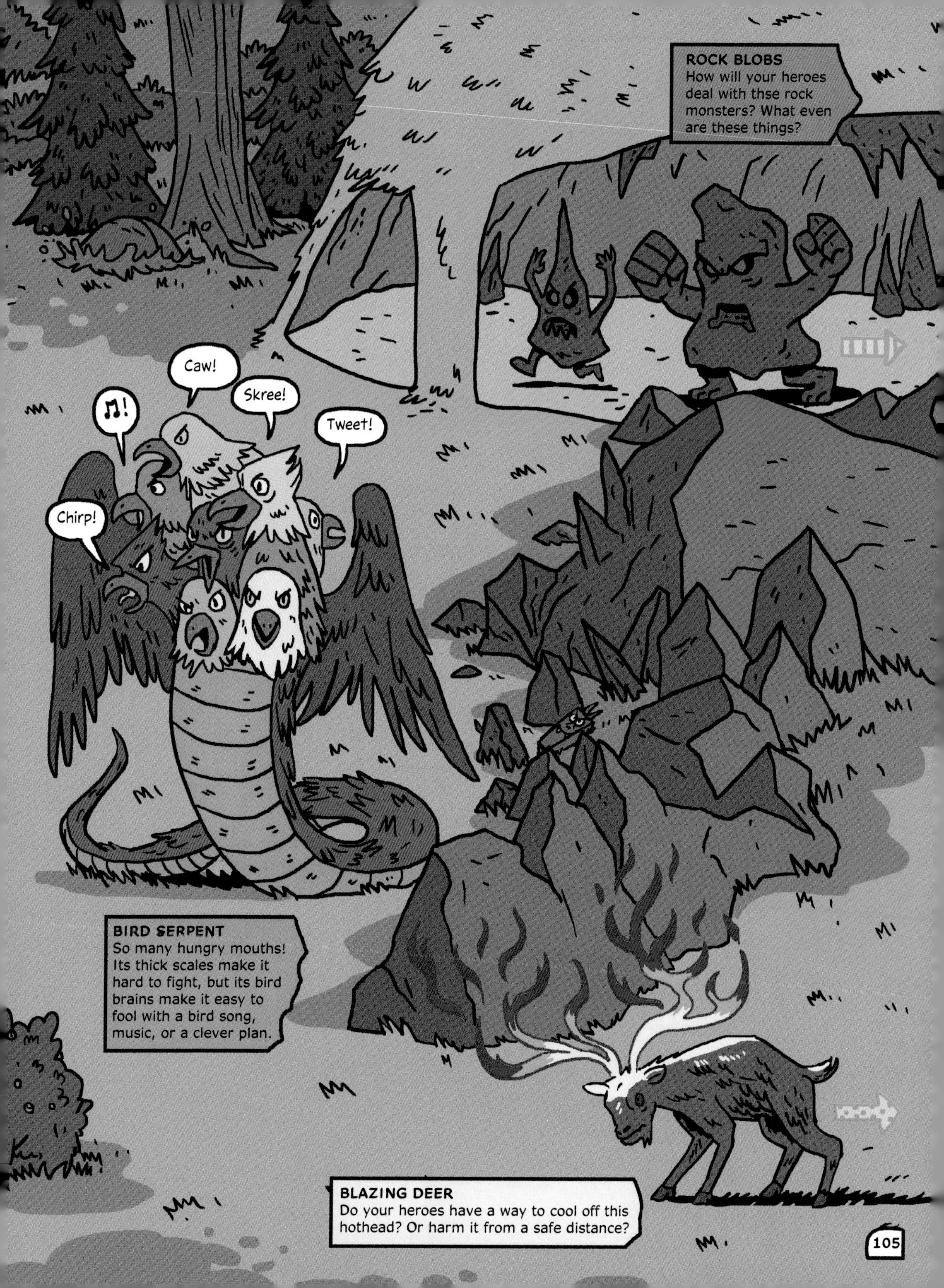
ROCK BLOBS
How will your heroes deal with thse rock monsters? What even are these things?
♫!
Caw!
Skree!
Tweet!
Chirp!
BIRD SERPENT
So many hungry mouths! Its thick scales make it hard to fight, but its bird brains make it easy to fool with a bird song, music, or a clever plan.
BLAZING DEER
Do your heroes have a way to cool off this hothead? Or harm it from a safe distance?

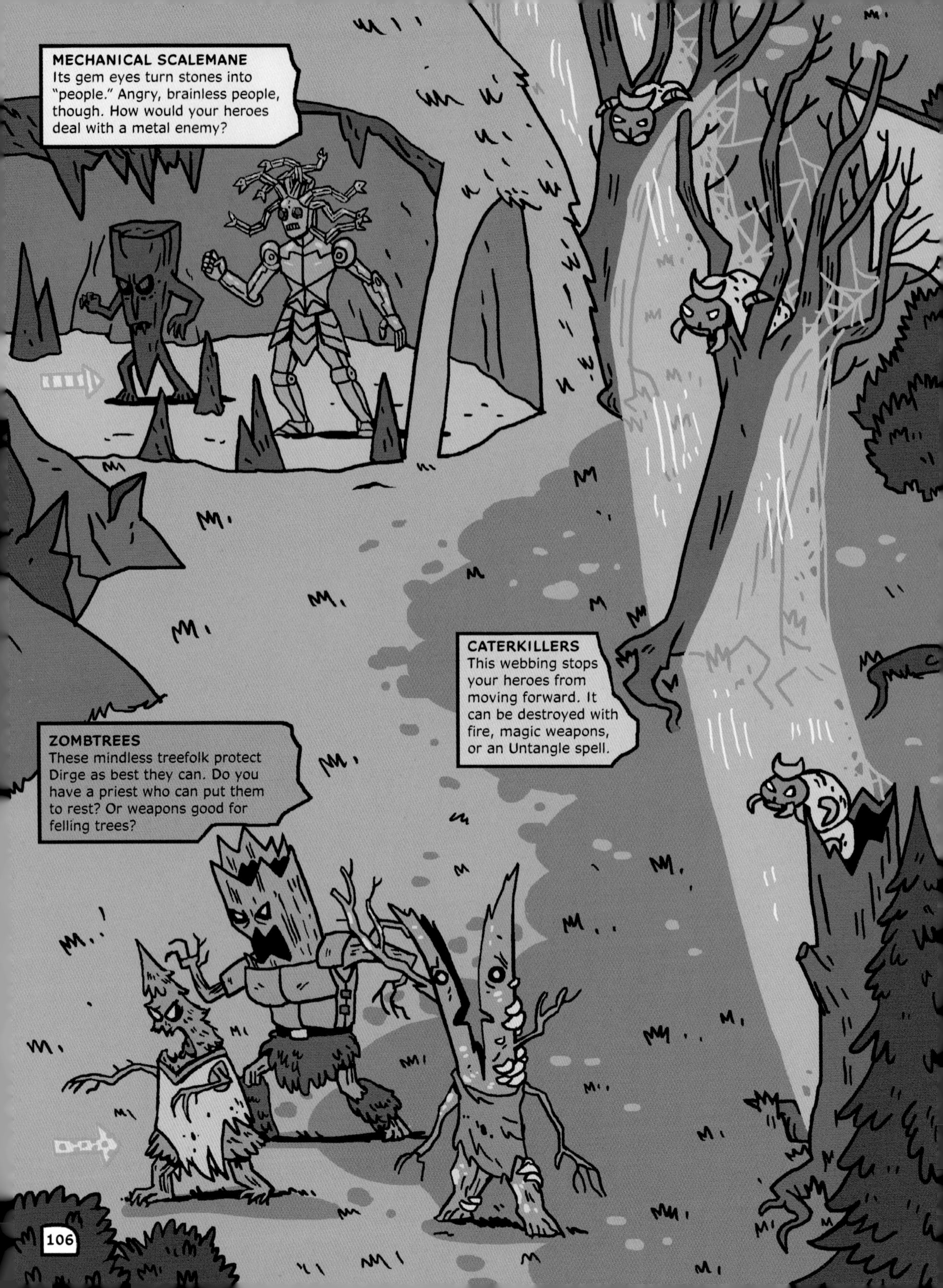
MECHANICAL SCALEMANE
Its gem eyes turn stones into "people." Angry, brainless people, though. How would your heroes deal with a metal enemy?
CATERKILLERS
This webbing stops your heroes from moving forward. It can be destroyed with fire, magic weapons, or an Untangle spell.
ZOMBTREES
These mindless treefolk protect Dirge as best they can. Do you have a priest who can put them to rest? Or weapons good for felling trees?

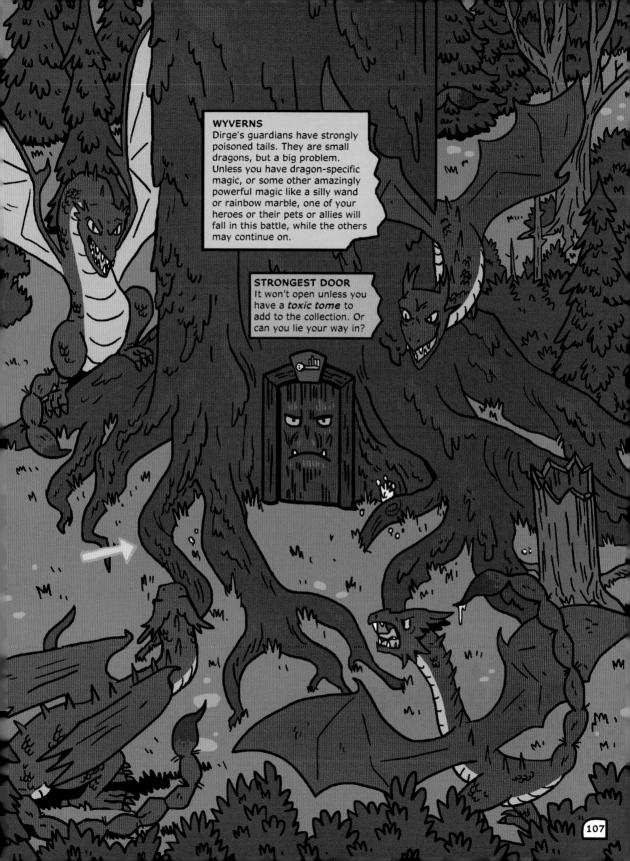

WYVERNS
Dirge's guardians have strongly poisoned tails. They are small dragons, but a big problem. Unless you have dragon-specific magic, or some other amazingly powerful magic like a silly wand or rainbow marble, one of your heroes or their pets or allies will fall in this battle, while the others may continue on.

STRONGEST DOOR
It won't open unless you have a *toxic tome* to add to the collection. Or can you lie your way in?

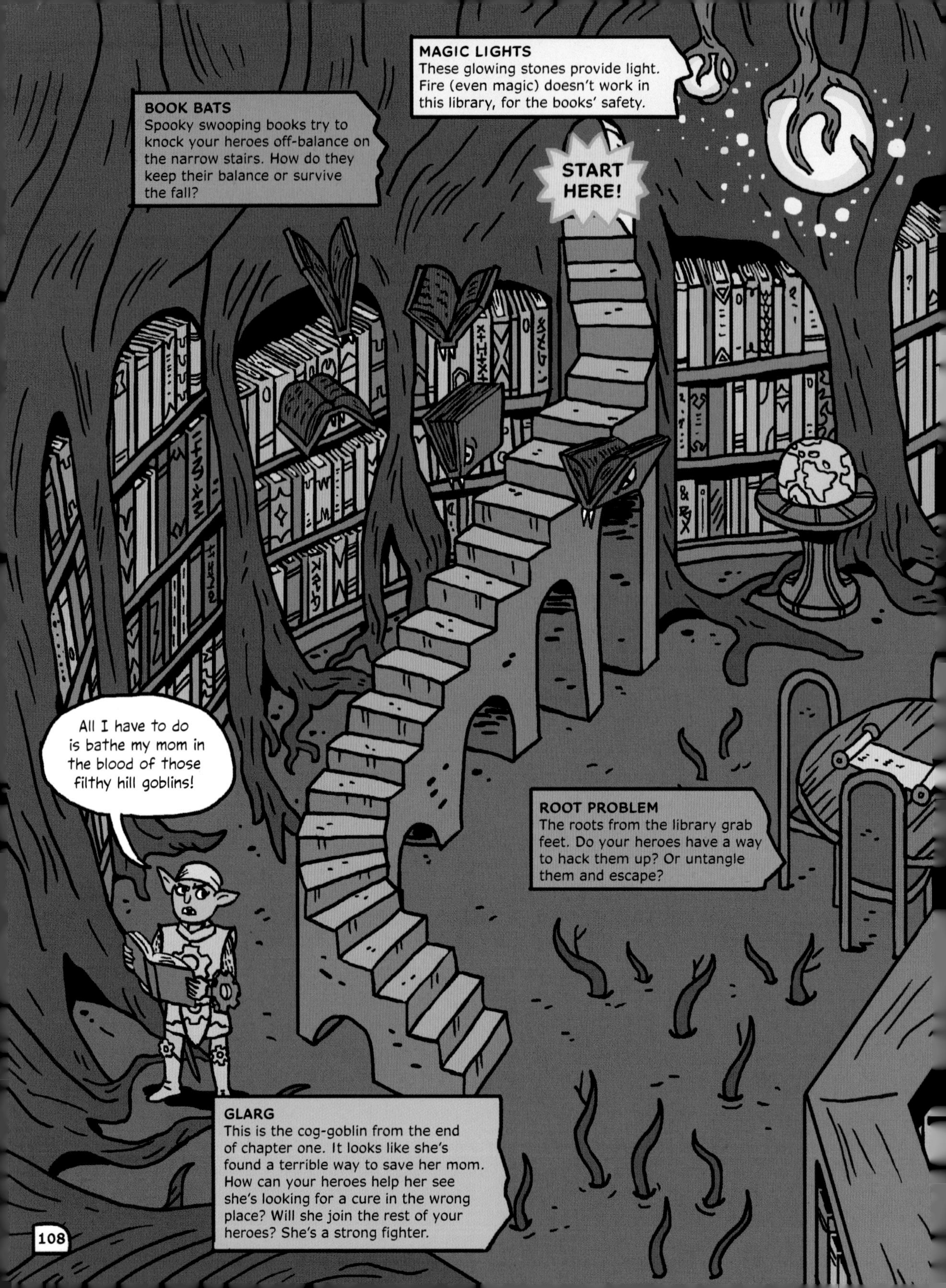

MAGIC LIGHTS
These glowing stones provide light. Fire (even magic) doesn't work in this library, for the books' safety.
BOOK BATS
Spooky swooping books try to knock your heroes off-balance on the narrow stairs. How do they keep their balance or survive the fall?
START HERE!
All I have to do is bathe my mom in the blood of those filthy hill goblins!
ROOT PROBLEM
The roots from the library grab feet. Do your heroes have a way to hack them up? Or untangle them and escape?
GLARG
This is the cog-goblin from the end of chapter one. It looks like she's found a terrible way to save her mom. How can your heroes help her see she's looking for a cure in the wrong place? Will she join the rest of your heroes? She's a strong fighter.

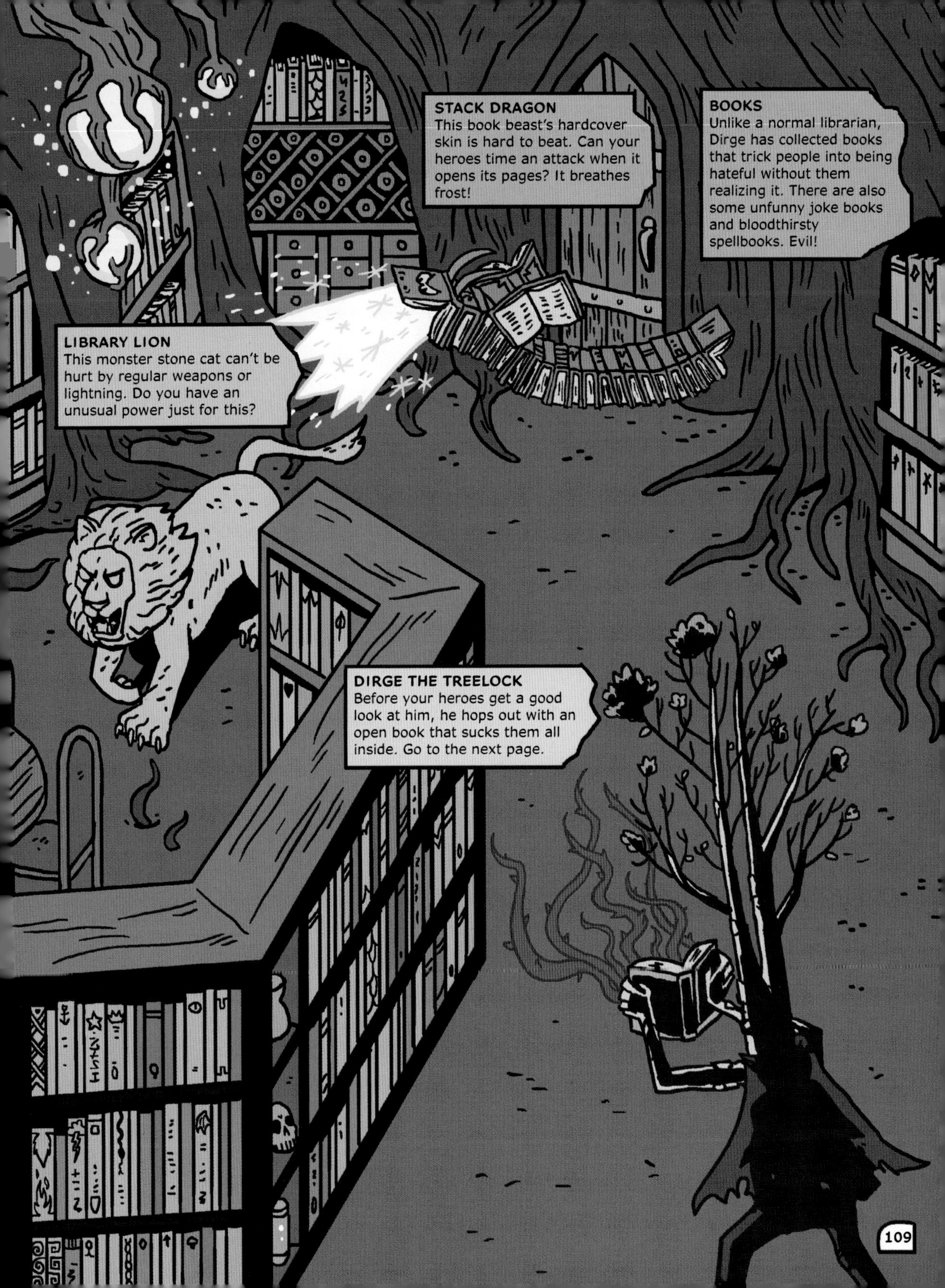
STACK DRAGON
This book beast's hardcover skin is hard to beat. Can your heroes time an attack when it opens its pages? It breathes frost!
BOOKS
Unlike a normal librarian, Dirge has collected books that trick people into being hateful without them realizing it. There are also some unfunny joke books and bloodthirsty spellbooks. Evil!
LIBRARY LION
This monster stone cat can't be hurt by regular weapons or lightning. Do you have an unusual power just for this?
DIRGE THE TREELOCK
Before your heroes get a good look at him, he hops out with an open book that sucks them all inside. Go to the next page.

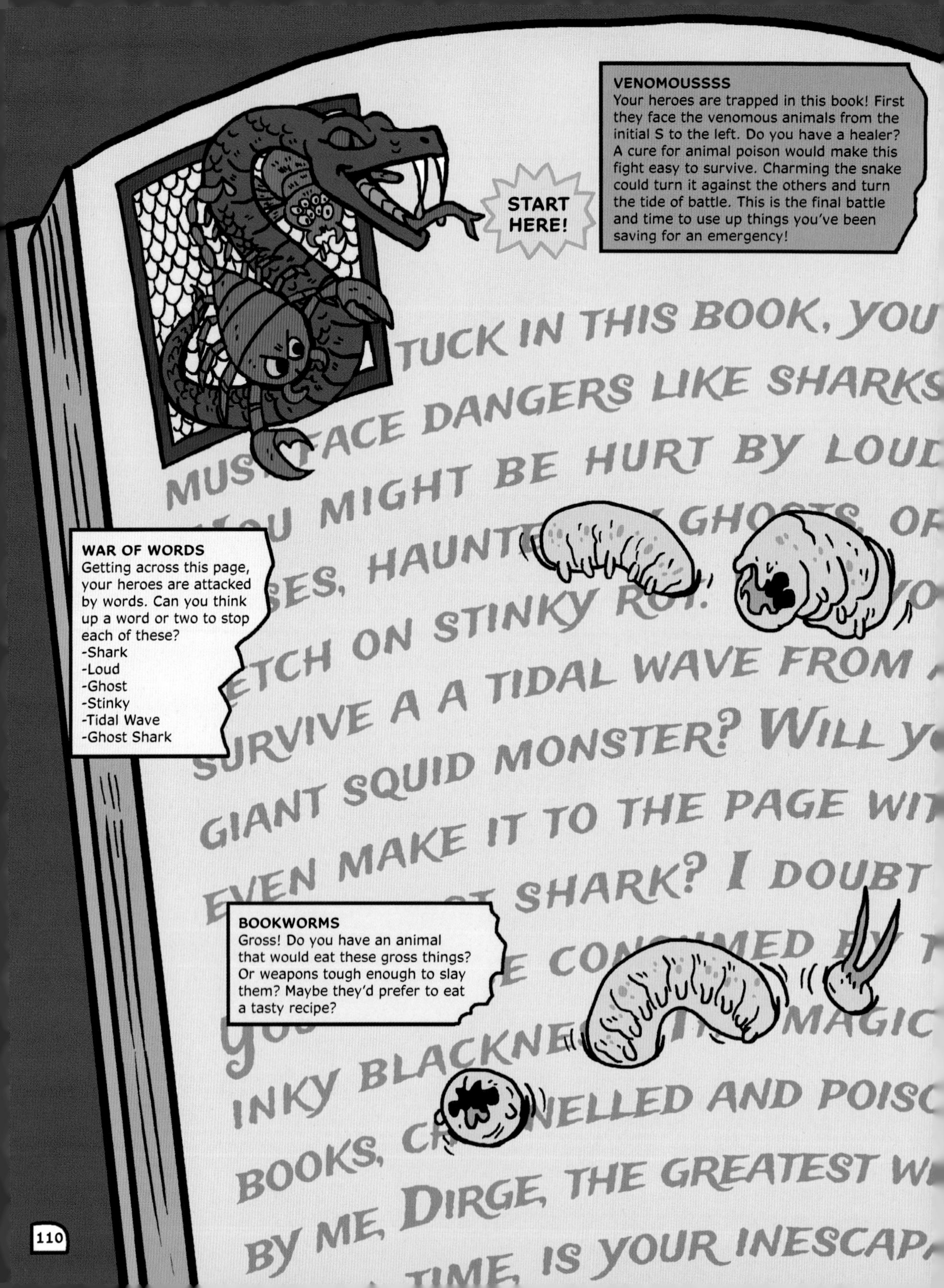
START HERE!
TUCK IN THIS BOOK, YOU
MUS FACE DANGERS LIKE SHARKS
OU MIGHT BE HURT BY LOU
SES, HAUNT GHO OF
ETCH ON STINKY RO
SURVIVE A A TIDAL WAVE FROM
GIANT SQUID MONSTER? WILL Y
EVEN MAKE IT TO THE PAGE WI
SHARK? I DOUBT
CO MED
MAGIC
INKY BLACKNE
BOOKS, C NELLED AND POIS
BY ME, DIRGE, THE GREATEST W
TIME, IS YOUR INESCAP

VENOMOUSSSS

Your heroes are trapped in this book! First they face the venomous animals from the initial S to the left. Do you have a healer? A cure for animal poison would make this fight easy to survive. Charming the snake could turn it against the others and turn the tide of battle. This is the final battle and time to use up things you've been saving for an emergency!

WAR OF WORDS

Getting across this page, your heroes are attacked by words. Can you think up a word or two to stop each of these?

- -Shark
- -Loud
- -Ghost
- -Stinky
- -Tidal Wave
- -Ghost Shark

BOOKWORMS

Gross! Do you have an animal that would eat these gross things? Or weapons tough enough to slay them? Maybe they'd prefer to eat a tasty recipe?

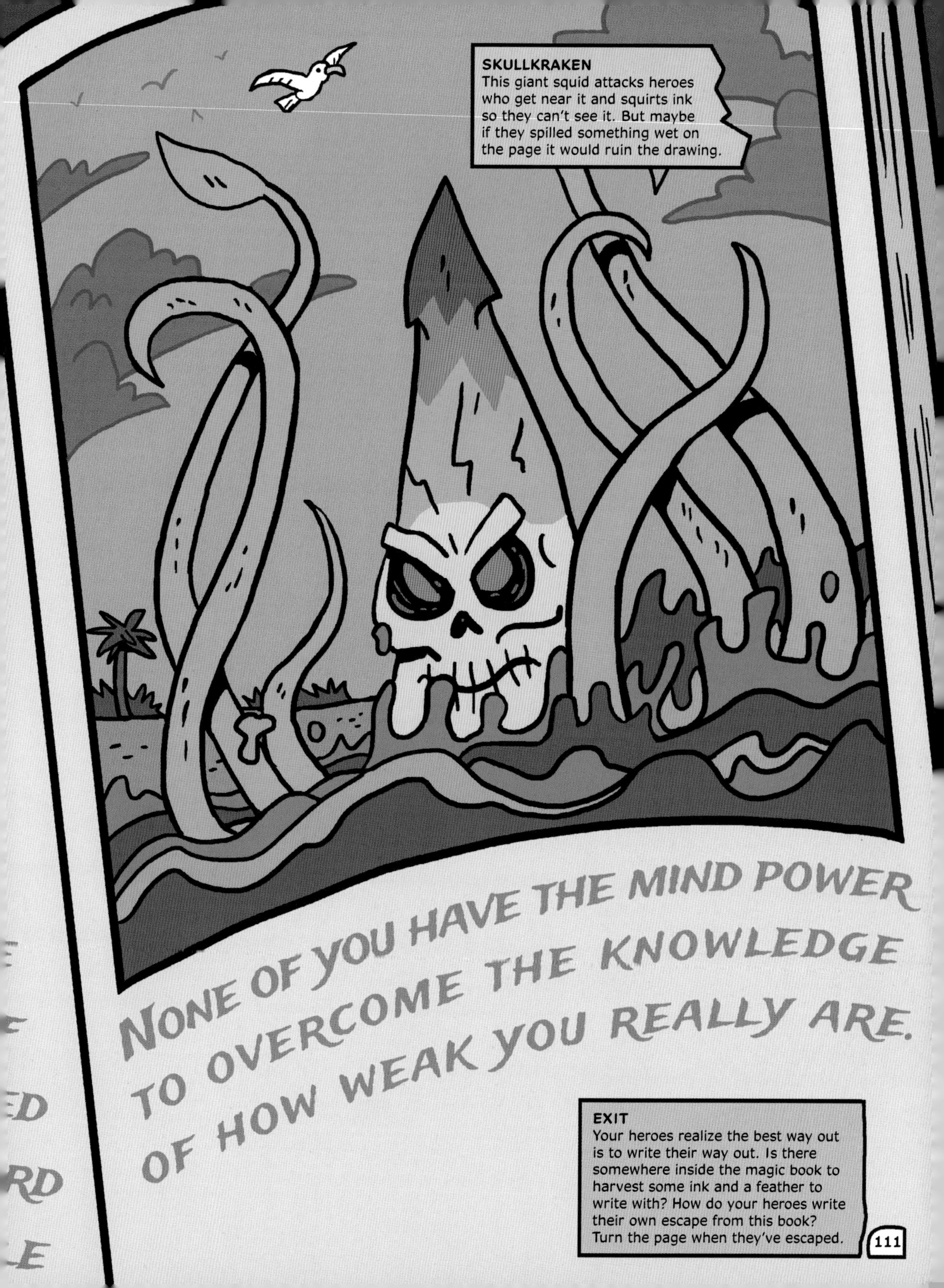
SKULLKRAKEN
This giant squid attacks heroes who get near it and squirts ink so they can't see it. But maybe if they spilled something wet on the page it would ruin the drawing.
NONE OF YOU HAVE THE MIND POWER TO OVERCOME THE KNOWLEDGE OF HOW WEAK YOU REALLY ARE.
EXIT
Your heroes realize the best way out is to write their way out. Is there somewhere inside the magic book to harvest some ink and a feather to write with? How do your heroes write their own escape from this book? Turn the page when they've escaped.

DIRGE

Your heroes are free from the book but now must face the treefolk wizard. What villain is worse than one who would use books for evil? In this big boss battle, Dirge attacks with long, sharp claws, cruelly chosen words, and magic spells that confuse the minds of your heroes.

Your heroes are ready for this, though. They must have some awesome powers, items, and allies to help them beat this wicked wizard.

How will they end it? Kill him? Capture him? Turn him to the good side and have him make up for his mistakes? What will your characters do? You decide how they win.

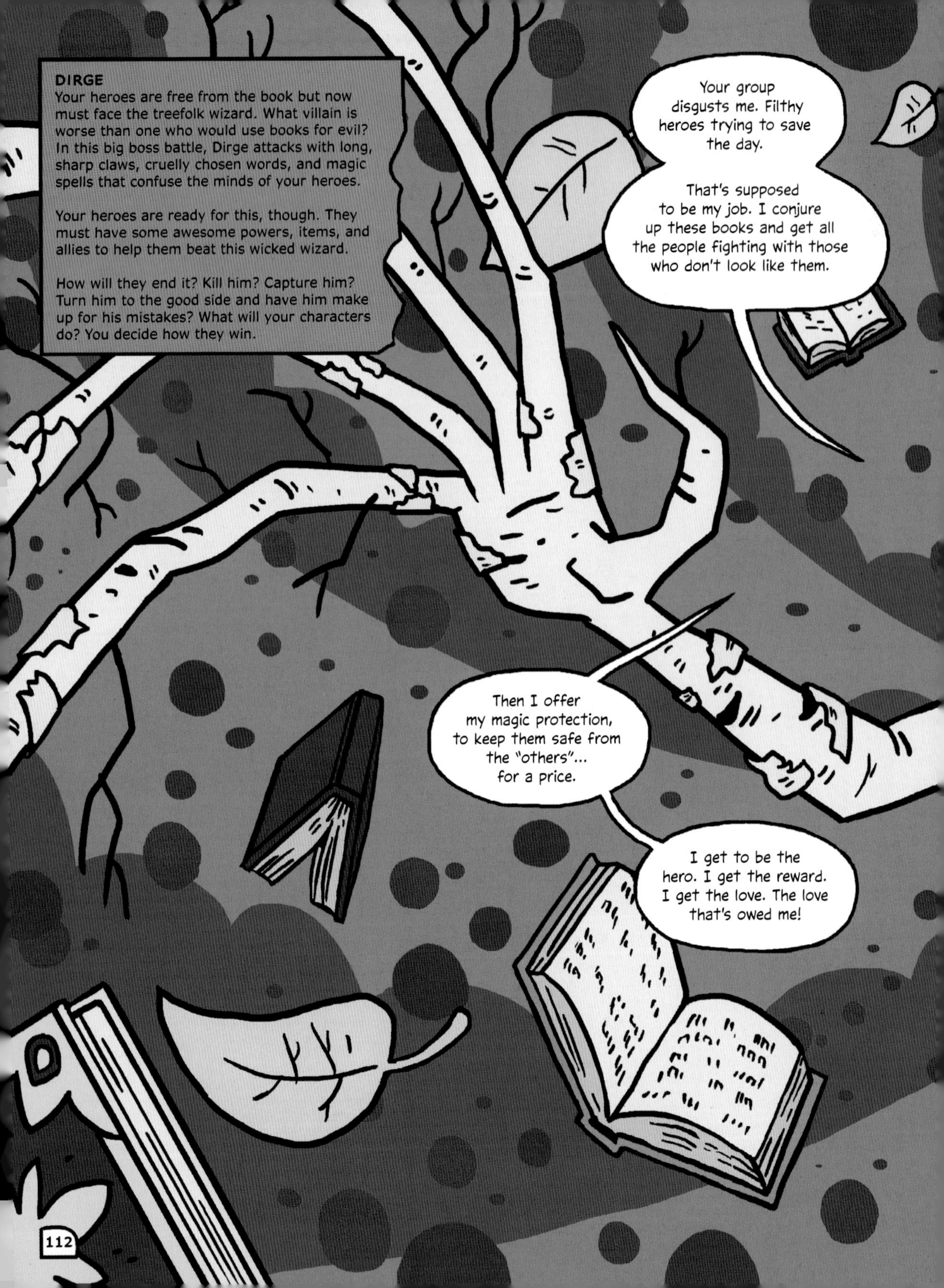
Your group disgusts me. Filthy heroes trying to save the day.
That's supposed to be my job. I conjure up these books and get all the people fighting with those who don't look like them.
Then I offer my magic protection, to keep them safe from the "others"... for a price.
I get to be the hero. I get the reward. I get the love. The love that's owed me!

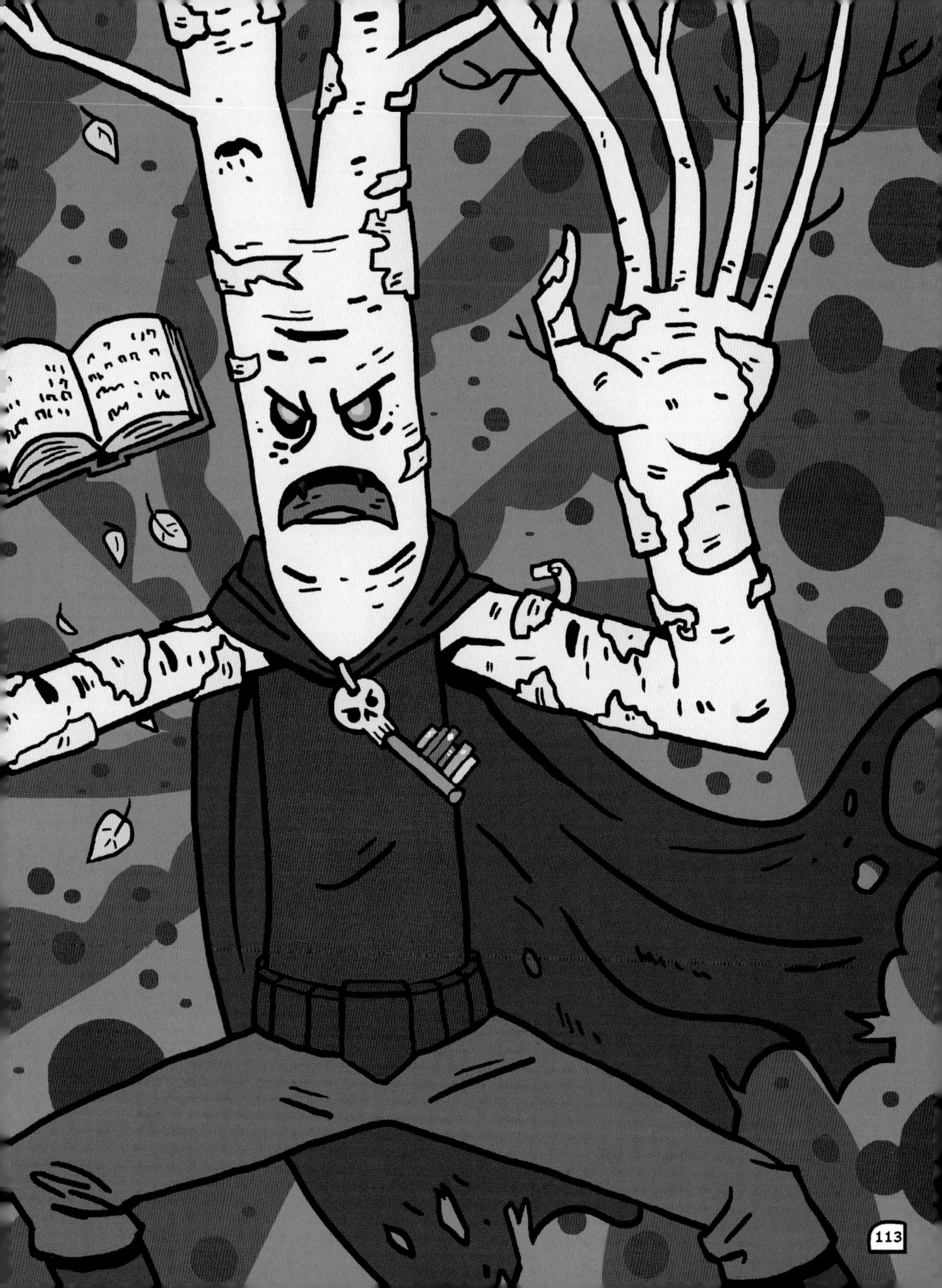

YES! YOUR HEROES DID IT! YOU ***COMPLETED THE QUEST!*** WITH DIRGE DONE FOR, YOUR HEROES CAN BURY THE BOOKS THAT SPREAD INTOLERANCE. WHEN YOUR GROUP RETURNS, QUEEN EVERGREEN IS OVERJOYED.

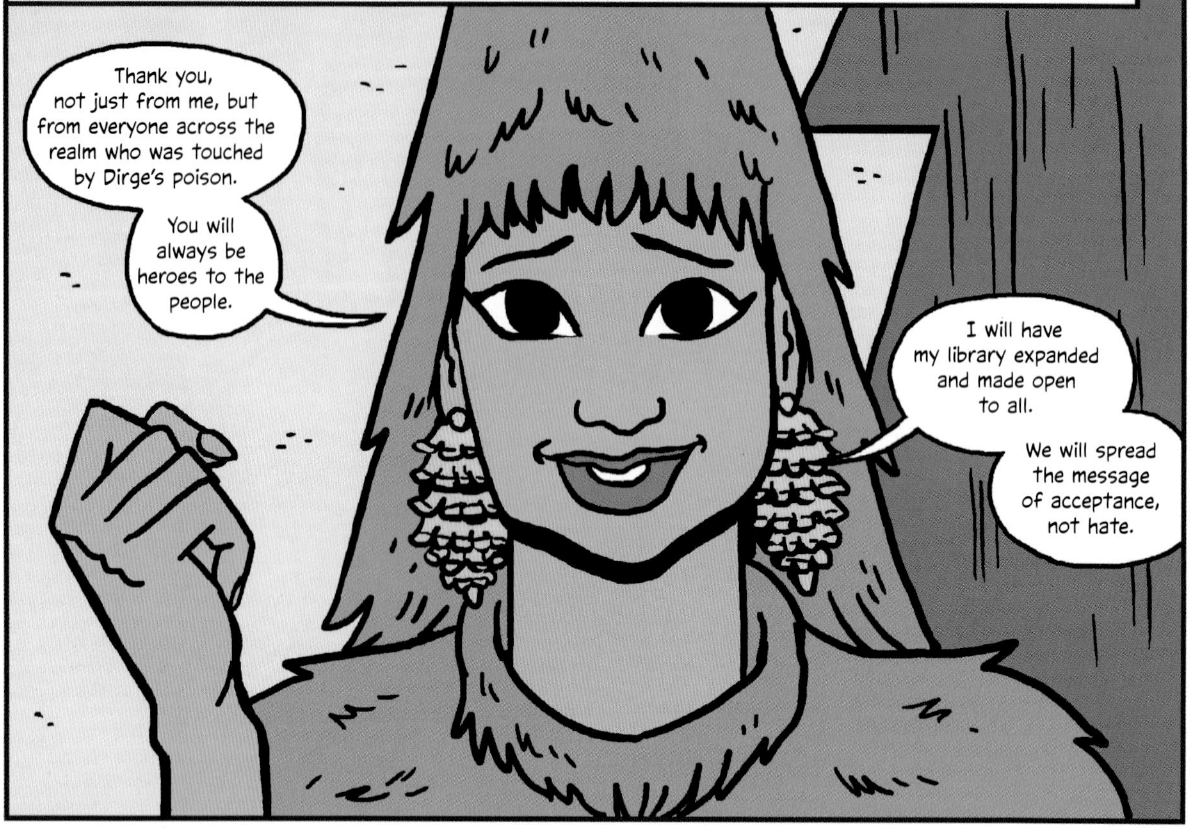
Thank you, not just from me, but from everyone across the realm who was touched by Dirge's poison.
You will always be heroes to the people.
I will have my library expanded and made open to all.
We will spread the message of acceptance, not hate.

TO SHOW THAT FLORIN AND KITH REALLY SHOULD BE EQUAL, THE QUEEN DECIDES THAT THERE WON'T BE ONE RULER OF THE QUEENDOM, BUT ***TWO EQUAL LEADERS,*** HER AND MARISHA. ONE KITH AND ONE FLORIN, NOW AND FOREVERMORE.

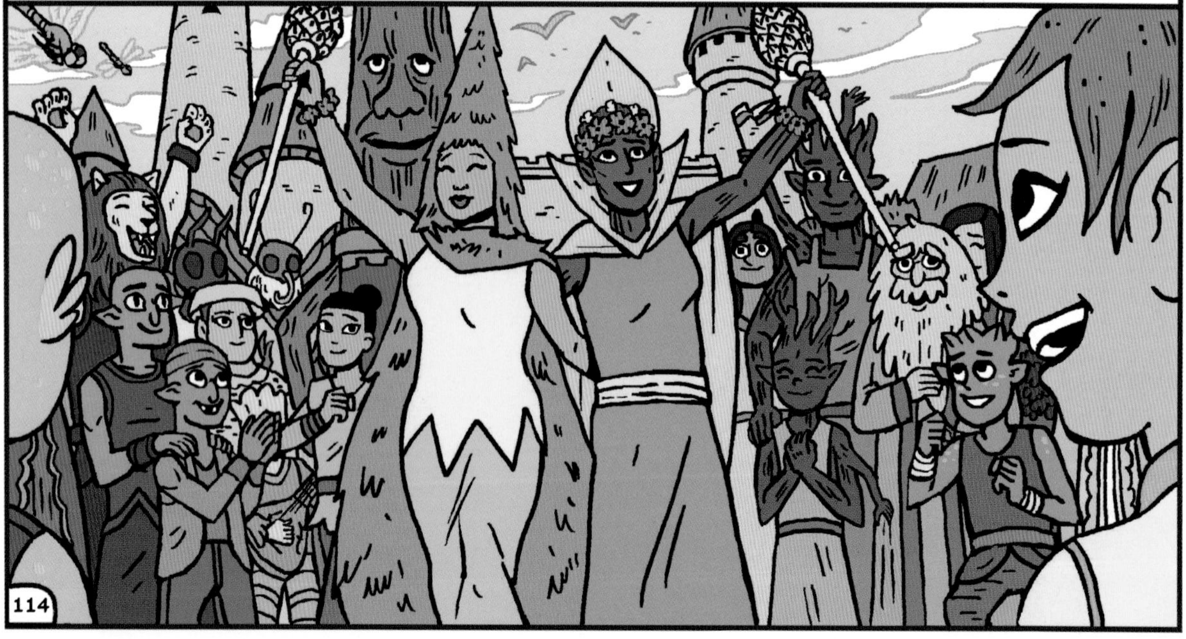

YOUR HEROES ARE OFFERED A ***REWARD.*** WHAT WILL EACH OF THEM ASK FOR? THEY MIGHT CHOOSE GOLD, MAGIC, KNOWLEDGE, A ROYAL TITLE, A FAVOR, OR WHATEVER YOU THINK THE QUEENS WOULD HAVE TO OFFER. IF YOU GAVE YOUR CHARACTERS ***PERSONAL STAKES,*** HAVE THEY GOTTEN WHAT THEY NEEDED YET? WHAT WOULD THEY ASK FOR?

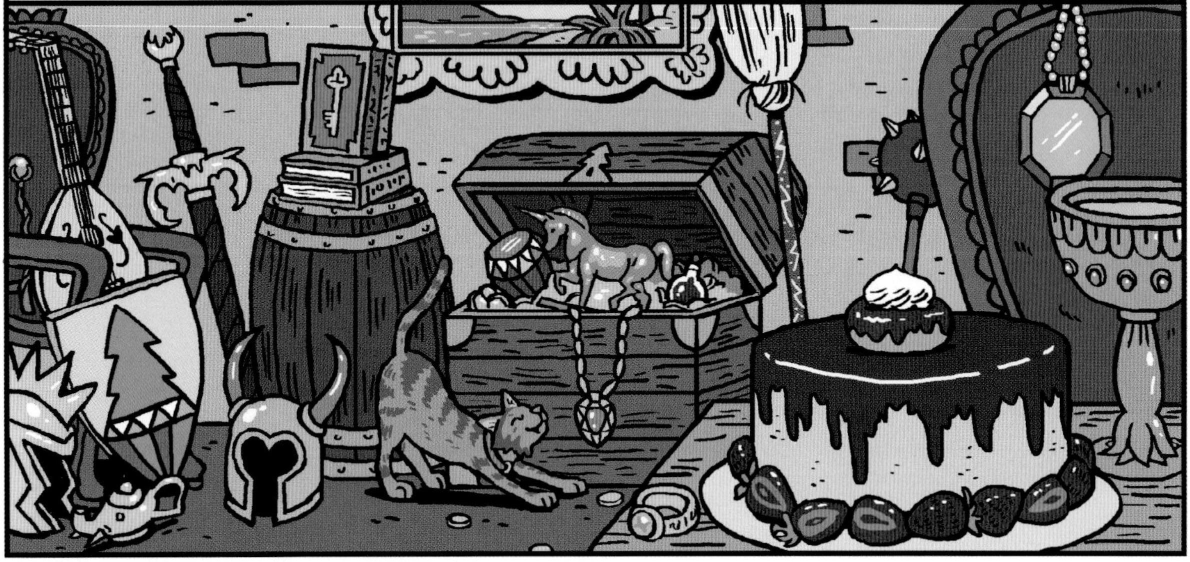

WITH THE MAIN PROBLEM SOLVED, THIS STORY IS OVER. BUT THAT DOESN'T MEAN THERE AREN'T SOME UNANSWERED QUESTIONS. THOSE ***LOOSE ENDS*** OFTEN GIVE US A CLUE AS TO WHERE THE MAIN CHARACTERS HEAD AFTER THE BOOK CLOSES. DO YOUR HEROES WANT TO HELP GLARG FIND A CURE FOR HER MOM BEING TURNED TO STONE? IS THERE AN ALIEN INVASION THEY WANT TO GO HELP STOP? MAYBE ANOTHER ONE OF DIRGE'S BOOKS IS STILL OUT THERE CAUSING TROUBLE. AS YOUR HEROES HEAD OFF INTO THE SUNSET, DO THEY GO ALONE OR TOGETHER, CLOSER THAN EVER?

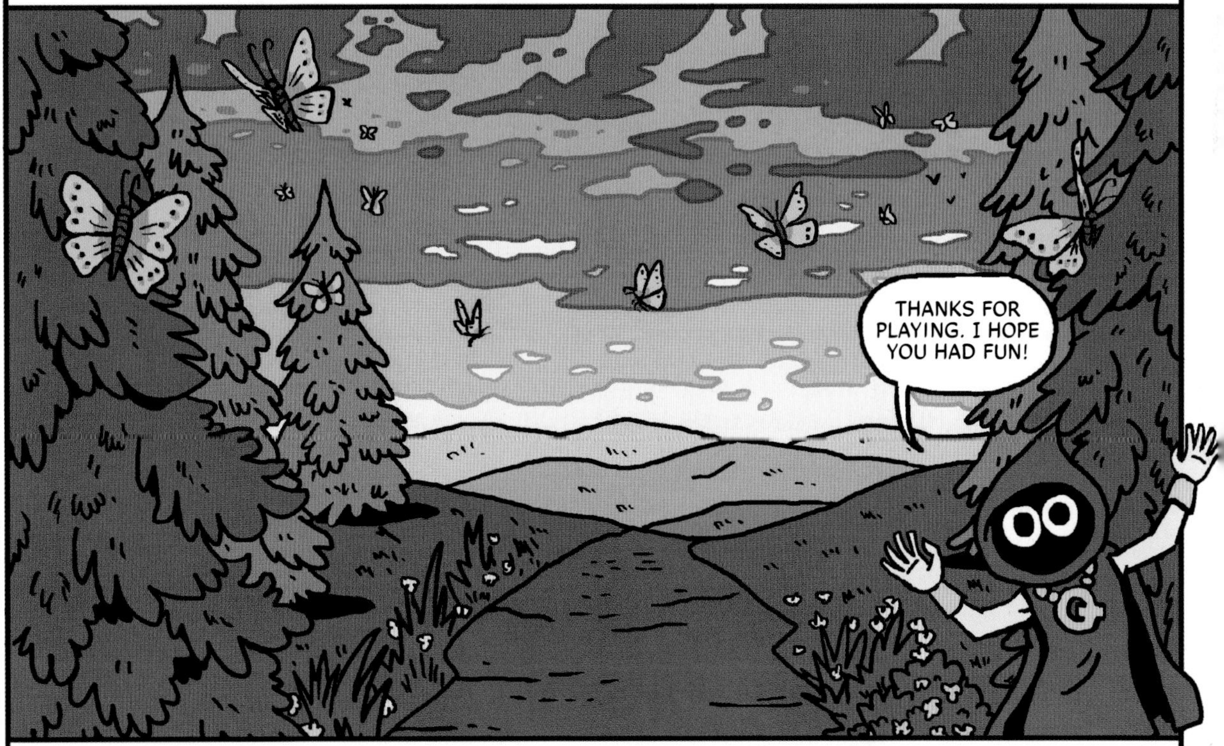
THANKS FOR PLAYING. I HOPE YOU HAD FUN!

WHEN YOU'RE DONE IMAGINING YOUR CHARACTERS' FINALE, MAYBE YOU'D LIKE TO PLAY AGAIN WITH DIFFERENT HEROES? TRY A DIFFERENT PATH? THE NEXT COUPLE OF PAGES WILL HELP YOU GET MORE OUT OF YOUR NEXT READ THROUGH.

Upping Your Game

RANDOM MODE

TRY LETTING LUCK SHAPE YOUR STORY! GET *TWO COINS.* FOR EACH CHALLENGE, FLIP THE COINS TO FIND OUT HOW SUCCESSFUL YOUR HEROES ARE. TWO HEADS MEANS THEY SUCCEED AMAZINGLY WELL! HEAD AND TAILS, THEY SUCCEED NORMALLY. TWO TAILS MEANS THEY FAIL SOMEHOW. MAYBE THEY NEED TO TRY AGAIN A DIFFERENT WAY, OR THEY GET INJURED AND CONTINUE ON AT A DISADVANTAGE.

FAILURE CAN OFTEN MAKE YOUR STORY MORE *INTERESTING.* IN FACT, MOST STORIES FEATURE A MOMENT WHERE THE HERO'S REGULAR WAY OF DOING THINGS FAILS THEM, AND THEY LEARN TO GROW AND DO SOMETHING THEY WERE AFRAID TO DO. LIKE A CHARACTER WHO ALWAYS FOLLOWS THE RULES BREAKING THEM, OR THE OPPOSITE. IF YOU CAN FAIL IN YOUR MIND, IN A STORY, OR IN A GAME, YOU'RE BETTER PREPARED FOR WHEN YOU FAIL *IN LIFE.* IT'S SAFE TO FAIL HERE.

EXPERT CHARACTER MODE

IF YOU'VE PLAYED THROUGH WITH ALL SIX HEROES, MAYBE YOU CAN MAKE UP YOUR OWN HEROES? OR TAKE FAVORITE HEROES FROM OTHER COMICS, MOVIES, BOOKS, GAMES, ETC. AND IMAGINE THEM TRYING TO COMPLETE THE QUEST. SEE HOW THE STORY CHANGES DEPENDING ON WHO THE HEROES ARE.

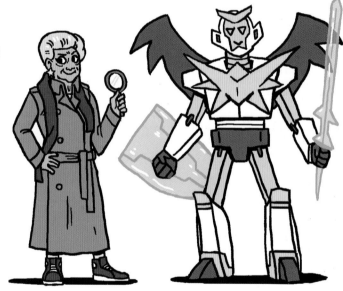

MASTER MODE

MAKE UP YOUR OWN PATH FOR THE CHARACTERS TO CONTINUE ON ANOTHER QUEST. IT MIGHT ONLY BE ONE MAP, OR A WHOLE BOOK. DRAW IT UP! OR DRAW COMICS OF YOUR FAVORITE MOMENTS FROM YOUR HEROES' QUEST. OR WRITE IT DOWN IN A JOURNAL, PRETENDING TO BE ONE OF THEM. WHAT MAKES YOUR QUEST DIFFERENT FROM ALL THE OTHER READERS' JOURNIES? BE INSPIRED TO EXPRESS YOURSELF THROUGH ANY HOBBY YOU HAVE.

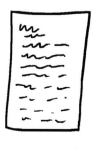

WHY DO WE PLAY RPGS?

ROLE-PLAYING GAMES, ALSO KNOWN AS RPGS, ARE GAMES A LOT LIKE THIS BOOK. SOMETIMES YOU PLAY THEM WITH DICE AND NUMBERS TO TRACK YOUR CHARACTERS' HEALTH AND ABILITIES—BUT IN THE END THEY'RE JUST STORIES YOU PLAY THROUGH, LIKE *COMPLETE THE QUEST.* SOME PEOPLE PLAY RPGS TO FEEL THE ACCOMPLISHMENT OF "BEATING" THE STORY IN THE *FASTEST* OR *GRANDEST* WAY. SOME LIKE CREATIVELY PROBLEM-SOLVING THE SITUATIONS LIKE *PUZZLES.* THEY PREFER THE *GAME* PART OF RPGS.

OTHERS JUST LIKE *TELLING STORIES COLLABORATIVELY.* THEY DON'T HAVE TO START WITH A BLANK PAGE, OR JUST SIT BACK AND LET A STORYTELLER DIRECT EVERY ASPECT OF THE TALE. THEY GET INTO THE *STORY* SIDE.

AND OBVIOUSLY, SOME ENJOY PLAYING THE *ROLE*, PRETENDING TO BE SOMEONE THEY'RE NOT. IMAGINING HOW EACH CHARACTER *FEELS* ABOUT EACH CHALLENGE. ABOUT EACH OTHER. YOU GET TO TRY ON SOMEONE ELSE'S SHOES FOR A BIT, IN A SAFE SPACE.

YOU'RE PROBABLY A COMBINATION OF ALL THREE. THERE'S NO WRONG WAY TO ENJOY THIS BOOK, EXCEPT MAYBE TRYING TO EAT IT OR SOMETHING. YOU'LL FIND WHAT MAKES RPGS SPEAK TO YOU.

I COULDN'T HAVE COMPLETED THE QUEST WITHOUT YOUR HELP!

STUMPED BY THE RIDDLES IN THE BOOK? THE ANSWERS ARE BELOW—AND UPSIDE-DOWN TO AVOID SPOILING!

PAGE 24: HOLES. PAGE 33: A BAT. PAGE 50: A TOWEL. PAGE 58: THEY WOULD "PICKAXE." PAGE 70: SHIELD, SWORD, HAMMER. PAGE 91: YOU WOULD GIVE IT A "ROCK."

SPECIAL THANKS TO: MY WIFE, AMBER, FOR SUPPORTING ME THROUGH THICK AND THIN, MY AGENT KELLY FOR SEEING THE POTENTIAL IN MY WORK, MY EDITOR JOHN FOR BEING ABLE TO VISUALIZE ALL THE LEVELS OF THE BOOK (AND HOW TO BROADEN AND DEEPEN THEM), AND MY PEERS AND FRIENDS WHO SAW EARLY VERSIONS AND RESPONDED TO MY ENTHUSIASM IN KIND!

THANK YOU TO OUR AMAZING PLAYTESTERS: Harrison and Hailey, Evangeline Weeks, Wilde Collins, Aaron Hanson, Connor and Kataryna, Adam Rex, Jeff Spirglas, Jethro and Augutus, Conan and Flint, Alexa Platto, Andrew James Soule, Anna L., Avi Irivine, Caroline, Evan Younger, Felix, Nathanial, Nate, Lindsay, Gabriel Vazquez, Noah Lauring, Sam V., Scarlett Wacholtz, Simone Larsen, Vida Josie, Steve Cober, Gabriel Clutterbuck, Nick Hendriks, and Leila Rahman.

IMPRINT
A part of Macmillan Publishing Group, LLC
120 Broadway, New York, NY 10271

ABOUT THIS BOOK
This book was drawn with a magical marker on power scrolls. The text was set in
CCLegendaryLegerdemain, CCVictorySpeechLower, and Trade Winds Pro.

The book was edited by John Morgan and designed by Carolyn Bull.
The production was supervised by Raymond Ernesto Colón,
and the production editor was Ilana Worrell.

Complete the Quest: The Poisonous Library. Copyright © 2021 by Brian McLachlan. All rights reserved.

Printed in China by 1010 Printing International Ltd., North Point, Hong Kong

Library of Congress Cataloging-in-Publication Data is available.

Paperback ISBN: 978-1-250-26830-3
1 3 5 7 9 10 8 6 4 2

Hardcover ISBN: 978-1-250-26829-7
1 3 5 7 9 10 8 6 4 2

Our books may be purchased in bulk for
promotional, educational, or business use.
Please contact your local bookseller or the Macmillan
Corporate and Premium Sales Department at
(800) 221-7945 ext. 5442 or by email at
MacmillanSpecialMarkets@macmillan.com.

Imprint logo designed by Amanda Spielman

First edition, 2021

mackids.com

Steal this book and you will be cursed
to slither the earth as a barf elemental.
Share your book with your friends and you will be blessed
to shine like a star diamond.

THIS BOOK IS DEDICATED TO ALL THE LIBRARIANS. THEY'VE SUPPORTED MY MISCHIEF, ENCOURAGED MY WRITING, EXPANDED MY BOOKVIEW, AND ENGAGED MY CHILDREN, ALL WHILE USUALLY BEING UNDERPAID AND OVERWORKED. PLEASE FORGIVE THE ANTAGONIST. AN EVIL LIBRARIAN IS PERHAPS THE MOST IRONIC THING I COULD THINK OF.